The
Good Ship
Lollipop

Patrick Benjamin

DEDICATION

For anyone who's had a broken heart.
For anyone who's had to learn to love and trust again.

To those who are still learning, hang in there.

ACKNOWLEDGMENTS

2020 was a challenging year to write a comedy. There wasn't a lot to laugh about. Still, I pushed forward, and I'm glad I did. The Good Ship Lollipop gave me something to focus on when the depression of being unable to see my friends and family was too much to bear.

Even though we spent most of the year apart, many people have supported me these last two years since I began my writing journey. Dallas, Geo, Jessie, Lornel, David (Vanity), Dan (Diva), Lewis (Carrie) –Just knowing you all were out there rooting me on, made all the difference. Friendship is a lot like oxygen. You don't have to see it to know it's there.

Rob, you are my sounding board, and I couldn't ask for a better friend or editor. Even when I didn't know how to communicate it, you understood exactly what I was trying to say. That's talent.

Laura, Kansas, Austin, and Lily: Blood is life, and you are a part of everything I do.

Jarrett, what can I possibly say at this point? These past eleven years together have been the absolute best moments of my life. Being married to a writer is not easy; I know that. I'm sure you sometimes feel like I'm married more to my computer than to you. I love you deeper than the ocean. Thank you for sailing through life with me.

Thank you all. I hope you enjoy

The Good Ship Lollipop

PROLOGUE
KYLE

I couldn't stop staring at his ass. I wanted to. I tried, but I was frozen. Physically incapable of looking away. It was a great ass. Well-formed and tight. The type of ass one only earned through countless hours at the gym, squatting and lunging.

It was there, naked, on my bed—our bed. Staring at me with its one, cosmetically-bleached eye. I didn't recognize the person attached to it. Granted, I couldn't see his face. It was nestled in the soft flesh of Dustin's scrotum. *My* Dustin.

Neither of them saw me. Dustin laid on the bed, his head propped up on a pillow. *My* pillow. His eyes closed, and his mouth open, he breathed deep from pleasure. The ass, and the man it belonged to, were too busy performing fellatio to realize I had even entered the room.

It was a Wednesday afternoon. Hump Day, coincidently. That morning, I'd left for my job at Pegasus Press, my stomach feeling off-kilter. I hadn't considered much of it. I thought it was likely indigestion or gas brought on from the Chinese food we'd eaten late the night before. Taking a swig of Pepto, I left to catch my train. By noon, my stomach was flip-flopping so much, it could have joined a production of Cirque du Soleil. So, I packed up for the day. As an editor, I had the luxury of working from home when I needed to. That day, my body was telling me I needed to.

I figured I'd come home, crawl into bed, and wait for my stomach to settle. Maybe even make myself sick. Because sometimes that helped. Watching the scene in front of me now, I certainly felt like I was going to throw up.

I didn't expect to find the bed occupied.

Dustin was also supposed to be at work. He had been working such odd hours for the last month. Leaving at the butt-

1

crack of dawn and sometimes not returning until way past sunset. Twelve-hour days, six days a week. He was determined to become a partner at InterPublic, the advertising firm that employed him. He even slept at the office a couple of times because he was so committed.

Committed no longer seemed like an appropriate word to describe Dustin. In retrospect, the late hours and sleep-overs should have been an obvious red-flag. At the time, however, it hadn't occurred to me Dustin would be so cliché. Although maybe it should have.

We had met at a karaoke bar. We were both there celebrating my friend Sapphire's birthday. I had been friends with her since college. There we'd bonded over our love of hot guys and cheap wine. Dustin was the twin brother of Sapphire's boyfriend, Justin. Dustin and Justin Salinger. I never understood why parents did that to their children. It would be hard enough going through life, looking identical to your sibling. I couldn't imagine having to share near-identical names as well.

I had mistaken Dustin for Justin initially. Sapphire had only shown me photos of her handsome boyfriend. So, it never occurred to me that the blonde, blue-eyed, broad-shouldered Adonis sitting beside her wouldn't have been hers. Once Justin emerged from the washroom, and I could see the men side by side, I recognized their subtle differences. Justin's face was rounder and more rugged. Less groomed. While Dustin's face and body were more chiseled. Firm abs, square-jaw with perfectly coiffed eyebrows.

Dustin and I hit it off right away.

We had similar no-nonsense temperaments and shared talent for sarcasm and wit. Dustin asked me out for that coming weekend and then again for the one following. After that, we were inseparable.

That had been fifteen years ago. Fifteen years, eight months, seventeen days, eleven hours. It was funny how precise your brain could be when it came to calculating the time you've wasted.

I thought we were the perfect couple. Everyone did. We both had successful careers, a beautiful apartment, well-to-do family backgrounds, and an active social calendar. We went to charity events and gala openings. We were invited to all the most fabulous parties.

More important than our glamorous lives was the fact that we loved each other. We were the kind of couple that wasn't afraid to be silly or sappy. We had the kind of love that made people sick, and we were happy about it.

Or so I thought.

Looking at the stranger's naked ass on my three-hundred-thread-count Egyptian cotton sheets, I was no longer sure of anything.

I stood there, equal parts mesmerized and horrified. At that moment, Dustin put his large hands on the stranger's head and pushed him deeper down onto his erection, making the stranger gag.

I certainly wasn't going to miss that nasty little habit.

I faked a cough. Dustin opened one of his eyes.

It must have taken him a moment to register what the sound was and where it had come from because it took two seconds longer than it should have for him to notice me in the bedroom doorway.

When he did see, he hurled the stranger off him. The stranger flailed, naked limbs knocking the lamp off the bedside table. Then he fell off the bed, his perfectly-formed ass colliding with the hardwood floor with a heavy splat.

"Kyle!" Dustin covered himself with the sheet, his dick still hard, making the fabric tent embarrassingly. "This isn't what it looks like." His voice sounded panicked.

"Oh? So, you weren't getting your dick sucked by a yoga instructor?"

"I'm a personal trainer," the stranger with the perfect ass dared to speak.

"You don't talk!" I snarled at him. Then it struck me how young he looked. "How old are you?"

"Nineteen."

"Jesus Christ!" I was disgusted. "Trying to earn your dick-sucking Boy Scout badge?" Turning back to Dustin, I flung, "Did you at least offer him an after-school snack?"

"I'm so sorry, sir," the kid looked terrified. "I didn't know he was involved with anyone."

Did that little shit call me, sir? I turned back to him. "Take your lunch money and go!"

I watched the nineteen-year-old scurry around the room, picking up his discarded clothes. "If you were going to cheat on me, Dusty, you could have at least done it with someone old enough to grow pubic hair!"

"Kyle, I am so sorry. It was a one-time thing, I swear."

"This was the third time," the personal trainer, who was now wearing pants, volunteered.

"Don't forget your backpack when you leave!" I growled.

He cringed and left the room. A few seconds later, I heard the apartment door open, then close. He was gone.

Look both ways before crossing the street, I thought to myself.

Dustin stood in front of me, still clinging to the sheet around his waist. His erection had finally subsided. "Kyle, it meant nothing."

Why did people always say that? It meant nothing. Like that somehow made it better. If anything, it only made it worse.

"Oh, thank God," I said with mock relief. "I was so worried that you threw away the last fifteen years of our lives over someone you actually cared about. What a relief to know that you sacrificed everything we had for one quick fuck with a young piece of ass. That makes me feel *so* much better!"

"Kyle…"

"Save it, Dusty." He hated it when I called him Dusty, but I didn't much care anymore. I could have called him far worse, but I knew Dusty would irritate him more than any of the other, more colorful names I could come up with. "I don't want to hear it!" I spun on my heels, placing my hands over my ears like a toddler before heading towards the door.

"I'll be gone for an hour. I expect you not to be here when I return!"

"Kyle! Don't do this to me!" he called after me.

Don't do this to *him*? Was he serious? At that moment, I hated him so much. I was tempted to shove him out of our apartment window. I would have smiled, a toothy, evil grin as he fell all twenty-three stories to the street below. I'd then take the elevator down so I could quickly do the Irish jig on his mangled corpse.

"How many have there been?" I dared to ask even though I wasn't sure if I wanted the answer. Or if he would give it to me honestly.

"Kyle…" That one word and the sad way he trailed off said everything I needed to know. It wasn't the first time Dustin had fooled around. There were others. The exact number was irrelevant.

"I made a mistake," he whined.

"Several, apparently."

"Baby, I am so sorry."

"So am I—baby!" I shouted defiantly, slamming the door just before I started to cry.

ONE
KYLE

"**N**o, absolutely not!" I nearly choked on a spinach leaf.

"You have to come," Sapphire insisted. "I want you to be my *Man of Honor*."

"A) That's not a thing. B) The answer is still no."

"I can't get married without you."

"Sure, you can. There's no law against it. People do it all the time."

When Sapphire offered to take me to lunch, I should have suspected something treacherous was afoot. Sapphire and I were like sisters. Sisters of different races and one of them with a penis, but sisters, nonetheless. Our relationship was something enormous and incomprehensible to most people. On paper, we had nothing in common. We had completely different backgrounds and cultural experiences that cultivated entirely different perspectives of the world around us. Despite those differences, we had found each other.

As close as we were, the girl had never offered to buy lunch. She seldom volunteered to pay for anything. That should have been warning number one. When she suggested my favorite Italian restaurant, Armando's, that should have been warning number two. When she volunteered to foot the bill to attend her destination wedding cruise, I should have known to prepare myself for the Armageddon of bad news.

"You spent fifteen years with the man. What are ten more days?" She spoke with her hands. A piece of chicken flung off her fork and onto the table beside us. The senior couple, who were trying to enjoy their eighteen-dollar salads, glared at us like we each had two heads.

"I'm so sorry," I mouthed to them.

"I can't believe you would miss your best friend's wedding over a tiny, little, uncomfortable inconvenience like this."

"A *cockroach infestation* is a tiny inconvenience. *Gonorrhea* is uncomfortable. What you're asking me to do is far worse."

"Don't be dramatic," Sapphire said, waving her hand. "Dustin is not that bad."

"Isn't he?" He was too tall, too fit, too classically pretty, and all too aware of the fact. He was narcissistic and untrustworthy, but he was also charming and exceptionally good at putting on an innocent act. He could flash his white teeth and his dimples and get people to believe anything he wanted. Still, if you looked into his eyes, you could tell he was soulless.

"Why would you want everyone to join you on your honeymoon, anyway?" I shifted focus. "I hate to tell you this, but if you can't stand to be alone with Justin for ten days, you probably shouldn't marry him."

"Very funny," she said dryly. "I want everyone there because I want my wedding to be an experience. An amazing memory we can all look back on together."

"I am not spending ten days, on a tiny boat, in the middle of the Caribbean, with *him*."

"It's a cruise ship," she corrected. "Besides, you won't be with Dustin. You'll be with me."

"Lies!" I wasn't buying any of it. "I know exactly what will happen. You and Justin will be too busy enjoying your Caribbean honeymoon to spend any time with me. Then I'll be trapped, in the middle of the ocean, with no one to talk to except Beelzebub's concubine."

"He's not going to be the only other person there, you know. Several other people will be in our group. You can make one of them your wingman. My father loves you. You can hang-out with him."

"Honey, don't take this the wrong way. If I'm on an exotic vacation, and the only man who wants to spend time with me is your sixty-five-year-old arthritic father, I might drown myself in a bathtub."

"Don't be silly," Sapphire dismissed. "You'll be surrounded by water. There'd be no need to draw a bath."

I did not look amused.

"I can't believe you're still so angry. It's been over a year." It had been eighteen months since the breakup, and yes, I was still harboring, hurting, and hating.

I hadn't seen or spoken to Dustin since the incident. As instructed, he had been gone when I returned to the apartment. With Sapphire's help and some very strategic planning, I had avoided him throughout the entire decoupling process.

I left yellow Post-it Notes on everything he could take and was extremely vindictive about it. He could have the Blu-ray player, but not the discs or the TV. He could take the kitchen table, but not the chairs. I even kept the Keurig, though I permitted him to take his pods. What kind of monster drank decaf anyway? I also instructed Sapphire to guard the jazz record collection with her life. I detested jazz music, and we both knew it. I planned to pawn or destroy the albums later.

The first few weeks after the breakup, Dustin tried tirelessly to communicate with me. He sent me text messages that I didn't answer and left voice mails that I refused to listen to. Dustin tried everything short of smoke signals. He even sent me an old-fashioned letter, which I didn't open and burned immediately. I had nothing to say to him and had no desire to hear what he had to say to me. I had never been an incredibly trusting person, and his betrayal had reinforced all those walls that I had been trying, for years, to dismantle.

Being the forgiving person she was, Sapphire tried to convince me to give Dustin a second chance. Still, I refused, steadfast in my determination that he'd had his chance. Since then, she had been careful not to mention him. Even though I knew full well that she saw him regularly. He was her fiancé's twin brother. She had to remain cordial. I did not and had no intention of ever being so.

"You simply have to come. We're going to so many beautiful islands: Turks and Caicos, Bonaire, St. Thomas, and Aruba. You've always wanted to go to Aruba."

That was true, but still, "If you put us on a ship together, I promise you, I will throw him overboard."

She smiled wide, her teeth gleaming white against the contrast of her chocolate skin. "That's fine! Just promise you'll make it look like an accident."

"Duh," was the most mature response I could muster. "I don't want to end up someone's bitch in a Caribbean prison."

"Don't you, though?"

Dirty, prison sex would have been the most action I'd seen in a while. Thirty-nine may have been young by hetero standards, but in the queer world, I was practically a spinster. Being classified as an *elder gay* meant that my dating pool had been reduced to a few categories. First, those men who were so weird or creepy that nobody wanted them, or second, those who were so bitter and jaded by relationships past that dating them was like trying to build a house out of straw. I was a card-carrying member of category two.

Of course, there was always a third group. Younger men. They were excellent in theory, with their zero percent body fat and their permanent erections. However, too often, their perfect bodies and sexual appetites only camouflaged the fact that they lacked any real substance. If brains were dynamite, most of them couldn't blow their nose. There were always exceptions. Old souls that knew how to converse about more than just Rhi-Rhi's new album or T-Swizzle's latest boyfriend. Those younger men wanted more than sugar daddies. Though, I still couldn't imagine having enough in common with someone who hadn't even been alive during the original run of *Friends*.

It wasn't that I couldn't get a date. Even close to forty, I was still cute. Not as attractive as I was at twenty, but I wasn't a hunchback or anything. My deep green eyes matched my red hair, which I kept cropped short to avoid the bozo-clown-realness it would become if left to grow-out. I was tall and still decently shaped, a little thicker in some places than I'd prefer, but that came with age. At least, that's what I told myself. I had a good understanding of where that put me in the queer hierarchy. Guys would still bang me; they just wouldn't brag about it anymore.

Admittedly, the realization that I was no longer prime real estate took some getting used to. Before Dustin, I had been a penthouse in Manhattan, but after fifteen years in couple-town, I was shocked to discover I was now a brownstone in Queens. Next stop? Condemned building in Jersey!

That being said, I was optimistic about my life, even if it meant spending it alone.

"The ship is huge," Sapphire was still talking. "You won't even really have to see each other. There are also excursions at every port: zip-lining, snorkeling, hikes, surfing. Come on. You can orbit around each other for ten days without committing a violent felony."

"Great, so I can spend the entire time by myself?"

"There's going to be thousands of people on this ship. It's a floating city. If you're so worried about being by yourself, you could always try making friends."

"You've known me for twenty years. Am I the type of person who *makes friends*?"

She thought about it for a second. "Good point." She took another bite of chicken. "I could introduce you to a guy from the station before the trip. Maybe you'll hit it off." Sapphire was the Director of Human Resources for an ABC affiliate in Chicago. Since Dustin, she had convinced me to go on a few dates with people she knew from work. All of them complete disasters.

"Please, no!" I exclaimed. "I beg of you, never try to set me up ever again. You have horrible taste in men."

"That's rude," she said, wounded. "Justin is amazing."

"Yes, yes," I nodded. "Justin is a gem. It's your taste in *gay* men that sucks dirty ass."

She made a face. "Gross."

"You think that's gross? The last guy you set me up with had a fetish for sock puppets. SOCK PUPPETS! He actually asked if I'd be willing to wear one while we fornicated."

"Fornicated?"

"His words, not mine. Do you know where he expected me to wear this sock puppet?"

"I assume on your hand?"

My eyes squinted as I shook my head. "If only. Let's just say there would have been no room for a condom."

Sapphire howled with laughter. "Oh my!"

"Yes, Sapphire, it was a cock puppet!" I exclaimed, my voice rising, my fork clinking against my plate. "He wanted me to wear a damned cock puppet!" The room was suddenly deathly quiet as I was met with a plentitude of scornful glares from surrounding tables. "Forgive me," I awkwardly offered to the room. One by one, they each returned to their over-priced entrees.

"Anyhow," Sapphire said, in between bites of her chicken breast. "You and I both know I'm going to get my way. So, you can continue to argue with me for another week and then give in. Or you can put on your big boy pants and agree to come. Then, spend the next few days pouting about how your mean best friend is forcing you to go on a free Caribbean vacation." She wasn't wrong. I would give in eventually. We both knew it. "Either way, you're coming. I'm the bride. The bride always gets what she wants."

If there was a way out of the situation, it wasn't coming to me fast enough. I decided to bite the bullet. "Okay, I'll do it, but I won't have any fun."

"God, I hope not. This trip isn't about you having fun. It's about your devotion to me."

"You're not going to be a bridezilla, are you?"

She smiled generously at me from across the table. "I won't be any more demanding than usual."

"That doesn't put me at ease."

Sapphire met my eyes again, this time with a half-hearted glare. "You're the *Man of Honor*," she argued. "It's your job to put *me* at ease."

"Once again, that's not a thing."

"It is for me," she laughed. "My only choices were you or my younger sister. It's bad enough my parents are forcing me to make her a bridesmaid, but can you imagine her as my maid of honor? I love Ruby, but she's an irresponsible slut."

"Easy."

"Alright," Sapphire reconsidered. "Maybe she's not."

"No-no, she is, but the correct term is *easy*." I had also known Ruby for years. Each time we hung out, she tried to convince me that I was only gay because I hadn't slept with her yet. "You can't go around calling people sluts anymore. It's inappropriate."

"No. Inappropriate was when she missed giving the eulogy at my grandmother's funeral because she was sucking off one of the pallbearers in a broom closet."

"Yes, that was unfortunate timing. but Ruby was grieving." I tried to justify it.

Ruby and Sapphire Johnson were ten years apart. Ruby was what Sapphire lovingly referred to as a flaw in birth control. She was twenty-eight and stunning. Sapphire was also beautiful but in an entirely different way. Sapphire was beautiful in the way women like Michelle Obama and Jane Fonda were beautiful. She was sophisticated, cultured, and when you looked at her, you could tell she was more than just the combination of a hot body and a gorgeous face. She was a woman of intelligence and class. One knew to treat her as such.

Ruby's beauty was far more superficial. Tall and leggy, with well-shaped assets—both top and bottom. She oozed sex-appeal. Often overly made up and frequently free with her body, she had no trouble gathering attention or earning a reputation. Men wanted to sleep with her, while women simultaneously hated her and wanted to be her, and she knew it. She used it to her advantage as often as she could.

The problem with relying solely on one's body was that it made people forget that you also had a brain. I had enough conversations with Ruby over the years to know that while she wasn't as intelligent as her sister, she wasn't the dim-witted sexpot she pretended to be. Well, she wasn't *just* a dim-witted sexpot.

I supposed, if Sapphire were too busy with honeymoon bliss, Ruby would serve as an entertaining, albeit unpredictable, source of company. I just hoped she wouldn't get me into trouble.

Ruby was young, impulsive, and never afraid to say exactly what was on her mind, no matter where or with whom she was. She enjoyed pushing boundaries and breaking the rules. On second thought, maybe I'd say screw it to any human interaction and spend those ten days alone, soaking up the sun by the pool. That would probably be the safest option.

The months leading up to the trip flew by in a haze. Luckily, the cruise line took care of most of the wedding details. They arranged the flowers, the cake, the venue, the minister, the reception, the food, the DJ. Everything one would need for their big day. The only thing Sapphire and Justin had to do was fill out a thousand forms and sign the cheque. This helped alleviate most of the traditional stress that came with planning a wedding.

For Sapphire, the absence of stress was the most stressful part. She was a typical type-A personality. She had an incessant need to control as much of the world around her as possible. It was a trait I often appreciated. Especially during the first few weeks after my breakup with Dustin, when she literally had to force me to bathe.

"I'm going to die alone anyway," I would sob. "Why do I

need to be clean?"

"Because life goes on," she had told me. "And frankly, you stink."

The lack of physical control over her wedding details often sent her into bouts of anxiety that I would have to quell.

She would cry, "What if they choose something as simple as roses? I don't want my wedding to be basic!"

"You clearly marked the orchids option on the form," I'd remind her.

"What if they do something tacky, like a chocolate fountain?" she'd ask.

To which I'd respond, "These people are professionals. They're not going to do anything distasteful."

"Can you call to make sure?"

I did, twice. There would be no chocolate fountain.

Each time she got this way, I was tempted, for a moment, to slap her like they did in old movies.

Snap out of it!

It would have been just as effective but much more entertaining for me.

The one area I thought she would be most concerned with turned out to be the detail she approached with the most calm; wedding dress shopping. If it had been my wedding, I would have been frantically trying on dresses, desperate to find one as close to perfect as possible. The last thing I'd want is to look unflattering on my wedding day. Sapphire seemed entirely unconcerned. This was likely because she had done her homework. Before Justin had even proposed, Sapphire knew exactly which designer and what style of dress she wanted. A Milla Nova design—mermaid cut with an illusion neck, capped sleeves, and full lace appliqué. She had bought it online and had it shipped from Paris.

Even with the perfect dress already tucked away, Sapphire still set aside a block of time so that she, Ruby and I could go dress shopping. We spent the day laughing as Ruby and

Sapphire purposely tried on the most hideous gowns ever created. At the same time, we guzzled up bottomless glasses of free, cheap champagne. After three hours, the shop attendants had been somewhat annoyed when we left without spending a dime.

As the trip came closer, my anxiety about seeing Dustin again grew exponentially. I wondered what he looked like after two years. I hoped he got fat. Fat and bald. Old, fat, and hairless. That was what I wished for him. The men in his family were prone to male pattern baldness, which brought me comfort knowing at least one of those three was possible, even if unlikely.

I decided, if the trifecta was too much to hope for, I'd settle for halitosis. Not just bad breath. The kind of bad breath that brought a sting to people's eyes and made them have to turn away from him when he spoke. The type of breath that smelled like something crawled into his mouth and died, was reanimated, rolled around in shit for several hours, then crawled back into his mouth and died again. It occurred to me that I might be a little extra.

During our relationship, Dustin had always been the more attractive one. He had the abs, the hair and at least three inches on me—in height, that is. I was always adorable but in a book-worm sort of way. I knew it was entirely superficial, but I wanted to look better than he remembered me. So I started to hit the gym. I even considered hiring a personal trainer, but I was still too traumatized by my last encounter with one and his perfect young ass. I wanted Dustin to see me and immediately feel a pang of regret for losing me. I wanted to look better without him than I ever did with him. There was a victory in that. I couldn't care less about him or what he thought about me. It wasn't about him.

At least that's what I told myself.

TWO
KYLE

Six months had gone by faster than I thought possible. In the calm before the storm, in this case, the days before my inevitable reunion with Dustin, I settled into calm acceptance. I would have to see him, worse, spend time with him. There was no sense stressing about that fact any longer. I was an adult, mostly. I would survive. Gloria Gaynor played loudly on my inner stereo.

To be safe, I flew into Miami late on Friday evening. Separate from all the others who had arrived the Monday prior. Being stuck with Dustin on a thousand-foot-long cruise ship was something I was prepared for. The boat was big enough. I could avoid him if needed. Being shoulder-to-shoulder with him, in coach, on a three-hour flight was a different story. A vision of me opening the doors, pushing him out, disrupting the barometric pressure of the plane, bringing it down in a fiery explosion of death and destruction, seemed all too possible to chance.

Wanting their wedding to maintain some sense of tradition, Justin had spent the night in a separate room with Dustin. So, I picked up Sapphire and Ruby at their hotel early in the morning. We headed to the cruise terminal at the Port of Miami together. The ceremony wasn't until three in the afternoon. Still, because they were getting married on the ship, it was necessary to get us checked in and through security before noon.

The ride to the terminal was bumpy but mercifully quick. I could have probably blamed some of my queasiness on nerves but chose to blame it all on the commute. We drove down a narrow avenue, lined on both sides with full-grown palm trees. The port of Miami was relatively young, established only in 1960, but it felt like the avenue leading towards it hadn't received much maintenance since then.

When the taxi slowed, making a final left turn, the cruise terminal came into view. It was a large grey building with very few windows and large rolling steel doors. It reminded me of a giant garage, where large limousines or buses would typically be stored.

When we came to a stop, two attendants appeared out of nowhere to greet us and retrieve our luggage. We were considered priority passengers because we were a wedding party, so the crew rushed us through the process. A few of the personnel naturally assumed I was the groom. Sapphire and I played along. Then, she pretended to be devastated when I revealed that I was actually a raging homosexual.

One attendant scribbled our names on several tags, attaching them to the handles of our luggage. "Go through the double doors. Follow the platform all the way up to the ship's lobby," He smiled. "Your bags will be brought to your cabin after they clear security."

When we were finally on board, everything sped up. An attendant ushered us to the salon, where a hairstylist wrangled my cowlicks into submission. At the same time, the girls were transformed into images of perfection. For obvious reasons, their beautification process took significantly longer than mine. So, when I was camera ready, I flipped through an old copy of *InStyle*, waiting for them to finish.

"I can already feel my hair frizzing in this humidity," Sapphire complained to us. At the same time, a cloud of attendants and stylists doted on her.

"It's so worth it," Ruby reminded her. "We could be stuck at home." Chicago in January was nearly unbearable, with its low temperatures and biting wind chills. Sapphire's frizzy curls were a small price to pay for tropical warmth.

"I want side-swept bangs and bouncing waves," Sapphire explained, her head full of large Velcro rollers. "I want to look like Beyoncé."

"It's a comb, not a magic wand," I offered flippantly, turning a page.

Sapphire yanked the magazine from my hand, swatting me with it like I was an annoying bug. She then flashed me a half-hearted glare, tossing the magazine back on my lap. "You, watch it," she warned. "Your one job is to compliment my bridal beauty."

She and Ruby were wearing matching white, fluffy robes and slippers. "You're a vision," I stated dutifully, although insincere. I winked at Ruby then resumed my reading.

"I thought your one job was to keep her hydrated and fed," Ruby said to me from under a hairdryer. "Much like a houseplant."

"Or a puppy," I added, sharing an amusing glance with Ruby.

"You know I can hear you, right?"

I nodded. "That would be the whole point."

Sapphire rolled her eyes then blew across her fingernails to dry the fresh coat of polish. "Be nice to me, or I'll pee on both of you."

"Justin might be into water sports, but I'm going to pass," I said with a grin. Sapphire looked satisfyingly repulsed.

I scanned an article on Lady Gaga. "You seem to be in a mood today," Sapphire noted. "I mean, you're always a sarcastic ass, but today you appear to be more vicious than usual."

I felt a pang of guilt. "I'm sorry," I said sincerely. "I'm just on edge about going on this trip."

"Nobody is forcing you to take a free dream vacation," Sapphire replied automatically before clapping her mouth shut. We both knew that wasn't true.

After riffling through most of the magazine, I tossed it aside then moved on to *People*. I flipped through it absently while the girls enjoyed their makeovers.

We continued our idle conversation, complete with innocent

barbs and inside jokes until the ladies were beautified. Then, we separated into dressing rooms. Being a man, I naturally finished dressing first. My white pants and royal blue suit jacket only took minutes to throw on, so I fiddled with my bowtie in the full-length mirror while I waited for the girls.

Ruby emerged first, motioning for me to zip her up. Her bridesmaid dress was impeccable, matching my jacket's blue perfectly, with a bright pink crinoline that peeked out from underneath the bell skirt. "Have you seen Dustin yet?" She asked.

"Not yet. Have you?"

Ruby nodded. "The five of us had dinner last night."

Ruby shuffled to an adjacent table, picking up a box of jewelry then handing me a rhinestone necklace from inside. I held the delicate piece of jewelry carefully. When she lifted her hair, I draped the jewels around her neck then fastened the clasp. "The five of you?"

"Yeah. Me, Sapphire, Justin, Dustin and Shawn," she said, putting in her dangling earrings.

Alarm bells sounded in my brain. "Shawn? Who's Shawn?" I already knew the answer. I just wanted someone to confirm it.

Ruby's eyes widened, and she stopped mid earring. She pursed her lips like she had spilled a valued family secret. "She hasn't told you?"

Sapphire appeared then, looking stunning and treacherous in her mermaid gown. Her veil was correctly pinned in her dark wavy hair, the epitome of perfection. I threw her a look that said I wanted to rip that veil off her perfectly Beyonce-fied head and set it on fire! She received the message loud and clear.

Panicked, she looked to Ruby, who shrugged off any responsibility, then back to me. "Now, Kyle, before you lose your shit, I didn't even know he was bringing his boyfriend until a week ago."

"You still knew he had a boyfriend."

"You would have known too if you stalked your ex on social

media, like a normal person."

"She's right," Ruby agreed. "I know every move my exes make."

"Something is wrong with both of you," I replied gently.

"There is nothing wrong with being informed," Ruby insisted. "I know who my exes are dating, what movies they've seen, and what vacations they've gone on. Thanks to Instagram, I even know what they have for breakfast each day." Then she added proudly, "I get a notification every time they post anything."

I was horrified. "That's batshit crazy. Dating you should come with a warning label."

"You know it," Ruby sang. "Hot stuff here. May burn you if mishandled."

"I was thinking more like, this girl owns a gun and refuses to take her medication."

"Also accurate," Ruby agreed. "It doesn't seem to deter men, though. Even with my crazy, they find me irresistible."

"No, Honey. They find you available."

Sapphire cleared her throat. "Slut-shaming aside, I'm not sure why you're shocked Dustin has a boyfriend. It's been two years. Why wouldn't he have somebody in his life?"

"I don't have anybody in *my* life," I pointed out.

Sapphire tilted her head. "Yes, I know, but you're a bitter old Queen."

"Damn right, I am." I wore it like a badge of honor. "You still should have told me. We've been sitting here for over an hour, and you haven't breathed a word about it."

Sapphire sighed. "Remember how we sometimes talk about things that are not about you? Today is one of those times."

I crossed my arms, pouting. "I can't believe you let Dustin bring a date, knowing how uncomfortable it would make me."

"I realize this may come as a shock to you, Hun, but this trip isn't about you. It's about me. So, can we get back to me?"

"In a minute. Right now, I want to hear about this boyfriend.

What's he like?"

"Why does it matter?" Sapphire frowned. She wasn't the biggest fan of Dustin either, but she had to be tired of having this conversation.

"You're not jealous, are you, Kyle?" Ruby taunted.

I laughed a little too aggressively. "Me? Jealous? Don't be ridiculous."

"Then why do you want to know?"

I realized I must have come across like a typical bitter ex, but I promised them I wasn't. "I don't care that Dustin has met someone. I just want to prepare myself. You know, batten down the hatches before hurricane Dustin. I don't want any surprises."

They both looked at each other, clearly skeptical. "Well," Sapphire began. "He's very—"

"Young." Ruby interrupted.

Sapphire glared at her sister. "I was going to say nice. Shawn is genuinely nice."

"And young," Ruby repeated.

"I think he's sweet," Sapphire reiterated

"Sweet, and young," Ruby repeated a third time.

Sapphire tried shooing her away. "He's not *that* young."

I ignored Sapphire and pressed Ruby for more information. "How young? A few years? Or is it a May-December kind of romance?"

"More like May-June," Ruby laughed.

"That's not so bad."

"May of the following year," Ruby clarified, and I gasped, horrified. "Dustin's May," she went on, in case I still hadn't figured it out.

"Yes, I got that. Thank you." I glared at Sapphire. "You were going to keep this from me?"

She shrugged. "You were going to find out eventually. I didn't want to upset you."

"*Upset me*?" I nearly squealed. "I think it's hilarious!"

"You do?" They asked in unison.

"Fuck, yes! I find the fact that Dustin is dating a preschooler delightfully entertaining!"

"You do?" They asked again.

"Absolutely!" I nodded.

"We thought you'd be pissed." Sapphire sounded relieved.

"Oh, believe me, I still am pissed that he has a date while I'm flying solo. Still, there is a certain joy that comes from knowing that he's dating a toddler." I just hoped it wasn't the same toddler with the great ass that helped to end us. That would be too awkward. Either way, the fact that he was still banging teenagers proved he hadn't changed in two years. It reinforced that I had made the right decision in leaving his cheating ass. Besides, it would give me something to harass him about the entire trip.

It might have seemed strange to some that this relatively small piece of knowledge brought me so much joy. I was confident anyone who had survived the demise of a long-term relationship would instantly understand. Some people wished horrible things on their exes. I certainly did. For a time, I wanted Dustin to experience something awful. Like death, destruction, dismemberment, or disembowelment. There came the point, though, for most of us, where anger made way for hope. A hope that your ex would one day find someone to share their life with. Someone beautiful and unique. Someone who would ultimately rip their heart out and feed it to him while it still beat.

I realized then I shouldn't have skipped breakfast. The notion of force-feeding human organs shouldn't have made my stomach growl.

With still an hour left before the ceremony, I figured we all could use a lite snack. Obviously, Sapphire couldn't roam the ship in her wedding whites, but I could go fetch something. "I'm going to head down to the lido deck for some food. Just something to tide us over until dinner. Any requests?"

"Nothing with sauce, dressing, gravy, or spices," Sapphire

listed.

"Nothing with dairy either," Ruby warned. "It makes her gassy." The last thing we needed was a belching bride.

"Also, no bread or anything deep-fried." Sapphire made a devastated face. She loved those things. Fried chicken, biscuits, macaroni and cheese, and fried okra were all staples on Sapphire's dinner table. Soul food, she called it. So, I knew it hurt her soul to have to abstain.

"And no desserts!" the sisters proclaimed, in stereo.

"Okay," I rubbed my temples, already getting a headache. "Carrot sticks. I'll bring back carrot sticks."

Sapphire frowned. "That's boring. You can do better than carrot sticks." I rolled my eyes, leaving the room before I threw something at her.

The lido deck was part of the cruise ship that featured all the swimming pools, bars, and dining options. It was on the ninth of the fifteen decks of the vessel. I took the stairs down six floors from the salon to the all-hours buffet. The ship was still very much in its boarding procedure. Only about half of the three-thousand passengers had made it on board. This meant very few people in the dining hall and even fewer people in the buffet line.

He was the first person I saw. Even though he looked identical to Justin, I knew it was him instantly. After more than a decade together, I was acutely aware of all the tiny, almost invisible differences between them. Dustin moved with a grace that Justin lacked. A dark cloud shifted across my mood at the sight of him.

Panic set in immediately. I wasn't ready. I thought I was, but I was wrong. I ducked behind the salad bar, hopeful he hadn't seen me, then walked on my knees, careful not to bob my head above the edge of the counter. This garnered a baffled expression from the woman in front of me.

"What are you looking at?" I hissed. "Nothing to see here! Turn around." The woman gave me one more look of judgment before turning away.

I reached one hand up along the edge of the counter, fluttering my fingers around, searching for the plates. I found napkins and cutlery. I even accidentally dipped my fingers in a creamy salad, either pasta or potato. I brought my fingers down, licking them clean. It was definitely potato. It was delicious, and I made a note to come back for a plate of it later. Once again, I reached my arm up, gritting my teeth as I continued my search.

A plate materialized in front of my face. I stopped dead, my eyes traveling slowly. First, from the plate to the well-manicured fingers that held it. Then to the wrist, which sported an expensive silver watch. I followed that up to the well-toned arm, noting the costly fabric of the suit it wore. I traveled my gaze up to the shoulders, broad and firm, my eyes lingering there several seconds longer than they should have. Then, unfortunately, I moved up higher and saw a smiling handsome face, examining me with entertained scrutiny.

I hated that face. Classically handsome, with tousled blonde hair, high cheekbones, a soft, friendly mouth, square jaw, and dimpled cheeks.

"Is this what you're looking for?" he said, waving the plate in front of me. His voice sounded different than I remembered. Vibrant and fluid like a full-bodied, expensive wine that was worth savoring. I hated that voice.

My mouth froze halfway open, unable to form words. Dustin broke out into a shit-eating grin. I still couldn't move. He looked down at me with those piercing eyes. I hated those eyes. Then he knelt to my level, meeting my face head-on. He had more eyelashes than any man had a right to. "Are you okay?" His blink was slow and cocky.

His eyes locked on mine. Something like annoyance or adrenaline spiked in my chest, almost like he bit me. "I'm fine." I didn't sound fine.

"Do you need help getting up?"

I realized that I was still crouched. Somehow, I had completely forgotten that I was still on the floor. Embarrassed, I panicked. "Found it!" I exclaimed, picking up an invisible something on the floor in front of me, then quickly rising to my feet. I shoved the imaginary item in my pocket to continue the charade.

Dustin rose too. "What did you find?"

"A contact lens." I squeezed my forehead, wincing at my stupid lie.

"You're not wearing contacts."

"How do you know?"

He arched his brow. "Because you're wearing your glasses."

Shit. I exhaled, wondering faintly why the hell I said that in the first place. Of course he'd bust me. "Alright, you caught me. I was hiding."

"From me?"

That jerked a laugh from me, but I didn't reply. We both knew the answer already.

"You look good," Dustin gave me a slow nod, up and down my body. I felt violated, like he was undressing me with his eyes—his beautiful, piercing eyes. I hated those eyes! Dustin, unfortunately, also looked good. Sexy even, but it had been months since I'd had sex, so the bar was low. I wasn't about to tell him that, though.

"You look older," I said smugly.

Dustin sighed, shaking his head. "I see you've decided to hate me for the duration of this trip."

After rolling my eyes, I met the gaze of the woman standing across from us, at the salad bar, who was clearly eavesdropping.

"Oh no, Dusty. Not only for the duration of this trip. Having sex with a toddler makes my disdain for you quite permanent."

The woman's mouth gaped open, horrified. Dustin turned to her, "He's exaggerating," he assured her. "He was nineteen."

That didn't seem to soothe the woman's judgment. He turned back to me, "Jesus, Kyle, you make me sound like a child molester. Are you trying to get me arrested?"

I lifted my chin defiantly. "Not intentionally, but I wouldn't stop them."

He scowled. "I was hoping we could be mature about this." I was hoping I could drive my knee right into his crotch. "Still," he went on, "I suppose I deserve this cold reception."

I wanted to say something sassy, but the only thought that came to mind was a simple truth. "Yes, you do." I pushed past him, placing several carrot sticks on the plate I had taken from him.

"How have you been?" Dustin asked. He wore a suit jacket identical to mine, but in dark grey—Justin's wedding color. I begrudgingly noticed how well it fit his frame. I may have hated his guts, but I wasn't blind. Dustin was beautiful. Seeing him dressed in black-tie was a bit too much confirmation for my liking.

"Never been better," I said. I added a handful of celery, cherry tomatoes and snap peas to the plate, making sure to skip over broccoli because, like dairy, it too made Sapphire gassy.

"How are your parents?" he asked me.

"Not really any of your concern, are they?"

Dustin was wounded. "Are you seeing anybody?"

"I don't see how that's any of your business either," I replied snootily, reaching for a few napkins.

He took a deep, defeated sigh. "I'm trying to make conversation. This is awkward for me, too, you know."

"Is it?"

"You know it is."

"Sorry," I said, feeling a brief moment of compassion. "My parents are fine. Dad had a minor stroke last August."

"I'm sorry to hear that." I did not expect sincerity, although I suppose I should have, considering the subject matter. It threw me temporarily. I knew how to handle sincere Dustin about as well as I would know how to handle a pack of rabid dogs.

"Thank you," I nodded. "There was no permanent damage,

thankfully."

"That's good to hear. How's your mom?"

"Mom is still my mom. You know her. Worrying too much, calling too much, generally being too much, but she's good."

A silence fell between us. Ten long seconds of nothing, then Dustin asked again, "Are you seeing anyone? Sapphire had mentioned someone named Simon or Simba or something?"

Simba? "Yes, I was dating an African lion. Things were going pretty well until he attacked a woman wearing black and white stripes."

He chuckled. "So, you're not seeing anyone?"

"Still none of your business, but no. I am not seeing anybody."

"You're here all alone?" There was a tenderness to his voice. That prick had the nerve to feel sorry for me!

"I've been assured that there are three thousand other people on this boat. I'm certain I'll make do," I retorted, pushing my glasses up my nose.

"You know what I mean. Flying solo at a wedding sucks. Vacationing alone also sucks. So, being single at a wedding that is also a vacation must be brutal."

Wow. "I was perfectly happy, flying solo, as you put it, but now you've pointed out how bleak and depressing my situation is. Thank you for that." My sarcasm had reached an all-new level. "Now, if you'll excuse me, I'm going to drown myself in a sink filled only with my lonely, lonely tears."

"I'm sorry," Dustin groaned. "I wasn't trying to be insensitive."

I gave a condescending chuckle. "You never have to try. Insensitivity comes naturally to you."

"I'd be happy to save you a dance later since you're all alone."

The thought of twirling around the dancefloor with Dustin made me want to gag.

"I don't plan on doing much dancing tonight, especially with you."

"Especially with me?" Dustin's face was so controlled that I couldn't tell if I'd genuinely offended him or not.

"Besides," I added, "I wouldn't want to make your boyfriend jealous."

He raised an eyebrow. "You heard?" He seemed surprised.

I nodded. "Did you need to get parental consent to take him across state lines?"

He looked a little embarrassed. "I see Sapphire has told you everything."

I shook my head. "Ruby, actually. Sapphire was uncharacteristically tight-lipped about you and your boy-toy."

"We are family now. Maybe her loyalties are shifting." It wasn't a question. "And for the record, Shawn is not a toy. We've been together for six months."

"Wonderful!" I made a showing of exuberance. "Were you his date to prom?"

"He's a sophomore at the University. While he may be young, he's very mature for his age. Much more mature than you are right now."

It was harsh but not untrue. I knew my digs were low. I felt a small twinge of remorse for razzing Dustin. A ridiculously small twinge. Almost microscopic. Yet it was large enough to make me reel myself in. "I apologize." It was almost sincere. Then, for a moment, I offered honesty. "The idea of you with a much younger man brings out the worst in me."

"Given our history, that makes sense."

Silence fell between us for what felt like minutes, awkward and palpable. I was tired of the exchange anyway. "Well, this conversation has been as compelling as toenail clippings," I said, resuming my snarky tone. "So, if you'll excuse me, Sapphire's probably having a coronary, wondering what's keeping me and her carrot sticks so long."

"You've been reduced to her carrot slave?"

"I prefer the title, Food Wench." Then I gave a perfunctory

nod before walking away. I could feel his eyes on me as I retreated. It took every ounce of my strength to resist the urge to turn back around and blow raspberries at him.

Forty-five minutes later, we were organizing in the corridor outside the ballroom. As we assembled, I did the mental math. Sapphire had Ruby and me in her bridal party. Justin's groomsmen were made up of one of his uber hetero, toxically masculine college frat brother, and Dustin. Shit. Unless Sapphire intended for me to walk on the arm of the Neanderthal, that likely meant that...

"We meet again," Dustin said, taking his spot next to me in the procession. He offered his arm. I pretended not to notice the tight curve of his bicep. Looking at his extended hand, my skin crawled. I refused to take it. Instead, I put my hands firmly in my front pockets, then held breath, releasing it in slow, controlled steam.

"Oh, come on. Lighten up," Dustin taunted. "We don't actually have to hold hands, but could you try not to look so nauseated."

I casually gave him the finger. "I could vomit just looking at you."

"That's sweet," he said tartly. Then he leaned closer, whispering in my ear, "Incidentally, you look fat."

Scrunching my nose against the obnoxiously pleasant smell of his cologne, I clenched my teeth. "I passed a kidney stone once that was less painful than this." He smiled at my comment, charmingly. I was not a violent person, but at that moment, the urge to bitch-slap that wicked grin off his face was nearly irresistible.

"This isn't a dream come true for me either, you know," he admitted, looking away from me. "Still reading books for a living?" he asked, changing the subject.

"Still convincing people to buy shit they don't want or need?"

"Yes. In fact, I finally became a partner," Dustin announced.

I remembered how badly he wanted that promotion. He had been working so hard. At times he had been convinced it would never happen. "I'd congratulate you, but I'm afraid I'd choke on the words."

"Oh, please risk it."

Before I could respond, the ship's wedding coordinator nodded to the DJ, and music began to play. I tried not to look entirely revolted as Dustin and I marched down the aisle. We walked shoulder-to-shoulder down the narrow path, making sure not to touch. My stomach was twisted, and my smile was too bright, but it was better than snarling like a rabid animal, which was what the proximity to Dustin made me want to do.

"Why are you making that face?" Dustin carefully whispered in my ear, his lips barely moving. "You look constipated."

I elbowed him in the side.

So soured by the man next to me, I hadn't taken the time to observe the setting. My breath caught in my throat. Never in my life had I seen anything so opulent. The wedding planners of the cruise line had made sure every detail was absolutely perfect. The ship's ballroom was stunning; arched ceilings, crystal chandelier and beautiful hardwood flooring, laid diagonally. The aisle was blanketed with yellow petals, leading up to a small, raised stage, anchored by four stone columns. Twenty or more tables with white silk tablecloths, trimmed with silver beads, were placed around the room. Atop each table was an elaborate centerpiece of exotic tropical flowers. Pink, blue, and grey ribbons hung from each chair's back, and tiny white lights, wrapped around each chair leg, twinkled.

Despite the balmy Miami heat, the room was cold. As pleasant as that was, I was still ungrateful. I was a stress sweater, and at that moment, I felt incredibly stressed. The fact that I couldn't blame the heat for the tiny drops of moisture forming at my temples only added to that stress.

The ceremony was simple yet elegant. Sapphire looked

gorgeous, while Justin looked happy and prepossessing. Rings were exchanged, vows were spoken, and Mrs. Johnson shed a few tears during both. In the end, Sapphire and Justin shared a tasteful, well-rehearsed kiss, which had the entire room erupting into cheers and applause.

Unlike traditional weddings, a wedding on a cruise ship was condensed for speed. After the ceremony, only three hours were allotted for the reception. Cake cutting, speeches and dance all had to be over with before the ship left port. That way, any invited guests who had not also purchased a cruise ticket could disembark. Had I known that was an option, I would have tried harder to say no to Sapphire's very generous offer to purchase my ticket. Her parents had ended up paying the travel expenses for the entire wedding party. I would have hated to see that bill—almost as much as I was going to hate the next ten days. Hell, a few hours and two run-ins with Dustin had already been more than I could stand. Sober anyway.

Sapphire and Justin had disappeared with their photographer to take wedding photos above deck, so I saw it as the perfect opportunity to hit the bar. I ordered something tropical to set the mood for the Caribbean week ahead and had just taken a sip of my Sea Breeze when I felt a tap on my shoulder.

"Kyle," Dustin's voice punched my name. "I'd like to introduce you to my boyfriend, Shawn."

Of course he would. I fully understood why, too. Who wouldn't want to wave their shiny new relationship in the face of the person who dumped them? Even I wouldn't have been above that kind of pettiness. I looked over my shoulder. "Charmed, I'm sure."

"I'm sure you're sure." Dustin positioned himself, so I had no choice but to turn and face the new man. Shawn stood there, in childlike cuteness, his hand extended. I gave him a well-faked smile, shaking it reluctantly.

"Nice to meet you, Shawn. I'm Kyle—the ex." I added in case he hadn't put two and two together.

"It's a pleasure," he shook my hand with much more exuberance than required. "Dustin has told me so much about you."

For a beat, I was speechless. The last thing I expected was for Dustin to mention me at all. To anyone. Ever. Least of all, to a new boyfriend. Wasn't that one of the new relationship rules? No talking about the exes? I wondered what kind of things Dustin had told him.

"Don't let anything he said frighten you," I assured Shawn. "I promise I'm not the wicked witch of the west."

Dustin chuckled. "You're sure as hell not Glinda."

"You're right. I'm Wanda, the so-so witch of the north-east. I'm good or wicked, depending on the person. Now go away, before I drop a house on you."

Shawn smiled wide, thoroughly entertained by our constant wave of snarky comments. "I love *The Wizard of Oz*!"

"Yes? Well, most children do." I nodded. Shawn appeared oblivious to my shade. "Shawn, Dusty tells me you're a sophomore in college?"

"Yes, sir," Jesus. He called me, sir.

"What's your major?"

"Physical Education," Shawn boasted. "I want to be a Phys-ed teacher or an adventure guide when I grow up."

When he grew up? I let out a single, incredulous laugh-breath, then quickly smothered it with my hand. After I regained composure, I said, "I'm sorry. That was rude of me."

"Yes, it was. You can buy Shawn a drink to make up for it," Dustin chimed in.

"I would, Dusty, but I don't think the bartender serves baby formula." I snarked, smiling robotically. "He looks like he just started shaving."

Dustin's brow creased as he stared at me. "How are you single? Frankly, it's a mystery."

I made a face in response, curling my fingers into fists to keep myself from slapping him. I knew I was being utterly, unreasonably, unnecessarily rude. I decided then that it was best to take my leave. I nodded to both before sauntering away.

It felt like a lifetime before the newlyweds returned, and we were all settled at the head table. Nestled between Sapphire and Ruby, I was still irritated about being paired up with Dustin, of all people. Having to walk down the aisle next to him had been incredibly infuriating. To be honest, I was also furious with Sapphire for putting me in that situation in the first place. I anxiously folded my napkin into a complicated shape on the table. It kind of looked like a bird. Ruby, sensing my anxiety, passed me a flute of champagne. I took it gladly, drinking it in one giant swig, then I flagged down a waiter, ordered two more Sea Breezes and instructed him to keep them coming.

"If my glass is empty for even a second," I warned him, "there will be no tip for you." I decided to spend the rest of the reception getting thoroughly drunk. Still, I needed his cooperation to make that happen. He nodded understanding, then scurried away.

By the time the toasts began, I was seeing double and feeling truly little. Sea Breezes packed a bigger punch than the name suggested. As best man, Dustin had the luxury of speaking first.

"Isn't Sapphire looking absolutely gorgeous?" He began, hunched over a wooden podium that was far too short for his frame. "Not only is she beautiful, but she's also caring, sweet, and she deserves one good-looking, sensitive, giving husband. Thankfully for Justin, I play for the other team, so she had to marry him instead."

Shocking myself, I let out a deafening cackle. Dustin certainly thought highly of himself, didn't he? Dustin paused, glancing over at me, wearing an amused smile.

"For those that haven't figured it out," he continued. "Justin and I met in the womb, and we've been inseparable ever since. Justin really is the best friend and brother I could have ever asked for. We've been each other's ride-or-die for the last thirty-eight years. I'm so proud of the wonderful man he's become and the wonderful husband he's sure to be to Sapphire. If you can look past his infatuation with The Care Bears and the fact that he went as Cheer Bear for Halloween in the fourth grade, I think you'll make it through anything!" There was a myriad of chuckles from the tables. "I am thrilled we can share the next ten days with so many friends and family. I can only hope for this much love and support when Shawn and I get married."

When he and Shawn did *what*? He's considering marrying that child after six months? We'd been together over a decade, and I could barely get him to commit to a weekend away! Sapphire gripped my wrist before I could reach for a knife.

Someone shouted out, "Are you getting married?"

Dustin laughed. "No-no, not yet." Not *yet*? "If we do, though, I can only hope all of you will be there to share in our joy. The way you're here for Justin and Sapphire." He took a sip of water. I screamed silently, wanting to throw something heavy or sharp.

Dustin and I made eye contact briefly. Just long enough for us to sneer at each other before he went on. I sat, seething, strangling my napkin like it had personally wronged me.

"There's an old saying about friendship that reads, 'It is one of the blessings of old friends that you can afford to be stupid with them.' Goodness, that couldn't be truer for Justin and me. I could go into all the funny stories that include some of those mistakes we've each made, but I promised Justin I would not speak badly about Kyle today." He winked charmingly at the crowd. I wanted to throw my plate at him, like a frisbee. I slipped my hands down, flattening them under my thighs to keep from doing so.

"Instead," he went on. "I'd rather focus on all the smart moves he's made. The smartest of those moves is marrying Sapphire." There was a barrage of awes from the guests. "Justin was the first to find his way out of the womb, the first to lose his virginity, and the first to find real love. Congrats, you two.

Salut!" He reached for his champagne, and everyone followed suit, raising their glasses in celebration. I did so under duress.

On his way back to the table, he leaned down, whispering to me, "Good luck following that."

I cleared my throat as I stood, pointedly, not looking at him. He laughed at my obstinance, resuming his position to Justin's immediate right. At the same time, I took his place at the podium. I put on my sweetest expression.

"Once in a while," I started, then the entire room cringed as the microphone shrieked painful feedback through the speakers. I shrank back, embarrassed, then adjusted the microphone before trying again. "Once in a while, in the middle of an otherwise ordinary life, love bestows on us a fairy-tale. A romance that is true and pure." Dustin tapped a fork against his wine glass. Soon a chorus of cutlery against crystal glasses forced me to pause and wait while Justin and Sapphire came together for a kiss. *What a jerk*, I thought to myself.

"I have never seen another couple as in love as Sapphire and Justin, and I am so honored to be part of their chosen family." Sapphire blew me a soft kiss. I pretended to catch it, placing it in my breast pocket. Cheesy, yes, but it was something we had done for years. Both of us too proud to admit that we loved each other; we had developed our own way of communicating it. "Love is not always perfect," I went on. "Still, when the right people are together, they will fight to make it work. Nothing in the world can tear them apart." I glanced pointedly at Dustin, sending him a subliminal: *You are scum, that's why we didn't last.*

"These two people sitting in front of us are the epitome of true love. I am so lucky to be a part of this special day and bear witness to this proclamation of love."

"How can you tell he works in publishing?" Dustin laughed. "So many big words." The room laughed along with him.

I gritted my teeth. "Sorry, Dusty. I forgot you get confused by words over two syllables long. Let me dumb it down for you." I made my best impression of a caveman. "Justin loves Sapphire, good."

This also caused the room to laugh and applaud. Sapphire did not seem as impressed.

"When I first met Sapphire, we were both fresh out of high school. We were young adults eager to find our way in the big world. Even then, I knew that she was someone special. She is one of the kindest, most generous people that I know. It takes an extraordinary person to tolerate me on my worst days."

"Amen!" Dustin shouted, raising his hand to praise one of the many deities before leaning over to clink glasses with his brother.

I tried—really tried—not to clench my hands into fists at my sides. Sapphire was my best friend in the whole world. It was her wedding, and I really was so happy for her I could have burst. Still, it was hard to anchor me fully, especially with Dustin interjecting, at every opportunity.

I cleared my throat. "Over the years, Sapphire and I have laughed together, cried together, and made so many amazing memories. She is one of the most important people in my life. I would do anything for her."

"Including take a vacation with an ex that left you for a younger--"

That was it! I had enough! "Oh my god, Dustin! Shut the fuck up! You cum-guzzling gutter whore!"

The entire room gasped collectively. My mouth gaped open as I slowly realized what had happened. Dustin had baited me into making a scene, and I had fallen for it. Hook, line, and sinker. I felt a firm hand on my forearm, pulling me away from the podium. It was Ruby. I returned to my seat, mortified and defeated.

"What Kyle is trying to say," Ruby attempted to recover. "Is, Sapphire, we love you, and we are so happy for you and Dustin—JUSTIN!" She corrected herself quickly. "And the life you're building together. Congratulations!"

Everyone took a ceremonial drink of their champagne, even though awkwardness had thickened the air in the room. Everyone that is, except Sapphire and me. I knew better than to partake while she was glaring at me with those disapproving eyes. I wanted to die. I was quite sure she wouldn't have wept if I did.

THREE
KYLE

With a resounding smack, Sapphire slapped her hand against my forehead.

"You said fuck in your speech!" She snarled. "You said fuck at my wedding! In front of my parents!"

Sapphire pursed her lips and cracked her knuckles. The same two things she always did when she was irritated with me. She and Ruby had hauled me into the women's restroom the moment the speeches were over. I stared down at the floor, unable to meet Sapphire's gaze. She looked like she was vision-boarding my brutal death.

"I'm not as surprised at this turn of events as you are," Ruby told her sister, coolly, with an inscrutable smile. "Although, I would be far more concerned with 'cum-guzzling gutter whore' if I were you."

Sapphire did not seem to find that funny. "Be quiet, Ruby," she ordered, her voice high.

As instructed, Ruby clamped her mouth shut. We weren't exactly afraid of Sapphire, but it was her day. It was her wedding. Sapphire was rightfully empowered with the knowledge that she was in charge.

"Fuck! Seriously? Fuck. In front of fifty of my friends and relatives!" Sapphire said with utter disdain.

"Oh, for Christ's sake," Ruby tried again. "He *said* it in front of them. He didn't *do* it in front of them."

"Ruby," Sapphire responded, her tone eerily calm. "For the last time, shut up."

She did.

"Are you out of what's left of your mind?" Sapphire demanded of me. "What on earth were you thinking?" She folded her arms across her chest, waiting for answers.

"I was thinking how nice it would be to smash a plate into

his face."

"Please, tell me another joke," Sapphire said. "While you're at it, please explain to me how this is funny."

I was going to tell her that I wasn't trying to be funny. I had very seriously contemplated throwing my plate at Dustin. Instead, I opened then closed my mouth a couple of times, unsure of what to say. I searched for words that weren't whiney or groveling and found none. "He started it," I stated finally. "He was interrupting me constantly. He pushed me until I couldn't take it any longer."

"Sugar, I do not care who started what," Sapphire's nostrils flared. To anyone less familiar with her temperament, she would have looked positively homicidal. Then her expression softened, and she gave me a passive-aggressive smile.

"As your best friend, I can agree that this isn't entirely your fault. He was trying to bait you. I acknowledge that. Still, you fell for it!" She sighed exasperatedly. I felt like she was continually sighing where I was concerned. I was amazed she had any oxygen left.

My amazement was not enough to appease my annoyance, however. I glared at Sapphire, conflict making my words come out tangled and thick. "How can you take his side on this? Anyone with eyes can see that he's manipulating me."

Sapphire watched, her expression mildly compassionate. She reached out, squeezing my shoulder. "Get it together, Kyle. He is my husband's twin brother, which means he automatically gets a free pass."

"Wow." I clenched my jaw. Why did Dustin get a free pass while I got met with severe scorn and ridicule? It didn't make sense to me. "Sapphire! I'm the victim here. You're supposed to be my bestie. You're supposed to be sympathetic."

"Sugar, I *am* your bestie. This is why I can tell you the unvarnished truth. The truth is, my sympathy ended the moment you decided to ruin my wedding."

"That's not fair! Didn't you hear the menacing laughter?"

"Yes, the most sinister of all sounds. The laugh."

"It certainly is when the whole room is laughing at your expense! It's even more horrific when it's an ex-lover cracking the jokes."

"Truly terrifying," Sapphire's voice said, clearly uninterested. She shook her head, then panic struck her as if she remembered she still had the rest of her reception to get through. "I don't have time to deal with this right now. So, here's what you're going to do," She said, fixing her hair in the bathroom mirror. "You're going to stay clear of Dustin. Completely. For the rest of the night."

"Um," I started.

"No!" she shouted. Ruby and I both winced as her voice bounced off the bathroom's ceramic walls. "I don't want to hear it! You're either going to avoid him completely or make nice with him. The choice is yours, but I know you. You won't be able to make nice, so just avoid him."

I blinked. "Do you really think that little of me?"

"There's only an hour left," Sapphire went on, ignoring me. "I'm sure you can last a while longer." She headed for the door, then stopped to kiss my forehead, where she had slapped her hand earlier. "You're a dumbass, but you're my dumbass. Please behave."

Then she was gone, heels clicking behind her. "I love you," I called after her.

"You exhaust me." I heard her reply before she vanished completely.

"All right, here's the deal," Ruby said, stepping in front of me. "Dustin's a dick. He's trying to sabotage you, and Sapphire is falling for it. I've got your back, girl. Do yourself a favor and let me handle him."

"Please, don't call me girl."

"I will call you whatever I want to, and you will like it. I'm the only person on this boat who is in your corner."

"Thank you, Ruby."

"Don't thank me. Just do as I tell you and lay low."

Trying to do as Ruby instructed, I chose a corner as far away from the dancefloor as possible to watch the couple enjoy their first dance. I hovered near the cake and the champagne fountain, wine glass in hand. Both sets of parents joined Sapphire and Justin for the second song, Sapphire, with her dad, Justin, with his mom, while the remaining two parents danced with each other. Halfway through the song, Dustin and Ruby joined the dancefloor together. It was sweet to watch the blending of the two families.

A few years ago, I would have considered them my family too. Dustin and I had discussed marriage only once. During that conversation, he had made it clear that marriage was not something he had any interest in. Granted, after being together fifteen years, marriage would have just been a formality anyway. Dustin's parents, Paul, and Kathy were great people. I missed the weekly Sunday dinners with them. I missed the sage advice Kathy would impart; on how to handle my own overbearing mother. I missed how Paul would treat me like one of the boys, when my own father still looked at me, at times, like I was damaged or wrong in some way.

I knew my parents loved me, and I loved them in return. Still, Paul and Kathy Salinger had also been parental figures in my life. For more than a decade, I was lucky to have them. Now, in many ways, I was an outsider—the one person in the entire group who didn't really belong. Dustin's statement from earlier echoed in my drunk mind.

Sapphire and I are family now. Maybe her loyalties are shifting.

He wasn't wrong; they were officially family now. Dustin was her husband's brother. From that moment on, Sapphire would be expected to side with him for no other reason but out of respect for her family. I wasn't family. It felt like I was losing something. My position as Sapphire's best friend no longer felt so steadfast or permanent.

"Would you care to dance?" Dustin asked, sliding up to me. I hadn't even realized the song had finished or that the DJ had announced the dancefloor open to everyone. I had been lost in my depressing thoughts.

"Shoo!" I said, free hand flapping in front of my face. "Begone, creature of the night."

Dustin had the nerve to laugh. "Very mature."

"Dusty, don't you have a date to attend to?" I gestured to Shawn, who seemed perfectly comfortable, confident, and entertained, sitting at a table with Sapphire's drunk aunt Lorraine. She was notorious for her outlandish stories and hilarious anecdotes. Shawn was in good hands.

"Kyle," Dustin said my name in a maddeningly smooth way. "I'm sure we can survive one dance together. We survived fifteen years."

"And I regret that," I very politely refrained from adding, *I didn't kill you, you bastard.*

"I'll even let you lead." Dustin smiled back, stretching out his hand to take mine, his eyes unreadable. He was annoyingly attractive, and he knew it. From across the room, Sapphire and I made eye contact. She was subliminally instructing me to play nice. I groaned, my shoulders sinking. With an eye roll, I allowed him to pull me onto the dancefloor.

Sapphire's wedding photographer was in the corner of the room, pointing his lens straight at us. So, I smiled winningly, saying through my teeth, "Let's get it over with."

Dustin rested an overly familiar hand on my waist. "Do you ever get tired?"

"Excuse me?"

"Of pretending you hate me?" He clarified.

I stared at him as we started to sway together. His eyes were big, soft and blue. He desperately needed to be punched in one of them. "You think I'm pretending?"

"I think you want to hate me. You even have reason to, I suppose. I don't think you do, though," Dustin said, naturally taking the lead, even after promising it to me.

"You're right. I don't hate you. I loathe you with every fiber of my being."

"You know," Dustin said between spins. "We had a lot of good times."

I wanted to set myself on fire. "Your point?"

"I think, maybe, if you tried, we could be friends."

Laughter erupted from me, loud and false. "Go fuck yourself."

"Hardly enough time," Dustin smiled.

"As I recall, you never needed much time."

"Please. Compared to you, I was a superhero."

"Indeed, Superman. Faster than a speeding bullet." I laughed again. A solitary snort escaped me as I took in air between cackles.

"Oh," Dustin narrowed his eyes. "You're drunk."

"I am not!" I lied.

"You only snort when you're drunk."

I made a concentrated effort not to roll my eyes. "Or when something is extremely entertaining. The suggestion that we could somehow be friends is earth-shatteringly hilarious."

"I'm just saying, we were friends before we were lovers. We could be friends again."

"Why would I want to be friends with you? You have the personality of a mop."

"You were always so free with compliments."

"You were always so free with everything else."

"Touché," He shrugged. "Be honest, though. Our bed was dryer than Black Rock City." The man had attended Burning Man one time, seven years ago. Still, he found a way to work it into as many conversations as possible. "If a man doesn't get it at home, he's going to look elsewhere after a while."

I was offended. "So, it's *my* fault you cheated?"

"I didn't say that."

"It was implied!"

Dustin laughed ruefully, "You're much easier to talk to when you're sober."

"You're just as unpleasant to talk to regardless of my level of liquor consumption."

"Dammit. This conversation isn't going how I'd hoped."

"Oh?" I made my eyes as coy and angelic as I knew how. "What did you hope, exactly? That you'd suggest that we try to be friends, and I'd instantly forget how you ripped my heart out? You think I'd jump at the chance to have you back in my life, in any capacity? Sorry Dusty, that ship has sailed. No, that ship has sunk."

"You know what?" Dustin whispered. "I'm not sure what I was thinking either. I should have known better than to even suggest it. I guess I was hoping we could salvage at least some sort of relationship since Sapphire and Justin have bound us together, forever."

"What are you babbling about?"

"You seriously haven't thought about it? We are going to be thrown together in random situations for the rest of our lives."

"Don't be absurd. We've managed to avoid each other successfully for two years, haven't we?"

"Yeah, and how difficult do you think that's been on Justin or on Sapphire? Splitting their time between us, balancing Christmases birthdays, and Friday game nights. Always being able to invite one of us, but not the other."

I always suspected that had been happening behind the scenes. Naturally, I assumed I was prioritized above Dustin. Now I realized he had been made to feel the same way. "You almost refused to come to this wedding because I was going to be here," he continued. "Do you think it's going to get easier once they have kids?"

Kids? No, it likely wouldn't.

"I'm not trying to upset you, only warn you," Dustin said, his tone polite.

"Warn me?" My tone was not as polite.

"Yes," he nodded. "Haven't you noticed that I have tried to be exhaustively civil today?"

I rolled my eyes poignantly. "Oh yeah, you've been a total prince—of darkness! You have been successfully sabotaging everything I've done today."

"You can't blame me if you fall for it." I wanted to scream. "Nothing wrong with a little healthy competition."

I pressed my lips together. "Competing over what? Nobody's winning anything."

"Nothing, except the glory of winning."

I looked at him, a grimace around my mouth and eyes. "You know what, you little shit, you can say or do whatever you want, but I'm not playing your games."

"Games?" He was insulted by my choice of words. "Look," he went on. "I don't particularly enjoy your company any more than you do mine, but I understand our situation."

I pinched the bridge of my nose where a stress headache was already percolating. "What situation is that?"

His tone shifted to one of professional level-headedness. "As we are now, there isn't going to be room for both of us in their lives. If we don't get in a position to stomach being around each other, one of us is going to get shut out." He paused a beat to see if I understood. When I didn't respond right away, he pressed forward. "I'm a blood relative. Justin and I shared a womb."

"Fuck off, I know that," I spat.

He pushed on. "I'm trying to help you, Kyle."

I was not convinced that was true. "Help me?"

"Yes. You need to be prepared for what's coming."

I stood with a vacant expression. I wasn't sure what Dustin was trying to say, so I wasn't sure how to respond. So I said nothing. It all became clear when he punched me in the gut with his next phrase.

"One of us is going to eventually be left behind," he said with certainty. "And it won't be me."

My mouth dropped open.

The song ended, and Dustin let go of my waist. "Thank you for the dance," he said tersely, turning to walk away.

I was furious. Dustin had the nerve to suggest that I could be tossed away, like garbage, simply because I did not share a bloodline. What about all those years of love and laughter? What about all those times I held Sapphire's hair when she celebrated too hard or held her entire body when she sobbed? Were they meaningless? Did twenty years of friendship mean nothing when compared to Dustin's new status as her brother-in-law? If that wasn't insulting enough, Dustin dared to think that he got the last word on the subject.

"How dare you!" I started after him. Without thinking, I reached out, pulling his shoulder back, determined that the conversation was not over.

Dustin turned to shake off my grip, and I staggered back, my drunk balance teetering, causing me to trip over my own feet. Not wanting to fall, I planned to steady myself by grabbing the nearest table, only to realize that table displayed the gorgeous, three-tiered wedding cake. Instead, I willed myself to fall backward and braced for the painful collision with the floor. My head crashed against the adjacent table, the one I hadn't noticed, knocking over the champagne fountain.

I was instantly showered in a loud explosion of glass and bubbles. Soaked and sticky, horror was added to my embarrassment when I saw the circular cake table shake from the crash's vibration. Then, in what felt like slow motion, I watched as one of the table's three legs popped loose. The entire table tipped suddenly, covering me in an additional layer of white and blue buttercream.

I saw Dustin drift away to hover near one of the walls, while somewhere in the room, I heard Sapphire scream.

FOUR
KYLE

"Ginger ale, please." I requested from the bartender, sliding him my sailor's card. There was no money exchanged onboard the cruise ship. Everything was charged directly to your room via a small, plastic card, just like in a hotel or resort. The card acted both as currency and as your room key.

The bartender poured a small plastic glass with soda. Placing it in front of me, he didn't even bat an eye at my appearance. I was still damp from champagne, with frosting smeared on my suit and clumped in my hair. I had wanted to change, but my luggage hadn't yet cleared security. I was definitely in the mood for something stronger than ginger ale, but I probably had more than enough booze in my system. So instead, I opted for something that would ease my stomach and perhaps sober me up.

I had been too mortified by the incident to stay for the rest of the reception. Sapphire couldn't even look at me. Not that I blamed her. It was supposed to be her dream day. She had been waiting for it her entire life, and I had singlehandedly managed to turn it into a wedding day apocalypse. The only way I could have possibly made it worse was by setting Sapphire's gown on fire. With my luck, had I stayed at the reception any longer, that likely would have happened too.

So I did the only thing I could think to do. I left. I mean, I couldn't go far. I was on a sea-faring vessel. Yet, I could go someplace that was elsewhere. I left Sapphire and Justin to salvage what they could in the last forty minutes they had before the reception was forced to end, and the ship had to get underway.

I had been tempted to leave the ship altogether, not go the

cruise, and arrange an immediate flight home. Yet, I worried that would be like adding salt to Sapphire's wounds. Her parents had forked over all that cash to pay for my trip, and they certainly wouldn't get their money back if I ditched-out last minute. To waste their generosity would add an additional offense to an already long list of horrible behavior. I knew, realistically, that everything had been my fault. As much as I really wanted to blame Dustin—like, really, really wanted to— all he did was throw the net. I was the one who ran right into it and got twisted up.

That had always been my fatal flaw—a complete inability to rise above conflict and, for the greater good, let things go.

When I was a kid, I was always tangled in the center of some sort of playground conflict. I would be the one to point out injustice or unsportsmanlike behavior. I was the morality police, penalizing anyone who failed to meet my expectations. It didn't matter how simple the offense. If you pushed someone off the monkey bars once, it was a crime from which there was no pardon. At least, not from me. I would regularly remind everyone, especially you, that you were a pusher and not to be played with. I was still that little boy in many ways, expecting everyone to hate Dustin for his transgressions against me alone.

I closed my eyes, willing the disaster of the day away and trying to forget.

"You look like you've seen some adventure this evening," a smooth, unfamiliar masculine voice from the end of the bar inquired. I noted his thick accent immediately, either Australian or New Zealand. They were too similar for me to distinguish.

"I have," I admitted. "The great buttercream wars. I wear the battle scars of my humiliating defeat."

"Any casualties?" He asked.

I sighed, then swallowed my ginger ale. "Only my dignity, and perhaps my best friend."

"You're kidding. Your best mate died?"

I decided that he was Australian.

"No, only her faith in me," I nodded to the bartender to pour me another glass. "I'd be surprised if she speaks to me again. I completely ruined her wedding," I admitted, looking to the stranger for a reaction.

His eyes widened slightly, then he laughed. "Now the cake behind your ears makes sense."

I heaved a dramatic sigh, still too disappointed with myself to find the humor in my appearance. It was at least two minutes before the stranger spoke again.

"Cheer up. We're about to set sail on one of the most beautiful bodies of water in the world. Things can't be all that bad."

"That depends who you're sailing with."

"By myself, actually."

I was surprised to hear that. "Who goes on a cruise by themselves?" I may technically have been alone, but I was with a group of people.

"I'll give you that," he said. "I'm here on bizzo." I must have looked confused by his slang. "I'm here for work," he clarified.

"You work on the ship?"

He shook his head. "No, I'm a photographer. I'm scouting several islands for an upcoming project."

"Wouldn't it be easier to fly to the islands?" I asked, pushing my glasses up the bridge of my nose.

"Easier, perhaps, but much more expensive," he said. "By taking a cruise, a get to hit-up all the same islands, while simultaneously avoiding a different airport and hotel every day. Plus, all my food is provided."

Made sense.

"Jax Abernathy," he said, offering me an outstretched hand.

Anyone with eyes could see that Jax Abernathy was a good-looking man. Broad and tanned, wearing a peach-colored sleeveless shirt exposing well-toned arms and shoulders. His hair was thick, chocolate brown, with bangs that came down in long whisps, almost covering one eye. He was roguishly handsome with soulful hazel eyes, perfectly groomed stubble and dramatic cheekbones. If I had to wager, I would have guessed early-thirties. He definitely looked like someone who had his life together. Someone highly evolved, who likely never had to dig in his car's ashtray for change. I shook his hand, pleasantly surprised by how soft his skin was. "Kyle Blackwood. Nice to meet you."

"Likewise. Have you been on a cruise before, Kyle?" He really was one of the best-looking hunks of man-flesh I had ever seen. He was all man, every sleek, well-muscled inch of him.

I shook my head. "This is my maiden voyage."

"A virgin?" He almost seemed excited. "I think you're going to love it."

"You've been on a cruise before, I take it?"

"I've been on several," he confirmed. "I haven't been on this particular ship before, but they're all grouse."

Again, I was confused. "The bird?" I asked, confident that couldn't be what he meant.

He laughed at me. "Sorry, I tend to forget myself. It means great. All the ships are great. They have incredible food and entertainment. Every night there's a different event."

"I guess that's why they call it a fun-ship."

"That's exactly right. So, what do you do, Kyle?"

"I work in publishing."

"Ahhh, a writer?"

My dream was to be a successful author one day. I was a massive fan of queer literature, but too much of it was all one-note. The protagonists were always full of angst or trepidation about coming out. Or they were struggling to find their place in queer culture. My deepest longing was to write something different. Stories where being queer wasn't the focus; it was just a secondary descriptor like hair or eye color. I didn't feel like revealing all that to a stranger, so I waved a dismissive hand. "Not exactly, no. I'm an editor. Basically, I make half-way decent writers sound like Pulitzer Prize-winning authors.

Nothing overly impressive."

"That sounds impressive to me. I imagine you'd have to be a rather good writer in your own right to accomplish that."

"Hardly. I just have an English degree and a basic understanding of what readers want."

"And what do readers want?"

I made a showing of thinking hard. "These days, people have short attention spans. They want a good story that they don't have to work hard to read, small words with a quick pace."

Jax nodded. "A wham-bam-thank-you-book-man, kind of thing?"

I half-smiled. "Essentially, yes."

"Sounds dull. I prefer a story with more grit and heart. A story that makes me feel something."

"Me too," I agreed. "Unfortunately, they don't make the best seller's list very often these days."

"Have you read *House of Impossible Beauties*?"

I had, many times. It was a fantastic, albeit little known novel that took a deep dive into New York City's queer ballroom culture of the eighties and nineties. "It's one of my favorites."

"Mine too. I love how the characters are trying to find their path; each equally lost in entirely different ways." Jax's knowledge of queer literature surprised me, so I said as much.

"I haven't come across many people who've read it." I had convinced my book-club to read it one year, during Pride Month, which they begrudgingly agreed to, at risk of coming across bigoted or intolerant. After all, Sapphire's suggestion of *Beloved* during Black History Month was agreed to without question.

"I love to support lesser-known authors and artists," Jax said, leaning in conspiratorially. "Especially members of the *community*."

"Are you a friend of Dorothy's?" I attempted to be subtle. Florida was on the cusp of the Bible Belt, so one couldn't be too careful when inquiring about someone's sexuality.

"Aren't you?"

"Is it that obvious?"

"Would you be offended if I said yes?"

"No," I shrugged.

"Then, yes." He smiled with a nod. A comfortable but brief silence fell between us. "So," Jax said, flipping the subject. "Do you mind if I ask how you came to be covered in wedding cake?"

"It's a long, boring story."

Jax laughed, with a smile so big that it almost lifted that air around me. "You're sitting at a martini bar, covered in cake, smelling like an Orange County housewife," he said, referring to the stench of cheap champagne that wafted around me. "I doubt it's a boring story, but if it's a long one, just give me the footnotes version."

I started to laugh but cut off when, as if on cue, Dustin and Shawn rounded the corner. Instinctively, I shifted my gaze downward, shrinking lower on the barstool. The duo didn't notice me. They were still dressed in their wedding formals but were heading towards the elevator. The reception must have ended because the guests were scattering to prepare for the ship's sunset departure.

"Were those the friends whose wedding you ruined?" Jax asked, motioning his head in the direction Dustin and his boy-toy had traveled.

I pulled my posture back up straight, but my face was still unsettled. "No, he was the iceberg to my wedding-ruining Titanic." It occurred to me that metaphors about sinking ships while about to set sail on the Caribbean Sea may have been in poor taste.

"Which one?"

"The one who's old enough to vote."

Jax took another look at Dustin and Shawn as they stepped onto the elevator. "So, what's the story? Did he push you into the cake?"

"Push me? Gosh no. Dustin doesn't have a violent bone in his body. The only things he knows how to push are my buttons."

"I'm sensing you don't like him," Jax said, clearly ribbing me.

I forced a smile.

"Is it that obvious?" I questioned facetiously. Then, I regaled him with the tale. I left out some of the more embarrassing or intimate details. I was spilling my guts to a total stranger, after all.

Telling a stranger about one of the most painful moments of my history didn't feel as uncomfortable as it probably should have. There was something therapeutic and nearly satisfying about telling the story to someone who was entirely impartial. I hadn't had the luxury of doing so before. After fifteen years together, everyone in my life had known Dustin. Known him well. It was hard to get them to jump on the Dustin-hate-train and fully commit to the journey. The people I had told had humored me, of course. They had given me a safe space to vent and cry. They had even offered advice when they had some to share. For the most part, however, they maintained neutrality, Sapphire being a prime example. She loved us both, so she allowed me to bash Dustin, but she rarely took part. That made it far less fun.

I had made a promise never to discuss the incident with dates either. Who would go out for a second time with a man who spent the entire first date bashing his ex? No one. So, I never spoke of it. Even though the number of men I entertained the thought of going on a second date with were very few. Jax was different. He had no vested interest in either Dustin or me. So, while telling the story to him, I received an unfiltered reaction for the first time. I told him everything. From the moment I caught Dustin cheating to the very second I was bathed in buttercream humiliation.

I didn't realize I'd been talking for an hour until I finished retelling what happened. "My gosh," Jax said, shaking his head, "What a wanker." It took a moment to decide if he was talking about Dustin or me.

When I finally determined he was referring to Dustin, I replied with a bristling, "You have no idea."

"Now, you're stuck on this ship with him for ten whole days?"

"Not unless I jump overboard. Which, at this point, is a very tempting option."

"Well, I wish you the best of luck," he said, lifting his drink to his lips, finishing it. He swished the liquid in his mouth before swallowing. I couldn't help but notice how square and defined his jaw looked. Like you could cut glass on it.

"Much appreciated. If you could say a few nondenominational prayers on my behalf, I'd be grateful."

"I would, but I'm more spiritual than religious."

"So am I, but I could use all the help I can get."

"I suppose that's true," Jax agreed. "Alright, one prayer. That's all I can agree to."

"One should be enough."

We shared a smile.

"Anyway," I said, rising from my barstool. "I should probably get changed. I'm sure the porters have delivered my luggage to my room by now."

"Are you going to watch the embarkation on the upper deck?"

"I don't think so. I'm not really ready to face my crew yet. I may watch from my balcony."

He nodded, understanding. "If I don't see you around, enjoy your vacation. Don't let that arse ruin it for you."

"I'll try not to. Thank you for the chat."

"Anytime." He nodded farewell as I headed toward the stairwell.

My cabin was on E-deck. While it was only two floors below lido, it was still a long trek to the ship's stern. Thankfully, my luggage was waiting outside the door to my stateroom when I arrived. I slid my sailor's card into the electronic lock and lugged my suitcase in behind me.

The room was a category-three stateroom, which meant it had an extra-long balcony towards the ship's right rear. Sapphire had googled the best side of a cruise ship, and that is where it told her to put us. The stateroom looked exactly like the photos she'd shown me, in hues of cream and tan. There was a wardrobe to the right and a small bathroom to the left when you entered the room. The bathroom was basically a closet with a stand-up shower and a small vanity, but I didn't really need much space to shower and shave.

Further into the room was a sitting area with a two-seater sofa and a smart-TV. The couch flipped upward to reveal storage space and two life-vests underneath.

To the left of the double bed was a small writing desk. It was topped with an ice bucket, a few plastic-but-glass-looking wine goblets and a single yellow orchid in a fancy vase. Poking out from the chalice was a card that read:

Thanks for being part of our special day
- Justin and
Sapphire

Pulling open the heavy-hinged balcony door, I stepped out into the warm February breeze. The temperature was balmy and not what I was accustomed to for that time of year. A loud foghorn sounded, announcing the ship's departure. Placing both hands on the steel rails, I leaned overboard to take in the full splendor of the ship's size. The Lollipop was one of the largest ships in Festival's fleet—fifteen decks high and over a thousand feet long. It amazed me that something so big could even float.

Slowly the ship pulled out of port. On the balconies around me, people shouted and waved to the spectators on the pier. Loud Latin music filtered through giant speakers on the lido deck, and I could feel the joy and excitement as people cheered and danced two floors above. Something bubbled inside me then, something light and more exuberant than the fear or irritation that had hounded me all afternoon and into the early evening.

Below me, the blue waters of Miami glistened like diamonds under the warm glow of the setting sun, and I had to shield my eyes from the glare. It was as though I had stepped through a portal and into a living postcard. If it were this gorgeous in port, I could only imagine the splendor once we hit the open ocean. As the Florida coast slipped further from view, it occurred to me how lucky I was to experience all of this, and on someone else's dime, no less.

A tiny kernel of sunshine sparked through my cloudy disposition as reality sank in, blending with a twinge of joy. I had ten beautiful, sun-drenched days ahead of me. I was about to experience the Caribbean in all its glory. I was confident I could find it in myself to try to enjoy every minute of it. After all, I deserved a vacation. Yes, this one was with my nemesis, but still.

How ungrateful and childish I must have seemed, allowing my disdain for Dustin to ruin such a fantastic experience and Sapphire's wedding, intentional or not. Was I really so shallow and selfish that I would make the entire vacation all about me? Was I really that person? The answer was yes, but I didn't want to be. I'd have to make amends for my behavior earlier that afternoon. I just didn't know where to start.

A shower—I decided, catching a glimpse of myself in the reflection of the glass partition between balconies. My ridiculously expensive blazer was still covered in smashed buttercream flowers. A shower first, then find Sapphire for an obscene amount of groveling.

After showering the stench of champagne and embarrassment out of my hair then changing into something clean, I felt surprisingly better. Well, not better exactly, but definitely more sober. I had just slipped on a pair of yellow shorts and a polo shirt when I heard an aggressive knock on my door.

"Open up, whore!" Ruby called archly. "There's a party upstairs, and you're missing it!"

She meant it as a term of endearment. Still, there was a certain irony of being called a whore by a woman whose vagina had served more people than McDonald's.

"I don't know," I replied while opening the door. "I'm not much in the mood for a party right now."

"Bullshit," she snorted, pushing past me and into the room. She had changed out of her bridesmaid gown and into a floral dress. It was a little too tight and a little too short for my taste, but she looked terrific. "You're going to get your party on, even if I have to drag you upstairs myself."

"How did you even know what room I was in?"

"Duh, I asked Sapphire. She booked us all on the same floor. Except for her room, of course. She and Justin are literally on the other end of the ship. I guess they didn't want us eavesdropping on their wedding sex-capades. I'm next door."

She was holding a bottle of wine in each hand. Contraband, since unauthorized liquor was entirely forbidden.

"That's not allowed on board," I reminded her.

"We're in international waters," she shrugged, plopping herself on one of the two twin beds, crossing her legs chicly.

"I don't think that's how it works."

"Whatever," she dismissed, opening a bottle of rosé—twist cap, how classy. "What are they going to do, make me walk the plank?"

"Probably not, since they're not pirates."

"So then, what's the harm?"

"They could fine you. Maybe even have you removed from the ship."

"Look at me," she said with extreme confidence. "Do I look like the kind of woman that men want to see leave, anywhere?

Especially lonely men, who've been away at sea?"

I laughed, rolling my eyes. "Jesus, Ruby. It's a Festival cruise ship, not the USS Arizona during wartime."

"War or peace is irrelevant. A man is a man." She drank straight from the bottle, then tried to pass it to me.

"What about a *gay* man?"

"Still a man. Even they love a beautiful woman, just for different reasons."

She thrust the bottle to me once more. Recognizing that she would get more persistent, the more I resisted, I took the wine from her and pressed the bottle to my lips.

"Good boy," she nodded, giving me a look I couldn't quite parse. I chalked it up to Ruby being Ruby: impulsive and adventurous, often working in mysterious ways. She had a way of organizing and orchestrating things Sapphire and I never saw coming until it was too late. "Drink up," she urged. "Once you're ready, we'll head up."

"Head up where?"

Ruby opened the second wine bottle for herself. "To party under the stars! Practically the entire ship is up there, dancing and drinking under the Caribbean sky, and you're missing it."

I sighed. "I shouldn't. My day has been eventful enough. I need to talk to Sapphire."

"Not tonight, you don't," Ruby scolded.

"Oh god, why? Is she so mad she won't even speak to me?"

"Aw, Kyle," Ruby said, reaching over, patting my hand. "It's sweet how you think everything is about you."

"I don't think—"

"It's her wedding night," Ruby interrupted my protest. "She and Justin have better things to do than to listen to you apologize repeatedly." She drank. "Besides, I think you're blaming yourself far too much. If you ask me, the whole thing is doomed from the start."

"Um, that's your sister and brother-in-law you're talking about."

"I don't mean them as a couple," She took another gulp from her bottle. "I mean the situation in general. Getting this many people, with so many issues, in a small, confined space is a recipe for disaster. Especially if it includes an open bar."

"Still, if it wasn't for me—"

"Enough! There will be plenty of time for self-flagellation if that's what turns you on. Tonight, the goal is to let loose and hopefully dislodge that stick from your ass."

"Excuse me?"

She glared. "Don't pretend you don't know what I'm talking about. I play stupid much more convincingly than you do."

She got no argument from me.

"Kyle," She clarified in between swallows. "You've been tighter than a teenage cooter since we got here."

"Gross. Please don't compare me to vaginas of any age."

"Not the point," Ruby replied. "You seem to think this entire trip is the Dustin and Kyle saga. That story is over. It has been for two years. Frankly, you're acting like a douche."

"That's…fair."

"Yeah, so?"

"So?" I prodded.

"So, stop it!"

"Dustin—"

"Dustin is your problem, not Sapphire's. Stop trying to make him her problem. Better yet, stop using him as an excuse for your bad behavior. You're a grown man. Take some responsibility for your own actions."

"Shit, I'm an asshole," I said as realization sunk in.

"Mm-hmm, you are."

"I really don't want to make this entire vacation about me. I want to be mature, but Dustin makes it so difficult."

"Of course he makes it difficult! He's your ex. If being friends with your ex was easy, everyone would do it."

"I don't want to be friends with him."

"No one is saying you have to."

59

"Good, because I'd rather be waterboarded."

"Still, you do have to be friendly."

"Absolutely not!"

"Absolutely yes."

"No!"

"Yes," she nodded.

"No!" I said again, on the verge of a tantrum.

"Yes!" She scolded louder.

I could tell she wasn't going to let it go. I was quiet for a moment, just long enough to take a swig from my bottle. Finally, I gave in. "Fine, but you better tell Dustin that, too."

"I absolutely did." I must have looked disbelieving because she added. "I told you I'd handle it, didn't I?"

"No," I told her between swallows of wine. "You said you'd handle *him*. I was hoping there'd be bloodshed or at least restraints."

"Kinky, but not my style. Dustin's agreed to retract his claws as long as you do."

Why did it feel like I was being forced to be the bigger man in this scenario? "This feels monumentally unfair," I drank again.

That's when I started to feel tingly.

FIVE
JAX

Wa frozen cocktail in one hand and my camera in the other, I stepped out onto the lido deck where the party was in full swing. The heavy ocean air stuck my shirt to my chest as I snapped pictures of the crowd. I marvelled at the spectacle—cruisers celebrating the departure from their respective worlds in their own different ways. Professionals, families, single twenty-somethings, and grandparents, all blowing whistles, drinking, cheering, and flailing to loud Caribbean music.

A large orange sphere hung low on the horizon. I snapped a picture of it, captivated by how large the setting sun looked on the cusp of the waterline. Even after the sun slipped from sight, the colours dazzled in the sky, painting the twilight with hues of pink, orange, and deep purple.

To my left, a young girl, six-years-old at most, twirled in a yellow sundress, the bold colour creating a pleasant contrast against her olive complexion. An attractive brunette woman stood nearby, keeping a watchful eye on the youngster. We made eye contact, and I gestured with my camera. She nodded, smiling.

Not wanting to get a distorted view of the girl from above, I knelt to her level. From that angle, I could capture a greater abundance of the scene around her, rather than just the simple, brown deck floor. Behind her, I could see the Prussian blue of the ocean peeking through the white metal banisters of the ship. The sky was caught in civil twilight, that breathtaking moment when the light started to fade. However, we could still comfortably go about our business without the need for artificial light. Although the demand was little, strategically placed deck lights slowly came to life around us, causing the ankle-biter to create intriguing shadows as she danced and spun.

I switched my camera to burst mode and held down the shutter button for several moments, hoping to capture her exuberance in real-time. Self-consciousness and embarrassment were foreign concepts at that age, so she continued to twirl with little regard to me. When I was confident I had enough photos, her mother and I exchanged pleasantries and e-mail addresses. I promised to send her the finished picture. Then, I moved on.

The lido deck was party central, and while I walked across it, *Cupid Shuffle* began to blare through the expensive sound system. I could feel the base of the music through the balls of my sandals and up through my legs. The dancefloor quickly filled up with people of all ages and backgrounds, thrilled to be free of the mundane of their real lives, if only for ten days. A senior couple ambled their way to the floor. I snapped a few candid shots of them as they tried to keep up with the more experienced line dancers around them. The gentleman held her hand while he explained the steps.

To the right, to the right...

He led her.

To the left, to the left...

She was concentrating on her steps, and he changed direction before she knew she had to, so they bumped into each other softly. They both chuckled at the collision. I had to restrain a laugh, and I hoped I caught the innocent exchange on film.

I loved people watching, especially with my camera. I enjoyed the challenge of hiding in the wings, patiently waiting to capture an intimate moment. Sometimes the moment was public, sometimes private, sometimes embarrassing, but always genuine.

I ascended a metal staircase up to the mezzanine overlooking the lido deck. Realistically, it wasn't a balcony area. It was another floor, all its own, that featured the mini-golf course, the water slides, and a running track. It was also the only place where I could get a full scope view of the party happening below.

I was panning across the floor when suddenly I saw him, the cute wedding-wrecker from earlier. Kyle. He had looked so defeated when we initially crossed paths, I was glad that he had decided to venture out after all. He was walking, or rather, teetering alongside a pretty woman with dark skin. Her dress was bloody short and tight, and she drew a little too much attention as she passed through the crowd.

Kyle's bright yellow shorts made him look cheerful and handsome. They also made it easy for my eyes to follow them as they walked around the dancefloor towards the rum bar. Although, to be honest, it didn't look like either needed more booze in their lives. He already carried with him a glass of something. It looked like a pina colada, and I wondered how many others he had in the brief time since our encounter. He seemed pissed as a fart but not yet sloppy.

He looked different outside of the formal attire from earlier. His arms weren't muscular like mine, but they were toned enough to prove he put forth some effort at the gym. His legs were surprisingly muscular and seemed to go on forever. For some reason, I expected that, in shorts and a polo, he'd look like a string bean with awkward limbs bending at odd angles. Maybe I assumed that because he was so tall.

I snapped a few candid shots of the pair of them. The first was one of Kyle laughing at something his mate had said. The second was one of his mate flipping her long hair over her shoulder as they moved through the crowd. I didn't take any photos that could be considered invasive or predatory, just evidence of fun being had by two mates.

The song switched to something Latin-inspired, with a fast beat and heavy percussion. Some of the line dancers cleared the floor, and new dancers took their place. One of those dancers was Kyle's mate, escorted to the floor by a debonair, although likely sleazy, bloke in chinos. Which left Kyle standing alone, in a corner by the hot tub, casually sucking the straw of his cocktail. He looked a little awkward but not uncomfortable. Like he was wondering what he was supposed to do while she danced. *Go dance too*, I pushed the thought towards him. The message was not received. Instead, he perched on one of the wooden pool chairs, drumming his foot along to the rhythm of the music. Clearly drunk and obviously bored. That's when I chose to throw him a lifeline.

As I approached, it became more apparent how uncomfortable Kyle really was. His foot drummed off rhythm, struggling to find the beat, while he visibly wrestled with what to do with his hands. He looked handsomely awkward, like a red-headed Clark Kent. "You don't dance?" I asked when I had finally reached his perch.

"You!" Kyle noted, his smile welcoming, but his tone was gobsmacked, and his inflection slurred.

"Me," I confirmed, returning his grin. I queried again, "You don't dance?"

"No, I do," Kyle replied. "Just not very well, and I think I've embarrassed myself enough this evening."

"I'm sure you can't be that bad."

"You know those embarrassing old men at parties who always end up thrusting their way onto a list of the world's most cringe-worthy YouTube videos?"

"Yes…" I said cautiously.

"I am their leader." I laughed, and he continued. "You know how they say, dance like no one is watching? Well, I dance like my body is on fire, and trust me, people *are* watching. It's like a car wreck they cannot look away from, no matter how grotesque."

"How can you be so hard on yourself?"

"Years of practice."

"Maybe more practice is exactly what you need."

"No," he said, shaking his head. "I'm already very good at bashing myself."

"That sounds like a good conversation for you and your therapist, but I meant to practice dancing."

"Oh…" he giggled like a little boy who had learned how to make foul noises with his armpit.

"C'mon," I said, craning my neck towards the dancefloor. "Dancing is a human right. You don't have to be any good at it to enjoy it."

"That's ok. I'm good here."

"You're just going to sit here bored?"

"Not at all. I'm going to sit here and judge."

"I see. So those who can't do, judge?"

"In my experience, everyone judges. Talent is entirely irrelevant."

"C'mon," I said again, holding out my hand to him. "It's not that hard. It's all about using your body to tell a story."

"My body doesn't tell a story. If it did, it would be something resembling a Steven King novel."

I laughed again, but when my hand remained outstretched, and Kyle realized I wasn't going to take no for an answer, he finally gave in to my request.

"You have to loosen up, mate," I chuckled, leading him to the dancefloor, then turning to face him. "It's all in the hips," I said, reaching down to put both hands on Kyle's pelvic bone. Instantly I felt him tense up. "Relax, I'm not going to hurt you."

"No, I know that," he assured me. "It's just, you know, we're two guys dancing together. I don't know how people are going to react."

"You really worry about shit like that?"

Kyle held on to his pina colada for dear life. "When I'm surrounded by a large group of strangers on the open water, I do."

"Do you really think they're going to throw us overboard?"

Kyle shook his head, smiling. "Of course not."

"So then, what's the problem?" He shrugged. "The worst that will happen is a couple of stares. Maybe someone will utter a colourful phrase or two. Unoriginal words that we've both heard and survived a hundred times."

His expression suggested that he knew I was right. More importantly, *I* knew I was right. Still, to put him at ease, I didn't touch him again. "Watch me," I told him, shaking my ass to the rhythm of the music.

"It's hard not to," Kyle said between drunken slurps of what was left of his rum beverage. I could see a rose tint come over his cheeks. Either from the booze or embarrassment, I couldn't tell which.

"Would you put that blasted thing down?" I begged, taking the empty glass from his hand, just as he tried to put the straw to his lips once more. He pouted briefly until I assured him that it was empty. "We'll get you another one later," I promised him. Then, I put the empty glass on a table and hurried back to him before he scurried off the dancefloor.

With extreme trepidation, Kyle started to bob his head a little. Then the song faded into another with an even more Latin flavour. I could feel the beat creeping in through my toes, travelling upward. "Dancing is not about how you move on the floor. It's about enjoying each movement, no matter what it looks like. It's about celebrating that you can move at all."

I watched him attempt to find the beat. I smiled wide. "Not like that," I said. Kyle stared at me blankly as I bent one knee and began to rotate my pelvis back and forth erotically. "You have to feel the rhythm," I instructed.

Kyle's face was shocked and confused, and it was hilarious to watch. "I can't move like that."

"Sure, you can. It's easy. Just try." He did. He attempted to mimic my movement precisely, but on him, it looked entirely different. It seemed sterile and wrong, lacking any spirit or charisma. The senior couple I watched earlier would have had more sex appeal on the dancefloor. Kyle could tell I was stifling a chuckle.

"Don't laugh at me," he whined self-consciously.

Immediately I composed myself. "You're right. I'm sorry." I looked at him, bewildered. "Have you seriously never dirty danced before?"

"Do I look like Patrick Swayze?" he asked, giving his hips a little shake.

"Not in this lighting," I chuckled, then pretended to reconsider. "Maybe a little like Jennifer Grey," I went on, mouthing the words, *the nose*, gesturing around my own face for effect.

"Rude!" Kyle pouted then went to suck on the straw of the glass he forgot he was no longer holding.

I pressed the back of my hand against my lips to stifle a laugh. "I'm teasing, obviously. Your nose is fine." I assured him. "I can't believe you've never dry humped to music before?"

"Well, I haven't," he said nervously. "Why? Did you want to dry hump me?" he asked.

I chose to smile coyly, "Not tonight. We just met. Check-in with me in a few days."

"Oh my God," Kyle laughed, the booze making him giddy. This time a very distinctive red hue painted across his cheeks. "I don't know why I said that. I think I'm a little drunk."

"I think you're more than a little," I laughed, closing my eyes, spinning around in time to the music.

When I reopened my eyes, Kyle was looking back at me, his expression unreadable. I noticed a bead of sweat gathering on his brow and upper lip, which struck me as odd since he hadn't moved much since I forced him on the dancefloor.

"Are you feeling alright?" I asked, genuinely concerned for his well-being. The bloke had gone from mildly intoxicated to looking like he was going to chunder in less than a minute. A change that abrupt couldn't have been typical, no matter his metabolic rate.

"I'm fine," he slurred. "I'm feeling a little dizzy."

"Do you need me to help you back to your room?"

"It's fine. I'm fine," Kyle guffawed at me automatically, almost looking offended. I tilted an unconvinced look at him. It didn't matter how many times he said it; I was quite sure he was not ok.

Kyle took a couple of wobbly steps backward, and his thongs fumbled. One fell off his foot, and he looked like he was about to fall back, so I quickly grabbed hold of his arm. "Whoa, Nelly," I said, pulling him upright. "I think we should go sit down."

What on earth was happening? How did he get so sloppy so fast? Still, even in his newly developed state, he was the most adorable bloke.

With a tug, I pulled him over to a lounge chair, forcing him to sit. He plopped down with more weight than I expected.

"My shoe," Kyle whimpered, pointing back out to the dancefloor. Sure enough, his sandal was still there in the spot where it had fallen off. Kyle had lacked the foresight and the motor function to slip it back on before we left the dancefloor. I quickly retrieved it and brought it back. I knelt in front of him, holding his sandal out to him. He slipped into it with ease then placed his foot down solidly.

"I feel like Cinderfella," he smiled at me.

I still knelt in front of him. "Are you sure you're alright?" I asked, rising to my feet.

Kyle stood abruptly then, grabbing hold of my shoulders, jerking me towards him. He planted his mouth stiffly over mine, but my eyes remained open and horrified. I hadn't expected it. Sure, I'd entertained the idea of kissing the handsome stranger at some point on the trip, maybe, but this was not how it was supposed to go. I gently pushed him away.

I recognized the expression on Kyle's face instantly: drunk disappointment. "I'm sorry," he mumbled. "I shouldn't have done that."

"It's alright," I tried to reassure him, but in his mental state, he couldn't hear it.

"I have to go," he muttered to himself. "I have to leave. I have to go."

I couldn't disagree with him at that junction. Kyle clearly needed to lay down. I turned around, scanning the dancefloor for the mate I had seen him with earlier. "Let's see if we can find someone to help you back to your room." I looked back over my shoulder to where Kyle was sitting.

He wasn't there.

I stared at the vacant chair as if it would reveal an explanation as to what happened and where Kyle had gone.

It revealed no answers.

SIX
KYLE

The mattress was incredibly uncomfortable. Even lingering in that place between sleep and awake, I could feel it, like rocks beneath me. My pillow must have fallen off the bed at some point because my neck felt strained from having laid flat too long. Around me, a low engine rumble vibrated, which I found strange. I didn't remember my room being so close to the engine room. My tongue felt like sandpaper, and my lips ached from desiccation. The painful thumping at my temples reminded me of the steel drum percussion of Caribbean music.

How much did I drink last night? I wondered. I remembered several sugary drinks at the wedding reception and a glass of champagne for toasting. Unfortunately, I also remembered the disaster that occurred just off the dancefloor—that poor cake. I recalled I was feeling sufficiently inebriated at that point. Still, once I had come back to the room and showered, I felt relatively sober.

Then, Ruby appeared at my cabin with wine. It had only been a bottle for each of us, and I didn't remember finishing it. In fact, I couldn't remember much after her arrival. Had we even left the suite?

Ruby had mentioned a giant deck party, but I had no recollection of attending. Indeed, I would have remembered a party of that magnitude. What the hell was wrong with me?

I could usually handle my liquor very well. I contributed that to the fact that I was rarely, if ever, completely sober. It took twenty-four hours for alcohol to entirely leave your system, and I averaged one drink every twelve hours. So, it was safe to say that I was always in some state of pickling. Then again, my only real calorie consumption that day had come in liquor form. I had only nibbled on a few carrot sticks before the ceremony but had been too nervous, or perhaps too annoyed, to eat during the reception. Then, afterward, I had felt so guilty that even the thought of food had made me queasy.

Kind of like how I felt at that moment, like if I got up or moved too quickly, I could vomit all over the room.

A low moan escaped my lips. My head was pounding. I opened one eye, then the other, and they ached as they fluttered to awareness. The darkness started to recede and was replaced with disorientation.

After a night of drinking, waking up was sometimes confusing, even when doing so in a room with which I was familiar. Doing so in an unfamiliar space made it worse. Not only did I struggle to bring things into focus. Because everything was foreign, once it did come into focus, it took a while for me to register what I was looking at.

I blinked in rapid succession as the blurry room swirled into clarity. Initially, I saw only the whites of the ceiling. Eventually, with my eyes open, I became fully conscious of my body and determined one thing to be fact; I was on the floor.

My gaze darted around, unable to find my bearings. Nothing looked familiar. I struggled to sit up, my head feeling cloudy.

What-the-actual-fuck was going on?

I didn't know where I was, but one thing was clear; I was not in my suite. Panic immediately set in. I fell back onto the floor, stared up at the ceiling, forcing myself to breathe.

Where the hell was I?

I turned my head to the right, my cheek smooshing against the cold, tile floor. Three washing machines lined one wall. I looked in the opposite direction. Two ironing boards and a single dryer lined the other. That seemed disproportionate to the number of washing machines.

I glanced around in horrified wonder. How the hell had I ended up in the ship's laundry room? Then, another realization struck me like a hammer blow. I was dumbfounded that I hadn't noticed until that moment.

I was stark-naked.

Slowly I sat upright, immediately nauseated. I rolled over to my knees and crawled from dryer to dryer, opening them in search of anything to cover myself up with, a towel or sheet perhaps. Shit, at that moment, I would have settled for a random forgotten sock. I found nothing. All the dryers were empty.

Afraid I would vomit if I stood up too fast, or at all, I crawled over to the door. Using the doorknob as leverage, I hoisted myself to a standing position. That simple act winded me something awful.

I leaned my head against the door, attempting to gather myself. I needed a plan to escape. Only one entry in or out, I made note. Which meant, unfortunately, that the door likely opened directly out into the floor's main hallway.

I was left with little choice. I was going to have to make a run for it. Putting my ear to the door, I listened carefully. I heard nothing—no voices, no footsteps, no sign of life at all. Cautiously, I poked my head out of the doorway and into the hall, looking left then right. Not seeing anyone on either side of the long corridor, I decided it was as safe as it was going to get.

Gingerly, I stepped out into the hall, cupping both hands over my junk. Remembering that my ass was also completely exposed, I pressed my backside against the wall, then carefully slid along it. I was suddenly very thankful I decided to get a full-body wax before the trip.

The hallway elongated in front of me. The beige wood paneling and blue carpet seemed to go on forever in an endless straight line. My room was 717, but as I shimmied past 702, another horrifying truth came to me. I didn't have my room key.

I nearly shat myself right then out of fear. I was naked, in a hallway, on a family-friendly vacation cruise. What was I going to do?

Ruby! Her name flashed into my mind like a bolt of lightning. She said her room was next door to mine, but in which direction, left or right? I had an image of me pounding on the wrong door, only to have it opened by a woman or worse, a small child, and me standing there, ass naked, exposing myself.

"I'm going to get arrested," I said to myself aloud.

I sidestepped my way down the hall to room 716. It was a fifty percent chance that I'd be lucky enough to get Ruby's door on the first try, knew that. Still, my options were either to risk it or stay stranded, naked in the hall. I tapped on the door, quietly at first as to not draw attention from the adjacent rooms.

"Ruby," I snarled in a loud whisper. "Open the door." Inside, the room was quiet, and the door remained latched. I banged again, a little harder. "Ruby? Are you in there?"

I heard a door open behind me, followed by a sudden feminine gasp.

Ruby! Hope filled me like helium until I whipped my head around to discover it was not her. Instead, it was the same woman from the previous day. The one I had snapped at and had overheard me suggest Dustin was a pedophile. She stood before me, horrified by my presence.

"Good morning," I offered, flashing her an embarrassed smile.

The woman said nothing. She simply retreated inside her suite, her eyes full of alarm. She closed the door. I heard her latch the security lock milliseconds later—poor lady.

My anxiety thickened. The air suddenly felt dense and hot around me, as though someone had jacked the temperature. I felt a single drop of sweat pool at my armpit, then slowly drip down my inner arm. Instantly, I felt disgusting.

Desperate, I decided to try once more. Taking a gamble, I moved two doors to the right to 718. I rapped at it in small spastic knocks, almost like a woodpecker. "Ruby!" I called.

Slowly, the door opened.

Praise Madonna! I nearly melted in relief until I saw who had answered the door. I immediately took it back. *Fuck*

Madonna, that decrepit old hag! To my horror, Satan stood before me. I wasn't sure whether to laugh or scream.

He was definitely not sweaty or disgusting. He looked irritatingly attractive. Even rumpled and half awake, shirtless in his plaid pajama bottoms, his hair messy and his feet bare, shoulders slumping as he yawned, he was handsome.

A strange, violent reaction wormed through me at the sight of his muscles. A dark smattering of hair over his broad chest caused my hand to curl into a fist. How dare he look that good first thing in the morning! He looked attractive and innocent. Even though I would bet money that he spent the night dreaming of drowning kittens.

As if he could read my mind, Dustin smirked then tugged a shirt over his head. Immediately, with his abs out of my sight, the fire of hate in my lower belly subsided.

"Kyle?" Dustin's voice sounded scratchy and bewildered. At that moment, I really resented the extra few inches of height he had on me. He really was physically perfect. It was totally unfair. Then, his eyes bulged wide, suddenly registering my full predicament, and he nearly squealed with delight. "What-in-good-god's-name are you doing?"

There was nothing in the world I wanted less at that moment than for Dustin to answer the door. Except, maybe, have his imagination run a marathon of reasons why I could be showing up at his room, naked in the wee hours of the morning. He stared at me in disbelief as I pushed past him into his suite.

Very slowly, Dustin blinked, then blinked again. "You're naked," he said helpfully.

"Your powers of observation never cease."

"I can't tell you how many times I imagined you showing up at my door, begging to sleep with me." He laughed, stretching, lacing his hands together behind his head.

Gross. "That is not what this is," I said emphatically.

His reply was a lazy drawl. "Then what is it?"

"Can you not be a dick and get me a robe or something?"

My eyes darted around the room, hopeful that Shawn was asleep. To my relief, he was nowhere to be found. Dustin tossed me a T-shirt, barely long enough to hide my dingleberries. "Thanks," I replied tersely, pulling it on and tugging it low in a futile attempt at modesty. "What are you even doing right now?"

"What am *I* doing? I was trying to sleep. Care to tell me what *you're* doing naked and in my room at six in the morning?"

Was it really that early? Thank God. Any later, and the hall would have likely been busy with traffic. I frowned, "I have absolutely no idea."

"Seriously?"

"Seriously. I woke up in the laundry room, of all places, with no recollection of how I got there."

"Seriously?"

"Seriously. In fact, I don't remember anything about last night; where I went, what I did, who I was with—nothing."

"Seriously?"

"Stop asking me that!"

"I still don't understand why you knocked on my door instead of going back to your room."

"Because I can't get into my room, genius."

"You don't have your room key?"

"Of course I do. I have it nestled safely between my butt cheeks." My sarcasm was palpable.

"What could I have possibly done to bring this upon myself?" he asked the ceiling.

I raised a brow. "Do you honestly want me to make you a list?"

"Okay." He exhaled long and slow, clawing a hand through hair so thick and luscious, it made me want to puke. "Use my phone to call guest services."

I barked out a laugh. "Wow, that is so generous of you."

His forehead scrunched up in a frown. "For someone who is clearly in need of assistance, you have a bizarre way of showing gratitude. I could easily toss your naked ass out, you know."

"Please," I scoffed. "Like you've ever been able to say no to an attractive, naked man."

"Did you call yourself attractive? Isn't that a tad vain?" Then he reconsidered. "You do look good, though. Have you been working out?"

I felt my face flash hot for half a second. "A tad. I even joined a gym."

I should have known that his flattering observation would be immediately followed by something foul. "Since when do you care how you look?"

A fire rose in me. "I think it started when I came down from the bell tower and had my hump fixed!" I flung back, then picked up the receiver, dialing zero. While waiting for someone on the other end to pick up, I inquired, "Where's your boyfriend this morning? Did you already drop him off at daycare?"

Dustin rolled his eyes. "No, he's at the gym."

I pressed a horrified hand to my chest. "Already?"

Dustin shrugged. "He likes to stay fit. Besides, he wanted to take out some pent-up frustration on the bench press."

The phone was still ringing in my ear. Why was no one picking up the damned call? "Pent up? Oh, are you having issues pleasing the guy half your age? They make little blue pills to help, you know."

I could see Dustin swallowing down his impatience. "We have no issues in that department, trust me." I didn't. "Actually, if you must know, he's frustrated by us."

"Us?" I carefully scanned his face, and he studied mine in return.

"Us," he nodded. "Shawn seems to think you bring out the worst in me."

I was stunned. "Me? Your douche-canoe sails perfectly fine without any help from me."

Dustin stared at me. "My what?"

I held my hand up to him, focusing my attention on the other end of the phone. Then, I turned my back to him, trying not to sound as desperate as I felt. "Hello?"

"Good Morning Mr. Salinger. This is the front desk. How can we be of service?"

"Hi, this is actually Kyle Blackwood from 717. I am locked out of my room and was hoping you could help me get back in."

"Of course, Mr. Blackwood. If you come down to the front desk, so we can confirm your identity visually, we'll be happy to issue you a replacement sailor's card."

"Visually?" My stomach dropped.

"Yes, sir. It's standard protocol."

How the hell was I going to stand in front of them, wearing nothing but a cotton t-shirt? I'd have to think of something. "Thank you so much," I said to him, exhaling for what felt like the first time since I woke up. "I'll be down soon."

"You're very welcome. Was there anything else we could do for you this morning?"

"No, that will be all. Thank you again." I hung up the phone, then turned back to Dustin. "What were you saying?"

"You're a bad influence."

"And you're Voldemort. What's your point?"

Dustin shrugged, then reached up, scratching his jaw. "Only that Shawn thinks we're unnecessarily rude to each other. He thinks that's a sign that we might still have feelings for each other."

I narrowed my eyes, expression blankly bewildered, and wondered what I had ever seen in him. "Only loathing with a sprinkling of nausea," I assured him.

"Can't you at least pretend that I don't utterly disgust you?

"You mean, lie?" I placed my hand over my chest, feigning horror at the very suggestion.

"Yes. At least for Shawn and Sapphire's sake?"

I couldn't care less about Shawn's sake. He seemed like a nice enough boy, but I felt no obligation towards him. Sapphire, on the other hand, already knew the depths of my hatred for

Dustin. She had asked me to play nice with him. Still, I doubted I could stomach faking enjoyment at being around him.

I pretended to briefly consider his suggestion before dismissing it. "I couldn't possibly."

"Why not? It won't kill you."

It might, I thought. "For starters, I'm a terrible liar, and you know it. Besides, those of us with souls consider honesty to be a virtue."

"Oh yes," he said, rolling his eyes. "We both know how virtuous you are," his words were drenched in sarcasm. "You're practically a priest."

"No, that would be you. You're the one with a fetish for young boys."

Judging by his expression, Dustin did not see the humor at all. "Just go," he ordered, ushering me to the door. "I did my good deed for the day. I let you use my phone. I'd rather not have Shawn return to find you pant-less in our suite."

"You could always give me pants," I urged.

He chuckled. "I could, but I like you this way. All powerless and wormy."

"Stop looking at my worm," I told him. Once again, I pulled the t-shirt low enough to hide my testicles.

"Here," he said, tossing me a white terrycloth towel. "Tie it around your waist. Pretend you came from the pool. No one will even know you're naked underneath."

"Clever man," I nodded, doing as he suggested. When I was finished, Dustin held his hand out to me, palm up, his fingers wiggling. "I'm not paying you for the towel," I said flatly.

"My shirt," he said, wiggling his fingers again.

"You can't be serious." I raised my head defiantly, but that only made him laugh.

"I'm very serious. I don't want you to leave wearing it. I don't trust you."

"Don't trust me? It's a fruit of the loom t-shirt. What on earth do you think I'm going to do to it?"

"I don't know. Maybe shred it, like you did my Prada suit." I had forgotten I'd done that. Fresh with rage and betrayal, I had destroyed his favorite suit in a paper shredder. It ended up getting stuck in the shredder, clogging it up something awful. I had to throw the machine out. Yet not before sending Dustin a photo of it and the mangled, pinstripe carcass protruding from its teeth. He had deserved it then. I was reasonably confident I wouldn't have done so now. Yet, I suppose I understood his lack of faith.

"Fine," I relented, pulling the fabric up and over my head.

Then, as if in slow motion, a series of simultaneous events occurred in rapid succession. First, my enormous head got stuck in the tight neck of Dustin's shirt. Second, I felt the knot in the towel around my waist come loose, and the sheath fall to the floor. Third, I sensed Dustin kneel in front of me to pick up the fallen towel. Fourth, I heard the muffled beep of a keycard sliding into a lock. Finally, I felt the presence of another body as the door opened, and Shawn entered the room.

There was a horrifying beat of silence where Dustin and I realized what had happened. We froze, somewhere between shock and embarrassment. My head was still caught in the fabric of Dustin's shirt. From the energy in the room, it was clear we both wanted to die of mortification.

"Baby! This is not what it looks like!"

That certainly sounded familiar.

"You have your ex-boyfriend's dick in your face," Shawn said matter-of-factly.

"I know, but look at it," Dustin urged as though presenting evidence of his innocence. "Babe, it's not even hard."

That may not have been the best time to offer a pleasant, "Good morning," but I did anyway.

I could feel Dustin glaring at me. When I finally freed myself from the confines of the t-shirt, I picked up the towel, once more securing it tightly around my waist.

Shawn nodded curtly in my direction. Understandably

uneasy with the scene before him. I tried to put him at ease. "Dusty was just giving me a hand with something." Perhaps not the best choice of words.

"Kyle, do you mind?" Dustin snarled. "You're not helping."

"Don't snap at me," I said, slicing one hand through the air. "This is your fault."

"How is this possibly my fault?" He hissed.

"If you had just given me pants…"

"Shut up, Kyle." Dustin rushed forward toward Shawn, eager to quell all his suspicions. "It's not what you think," he continued. "Kyle barged in here, completely naked, like a crazy person."

That was an unflattering description. Even if mostly accurate. Shawn turned his attention to me. "Is that true?"

"Technically," I admitted.

"Are you drunk?" he asked.

"Not presently." Shawn raised an eyebrow, urging me to explain. "I just came to use the phone, I promise."

"To use the phone?" He seemed understandably unconvinced. "Naked?"

"Yes. I appear to have had a sleepwalking incident last night. I woke up, locked out of my room."

He tilted his head, understandably puzzled by what I'd said. "So, you came here? When Ruby's room is right next door?"

It took a moment for his words to sink in. When they did, I whimpered in agony. Fuck. If I had only gone one more room to the left, this could have all been avoided. "I didn't know that."

Shawn seemed placated. His demeanor softened almost instantly. "Sorry for making assumptions," he said. Was he actually apologizing to me for finding me naked with his boyfriend? The younger generation seriously confused me.

"For the record," I offered. "Being here, like this, is one of the most depressing moments of my life."

Dustin snorted. "More depressing than cruising some of the

most romantic destinations, completely alone?"

My eyes narrowed. I really hated that man.

Shawn slapped Dustin playfully on the shoulder. "Be nice. It's hard to be alone on trips like these, especially at his age."

At my age? Mother fucker, I cursed internally.

"There's no need to rub it in, unnecessarily," Shawn continued. It was then I was convinced Shawn was either a savant of passive-aggressiveness or he was an imbecile. "Kyle, would you like to have breakfast with us?"

Imbecile. Definitely imbecile.

"I'm not really dressed for breakfast," I replied, gesturing dramatically to the towel around my waist. "Thank you so much for the invitation, though." *Not!*

He laughed. "I don't mean right now! I just came from the gym, so I have to shower first anyway. That should be more than enough time for you to sort out this little predicament of yours."

"Shawn, babe, I don't think that's a good idea," Dustin opposed.

He seemed genuinely confused. "Why not? He has to eat, doesn't he?" He turned to me with concern. "You do eat, don't you?"

"Only the flesh of the innocent," I gave a toothy, insincere grin.

"Well then, it's settled," Shawn said with a nod. "We'll meet you in the dining room in an hour."

"Fabulous," I gave in, smiling. My voice was thick with defeat, and I hoped I looked less annoyed than I felt.

SEVEN
KYLE

The guy at the front desk was very accommodating. Although he did smirk at me, like he may have known my secret. Which I dismissed right away since I had only encountered one poor, unsuspecting woman that morning. It occurred to me then, like an alarm in my head, that the cruise ship likely had security cameras in the hallways. Worse, a security team whose job it was to monitor those cameras. The morning incident instantly felt a lot less private and a whole lot more embarrassing.

All through breakfast, I hardly spoke and held myself as if moving the wrong way, or too quickly, would somehow cause the entire table to burst into flame. In other words, I was extremely uncomfortable.

Across from me, Dustin and Shawn sat side by side, coupled. Dustin had ordered Eggs Benedict while Shawn opted for sausage links, hash-browns, and whole-wheat toast. When their plates arrived, I watched as Dustin put one half of his Benedict onto Shawn's plate. In exchange, Shawn gave him two of his four sausages. While he did that, Dustin delicately cut the crust off Shawn's toast, like he was a picky four-year-old. Neither of them missed a beat of conversation as they went through the motions. Their breakfast routine was seamless and well mastered. I picked at my omelet while watching them.

"I was in line for a smoothie," Shawn was telling me how they had met. I hadn't asked. "I had just come from the gym, when the next thing I knew, this gorgeous guy was complimenting me on my well-shaped glutes. I knew instantly that he was someone special."

Apparently, the way to Shawn's heart was through his ass. "Aww," I fawned, making a theatrical showing of fluttering my hands around my collarbones. "Love at first sight."

"Not quite," Shawn continued, clearly missing my sarcasm. "Our first date was a complete disaster," he admitted, spreading peanut butter on his crust-less toast. "He took me to a concert. Some band I had never heard of, then got insulted when I didn't know who they were." He took a bite of his toast. "Should I know who Matchbox Twenty is?"

I made my eyes round like he just told me the most fantastic story. "What year were you born?"

"Ninety-nine."

"Then, no, you shouldn't know who they are." With a deep breath, I gave Dustin a look that asked, *what did you expect?* I struggled to keep my more sarcastic, bitter thoughts from bubbling to the surface and out of my mouth.

Dustin grimaced at me, wrapping a strong arm around Shawn's shoulder. "That's why we're perfect for each other. We introduce each other to new experiences."

Oh, give me a break. What kind of new experiences could Shawn, the man-child, possibly bestow upon Dustin? As though reading my thoughts, Shawn said, "I taught him to ski and introduced him to *Panic! at the Disco*," he sipped from his glass of water. "I even got him to go skydiving with me."

I looked at Dustin with a raised eyebrow. "You hate to fly. Now you're jumping *out* of airplanes?"

"Occasionally," he smiled.

"Any other new hobbies?"

"Not yet," He leaned in, grinning. "Our relationship is still new. I'm sure there are countless things Shawn and I can learn from each other throughout our lives together."

That comment made me want to gag, while it seemed to make Shawn giddy. He leaned into Dustin, giving him a peck on the cheek.

Seeing it as an invitation for more, Dustin tilted Shawn's chin with his fingers until their lips touched. Then, they proceeded to engage in one of the most prolonged, sloppiest looking kisses I had ever seen. At one point, I thought I actually saw Shawn lick Dustin's teeth. I held back a dry heave. I supposed kissing like that eliminated the need for toothpicks. Having kissed Dustin for over a decade, this new technique had Shawn written all over it.

I awkwardly waited for them to finish, but they didn't appear to have any intention of stopping.

I motioned for the waitress to clear the plates on our table. I was confident Shawn and Dustin were finished with theirs. I had indeed lost my appetite. Between their closed eyes and low hums, they hadn't even noticed her tend to the table.

I cleared my throat, but it garnered no reaction. *Maybe I should leave*, I pondered. Would Dustin or Shawn even notice? I coughed, deliberately loud, but that also went unnoticed.

"Good morning," a deep, accented voice came from my right. I looked up, instantly recognizing him but unable to remember his name. He was wearing different clothes than when we had first met, but he still looked like a million dollars: same deep-hazel eyes and square-jawed manliness.

"Hey, you!" I shouted, "Join us!" I demanded, yanking on his arm, pulling him into the seat next to me. The table shook slightly, causing our coffee cups and water glasses to jostle. *That*, Shawn and Dustin noticed. They turned, irritated with us as if we had splashed cold water on them. If they had continued making out much longer, I might have had to.

"Kyle," Dustin asked, composing himself. His lips were red from friction. "Is this a friend of yours?"

I nodded my head, a little too enthusiastically, but offered no further explanation. All three of them looked at me like I had spontaneously grown fur.

"Does he have a name?" Dustin coaxed me.

I shot him a glare. "Of course, he has a name."

He waited. They all did. "And it is…?" Dustin prodded.

"Jax Abernathy," Jax offered, registering that I had no idea what his name was and could not introduce him. He offered

Dustin and Shawn his hand. They both shook it, although Dustin did so with reservation.

"How exactly do you two know each other?" Dustin asked. The question itself didn't irritate me, but there was an implication in his tone. It demanded details. Details that were none of his business. A muscle flexed in my jaw.

I realized there were two ways I could respond:

I could admit that we met at The Alchemist martini bar, while I was covered in cake. I could be honest and say that Jax had been kind enough to listen to me vent and whine about Dustin, who I wished would be slowly eaten to death by crabs. Or I could lie. Ultimately both were unflattering. Option one left me with my integrity, but not my pride. Option two would leave dignity intact but make me a lying sack of shit. I knew there was an obvious right choice, but I did not make it. I couldn't believe what I was about to say.

Jax started, "We—"

"Fucked," I finished. Of all the stories I could have come up with, I didn't know why I chose that particular one. I had no shortage of meet-cutes to choose from. I worked in publishing, after all.

Shawn smiled in approval, Dustin looked skeptical, and Jax whipped his head my way. He looked horrified like I had just boiled his pet rabbit. "Are you mad? Why would you blurt that?" He demanded.

Dustin laughed incredulously, "You did *what*?" He asked, raising his eyebrow.

For the love of all that is gay, why do you do this to yourself? I scolded myself even as my mouth continued to spew the lies. "Just because you're my *ex-boyfriend* doesn't mean everyone finds me hideous." I emphasized ex-boyfriend, in case Jax didn't recognize him from the previous day. "I mean, I may not be a spring chicken anymore, but I'm not a haggard old troll. People do still find me attractive, you know. I can have sex if I want to—and I do. All the time. Indiscriminately. I'm not the lonely spinster you think I am." Ok, I was rambling. Lying and rambling, which was a horrible combination. When I finally came up for air, everyone at the table was staring at me like I was a crazed lunatic. Maybe I was.

Luckily, Jax picked up on my discomfort and decided to take pity on me. Rather than call me out for my baseless and scandalous lie, he cleared his troubled expression, composed himself and smiled. However, if I was reading his eyes correctly, he regretted saying good morning to me at all. No nice gesture went unpunished when I was around.

Dustin looked directly at Jax, with the determination of a police detective. "Is this true?"

My voice rose. "Why would I lie?" *I don't know, Kyle, why would you lie?* I berated myself.

Dustin turned to Jax for confirmation. "A gentleman doesn't kiss and tell," he drawled in his smooth Australian voice. Evasive, but not a complete denial. He was a good man.

Dustin looked to me, frowning. "I guess that means you're not a gentleman."

"He bloody well wasn't last night," Jax wiggled his eyebrows. To my surprise, he mimicked the couple's body language across from us, pulling me close with faux intimacy. Immediately, I felt myself blush before reminding myself that it was complete bullshit.

Dustin fixed me with shrewd eyes. "You expect me to believe that in less than twelve hours on board, you not only met someone, but you've also had relations?"

I scoffed at his choice of words. "Why yes, Grandfather, we had relations, but with God as my witness, if he gets me in trouble, he's promised to marry me." I mocked him, in my best impression of a southern belle.

"It doesn't sound like you, that's all. You're rarely interested in sex."

"With *you*," I clarified. "I was rarely interested in sex with *you*."

Shawn seemed to take our banter seriously. "Why's that?"

I looked into his bright, inquisitive eyes. He seemed to genuinely expect an answer, so I gave him one. At least with that, I could be truthful. "Dusty was usually too busy having sex with everyone else. It was a turn-off."

The pastry cart's squeaky wheels made their way to our table, cutting through the awkwardness that was quickly developing. "Would any of you like a croissant or muffin?" The pretty waitress asked. Collectively, we waved her off. She gave us all a quick smile then left us alone.

"Less than twenty-four hours on this ship and I'm already convinced one of the crew's primary goals is to make all of us fat before we even make it to a beach." I quipped.

Dustin leaned back in his chair, draping his long arm over Shawn's neck and shoulders. "Looks like some of us have a head start in that department," he whispered before taking a drink of his coffee.

I meant to glare but was momentarily distracted by the way his Adam's apple moved as he drank. I imagined taking a knife and performing a tracheotomy on him, right there at the table.

"Anyway," Jax swerved, "What is everyone's plan for the first full day at sea?"

Our first call to port was Aruba. Unfortunately, it took a full day of sailing to get there. A full day trapped onboard the cruise ship sounded incredibly dull to me, but it would allow me to explore.

According to the ship's guide, there were endless ways to enjoy ship life. A leisurely brunch, a full spa day, or napping in the sun by the pool were relaxing options. There were waterslides and ping-pong tables on the top deck. Or, if I wanted something equally stimulating but less physically demanding, I could always spend a few hours throwing my money away in the casino. The shopping center on board was also calling my name. It had everything from cheesy souvenirs to expensive jewelry and designer sunglasses. One of the pubs had karaoke with a live band every day at noon. There was even a comedy club with a different featured performer twice a night. That was in addition to the fantastic Broadway-quality evening shows featured in The Liquid Lounge—a giant auditorium with two floors of stadium-style seating. The piano bar on the promenade had a wine tasting event that tempted my inner party monster. However, I was still feeling slightly hungover from the night before. Which puzzled me since I really hadn't drunk that much. Not by my usual standards anyway.

"I think I want to lay poolside most of the day," Shawn announced. "Just me and a pina colada," then he kissed Dustin's cheek. "And my bae, of course."

His bae? I couldn't help but roll my eyes.

Watching the two men together, I admitted they both seemed incredibly happy. Irritatingly so. Shawn's youthful optimism balanced out Dustin's experience and cynicism, which resulted in a culmination of wonder and wisdom. If I weren't vehemently opposed to Dustin achieving any semblance of joy, I would have been incredibly supportive of the union, even with the significant age difference.

"What about you, Kyle?" Jax inquired of me.

"I haven't the slightest idea yet." To be honest, I likely would have hidden in my room, where I could avoid further disaster.

"You could lounge by the pool with an alcoholic beverage in your hand, like Shawn?" Jax suggested.

"People," I stated simply.

Jax laughed. "There's the casino?"

I frowned. "Also, people."

"What's wrong with people?" He asked through a hesitant smile.

"I don't particularly like most of them," I admitted.

"The spa has an embarkation sale. Half price full-body massages," Shawn suggested. "They have couple-massages too," he nudged Dustin.

I shook my head emphatically. "I think I would prefer an activity that is a little less naked."

Dustin chuckled at my expense. "I suppose you've been naked, publicly, enough for one day."

I flipped the bird in his general direction.

Jax looked between us, obviously confused. "Am I missing something?"

"I'm sure your new lover will tell you all about it," Dustin grinned. His tone blatantly said that he still thought I was full of shit.

I chanced a glance at Jax to see his reaction to what Dustin said, but he gave none. He sat motionless, smiling, like a gorgeous Australian statue. Still, something about his smile made me wonder if he was contemplating murdering me and hiding my body. I turned the question back on him. "What do you plan on doing with your day?"

"Taking photos," he said simply. "Lots and lots of photos."

"Of the ship?"

"Of the sea, mostly, but yes, also of the ship, the sky, the sun, the people. Everything."

"Jax is a professional photographer," I informed the others.

"Would I have seen any of your work?" Dustin asked.

"Quite possibly," Jax shrugged without offering anything further.

"I work in advertising," Dustin went on. "We're always looking for new photographers. You should send me some of your stuff. I'd love to see your package."

"Would you?" Dustin nodded. "I might be able to arrange that. I should warn you, it's rather big."

"I don't mind. The bigger, the better," Dustin said with a grin, leaning forward.

I looked back and forth between the two of them dramatically. What the actual hell? They were flirting! I supposed I couldn't be upset with Jax. Dustin was gorgeous, and our tryst was a complete work of fiction. *Harry Potter* was more firmly rooted in reality than the notion of Jax and I together, but Dustin didn't know that. As far as he knew, Jax was the one guy on that heavily-heterosexual ship that had any interest in me whatsoever. Still, there Dustin was, actively trying to steal Jax from me, right before my eyes. And, in front of his boyfriend, no less! Although Shawn seemed entirely oblivious as he twirled his fingers around the collar of Dustin's polo shirt.

I moved my chair a little closer to Jax, laying claim to him. Then, I coughed. Both men looked at me briefly, and I raised a brow in Dustin's direction. He darted his eyesight in panic, realizing he had been caught. Quickly, he leaned back in his chair, as if the additional foot of distance between him and Jax would erase the very blatant sexual innuendo.

"Anyway," he reached up, scratching the back of his neck—the tender rocking of the ship masking the rage vibrating through me. "Obviously, I can't guarantee anything, but it's always great to make another business contact."

Sure. Business. Right. I was careful not to utter the words rolling through my mind, but my expression said clearly how little I bought the exchange as business. I tilted my head, scowling. "I'm fully aware of how much you enjoy doing business with people. You're always getting busy with someone."

Dustin gave a douchey little shrug then said, "I can't help it if my services are in high demand."

I stifled a chortle. "Yes, but we both know your deficiency rating."

"All of my clients are extremely satisfied," he said defensively.

"I'm sure they are. After the rash clears up."

"How dare you!" he scoffed. "I have never had a disease."

Without missing a beat, I snarled, "Oh, please, I need antibiotics just to sit next to you."

Shawn leaned across the table, "Are they still talking about advertising?" he asked.

"I don't think they ever were," Jax informed him. Poor, naïve Shawn.

"You realize you're making yourself look petty, right?" Dustin flung. "It's not my fault that you're basically a spinster while I continue to be a man magnet."

I gestured toward Shawn. "Does he know what a maggot you are?"

Dustin sighed like I was the most irritating person alive. "I said magnet."

"I know."

Jax exhaled slowly then rose from the table. "I think that's my cue. You all have a good day. Kyle, can I have a word?"

Fear flowed through me. "Um…sure," I said hesitantly, following him out into the hall.

Jax herded me further, out the hall, up one flight of stairs, until he was sure we were far enough away from Dustin and his boy-toy. "Care to tell me what that was all about?" He asked without turning to look at me.

"I'm…you know…so…sorry," I stumbled. "Dustin and I have a way of going for each other's throats."

He glanced at me over his shoulder as we continued walking. "No, not that. I have an ex too. I know how they can be." Only one ex? I was sure a man who looked like he did would have several in his wake. "I'm referring to your announcement that we—"

"Oh? Slept together?"

He stopped walking abruptly, turning to see me this time, his hazel eyes narrowing. "I think fucked was the word you used."

He was so carefully balanced between passive-aggressive anger and indifference that I was all mixed up about how to respond. It made it impossible to gauge the correct reaction. So, to be safe, I decided apologetic was the way to go.

"I don't know why I said it," which was the truth. "Sometimes, my mouth runs off without checking with my brain first. Honestly, I think I was reaching for any response that wasn't '*we met while I was covered in cake'*."

He gave a half-amused snort, then turned to continue down the long corridor. "You could have said we met at the pool party last night."

Pool party? "That would have been better, yes. Except, I don't actually remember being there."

"Had a little too much to drink, did you?"

"I actually woke up in the laundry room this morning," I admitted. "Naked."

He glanced at me again. "Seriously?"

I scowled. "Why do people keep asking me that? That's not something I would make up."

"Yet, you would make up us sleeping together?"

Guilt edged in a tiny bit. "I realize how that looks, but that was entirely out of character for me, I swear. Normally, I would never, but I panicked." Then I added unnecessarily, "Dustin was looking so smug and annoying. I wanted—"

"To make him jealous?"

I cringed. "Yes, but not in the way you're probably thinking." I softened my voice, knowing full well that he had every right to be furious with me. Yet, not only had he not immediately left the table, but he had also played along with my lie. "I'm sorry, Jax. Truly, I am. I haven't done a lot that I'm proud of in the last twenty-four hours," I admitted, frowning.

"I suppose I can forgive you," he said magnanimously. "To be honest, I rather enjoyed the look on his face when you said it."

I giggled. "Dustin did look pretty dumbfounded."

Jax laughed too. "It looked like he might have thrown himself across the table."

"If he did, it would have been to throw himself at you."

Jax looked puzzled. "Why do you say that?"

"Let's just say the flirting was strong between you two."

He laughed like I had said something hilarious. "He may

have been flirting, but I was seriously talking business."

"My package is *soooo* big, I hope you can take it all," I mimicked, in my best effort to sound sultry.

"That's not at all what I said, and bloody well not how I said it."

"If you say so," I placed my hands palms out, fingers up, the universal sign that I meant no judgment. "Still, I know flirting when I hear it."

He outright laughed. "You must imagine that you hear it quite often then."

"Imagine?"

"Yes, imagine. My friends and I say far more inappropriate things to each other, and I have no desire to get into their pants. Sexual innuendo is not how I flirt."

"Oh?" I was intrigued. "How do you flirt?"

"Your imagination is a muscle. Use it," Jax grinned. "Just trust, if I'm flirting with someone, it stands out like dog's balls, but it's not anything as direct as talking about my package or any such nonsense."

Dogs balls? Gross. Yet somehow, his accent still managed to make the phrase sound charming. When I didn't say anything else, he asked, "Do you honestly not remember anything from last night?"

"I remember my friend Ruby coming to my cabin, and I vaguely remember leaving the room. I think there was music. I *know* there was wine, but other than that, it's all a blur."

"Interesting."

"Why? Did you see me last night?"

"For a brief moment."

"Did it look like I was having fun, at least?"

He nodded. "I'd wager you were, yes."

"I didn't do or say anything stupid, did I?"

He gave me the biggest grin I'd ever seen. "At one point, you were dancing naked on a speaker."

I nearly screamed mortified. It certainly would explain why

I woke up naked that morning. My face froze in horror while I tried to decide if Jax was serious. Seeing my expression, he laughed out loud. "I'm only teasing. Really, I only saw you for a few moments, but you seemed like you were having well-behaved fun."

Well-behaved fun made me sound like an exhaustingly dull Boy Scout, which was neither flattering nor exciting. I certainly didn't want the sexy Australian stranger to see me as an innocent bore. "I'm not always well behaved," I felt the need to declare. I wasn't sure who I was trying to convince more, him or myself. "I can get crazy sometimes."

Definitely him.

Jax, unfortunately, seemed unconvinced. "Oh, really? Anything more shocking than getting in a verbal smackdown with your ex?"

My nerves dumped buckets of adrenaline into my veins. I didn't expect Jax to call my bluff. "Well..." I struggled to find examples. "Sometimes, I skip flossing," I said lamely.

He let out a hearty laugh. "Oh, wow. You live on the edge."

"You have no idea," I went on flippantly. "I've also been known to rip the tags off my pillows."

He blinked. "You're practically criminal."

We both chuckled at our exchange. Jax and I had a similar sense of humor, and I filed that away in my mind. As we bantered, I was amazed at our smooth, natural rhythm. Talking with Jax was far more comfortable than talking with some people I'd known all my life. That was unique to me. I didn't usually feel that at ease with people. Especially not people I'd just met and had known a combined total of ninety minutes.

A comfortable silence fell between us. Without realizing it, we had journeyed the entire length of the ship. We stood shoulder to shoulder at a wall of elevators.

"Thank you again for your discretion today," I spoke with deep sincerity. "I don't know many people who would have played along with my lie."

"Believe me, I almost didn't."

"Why did you?"

A second passed, the time ticking by in my head while he appeared to struggle with an answer.

"I don't know," he said finally, a quirk of a smile on his lips. "It's not like me to pretend to sleep with a stranger, but I saw how smug Dustin was being. After your rough day yesterday, I decided I could spare a good deed. Besides, it's good karma."

"If you believe in that sort of thing."

"You don't?" He challenged.

I shrugged. "I'm not sure. I've seen a lot of bad things happen to good people. Makes it hard to believe in."

"That's not always karma. Sometimes that's just bad luck."

I put on a confused face. "What's the difference?"

"Karma comes from the universe as a result of your actions. Luck is completely random."

He flashed a toothy smile complete with dimples. For a moment, I forgot whatever witty comment I had been brewing. So instead, I threw out, "Either way, I owe you one."

He laughed once. "Yes, you do. Don't think I won't collect."

That sounded ominous. "Should I be nervous?"

His eyes dazzled as he boarded the elevator. I didn't join him. "You should be afraid," he warned with a grin. "Very afraid." He leaned in and winked.

I laughed at his playful act. Then the elevator doors closed between us, then he was gone.

I felt something stirring alright, but it wasn't fear.

EIGHT
KYLE

Later that afternoon, I met up with Sapphire and some of the others on the Serenity Deck. Because it was an adults-only location, the deck and its décor were more luxurious than the other family-friendly parts of the boat. There were several designated group-sitting areas with oversized, plush loungers and large square, glass patio tables at their center. Each pod had a built-in awning that could be moved and manipulated with the movement of the sun. Which was entirely convenient for me since my red-hair and pale complexion made the sun a dangerous adversary. I traded my usual frames for a pair of prescription aviator shades, then lathered my arms with a store-bought lotion with outrageously high SPF.

That portion of the ship was also significantly quieter. Caribbean music still played softly on speakers throughout, but at a volume that welcomed conversation and relaxation—a direct contrast to the party vibe that flowed viscously through the rest of the vessel.

It was still relatively early, but there was already an afternoon crowd occupying most sitting areas. A person really had to be there at the crack of dawn to secure one. Luckily, Sapphire was organized like that. She had skipped breakfast to ensure she got one for the group. Sapphire had selected a table, in the middle of the deck, at the apex of all the action. She loved people watching almost as much as she loved peace and quiet, and the location offered the perfect vantage point to enjoy both.

"Look who finally decided to show his face," Sapphire taunted, adjusting the brim of her giant hat. "I haven't seen you since you destroyed my wedding cake."

"I still feel awful about that," I groaned.

"Good. You should," Sapphire replied curtly as she put on her sunglasses.

"I'll make it up to you. I promise. I don't know how, but I will."

She nodded. "Yes, you will. Maybe not today, maybe not tomorrow, but soon, I will come to you for reparations." She peered at me over the frames of her sunglasses. "When that time comes, you will not argue. You will not whine. You will pay penance, and you will pretend to enjoy it. Capeesh?"

I nodded.

"Good boy," she praised condescendingly, putting her shades back in place then returning to her book. "You may sit."

"Actually, I was on my way—"

"I said, sit." She barked, and I complied. Beside her, on the oversized lounge chair they were sharing, Justin laughed without looking up from his tablet.

"Don't chuckle too loudly there, dude," I warned him. "She's legally yours now. It's only a matter of time before she starts barking at you too."

He chuckled. "Like a rabid dog?"

"Hush, Dear," Sapphire instructed, placing her hand on her husband's thigh. She was wearing a vintage one-piece bathing suit, blue with white stripes across the top and accented with tiny red buttons. It hugged her curves splendidly, making her look chic and sophisticated. The giant white floppy hat and oversized sunglasses helped to solidify that image.

Justin appeared unfazed by her parental tone. Sapphire always ran the show. That was the dynamic of their relationship. That was the dynamic of Sapphire and anyone she had a relationship with. Including me.

Being her bestie was not without its tribulations, and I knew she'd say the same about me. Overall, we had our relationship down to an exact science. We understood each other in ways our significant others—if I had one—likely never could. Even with that level of understanding, I couldn't imagine being married to her. Justin deserved a Purple Heart for undertaking the challenge.

He had always been more subdued and even-keeled than his brother. Dustin enjoyed being the center of attention. He strived to pull focus whenever possible. Justin, however, much preferred to sit back and let life unfold around him. Only speaking up when necessary, exciting, or convenient. Occasionally he offered a one-liner or even a crude joke. Still, mostly, he was quiet and kept so by the much larger personalities of the people around him.

Speaking of enormous personalities, the largest one of the

group, Ruby, appeared then with a flourish. I had literally just started to wonder where she was hiding when she materialized. Think of the devil, and she will appear. She certainly looked sinful in her barely there bikini. It strategically covered all her naughty bits but blatantly reminded everyone that they were there, and they were fabulous.

She had a way of shifting the very air around us with her presence. It seemed to dance with her, like a lover. It gently billowed her hair out and away from her face, as though she were Jennifer Lopez and nature itself was her personal industrial cooling system. Sapphire's thick mane certainly never did that. It was too heavy and course to move in the air. It would take hurricane-force winds to even get it to rustle. It was just another endless example of the differences between the two sisters.

"Good fuckin' morning, everyone," Ruby said, giving the group a huge smile, then striking a pose beside us.

"It's the afternoon," Sapphire replied, her tone instantly clipped. "And must you always be so vulgar? You sound like a sailor."

Ruby grinned evilly. "I should. I was pumped full of seamen last night."

Dustin, to whom I had been happily oblivious, laughed from his lounger, while Justin nearly choked on his slushed rum drink. I turned to her, shaking my head in disgust. Affectionate disgust but disgust all the same. "You must be exhausted," I said sarcastically. "I hope you stayed hydrated."

Sapphire looked disapprovingly at Ruby, comfortable with her role as the perpetual judge. In many ways, she behaved more like Ruby's third parent than her sister.

"Grow up. Dad is right there," she said sharply, gesturing to their father, who, sure enough, was relaxing two feet away, leaning against the inner wall of the hot-tub.

"Calm down, Sapph," Ruby shrugged, taking a perch on the arm of my lounger chair. "You know very well he never wears his hearing aid at the pool. Right now, he's as deaf as Grandma."

"Grandma is dead," Sapphire reminded her.

"Exactly," Ruby said curtly.

The salty ocean breeze was warm but strong that afternoon,

and it brought with it the slight fragrance of greasy food from the burger shack in the eastern corner of the deck. Ruby gestured to a nearby waiter and ordered a strawberry daiquiri before taking stock of the group of us.

"Look how fabulous we all are," she said. "Makes you wonder how many people on board secretly hate us, doesn't it?"

"Not really, no," I replied, confused. "Why would people hate us?"

"Look at us," she said, gesturing to encompass the whole group. "Two strong, gorgeous Black women and their gay BFFs."

"That doesn't mean they automatically hate us," I argued.

"Most of these people are from the bible-belt," Ruby pointed out. "We launched out of Florida, for fucks sake."

"You raise a good point. We are a Republican's worst fear," I laughed a little grimly, humoring her. "We are a smorgasbord of minority."

"Not me," Justin spoke up, having returned to whatever he was reading on his tablet.

"Every group needs a token straight, cisgender, white man," I acknowledged.

"It's true, dear," Sapphire laughed, touching his thigh again. "Without allies like you, we wouldn't have the right to vote."

"Or marry," I finished.

"Or work," Sapphire countered.

"Or adopt," I continued.

"Or own property," Sapphire countered again.

"Where's your boy-wonder, today?" Ruby asked Dustin, taking note of Shawn's absence from the group and desperate to stop Sapphire and my conversation, which was quickly becoming a competition.

Dustin shrugged. "I'm not sure. He went to the gym again after breakfast and said he'd meet up with me later."

"And you didn't go with him?" There was no accusation behind Ruby's comment, just observation. "I thought you were a gym bunny too?"

"A bunny?"

"You know what I mean," she hedged. "Aren't you Mr. Health these days?"

"Not when I'm on vacation. Even I'm not that dedicated. I'm

here to enjoy the sun and sights, not the treadmill."

"Someone should send Shawn the memo that the mission here is to party," Ruby laughed. "No one likes an overachiever."

"Or an underachiever," Sapphire slung at her sister. "You party enough for all of us."

"Don't be jealous, just because I have an active social calendar and an open mind."

"It's your open legs that concern me," Sapphire quipped.

"Is it my fault that I'm such a fine piece of ass?" No one could ever fault Ruby for lack of confidence. "What's the point of looking this good, if not for men to enjoy?"

My lip curled upwards. "What an empowering, feminist statement."

She shrugged dismissively. "I still want to dismantle the patriarchy, but occasionally I also want to be treated like a piece of meat. I'm a double agent. I want to tear them down from the inside, like a Trojan horse."

"Is that the brand of condom you prefer?" Sapphire asked her. "I'm surprised they haven't asked you to be their mascot."

Ruby looked like she was about to say something further when I intervened. "Now, now girls play nice. Let's make a deal. Sapphire, you will not comment on Ruby's spirited escapades. Ruby, you will not comment on Sapphire's anal-retentiveness." I looked back and forth between them.

Sapphire's eyebrows shot up, and I instinctively felt like I should run for cover. "I am not anal-retentive," She said, offended. "And considering that I'm still technically mad at you, you'd be wise to keep your mouth shut."

I bit my lower lip immediately. My remorseful expression turned to shock when I heard Dustin say, "You know Sapph, I'm as much to blame for the cake as Kyle." That was unusually generous of him to admit, and my face said as much. "You can't hold it against him for the whole trip."

"I certainly can," Sapphire assured Dustin, as though I wasn't sitting two feet away from her. "Kyle knows how much I love him, but after the way he behaved yesterday, I may not invite him to my next wedding."

Justin looked up from his tablet, interest suddenly peeked. "Next wedding?"

"Hush, dear," Sapphire placed her hand on Justin's thigh

again.

"I am so, so, so sorry," I groveled in Sapphire's direction. "You have every right to hate me."

She lowered her gaze at me. "I could never *hate* you, but I am mad at you. I know it's just cake, and I will get over it, eventually. Until then, I intend to milk it. Understand?"

I nodded, knowing full well that she was capable of milking situations for a very long time when she wanted to. She squeezed my ankle then—a comforting gesture to reassure her affection for me.

"Yeah, I do," I told her, recognizing that she didn't want me dead anymore, so I should consider that a win. Yet the eternal pest in me couldn't resist poking the bear. "As long as you admit that you are, in fact, extremely anal-retentive."

She scowled. "That does not feel like a fair trade."

I shrugged. "The truth isn't always fair."

"Fine. I'll admit that. As long as you admit that you're a frigid snow queen."

"I've never denied it. It's one of the qualities I love most about myself."

"Of course, what's not to love? Your resting bitch-face, your endless sarcasm, your complete disregard for common pleasantries."

I looked at her, trying to choose between a million choice words, before tipping my head to the side, offering up a remarkably simple, "Thank you."

"Only you would see those as compliments."

"Correction. I *choose* to see them as compliments."

"Well, most people see them as obstacles," Sapphire challenged. "It's why some people don't like you."

"Rude! It takes a while for me to warm up to people, that's all. People like me once they get to know me."

"I know you, and right now, I don't like you."

"You love me."

She laughed. "God knows I do, and only God knows why."

I blew her a kiss.

"Give him a break," Dustin interjected. "People like him fine. In fact, he's already made a friend onboard. Isn't that right, Kyle?"

I shot daggers in his direction. I hoped they told him to keep his mouth shut. The last thing I needed was the entire group knowing about Jax, or worse, thinking we'd slept together. That was a lie meant only for Dustin's ears. A lie I thoroughly regretted. Most untruths were like matches. If they were held close and properly monitored, they were relatively harmless. However, the more people who knew and believed the lie, the harder it would be to manage, and the more likely it was to burn me in the end.

"We don't need to talk about that, Dusty."

"Oh?" Ruby asked, wiggling her eyebrows. "Why so secretive?"

"Yeah," Sapphire agreed, hotly. "If Dustin knows something, so should I."

"What are you, nine years old? You don't automatically need to know something because someone else does."

"You hate him!" Sapphire blurted before giving an apologetic smile in Dustin's direction. "Sorry, Dustin, but he does."

"I do," I agreed, turning to nod at him.

"That's why it hurts me so deeply that you would tell him something and not me," she said, laying it on real thick.

"Sooooo deeply," Ruby chimed in. True sisters, enemies one second, allies the next.

"Does our friendship not matter to you anymore?" Sapphire pouted.

"Yeah," Ruby continued her chorus of back-up. "Does your friendship not matter anymore?"

They sent sad, puppy-dog expressions my way and waited for me to crack under the weight of them. When that didn't appear to be working, Sapphire went for the jugular. "Since you ruined my wedding, the least you could do is tell me."

Somehow I knew she would play that card. I held my hands up in sarcastic surrender. "He's someone I met on the ship. It's not a big deal."

"That's awesome, Kyle," Sapphire said, clapping her hands together. "You made a friend!"

I smiled despite myself. "That is not some amazing feat. I have friends."

"You have us," Sapphire said simply.

"Stop it," I whined. "I have friends that aren't you."

"Oh?" Sapphire asked. "Name two."

"I don't have to prove anything to you," I told her defensively. Which the entire group knew was code for, *I can't think of a single fucking name.*

Sapphire adjusted herself on her chair. "It's really nice that you're making friends who aren't us. We want to know everything."

"For the record, I don't," Justin admitted, raising his hand, already bored by the topic. He continued to stare blankly at his tablet. I couldn't decipher if he was reading or watching something.

"There's not much to tell," I said, ignoring him. "We met the other day at the martini bar. We only chatted for about an hour."

"Wait a minute," Dustin snapped his head. "You said that you slept together."

Shit. I was faced with a choice. Come clean or carry the lie further. I had to decide and quick. They were all looking at me.

"Thank you, Dusty," I tried to set him on fire with my mind. "I was so eager to share that information with the rest of the group."

"You seemed really eager to share it with me this morning," Dustin replied immediately. "If you wanted something to be discreet, you should have shown a little discretion in the first place."

He wasn't wrong. I had blurted it out like a crazy person, right there at the breakfast table. The fact that he was right only annoyed me further

Ruby stopped short, her cocktail halfway to her mouth. "You did what now?"

"Wait a minute," Sapphire took off her shades, pressing one of their arms to her chin. "You had sex?"

I was offended. The notion wasn't nearly as ludicrous as their tones or expressions suggested. It shouldn't have been such an earth-shattering concept. I was entirely capable of having sex—I had all the equipment.

"Kyle," Sapphire snapped her fingers impatiently when I didn't immediately disclose the details. "You had sex?"

No.

"Yes," I nodded.

"With a man?" She inquired further.

No.

"Of course," I nodded again.

"A man on board?" She asked for clarification.

No.

"Yes," I said, exasperated.

"Top or bottom?" Ruby chimed in, smirking naughtily while biting her straw suggestively.

None of your business.

"None of your business," I scolded her, grateful that my reply matched my inner monologue for once.

"Bottom. Kyle is always a bottom," Dustin leaned in to whisper in her ear, but I heard it clear as thunder.

I snarled. "That is nobody's business either! Even if it were, that is categorically untrue!"

"Prove it," he challenged.

I squinted in his direction. "How on earth would I do that, genius?"

"Ignore him," Sapphire ordered, chopping her hand through the air between us. "Let's get back to the good stuff. You had sex?" Her grin stretched unnaturally wide.

I huffed a laugh. "This really shouldn't excite you this much."

"Are you kidding?" She bounced. "This is a big deal! You never have sex!" Her excitement drew the attention of several strangers around us, who tried, unconvincingly, to mask their amusement.

Oh my god. Mortified, I closed my eyes, praying for the sweet release of death. "Would you please calm down?" I begged. "It was a roll in the hay, not a walk on the moon."

"Sorry," she said as though she had only realized that other people could hear our conversation. "You didn't really tell us anything yet, though," she noted.

I groaned, rubbing a hand across my face. "What do you want, a diagram?"

"Yes, please," Ruby grinned slyly. At least she said please.

Sapphire ignored her. "Just a few details. What does he look like? Age, height—"

"Length, girth," Ruby finished Sapphire's train of thought, although I was sure those were not the next stops on Sapphire's track.

"Haven't you had enough?" I asked, turning to Ruby. "We've been on this ship only twenty-four hours, and you've already been under more sailors than a nautical toilet."

Ruby cackled. "Hate to break this to you, sugar, but we appear to be tied in that department." She held up her index finger, indicating that she'd only slept with one person on board thus far. "Personally, I couldn't be prouder of you."

Ruby being proud was not a good sign. Her moral compass rarely pointed true north.

"Are you quite finished?" I asked, reaching the peak of embarrassment. "Can we please change the subject now?"

"My intention was only to loosen you up," Ruby went on. "Had I known how loose you'd get, I would have spiked your drink the moment we got here."

Alarm bells sounded loud in my brain. The rest of the group turned to Ruby. The expressions they wore suggested they were as alarmed as I was.

I tilted my head in guarded confusion. "Come again?"

"I plan to, later tonight," she grinned widely.

"Focus, Trampy-McSlutty-Tits," Sapphire barked at her sister. "What do you mean, you spiked his drink?"

"G," Ruby said simply. Both Sapphire's and my mouth tapped open instantly.

"You drugged me?" I yelled in disbelief, although it shouldn't have surprised me. Ruby would be the type to do so without any reservations about it.

"Relax, you make it sound like a crime," Ruby said, by way of admission.

"It *is* a crime!"

She looked at me with slight bewilderment. "Oh, come on, Kyle, you must have known," she said casually. "You drink often enough. You must have noticed the wine was hitting you differently."

"I thought it was stress or the heat, or the fact that it was a long day. It never occurred to me that you had roofied me!"

"Oh, don't be so dramatic," Ruby waved a hand dismissively. "You had fun, didn't you?"

I wanted to scream that I didn't remember anything at all. At least I finally understood why that was. Now the only mystery was how and why I ended-up naked in the laundry room.

I had to tread lightly with my anger. Revealing that I didn't remember would mean admitting the lie I'd told about sleeping with Jax. Sapphire had been so excited. I wasn't sure I would be able to stomach her disappointment at the truth. She had been uncharacteristically giddy about my dry spell coming to an end. Also, I still vividly recalled the smug, knowing look on Dustin's face when I told him I'd slept with Jax. Immediately, he didn't believe it. So, to admit now that he was right was a victory I had no desire to give him.

"I have to go," I announced suddenly.

"Go where?" Sapphire blinked, her tone serious. "We're surrounded by water."

"Anywhere," I replied, realizing it was a ship at sea, and my options were limited. "I have to be elsewhere. Now. Away from *her*." I nodded towards Ruby.

"Don't be a baby," Ruby said dryly. "I was high too."

"That doesn't make it ok!" I tried to gather my composure. "I could have you arrested, you know."

Ruby couldn't help laughing. "Great! Do it. I dare you! I love a man in uniform."

"I'm serious, Ruby!"

"No, you're dramatic," she said, holding her hand over her heart, making a sad face.

"Dramatic?" I grimaced in frustration, casting my eyes to endless water, hoping a giant wave would come to swallow her whole. "I can't even… with you…right now," I mumbled, getting up to leave.

"Kyle, sit down," Sapphire nearly begged, laying a hand on my shoulder. "Where are you going to go? Really?"

"Someplace where I can trust that I won't be violated when I'm not looking," I scowled, then spun around on my heels, fueled by righteous indignation. As I stormed off, I could have sworn, out of the corner of my eye, I saw Sapphire smack her sister.

NINE
KYLE

Retail therapy was real and glorious. Even though I was limited to only the dozen or so shops on the cruise ship, I still managed to find a few small tokens to bring back to my parents.

Losing myself in the serotonin-inducing activity of purchasing overpriced baubles was a great distraction. Still, in the back of my mind, my annoyance with Ruby vibrated. What had she been thinking? How could she have thought, even for a second, that slipping an illegal narcotic into my beverage was a good idea?

Easy. It was Ruby. In her mind, it was likely no different than aspirin. Why would anyone be upset over aspirin? I knew I would forgive her. I was just making her sweat for a while. I also knew she meant well in her convoluted way. It wasn't like anything bad had happened to me. Although it could have. In fact, it might have. It wasn't like I remembered much of the evening.

Since breakfast, a few flashes started to return to me. I wasn't entirely confident they were memories. They could have been dreams. In those moments, I was dancing. Dancing with Jax. Dancing was not something I did well, so I typically avoided it. For that reason, I didn't fully trust that the memories were accurate. Instinctively, I was embarrassed. Even though I couldn't remember if I had reason to be. When it came to dancing, embarrassment was my default setting.

The day had been emotionally draining. First, waking up naked, with no memory. Then the frustrating breakfast with Dustin and his Boy Wonder. Facing Sapphire for the first time since I ruined her wedding had been incredibly stressful. Finally, the realization that Ruby had drugged me had been the cherry on top of a shit-sundae. It was only mid-afternoon, yet it felt like the one day had lasted years.

Usually, whenever I had one of those endless-type days, my go-to was Sapphire. I would call her up, and we would talk through all the issues of the day. For as long as it took. Sometimes hours. That wasn't an option, not when Sapphire was part of why my day felt so stressful. I couldn't very well vent to her *about* her and risk making her feel bad for making *me* feel bad. I had ruined her wedding. I deserved to feel terrible.

I browsed at overpriced coffee mugs, trying to decide between two different ones when I heard a familiar voice behind me.

"I like, *All I need is Vitamin Sea.*'" I turned to find Jax smiling in my direction.

I picked up the mug. "Are you sure? Because I'm leaning towards, *Life is Better in Flip-Flops."*

"Rookie mistake," he said, taking the mug from my hand, putting it back on the shelf. "Life is actually better barefoot. At least *vitamin sea* is punny."

"Good point," I smiled back. Taking Jax's advice, I walked the *vitamin sea* mug up to the counter. The cashier wrapped it in grey paper, then placed it in a plastic bag for me. "How has your afternoon been?"

"Uneventful. Yours?" He asked as we headed out of the store.

"I wish I could say the same," I sighed. "Let's just say it has been a day."

"Want to talk about it?"

Yes. "No-not really, but thank you."

He frowned immediately. "That bad, huh?"

I shook my head, biting my bottom lip. "No. Just...you know." I realized I really didn't want to discuss it.

"I don't, actually, but I can imagine."

We began walking down the hall. Automatically, we matched pace. "So, do I keep running into you by accident, or are you stalking me?"

"Stalking," he grinned wide. "I fully admit it."

"Wow. I don't know what I did to warrant a stalker, but I'll take it."

A brief silence fell between us.

"Did you want to grab dinner?" Jax asked promptly.

"Tonight?" He nodded. "I don't think I can. My friend Sapphire wants us all to have dinner together. It's our first dinner."

"You didn't bog last night?"

I laughed. "I might have. If only I knew what that meant."

He laughed too. "Eat."

"Oh! Well, yes, of course, we ate last night, but that doesn't count."

"Why not?"

"Because that was the wedding we dare not speak of."

"Ah, yes. That makes sense. So tonight is a little bit of a—"

"Do-over," we said simultaneously.

"Thank you for the invite, though," I said honestly. "I'd much rather have dinner with you."

"You barely know me," he said. "I could be a serial killer."

"I know. That's how much I don't want to have dinner with some of those people. I'd rather risk being murdered."

"It can't be that bad."

I shrugged. "Sometimes."

"What are you doing after dinner?"

"Probably wallowing in self-pity. Why?"

"They're playing a movie on the upper deck, later this evening. I haven't looked into what's playing, but it has to be better than self-pity."

"What time?"

"Movie starts at nine."

My eyes widened. "At night?"

He found the alarm in my voice rather amusing. "Yeah, it's a movie under the stars. Night is when they come out."

A movie under the stars. How painfully cliché.

I hesitated. "It's just that it's rather late."

"Are you under a curse? Do you turn into a pumpkin at midnight or something?"

Another laugh. It was nice to be around someone who could make me smile amid my negative thoughts. Although Jax might have been onto something. Maybe I *was* cursed. "I'd love to go," I nodded in agreement to his invitation. It just meant I'd have to find time to nap beforehand.

"Great!" He beamed. "I'll pick you up at your room."

"You don't have to," I dismissed. "I can meet you somewhere."

He eyed me suspiciously. "Do you not want me to know

what cabin you're in? You don't have a secret wife and ankle-biter, do you?"

"I might," I teased back. "There are a few nights from my twenties that are fairly hazy."

He bumped me in the shoulder with his own. "Alright then, where should we meet?"

"Anywhere you like."

"There's the Havana Bar. I haven't been yet, but the Latin music coming from inside has been calling my name."

I was immediately hesitant.

"Oh, yes, I forgot. You don't dance."

I didn't remember telling him that. Maybe the memories were real?

"I don't," I assured him.

"Alright," he smiled. "How about we meet on the upper deck, around seven? We can have a few drinks and enjoy the sunset before the movie."

I nodded. "Looking forward to it." I really was.

The hallway came to a tertiary fork, and we parted ways. Jax went down the center staircase, towards the atrium, while I veered to the left, making a beeline towards the small coffee kiosk. I ordered a venti cinnamon dolce latte before returning to my room.

When I reached the door, I struggled to fish my keycard out of my pocket while holding my shopping wares and caffeinated beverage. I clutched one of the bags in my mouth with my teeth while swiping the keycard against the door. The lock flashed red.

I tried a second time, almost fumbling my coffee all over the entryway in the process. Again, the lock turned red. *What-the-actual-hell?* It was a brand-new sailor's card. It had worked perfectly that morning, so I attempted once more. Red.

"Are you struggling?" Dustin's voice was instantly recognizable. Usually, it grated on my every nerve. At that moment, however, I welcomed it.

I endeavored to respond, but the shopping bag in my teeth made my words come out in an incomprehensible mess.

Thankfully, Dustin had already deduced my plight. "Here, let me help you," he said, taking the card from my one free hand.

Of course, the lock flashed green on his first swipe. I would really have appreciated it if Dustin stopped proving me wrong or inept. He held open the door for me, and I went straight to the desk, offloading my cargo. He followed me into the room, placing my sailor's card down next to my coffee.

I turned to him, a surge of gratitude going through me. "Thank you. I'm not sure what I was doing wrong with that stupid lock."

"They're finicky. Shawn and I have both had issues with ours too." Good. I was glad to know it wasn't just me being incompetent.

Dustin stood there, staring at me. "Well, thanks again," I said, wondering why he was still standing in my room.

He eyed me suspiciously, his eyes narrowing as they made a circuit of my face. "Are you ok? You look…happy."

An average person's response would have been something like, *Yes, I am happy. Thank you for noticing.* Yet, when it came to Dustin and me, defensiveness was the default reaction. "Is that unusual?"

Dustin grinned at me before seeming to remember that he didn't like my face. "For you? Yes. Especially considering the way you stormed off this afternoon."

I rolled my eyes. "I didn't storm off."

"Are you kidding? If you could, you would have shot lightning out of your fingers, like Darth Sidious."

"Ooh," I hummed. "Good reference."

"I knew you'd appreciate it," He laughed, his smile lingering as he looked at me. "So what has you so smiley all of a sudden?"

"I don't know what you're talking about," I turned away from him. It was easier to lie when he couldn't see my face. "Even if I did, it's none of your business."

I glanced over at Dustin, at the suspicious quirk of his lips. He wasn't buying it. He was looking at me in a piercing way that made me feel like a bug stuck under a magnifying glass.

"What?" I snapped at him.

"It's your new Australian friend that has you all cheerful, isn't it?"

I very deliberately tried to look cool but did an unbelievably lousy job at it. I fought a telling smile.

Dustin shrugged. "Whatever's got you smiling, I'm glad to

see it." He met my eyes for a brief pulse, almost like he wasn't sure I'd believe him.

I swallowed the sassy retort that was building in my throat. Instead, I simply said, "Thank you."

"I was starting to wonder if you remembered how."

"To smile?"

He nodded.

"I smile all the time, Dusty. Just not usually in your direction."

I could sense him weighing several thoughts out at once, as he often did. "Do you think we might be able to call a truce?"

A bubble of hysterical laughter emerged from my throat. "Are you serious? You spent the entire day sabotaging me. Now that I'll forever be known as the dick that ruined your brother's wedding, you want to call a truce? How convenient."

"Convenient?" He repeated, his eyes wide. "Nothing about this is convenient, Kyle. I'm trying to ensure we each have some sort of good time."

I pinched the bridge of my nose, trying to channel professional Kyle, who could keep his cool even when challenged by condescending novelists. "That should be easy. Just stop pushing me," I said, turning the blame back where it was deserved.

"So I take it that's a no to the truce?"

I folded my arms righteously. For as frequently as I wanted to open-hand smack Dustin, I could also appreciate how awkward it must have been for him as well. He was being forced to endure a vacation with the man who dumped his lying, cheating ass.

"Ugh," I rolled my eyes, knowing full well that I'd likely come to regret it. "Fine. Truce, but I'm not going to braid your hair or sing kumbaya. I still hate you."

Dustin hummed in suggestive agreement, and the two of us let the rhythm of banter fall away.

"Hey," Dustin said spontaneously. "About Ruby, are you ok?"

"You mean Pablo Escobar?" He laughed at my comparison. "I can't believe she would do that."

"Can't you? It's Ruby. The girl pops pills like their M&M's. If she knew how to sing, she'd be the Black Judy Garland."

"Dorothy Dandridge." He stared at me, confused. "She was the Black Judy Garland. She also died of an overdose."

"Oh," he nodded. "Well then, that would be Ruby. Nothing that girl does surprises me. Although, I'm sure she didn't mean anything malicious by it."

"I know," I agreed. "I'm almost over it already. Shopping helped," I gestured to the bags I had placed on the desk. "I'm going to let Ruby sweat for a while. Maybe see if she comes to apologize. It's not like anything bad happened to me. I survived."

"And got laid," Dustin added.

I hesitated, almost forgetting the lie I had told. "Right," I said finally. If Dustin had caught my hesitation, he didn't let on.

"Ruby's motto has always been *bad for the body, good for the soul*," he added.

"That's funny because sometimes I wonder if she even has one."

He chuckled at that, then said, "For a moment, I thought you were going to make a comment about *my* soul, or lack thereof."

"I'm not going to lie, I was tempted, but we literally just called a truce. I am a man of my word."

Dustin put his hands in his pockets, in that way he did when he was feeling victorious about something but was trying not to act like it. Obviously, he viewed our cease-fire as some sort of achievement that he was responsible for. Perhaps Sapphire or Justin had sent him to wave the proverbial white flag. I was really tempted to tell him that a soldier shouldn't look so arrogant during a temporary armistice. It meant nothing. I would still happily drop a bomb on him at the earliest convenience, and I was confident he'd do the same to me.

Truce? Yeah right. We were both grenades, ticking away. It was going to be a long two weeks.

At least I had a cute Australian to distract me.

TEN
KYLE

While breakfast and lunches were reasonably casual, dinner on the ship was served in a space that looked more like a formal ballroom than a restaurant. The stunning two-story room was filled with crystal chandeliers and a giant window spanning three walls, looking out over the ship's stern. Everything was marble, wainscoting and dark cherry wood with gilded fixtures and golden accents. It was gorgeous, although a little over-the-top.

Dinner was served in two seatings, five pm and seven pm. Since night settled so early on the water, if you were lucky enough to be a premium passenger, your party was seated at the earlier dinner. This way, you could enjoy a beautiful view of the ocean while you dined.

Tables were also assigned based on the party you booked with. So if you reserved as a group, you ate as a group. No exceptions.

Unsurprisingly, given the events of the previous twenty-four hours, dinner was tense. Tense and mostly silent at first. Sapphire and I were both upset with Ruby. Sapphire and Justin's parents were all still irritated with me for the night prior. Even though their children had already forgiven me, for the most part. Dustin and I were also permanently annoyed with each other, even though we had agreed to a truce. So, as one could imagine, the conversation was sparse and peppered with animosity.

At one point, Sapphire, who was pushing her salad around her plate the way she did when she was full but felt guilty about wasting food, snarled at Ruby, "Stop slurping your soup! You sound like you lost your lip in a violent accident." Which didn't really help alleviate any of the tension.

At first, the conversation was minimal, but the alcohol was free-flowing. So by the time most of the table had let go of hostilities enough to actually begin enjoying themselves, four bottles of wine had been consumed. Like a cloud lifting, I felt the lingering tension dissolve.

I, however, was careful not to overindulge in the wine. I had a movie date after dinner, and I was somewhat confident Jax wouldn't have enjoyed me inebriated or sloppy. The prospect of meeting up with him infused me with energy and alleviated my agitation. In fact, I felt a feeling I identified immediately as optimism.

I noticed that Sapphire, too, was pacing herself. The woman was usually seventy percent wine on any given day. Still, her glass sat empty in front of her as she sipped on water.

"Not having any wine tonight?"

She shook her head. "My tummy has been acting up all day."

"Seasickness?"

She nodded. "I think so. I've been chewing ginger tablets like Tic-Tacs."

I made a sad face in her direction.

The rest of the table spoke about mundane things. Topics I forgot about as soon as the discussion was over. Mrs. Salinger started talking about the weather, which led Cody into a story about when he was hiking with a friend in Yellowstone and was caught in a freak lightning storm. I half-listened, making noises at the appropriate moments, but inside, the thought of Jax waiting for me left me too excited to focus. I took a deep breath, trying to shove down my excitement.

By the time dinner was over, it was nearly seven. Which was precisely when Jax and I were supposed to meet. I scurried back to my room to freshen up. That meant trying on every article of clothing I had brought with me. Because, for some reason, I was no longer convinced my casual shorts and blue t-shirt was date-worthy.

After several wardrobe changes, I ended up back in the exact outfit I had started with, and consequently, fifteen minutes behind schedule.

The sun was low in the sky when I finally joined Jax on the upper deck. He stood at the railing, arms crossed, staring out at the sun as it started its descent. The sky ignited in a stunning parfait of pastels, and he looked like a painting, bathed in its golden light.

I felt the unmistakable stirrings of a crush. Even from a distance, I saw something in Jax sparkle, something with which I had become all too familiar in the short time we'd known each other. I was drawn to it. I couldn't take my eyes off of him as I shimmied up beside him.

"Sorry I'm late," I offered, grinning. "I had a bit of freshening up to do."

His face brightened when he saw me. "You look absolutely perfect, Kyle." My stomach ignited as his accent breathed new life into my name.

"Thank you," I blushed. "You don't look so bad yourself."

"So, I've been told." A smile hinted at his lips, and I couldn't help the blush that enveloped my face. "You're just in time for the show," he gestured to the setting sun before us.

We watched together as the sky continued to transform every few seconds, an unreal canvas continually changing in front of us. It made me feel like a little boy again, but instead of imagining a castle in the sky, I was living in it. Indeed the only thing we could see all around us was the dramatic, painted sky. It was one of those perfect sunsets, where the light got progressively lower and lower until there was nothing but a tiny dot of light, then it disappeared completely.

"How was dinner?" Jax asked, the shadow of the setting sun deepening his jaw. For a moment, I was tempted to reach out and touch him, but I resisted the urge. Instead, I said:

"I avoided wearing any of it, so I'd say it was a success."

"Progress," he nodded.

"Progress," I agreed. "What did you get up to the rest of the day?"

"Absolutely nothing. Which was exactly what I needed. Just the sound of the ocean, a good book, and me."

"Sounds like my type of afternoon." It really did.

"Would you like a drink?" He asked, gesturing to the tropical rum bar to the left of us. "We have some time before the movie starts."

"A Coco Loco would be wonderful, thank you."

"What the hell is that?"

"Basically rum, banana liquor with a dash of coconut milk blended with ice."

"It sounds dreadfully sweet. I bet it comes with one of those tacky little umbrellas, doesn't it?"

I narrowed my eyes. "No, it absolutely does not." Then I admitted. "It comes in a tacky souvenir glass. Every day, a different cocktail has a different collectible glass. I'm going to try to get the full set."

Jax laughed. "Why on earth would you want that?"

"I don't, but they make perfectly cheap souvenirs for work friends."

He nodded, understanding. "One coco-nutty coming right up."

"Coco loco," I corrected.

"I know, but mine sounds better," he winked, then headed to the bar.

He returned with my drink in its fabulously tacky souvenir cup. It was tall, slender with colorful confetti accents, and *Festival Cruise Line* stenciled in bold letters across the front. I nearly giggled when I saw it.

As he stretched his arm out to pass me the cocktail, my eyes were like magnets, following the lines of his body. The fabric of his shirt pulled tight across his chest and strained along the curve of his bicep. It planted a seed of desire in the pit of my belly.

What a masochist I was to indulge myself in his company,

knowing I couldn't have him. To endure his presence when every word, every motion, every mundane part of his body had me salivating was torture. I searched his face, looking to see if he was as affected by me as I was by him, but I found nothing.

"So, aside from your love of hideous glassware, what else is there to know about you?" Jax asked me.

"What do you want to know?"

"Let's start with a basic bio."

"Alright. Thirty-nine, Gemini—not that I put much weight in astrology. I grew up in Naperville. Yes, it was as dull as it sounds. Now I own an apartment in Somerset, which is a far more entertaining part of Chicago. It's only a ten-minute drive from Boystown."

"Ah yes, the infamous gay mecca." He said, stretching. His shirt rose a bit, and I caught a peek of his stomach.

Jax had a really sexy stomach. I wagered he'd look great with his shirt all the way off, hovering over me, arms outstretched, fingers wrapped around the headboard while he pumped vigorously.

Whoa. Where did that come from? I tried to regain my composure enough to speak, but my words came out jumbled and with a slight stutter. "I'm close…um…not too close. You know, just close enough. I can go…um… out when I want, but still far enough away—far enough that I'm not…um…tempted to go out every night. Not like I did in my…um…twenties." Good god, I sounded like *Rain Man*.

"You went out heaps?" Jax pretended not to notice my sudden speech impediment.

I nodded, finally composed. "Dustin and I were bar-stars in our younger years. I'm quite sure he still is."

"You aren't?"

"No," I replied matter-of-factly. "I go out to a club maybe once or twice a year."

"Why's that?"

"I think, as we get older, there comes the point when bar-stars burn out, or we risk getting labeled bar-trolls."

"You're no bloody troll. Unless you're talking about those cute, singing ones from that movie."

I blushed. "Thank you." The man was obviously a shameless flirt, but I was happy to soak up whatever compliments he threw my way.

After pit-stops at the bar and the popcorn stand, Jax led me to the deck's center where patio chairs, fifty or so, were scattered out in rows. He gestured to one, close to the middle of the cluster, and I nodded. Usually, my favorite place to sit in a movie theatre was at the back. Still, without the steady incline of stadium seating, the middle was quite literally as good a seat as any.

Jax turned to me. "I hope you don't mind sad movies."

"Honestly? I enjoy them."

"Really? I pegged you for a romantic comedy bloke."

I laughed like he had said something absurd. "Not at all. It's probably my least favorite genre."

"Why is that?"

"They're so cliché and unrealistic. They set the bar for romance so high that it's impossible to achieve in real life."

"I like them," Jax admitted proudly. "They give me hope that things like fate and destiny exist."

"Fate and Destiny are the names of strippers."

Jax's laugh was high and clear. "So, you don't believe in romance?" His eyes moved all over my face like he was reading a news story for the latest update.

"Of course I do. It's just that romantic movies are so over-the-top. If anyone actually did the things shown in romantic movies, it would totally backfire."

"Such as?"

"Like sweeping someone off their feet then carrying them up a flight of stairs," I grinned. "I'll tell you this much, if anyone were to try that on me, they better make sure they can effortlessly lift my weight. If there is so much as a grunt, I will fuck a man up."

Jax laughed wholeheartedly. The sound caused something buoyant to fill my chest. I felt like I could swim the length of the ocean without stopping for air. "You're a funny bloke," he told me.

I blushed, suddenly modest. "I tend to make jokes when I'm uncomfortable or nervous."

"Are you saying you use comedy to mask feelings of inadequacy? That's ground-breaking. You should give a Ted Talk," he teased.

My grin went crooked and a little shy as I took a drink of my cocktail. "Sarcasm is my superpower," I admitted. Then my expression turned quizzical. "What's yours?"

"My superpower? What do you mean?"

"You know, if you could narrow down your personality to your one most dominant trait, what would it be?"

He thought for a moment. He could have said anything; honesty, intelligence, or romanticism, but he almost instantly settled on one word. "Compassion."

"That's a good superpower to have." Jax grinned and I couldn't help but smile back. "I wish mine were as noble."

"I wouldn't consider it noble, necessarily. I just seem to know what people want or need. I enjoy helping them get it. So really, it's self-serving."

I shrugged. "Compared to my sardonic disposition, you're practically a saint."

Jax laughed. "Trust me, I'm not. I'm an average horny little devil." He smiled again. He really had a great smile. It was infectious, and I found myself instantly reciprocating the expression. "You're really cute," he said to me, suddenly.

The compliment hung in the air between us, and my smile slowly turned into something that straddled surprise and confusion. I stared into Jax's eyes, trying to see if he was honest. "You think I'm cute?"

"Of course. You must have figured that out already."

His confession caused a sudden stutter in my heartbeat. I blushed, hoping the look on my face didn't reveal the truth; I absolutely had not figured that out. What could I have said except, "Thank you. I think you're cute too."

He smiled again. "So, what is your favorite?" He asked, returning back to the original topic of conversation.

"Movie?" I asked unnecessarily. "I'm not sure I can narrow it down to one."

"Give me a list then."

"Okay," I took a contemplative breath. "Some of my all-time favorites are, *My Girl, The Lovely Bones, Schindler's List.*"

"So, only sad movies?"

I was momentarily taken back by the question. They were all dreadfully depressing, weren't they? I felt a sudden need to look less dismal. "I also like a lot of classic gay films," I assured him.

"Such as?"

"*The Wizard of Oz, Death Becomes Her, Rocky Horror, Priscilla, But, I'm a Cheerleader.*"

"I haven't seen that last one."

"It's my favorite of the genre. It's deliciously awful! Honestly, it's probably one of the worst films ever made."

"I'm not sure you fully understand the concept of favorites."

"I know, it doesn't make any sense," I laughed. "It's tacky and campy. The writing is awful, and the acting is even worse, but I absolutely love it."

"Note-to-self, never let you pick the movie."

I laughed more heartily. "That's not typical, I assure you. I also love films like *Inception* and *Scarface.*"

"*Scarface* is a classic. Michelle Pfeiffer coming down the elevator in that teal dress made me wish I were straight. At least for a moment."

"Most definitely," I nodded.

"Alright, opposite question. If you had to pick one of your least favorite films, which would you choose?"

"That's easy. *My Best Friends Wedding.*"

"Really? Why?"

"Because it's so unrealistic!" My voice came out nearly confrontational. "Julia Roberts spends the entire movie lying, scheming and manipulating, trying to get her best friend to fall in love with her. Then, in the end, her best friend *and* his new wife both act like it's absolutely fine. Like she hadn't spent the last week trying to destroy their entire future together? It's absurd. Cameron Diaz should have put an end to Dylan's friendship with Julia immediately. The woman can't be trusted."

"You do realize these aren't real people, and it didn't actually happen, don't you?"

"Of course I do, but they *could* be real people, and it *could* happen. It probably has."

"You've given this heaps of thought, haven't you?"

"I've had to argue this point before."

He laughed. "I've always preferred *Pretty Woman,* myself."

I scoffed. "Don't even get me started on that one." Jax examined me quizzically, so I went on. "Aside from being a complete rip-off of *My Fair Lady*, it makes absolutely no sense. You expect me to believe that a gorgeous, distinguished millionaire would need to hire a prostitute? Or that he would actually fall in love with a random street-walker?"

"I don't know," Jax shrugged. "It could happen. Love rarely follows any steadfast rules of order. The heart is wild and unpredictable. It wants what it wants, regardless of right or wrong."

I didn't respond immediately. I met Jax's gaze, searching. Then I said, "I didn't peg you for a hopeless romantic."

"What's hopeless about romance?"

"Besides almost everything?"

He seemed surprised by my retort. "I didn't peg you for such a cynic."

"I prefer the term realist."

His gaze remained leveled on mine. "I see. So you agree

romance exists, but you don't think it's real?"

"Real?" I repeated the word, considering his question and my subsequent response carefully. "As in, is romance genuine? No, I don't think so. It's contrived, deliberate and usually goes hand-in-hand with an agenda."

"What sort of agenda?"

"Sex," I said simply. "Or were you hoping for an answer more sophisticated?"

He laughed. "So you honestly doubt that romance can come from a place of genuine emotion? You don't think someone might want to be romantic for no reason at all except to show affection?"

"Not at all. I think it is absolutely possible. I just don't think it happens very often."

"That sounds a little jaded."

"Maybe," I agreed. "I feel like we meet people in life and want so much for them to like us that we do things we wouldn't normally do. We suck in our stomachs or pretend we don't fart or tell them a bunch of things we think they want to know or do a bunch of cheesy, romantic things we think they want us to do."

"That's called courtship. Isn't that how people fall in love?"

I shrugged. "Perhaps, but they end up falling for the person we're pretending to be, instead of for the person we really are."

"I disagree. Putting your best foot forward isn't pretending."

"Maybe not, but it sounds like work to me."

"Relationships *are* work."

"Maybe they shouldn't be. I think relationships should develop organically and be maintained through honesty."

"No assembly required, kind of thing?"

"Exactly. You can't fake or force a connection. I think, at the very least, romance is often used in an attempt to do just that."

"On that, I suppose we can agree." We held each other's stare for a moment before I looked away. "Alright," Jax said. "Back to the original topic."

"Which was, again?"

"Movies. That is until Julia Roberts sent you on a tangent."

I smirked, embarrassed.

"What's your favorite movie quote?" Jax asked suddenly.

I thought for a moment, then answered with more finality than I'd responded to his previous questions. "Worrying is like a rocking chair. It gives you something to do, but it doesn't get you anywhere."

"I've never heard that before. It's bloody profound. What movie is that from?"

"Guess."

"I have no idea," he said honestly. "Knowing your love for depressing film, I assume something dramatic like *Sophie's Choice* or *The Help*."

My eyes glittered with mischief. "You'd think, right? You'd be wrong, though."

"Alright, I give up. What film is it from?"

"*Van Wilder*." Jax's handsome face morphed into a visible look of shock. "I know, something that poetic is actually from a shitty Ryan Reynolds movie."

We laughed together. It was a delightful, comfortable exchange. "I've surprised you've ever seen that movie."

"I haven't," I admitted. "I read the quote in a meme."

He looked at me like he had just caught me cheating at cards. "That is not fair!"

I shrugged. "Of course it is. You only asked for my favorite quote. You didn't specify it had to be from a movie I've actually seen."

Jax tilted his head close to me, tight, and it looked for a moment like he might have been aiming to kiss me. Instead, he whispered playfully, "You're a trickster."

"Guilty," I grinned. "What's your favorite movie quote?"

Jax opened his mouth to reply, but then his expression turned sour. "Gentlemen," he said in greeting as Dustin stepped up to our lounger chairs, cocktail in one hand, Shawn's arm in the other. Of course, they would approach us at that moment, Shawn looking boyishly cute, Dustin looking devilishly handsome.

I gave the two men a flaccid nod, keeping my smile where it was, although I felt it tighten unnaturally.

"Hey, you two!" Shawn's voice was so animated; it was like having a real-life cartoon character standing before us. "This ship is amazing, isn't it?" He exclaimed. "Did you see the adorable towel creations they left on the bed while we were at dinner? We got an elephant. What did you get, Kyle?"

"I haven't been back to my room yet," I lied. Housekeeping had left me a monkey, but Shawn didn't need to know that.

"I hope they make a different one every night," Shawn said, almost giddy, holding on tightly to Dustin's hand. "I should snap it. I'm sure my followers would think it's super cute!"

Shawn's energy was fast becoming irritating. I split my attention between the two men, genuinely curious how that relationship worked. Dustin was not a cheerful person. Shawn seemed to be made of sugar, spice and everything annoying. While Dustin, much like me, was sixty-percent sarcasm and forty-percent gin. In fact, the Dustin I knew would have found Shawn's exuberance and flighty demeanor exasperating. So why did they seem so happy?

"Going to watch the movie?" Shawn asked.

Why else would Jax and I be sitting there, with popcorn in between us, staring at a giant white screen? Was I that stupid at twenty-one, I pondered.

"Yes, we thought a quiet evening would be nice," Jax said politely, smiling a welcoming smile towards them. I tried to send subliminal messages in their direction that were less welcoming. They were not penetrating.

Keep walking. Don't sit down. Don't sit down. Don't sit down. Don't—Mother fucker!

Shawn led Dustin down the tiny space between our loungers and the row in front of us. He gestured to the vacant chairs to my left. "Are these taken?"

Yes! I wanted to scream but didn't. Instead, I gave a dismissive shrug. Jax looked at me, his one eyebrow raised. I sent him a barrage of panicked brain waves. Jax received my subliminal message and responded with one of his own. Except he was saying; *It's not a big deal. Let them sit.* I exhaled through my nose in long, patient steam. The two men took a seat, Shawn to my immediate left, Dustin at the end.

"Have either of you seen this movie before?" Shawn's eyes slid to Jax then back to me. "*Me Before You.* I've never heard of it."

Sandwiched between Jax and Shawn, I found the entire situation incredibly weird and uncomfortable. There were no other words to describe it. I blamed Shawn. Who, in their right mind, wanted to spend that much time with their current boyfriend's ex-boyfriend? Like, seriously, sit someplace else! There were dozens of vacant chairs.

Jax nodded. "I saw it in theatres, actually. It was quite a moving story. I think you all will enjoy it."

Beside Shawn, Dustin looked as perturbed as I was. He obviously didn't want to be there any more than I wanted them there. His reaction was subtle but distinct, yet it wasn't enough for Shawn to register. I wasn't sure if that meant Shawn was simply oblivious to Dustin's body language entirely or if I was still acutely, disturbingly aware of it.

"What's the movie about?" Shawn queried.

"A young woman falls in love with a quadriplegic bloke who wants her to help end his life."

Dustin grimaced, his eyebrows drawn. It was his unmistakable, *are you fucking serious?* face, but only I caught it. Dustin was never a fan of what one would call a chick flick.

"That's so romantic," Shawn said softly.

Was it? Was it really? Nothing about assisted suicide sounded romantic to me. Sad? Definitely. Romantic? Not so much. Either way, I knew I would cry and instantly regretted agreeing to the movie at all.

I may have come across as a sour patch kid on the surface, but it was all a façade. I was a softy underneath my shell, often weeping uncontrollably at movies and music. Even some commercials inspired an emotional response.

Some people were beautiful criers. They looked stoic and poised as one solitary glistening tear cascaded down their cheek, leaving a salty trail of emotion. Unfortunately, I was not one of them. When I cried, it was a monsoon of bodily fluids; tears, snot and saliva. They erupted out of me, like a free-flowing geyser of ick. I became a blubbering fool, one hundred percent of the time. Dustin had seen it many times, but it was a part of myself that I wasn't quite ready to show the others.

"It's such a calm night," Shawn said randomly. "Barely even a breeze." The rest of us nodded or hummed in agreement. "I've never watched a movie outdoors before," he went on. Then he turned to Dustin. "It's kind of like the old drive-in theatres you had when you were young, huh?" I stifled a laugh. "It's like, a dive-in. Get it?"

I tried not to glare. I was tempted to ask Shawn if he intended to talk incessantly through the whole film. I refrained, even though I had a horrible, sinking suspicion that he was precisely the type to do so.

An awkwardness settled over the group of us. Shawn seemed utterly unaware of it, but one look at Jax and Dustin and I had no doubt that they felt it too.

"Have you checked out the comedy club yet?" Jax asked, drawing my attention back to him and away from Dustin and Shawn. I shook my head. "The featured comedian is supposed to be really funny. We could check it out tomorrow afternoon if you're free?"

"That sounds great," I said automatically, then remembered. "Shit, I don't think I can. Sapphire has our entire day planned tomorrow."

He tilted his head. "Oh?"

"Yeah. After two days at sea, Sapphire has planned an entire island adventure for us."

"It's going to be so much fun!" Shawn cut in.

It took everything in me not to reach out and throttle him. Instead, I pasted the brightest smile I could conjure onto my face. I hated how comfortable Shawn felt infiltrating our conversation. I knew he didn't mean to be intrusive. He only wanted to be involved. I tried to be polite with him, but my words came out heavy with irritation. "Oh yeah," I said dryly. "it's going to be a blast."

Jax smiled wide, his dimples making an appearance. I wasn't the only one who noticed. From the corner of my eye, I could see both Shawn and Dustin take a mental snapshot to add to their spank-banks. "There's a glow party tomorrow night," he suggested. "It's supposed to be tacky, but fun. All black light and neon. Maybe we can go?"

"That would be great!" Shawn smiled enthusiastically.

"Pretty sure he was talking to me," I snapped. Shawn shrunk back to his seat. Dustin gave me the stink-eye for talking to his boyfriend in that tone, but he didn't scold me. Most likely because he knew my response was justified.

The ship was scheduled to depart again around sunset, which meant we'd all have to be on board shortly after dinner. The glow party could work, so I told Jax as much. It just meant I'd have to get over my aversion to dancing. Copious amounts of liquor would help with that.

Jax smiled brightly. "Excellent. I have a feeling that you'll need a beverage or two after a full day with…" he raised his eyebrows in Dustin and Shawn's direction.

For a man who had just met me, he already knew me well.

The conversation fell away as the movie's opening credits started to play. Midway through the film, a sudden burst of air rustled my hair. It was warm and smelled like the ocean, but it still caused me to shiver. Or perhaps it wasn't the wind. It may have been the way Jax's fingers had started to inch their way closer and closer to my own that caused my spine to tingle. Then, finally, Jax reached across the last inch of distance, lacing his fingers through mine.

I blushed, embarrassed, feeling my pulse quicken by Jax's simple touch. His fingers were long and soft, his hand warm and strong. Not at all dry or callused like I imagined it would be. I cataloged the details of his hand, the creases in his knuckles, his large nail beds, the meat of his palm. I felt like a thirteen-year-old on their first-ever date, at an age when the simple act of handholding felt adventurous and covertly sexual.

I made the grave mistake of meeting Jax's eyes. They were locked on mine, his lips parted, his body leaning and his hand resting solidly over mine. "You have goosebumps," he noted.

I didn't let go of his hand. I drew the smallest of breaths, leaning into him as well.

"Should we leave you two alone?" Shawn teased, grinning ear to ear at our body language. Clearly, we were not as subtle as I thought.

I wanted to scream, *YES! Yes, you should leave us alone!* Instead, I released my hand from Jax's as awareness snapped through me like ice. What was I doing? This was not familiar territory. It was not like me to hold hands with random strangers. I was not the type to partake in…what? A vacation fling? Especially not with men who looked like a walking Ken doll. Yet, that was precisely what was happening. It was an entertaining thought, but like most entertainment, I worried it was complete fiction.

I told myself not to overthink it—which was easier said than done.

ELEVEN
KYLE

Morning sunshine gradually burned away the cold overnight humidity, welcoming us to the waters outside of Aruba with intense warmth. Of all the stops on the ship's itinerary, I had been looking forward to the tropical island of Aruba the most. It was a relatively tiny island, but its intensely famous, pure golden beaches faced the Atlantic Sea. I had read that schools of dolphins frequently passed by, close enough to touch, if one was brave enough to attempt it.

The ship had reached port during the early hours of the morning, so we were already docked. I knew this, even before I crawled out of bed by the absence of rhythmic rocking the ship typically made while in motion. My cabin was chilly from the air conditioning as I stepped out of bed, making my way to the coffee pot. It was only a one mug percolator, and the coffee the cruise ship supplied was a step above crude oil. Still, if I was going to survive the day, especially after my late night, I needed to be caffeinated.

After the movie, Jax had walked me back to my room like a gentleman. We had bid farewell to the other two immediately. So eager to get away from them, I had practically left poor Jax behind. I hoped he understood my discomfort had absolutely nothing to do with him. Having an ex-lover and his new trophy always under my feet grew tiresome very quickly.

Jax and I had laughed and talked about trivial things as he escorted me to my room, but then he brought up the inevitable.

"So, you and Dustin," He trod lightly on the topic. "There's heaps of awkwardness there."

We were walking down a long narrow corridor. I was slightly ahead, leading the way. After a moment's deliberation, I nodded. "Yeah, I'm sorry you had to endure that."

"It's quite alright. It was more comfortable than brekkie. You two seemed surprisingly well behaved in comparison."

"In the interest of survival, we've agreed to a temporary ceasefire."

"That's probably wise."

"Yes, but also confusing. I'm not sure how to navigate being around Dustin. It's like I've forgotten how to do something so simple and basic."

"Like using chopsticks?"

I looked at him, confused by his comment. "I actually have no idea how to use chopsticks," I admitted.

A laugh bubbled in his throat. "Honestly?"

I shrugged noncommittally. "I've tried, but I've never been able to master it. So I don't use them."

"What if you're at an important dinner that requires them?" Another smile tugged at his lips, and I could sense the mirth hidden beneath his words.

"Haven't been to one yet. Besides, even a restaurant in the heart of the Asian village has forks on the table for us inept white people."

"What if you're meeting with an Asian author? Doesn't it look unprofessional of you to not even try?"

"It hasn't ever worked against me. Besides, how professional would I look with Kung Pao chicken dumped in my lap?"

Jax bit his bottom lip, trying not to smile at my expense. "Good point."

"What about you?"

"Can I use chopsticks? Of course."

"No," I laughed. "I mean, is there anything that you can't do?"

"I'm sure there's an entire list of things I can't do."

"No," I said again. "I mean something that seems so easy to everyone but you."

Jax thought for a moment. "Honestly, I don't think so. Most things come pretty easy to me."

I wasn't surprised. "I guess it was too much to hope that you would be less than perfect."

"You think I'm perfect?" He asked, purposely adding a smooth drawl to his voice.

"Close to it, yeah. At least from what I know of you so far. You're handsome, charming and smooth. I bet you've never tripped or fallen in your life."

"Maybe when I was an ankle biter."

"That hardly counts."

He cocked his head to the side. "Why not?"

"I don't know. It just doesn't."

That elicited another laugh from him. "That doesn't make any sense. I'm far from perfect, even if I do have great balance."

"Alright then," I challenged. "Tell me one thing that you can't do well."

"Anything?" I nodded, and he contemplated for a moment. I imagined him going through an internal list of everyday things. "Well," he said finally. "I can't sing."

"That's not that bad. Lots of people can't sing."

"No. I mean, I really can't sing. It's brutal. Imagine nails on a chalkboard meeting stray cats in heat mating to the sound of an untuned violin."

"That sounds like something I'll need to witness to believe." I tried to keep my face neutral, but Jax could see the extreme amusement his words had caused within me.

He straightened. "Oh really?"

"Absolutely. I need to experience this firsthand, just to confirm if it is, in fact, the agony that you describe."

"You don't believe me?"

"Not entirely," I admitted with a smile. "There's karaoke on the ship, isn't there?"

Caution crept into Jax's voice. "Yes."

"Well then, we definitely need to hit up karaoke night before this trip is over."

He stretched his arms behind his back, clasping his knuckles together then cracking them. "The prospect of my embarrassment appears to be giving you a surprising amount of joy. You're practically giddy."

"I definitely am," I admitted, stopping suddenly in front of the closed door. I leaned against the wall, trying my best to look at Jax flirtatiously. "Well, this is me."

"Well then, I guess this is where we part ways for the evening."

That was the point when, if I had been braver, I would have invited him in. I could have offered the suggestion carefully, like aiming a shot into a very distant, tiny basket. I could have simply said *unless you want to join me for a nightcap?*

Yet, despite the heat pooling in my stomach, I did not extend the invitation. Instead, I stood there awkwardly, picking a rogue piece of fluff off of Jax's shirt, like a goddamned grooming gorilla. Really, it was just an excuse to touch him, and I hoped he might have taken that as a signal to do *anything* in return.

He didn't. All he did do was say:

"Thank you for joining me tonight. I had fun."

"So did I," I responded truthfully.

Again, I waited. Again, Jax did nothing.

Do something! My brain screamed. Although I wasn't sure if it was screaming at me, at Jax, or both.

"We're still on for tomorrow night?" Jax asked.

Quick, my brain instructed. *Do something to draw attention to your lips. Pout! Make the duck face!*

I will not make the duck face, I argued with myself. *That seems desperate.*

You are *desperate!*

I am not!

You are too! I'm telling you, make the fucking duck face!

I refuse to make that face. If Jax wanted to kiss me, he would make a move.

You want to kiss him, and you're *not making a move,* my brain pointed out.

Dammit, stop using logic!

"Kyle?" Jax's voice cut through my internal argument, and I realized, embarrassed, that I hadn't responded to his inquiry.

"I'm sorry, what?" I asked, like an idiot.

"Tomorrow night? The glow party? You still want to go, right?"

"Oh! Yes," I nodded. "Absolutely."

"Ace!" Jax beamed, which I assumed was good. "Well then, good night."

Kiss him! Kiss him!

"Goodnight," I smiled through the disappointment, turning to slide my keycard in the door. I hoped it wouldn't open. I hoped it would be problematic like it had been earlier in the day. Instead, it flashed green, unlatched the lock with a soft click. I turned to look at Jax once more then gave a tiny wave before disappearing inside.

You wuss, my brain taunted. *You don't deserve a penis!*

"I know," I responded to myself out loud.

I'd call you a douche, but that would suggest you'd ever go near a vagina. To my alarm, my internal voice sounded a lot like Ruby.

After berating myself sufficiently, I started to undress and prepare for bed. I had just removed my shirt when I heard a tap at my door. It was likely Ruby, wanting to regale me with more stories of her sexual adventures on the open water. She usually would shout some form of profanity to announce her arrival. Still, it was late, so she was likely being uncharacteristically thoughtful.

I flung open the door and asked, "What happened to you calling me a whore?"

It wasn't Ruby. It was Jax. He stood there, one arm extended upwards, leaning against the door frame. "I'll happily call you whatever you like, but whore seems a tad extreme. Can we start with dirty-boy then work our way up from there?"

My face was on fire. It felt like my eyes might pop right out of my head, like a loony toons cartoon. "I'm so sorry. I thought you were someone else."

"You were expecting another bloke to show up at your door at midnight, to call you a whore?" Jax asked, a trace of alarm in his voice. "Should I be jealous?"

I laughed, suddenly incredibly nervous. "Yes—er—no—um," I fumbled. Then I paused, took a breath and tried again. "I mean, no. I wasn't expecting anyone. I assumed you were my friend Ruby."

"Does she frequently call you a whore?"

"Against my wishes, yes." I nodded. Then, as the initial shock of opening the door and discovering Jax wore off, I remembered something equally embarrassing.

I was shirtless.

Immediately, I reached into the adjacent closet, grasping the first article of clothing I could feel, and quickly brought it up to cover myself.

Jax raised an eyebrow, stifling a laugh. I looked down to see what was so funny, only to discover that I was covering my exposed nipples with a pair of underwear. I withheld a horrified scream then quickly tossed them aside. I said a silent prayer of thanks that they had at least been a clean pair, then folded my arms across my chest, trying to act casual, which I failed at, miserably.

Jax laughed. "Do I make you nervous?"

"Not at all," It was evident to both of us that I was lying. "What are you doing back here?"

"I got half-way down the hall, then it struck me that you and I are complete wankers."

My eyes bugged out again. "Excuse me?"

"I was standing here, too chook to do the one thing I obviously wanted to do. That's not like me."

"It isn't?"

"No, it isn't," he said pointedly. "Yet, for some reason, I stood there like a dipstick, waiting for you to send me a signal."

"A signal?"

"A bat of your eyelashes or pursing of your lips—something. Anything to let me know you wanted me to kiss you."

See, my brain taunted. *You should have made the duckface.*

Shut up, I ordered it. "Did you want to kiss me?" I asked timidly.

"Did I? You really are bad at this, aren't you?" I didn't respond. "A bloke does not walk you to your room, stand awkwardly in the hall for five minutes, say goodnight, then return ten minutes later unless he wants to kiss you."

I giggled at my idiocy. Jax laughed too.

Then he stepped closer, lust shimmering behind his gaze. My breath caught as he encroached. He brought his hand up my bare chest, then curled it around my neck. Then with urgency, he pulled me in, capturing my lips with his. He kissed me long and tender like one would see in an old black and white film.

Our kissing escalated until we were both out of breath.

Adrenaline coursed through me and my heart thundered. I kissed Jax repeatedly, while he punctuated the tenderness with gentle bites to my lower lip. He growled in response, kissing me back with more ferocity than I anticipated. I felt like my body was short-circuiting. Every single neuron in my body was firing. I was sure there was still a ball of rational thought bouncing somewhere inside my head, but I was incapable of catching it.

Then, as quickly as the kiss began, it was over. Jax backed away, breathless and pleased with himself. "Now I can go to bed happy," he said, backing out of the doorway then down the hall. "Thank you for a lovely evening."

I ventured out into the hall, making sure to keep one hand pressed against the door to prevent it from closing. "That's it?" I called.

He smiled, nodding. "For now." Then he turned his back to me and continued to walk away.

I couldn't stop smiling, even as I went to bed.

Not surprisingly, sleep evaded me. The stimulation of my brain proved more dangerous than that of my body. Bodies could be satisfied easily. The mind was more complicated and demanding. I spent the night thinking about Jax and the way his lips felt against mine. Strong yet tender. Foreign yet somehow familiar. So if I was going to survive the day ahead of me, I needed caffeine. STAT.

Sapphire had our day all planned, such was her way. First, she had arranged for the entire group of us to experience an island tour. She had circled several landmarks on a map that we simply had to make time for, including a sunken shipwreck and a volcano. The Antilla Shipwreck sounded pretty cool, but I didn't entirely trust myself to be around an open volcano with Dustin and not toss him in. I wondered if sacrificing a man-whore would have the same benefits as offering a virgin.

When the tour was over, we'd head to Palm Beach, where Sapphire had reserved us two beach umbrellas and barely enough lounge chairs for the seven of us. The beaches of Aruba were so heavily populated, groups actually had to book ahead of time. We'd spend two hours basking in the blistering sun and sand. No more and no less. At fifty dollars an hour for each umbrella, and an additional twenty dollars an hour for each lounge chair, I didn't blame Sapphire for putting us on a time-limit. That was a four-hundred-dollar experience, and it didn't even include food or drinks.

After the beach, we'd hit up the market on our way back to the cruise terminal. It was only right that we supported the local vendors after spending a day enjoying their island. Besides, I had several people back home still to buy trinkets for. It was going to be a full day.

Outside my room, I could hear the muffled hustle and bustle of people eager to disembark and explore the island. Not quite ready to face them, I took my cup of coffee and a granola bar out onto the balcony, nestling into the chair there. I took a single scalding sip before resting my steaming mug on the adjacent side table. I inhaled deeply, taking it all in.

The sky was wide open and cornflower blue for miles. The sun was still low but already radiating sweltering heat. It was definitely going to be a sunglasses and bare arms kind of day— also sunscreen, layers upon layers of sunscreen. My delicate ginger complexion would ignite like a match under that sun. I'd likely need to slather SPF60 on like mayonnaise.

Then, a small black and yellow bird landed to perch on the railing of my balcony. "Hello, little fella," I cooed in his direction. He chirped back in response.

With the sun blinding bright and the ocean calm and endless, I felt an incandescent spark of determination that hadn't been there the night before. I felt like under that sun, on that water, I could set anything adrift, and it would just float away, out of sight, like it never was. Even Mother Nature's creatures were welcoming me to the island. So, I decided right then that my bitterness would be that thing I sent away. I would spend my vacation being confident and optimistic.

In the two days we'd spent at sea, I'd been anything but forgiving. Where Dustin had been concerned, I'd been moody, bitter and condescending. With Ruby, I'd been angry, judgemental and dramatic. Yes, they had both wronged me in their own ways, but in this place, an island I had only ever read about and dreamed of visiting, I was prepared to let that all go. I would forgive Ruby for drugging me, and I would forgive Dustin for being a cheating, egocentric, narcissistic ass. As the words made their way into my brain, I realized that I was not off to the best start. I'd have to let those thoughts about Dustin go too.

Most importantly, I would be brave and open with Jax. There must have been something he really liked about me, or he wouldn't have kept inserting himself into my vacation plans. I needed to stop questioning it and simply accept his presence as a gift from the universe.

Breaking off a piece of my granola bar, I held it out to the bird. Clearly considering food to be more important than fear, he fluttered down off his perch, landing on the table beside me. I put the granola piece down in front of him. He chirped once before beginning his meal. I needed to be as courageous as that bird so that I might feast on the granola bar that was Jax Abernathy.

"I will be a beacon of positivity and light," I said out loud to myself, picking up my coffee, enjoying the hazelnut aroma. "I will be open to new possibilities."

My new black and yellow friend finished his meal, chirping gratefully in my direction, then took flight.

"Look at me," I marveled. "I'm Snow-fucking-White. Friend to all woodland creatures." I considered the encounter a positive sign of the day to come and nearly felt inspired to break out into song.

Whistle while you work...

Seconds later, I felt a plop of bird-shit hit my shoulder, and I re-evaluated.

When I was showered, dressed and ready to face the day, I met the others in the hallway. Justin's best friend, Cody, was utterly disheveled and half-asleep, while Justin and Sapphire looked well-rested and fresh. Sapphire, in particular, seemed very smug about it. Ruby emerged from her suite looking fabulous and sensual as usual in a two-piece bathing suit with matching silk wrap, and of course, her trademark high heels. She eyed Cody up and down immediately, almost predatorily. She reminded me of a cat ready to pounce on a canary—Cody, the canary.

"Come on," Sapphire hollered, banging on Dustin's closed cabin door, somehow managing to make it look delicate. "There is a strict itinerary, and it must be respected!"

The door slowly opened, then Dustin stepped out into the hall, looking hungover but handsome. "Relax, General No Fun, this is supposed to be a vacation, not boot camp."

"I said I needed both of you to be dressed and ready by..." Shawn joined us in the hall, and Sapphire immediately lost her train of thought. Her face was taken over with a horrified gasp that she tried to mask.

What-the-actual-fuck was Shawn wearing?

He stood there, in what could only be described as a pair of minuscule denim briefs. They were at least two sizes smaller than was decent and looked downright painful. His legs, specifically the muscle high up on his thighs, were a rather interesting development.

If the bottom half wasn't offensive enough, which it was, the top half was equally bad. Fluorescent pink with a mesh panel across the center, Shawn's tank-top made him look like he got snagged in a fisherman's net. Not just any fisherman. A fisherman who was likely on E and owned a boat with a shiny disco ball on its helm.

I directed my attention to Ruby, who stood beside me. "What is he wearing?" I whispered to her under my breath.

Ruby's eyes grew brighter, her grin spreading. "He looks…jovial." She whispered back, spitting out the word 'jovial' like most people would say 'smegma'. We giggled together, like schoolgirls.

Sapphire gave us both a look of warning before turning back to Shawn and Dustin. "I assume you're both dressed and ready?" She asked. Ruby and I, knowing Sapphire as well as we did, could immediately identify the scrutiny in her tone.

Like with most things, Shawn seemed oblivious. Dustin was not. I caught his small, irritated scowl as he took Shawn by the hand, heading past us, down the hall, to press the elevator call button.

"It's as if Liberace and Freddie Mercury had a baby," I whispered to Ruby and Sapphire both as we followed suit. Sapphire rolled her eyes, not in a scolding way, but an indication that she agreed.

The elevator doors opened, then the seven of us crammed inside. Our group's older members had opted to stay on board, scattered throughout the ship, poolside, or in the casino or bingo hall. Yes, the cruise ship had a bingo hall. It amazed me that the parents would have traveled all that way just to stay inside, doing the same, droll things they could have done at home. Sapphire insisted that the parents wanted their time away from us as much as we did them. Besides, all of them being in their late sixties, they would have slowed us down, and Sapphire had us on a tight schedule.

In the tiny square car, we stood together. The world's unlikeliest group: two women of color, a set of identical twins, two gay ex-boyfriends, a toxically masculine man and Shawn. Shawn, who looked like a discarded member of the village people. Having no shame and no filter, I addressed the elephant in the elevator. "So, Shawn. What's with the ensemble?"

"Kyle," Dustin warned ominously.

I raised my hands in peace. "I'm only asking what everyone is thinking."

Shawn looked down at his wardrobe as if only now registering how different it was. "I read that Aruba was a party island," he said in explanation.

I nodded. "I see."

"Kyle," Dustin warned again.

"It's an adorable outfit," Ruby assured Shawn. "I'm just not sure if pole dancing is on the agenda."

"Especially not at eight AM," Sapphire added, helpfully.

Shawn looked immediately self-conscious, and I felt a sting of guilt. "I can go change," he offered.

"Don't be silly," I said, feeling a brief moment of generosity. "You actually look very cute."

"I do?" he asked, blushing and grinning at me. It was a lot to take in.

"You do. It's just a lot of flesh for this early in the morning, for us old people."

"You're not old," Shawn assured me. "You're only thirty-nine."

"My liver is ninety-three. As is Dustin's."

I waited for Dustin's annoyed reaction, but it didn't arrive. Instead, I realized with surprise that he was smiling.

"What are you smiling at?" I poked him.

"It's just, I was expecting you to be someone else this morning."

I scoffed. "Oh? Who's that?"

"Someone petulant, sarcastic, handsome, but not pleasant until the afternoon? Someone mean. Have you seen him?"

Mean? I pondered, confused. I scrabbled back through our mental history, trying to see it from his perspective. Was I mean?

"I'm still me. I'm just heavily medicated this morning."

Shawn laughed. "You two are so funny. Seriously though, I can still change if it would make the rest of you more comfortable."

I leaned in closer to him. "Fuck the rest of us," I told him with a wink. "I was a bitch for even saying anything in the first place. You wear it, and you rock it."

Shawn really was a good boy. Boy and not a man because even at twenty-one, he had a teenager's mind and reactions. He was sweet, bright-eyed and hopeful, a little annoying but endearing all the same.

"Besides," I added. "If you go change, you'll put us behind schedule, and if you put us behind schedule, Sapphire might kill you."

"Not might," Sapphire corrected. "I *will* kill you. Dead. Murdered. Stabbed. I will chop you up into such tiny pieces that the only way the police will find your body is if they pan for it like gold."

I swear I saw Shawn gulp.

We piled into the van Sapphire had arranged to pick us up at the pier, then we began our journey. I sat in the passenger seat of the van. Sapphire and Justin sat in the bench seat directly behind me, Cody and Ruby sat behind them, while Dustin and Shawn claimed the back. I wondered if that was a product of Sapphire's ultimate plan to keep Dustin and me as far away from each other as possible.

As we drove, the trees whizzed by, and I marveled at how small the island was. Aruba was only thirty-two miles long and six miles across. So, even though the island was primarily flat, I could still see all four sides, surrounded entirely by water. Throughout the tour, the others chatted about mundane things I didn't care to pay attention to. Instead, I focussed on what the guide was saying and, by doing so, learned several interesting things.

I learned that Aruba was a tiny island yet had one of the world's most ethnically diverse populations. Even though it had a population of only a hundred thousand, it was home to over ninety nationalities. I also learned that nearly twenty percent of the island was a dedicated national park. At the Antilla shipwreck, I was told that Aruba was the world's diving capital and was home to some incredibly unique coral types. The Volcano was the last stop on our tour. The guide led us up the five-hundred exhausting steps to the top of Hooiberg, Aruba's third-highest point. He then announced that we could see Venezuela to our right

All-in-all it was a highly informative tour. Although Shawn and Dustin had been too busy making out behind the group to retain any of the information.

By noon, we were on our way to the beach. Realistically, the entire island was one giant beach, so I didn't understand why Sapphire had been adamant about hitting up one above all the others. Yet, when the road we were on veered left, around a tall hill, and our destination came into view, I totally understood.

Glistening white sand emerged bit by bit like the sun over the horizon. As we grew closer, I could tell that this beach was unlike any of the others. Not a single rock could be seen for at least a mile— nothing but pure sifted sand, and the water, oh my god, the water. The blue sea dazzled brilliantly, capturing the rays of the sun so perfectly that I had to shield my eyes from the glare.

Even while still on the cusp of the morning, the beach was already packed. People littered the area, some playing in the sand, others frolicking in the water, some merely sunbathing. Some people with boogie boards, some with jet skis, others had picnic baskets and foam noodles. Each group of them cluttered so tightly that it took almost a half-hour to find our spot on the beach as we weaved through clusters of people, beach towels and playing children.

The day was glorious. Only a handful of wispy clouds dared to periodically block the sun, which was sweltering. Fortunately, there was enough breeze to keep us from burning to ash. The view of the ocean sucked the breath directly out of my throat. The intensity of color was like a slap to my face. It was about as far from the real world as I could imagine. I breathed in the sense of possibility as I took my first barefoot step onto the pure white sand.

The Caribbean air filled me with hope and promise that the next ten days would be exactly what I needed if I allowed it. I glanced over at Dustin to see if he appreciated the view as much as I did, but he looked like he thought he'd seen better.

Sapphire hurried over to an empty lounger made sloppily of light-colored wood. She plopped her bag onto the sand and hopped on. Ruby and I immediately claimed the other two chairs adjacent to her. Dustin, Shawn and Cody laid out their beach towels alongside us, determined to achieve optimum tanning.

Tanning was not on my agenda. Even coated in sunscreen,

the sun was my enemy. The reason gingers were rumored to have no soul was because we really were like creatures of the night. Sometimes just a sliver of light exposure was all it took for my muffin-top to spontaneously combust. The thought of my muffin-top caused me to drape my beach towel protectively over my waistline.

I laid on my chair, eyes closed, basking in the warmth since not the sun directly. After several minutes, I heard a distinct wheezing sound coming from my left, like the inflating of a balloon. I opened one eye, then the other, turning to the source of the noise.

Of course it was Shawn.

"What are you doing, and can it stop?" I demanded dryly.

"I'm blowing up a beach ball," he said between puffs, the plastic nozzle clenched between his teeth.

I was not an imbecile. Obviously, I could tell it was a beach ball. "And why are you blowing up a beach ball?"

"Because we're on the beach," Shawn shrugged.

"And," Dustin added, "We're going to play water volleyball."

"You could join us," Shawn offered.

Dustin waved his hands dismissively like it was the most preposterous suggestion. "No, babe. Kyle doesn't do water sports."

I threw Dustin a dirty look and chose not to comment on the blatant double entendre.

"Kyle doesn't do *any* sports," Cody called over from where he stood with Justin.

Cody had removed his shirt, and I had no objections. *What powerful demon did he worship to end up being shaped like that*, I wondered. The man was a Neanderthal, but he was jacked. From a purely objective perspective, the man was beautiful to look at, with his aforementioned muscles and military-inspired quaff.

"No," I looked directly at Shawn. "I shan't be joining you."

A look of disappointment flashed across Shawn's young face. "You're just going to sit here?"

"Yes," I nodded. "It's called relaxing. Grown-ups do that."

"Boring is what it is," Dustin taunted. Yet, I could have sworn I saw relief pass over his face when I said I wouldn't be participating. It was quick, but it had been there.

"What about you, Ruby?" Cody asked, nudging her perfectly pedicured foot with his knee. "You want to play volleyball with us?"

"Do I look like Serena Williams to you?"

"She plays tennis," he replied smoothly.

"Same difference."

"Not really. They're completely different balls."

Ruby pulled down her oversized sunglasses to meet Cody eye-to-eye. "Honey, the only balls I have any interest in playing with are yours."

He scurried away from her like he had been offered a hand job from Freddy Krueger. I couldn't recall ever seeing Cody move so fast. Evidently, Cody wasn't used to being pursued by an alpha female.

"Sapphire?" Dustin posed the same invitation to her.

"This hair doesn't get wet," she said simply.

"That's because there are too many chemicals in it. Submerging your hair in the ocean would cause an environmental emergency," I teased.

Sapphire gave me the finger, stuck her tongue out in a childish way, then returned her focus to Dustin. "Thank you so much for the invitation," she told him politely.

"So you three are just going to sit here?" Justin asked.

"Yes," we answered simultaneously.

It registered then, to them, that it was a losing battle. We weren't going to change our answer. We also weren't going to budge from our expensive, shaded loungers.

The boys split up into two teams, Dustin and Shawn against Justin and Cody. Shawn was probably the most athletic out of all of them. He had the most muscle and, due part to his youth, had the least percentage of body fat. He and Dustin frolicked briefly in the sand while Sapphire lathered Justin in sunscreen like a mother would a small child. She watched me, watching Dustin and Shawn playfully toss dirt at each other, talking and laughing the intimate chatter of two people in love.

She sent Justin on his way then let out a highly fake "Aww" in Dustin and Shawn's direction. Then she met my eyes directly. It was a loaded, silent exchange. I wondered if the distaste I read on her face was about Dustin moving on so quickly and flaunting it in front of me. Or if it was about him moving on with someone who so clearly didn't belong with the group.

One by one, the men filtered into the glistening water. Justin's body was the least sculpted out of all of the guys. Except for mine, of course. My love of red wine and my utter disdain for physical activity were to blame for the small spare tire that had taken up residence around my waist. In preparation for the cruise, I had begrudgingly started going to the gym, but that was only cardio. It had helped to partially deflate my spare tire but had zero effect on muscle mass.

Shawn's denim briefs had turned out not to be denim at all. Instead, they were a nylon-Lycra speedo, made to resemble denim shorts. I couldn't decide if that made the ensemble better or worse. Then Shawn entered the water, and Ruby, Sapphire and I all gasped, deeply, in unison.

"Dear God," Sapphire choked. "It's even worse when it's wet."

It was. Profoundly worse. The moment the fabric got damp, it molded around Shawn's bulge in an impressively indecent display of manhood.

"It looks like a hamster stuck in a water balloon," I quipped.

Sapphire brought her hand to her mouth, hiding a laugh. "It's a hate crime against all swimwear."

"I feel violated," I added. "It's just so…"

"Ugly?" Sapphire offered.

I shook my head.

"Unsightly?" She tried again.

"No," I hummed. "I mean, yes, it is, but that's not the word I was thinking of."

"Big?" Ruby volunteered. "His dick does look huge."

I gave her a dirty look.

"What?" She shrugged. "It does."

I shook my head at her. "Is that really all you think about? Cock?"

"When it's staring right at me, yes," she said defensively.

"I think your obsession with sex is a cry for help."

"No," she argued. "It's a cry for an orgasm." We both rolled our eyes at her. "Now, if you'll excuse me. There's a group of guys at the tiki bar that look like they are eager to buy me a drink."

My mouth happed open. "It's barely noon."

Ruby tipped her head dismissively. "It's five o'clock somewhere." Then she sashayed towards a cluster of tchotchke looking guys, who were wearing far more gold jewelry than necessary at the beach.

Sapphire and I watched as our boys tossed the beach ball back and forth over a rope net. With every spike and volley, their sinewy muscles stretched and flexed, revealing even more definition. As the game progressed, each man got more determined to show off their strength and skill. Testosterone was funny that way. No matter how civilized the man, we were all primitive creatures full of animalistic urges and responses at our cores. The instinct to dominate and prove oneself the most viral was ingrained in our DNA.

I couldn't believe I was enjoying myself, just watching them. At one point, Dustin took the beach ball directly to the face, and I muffled a giggle. That had been immensely entertaining.

"Stop making that face," Sapphire ordered. She was lying on her lounger, lids closed, with an earbud in one ear.

I laughed. "How do you know I'm making a face? You're not even looking at me."

"You're gawking again," She said, opening both eyes to address me. "I can sense it."

I denied it immediately. "I am not."

"You are too. You're looking at the boys like you're trying to set them on fire with your mind."

"That is not an expression I know how to make." I sort of wished it were.

"I have caught you doing it at least twice," she said.

"I can't help it. It's like a convention of wet Andrew Christian underwear models."

She followed my gaze to where the men were still playing volleyball, all muscular and wet. "It is hard to look away," She agreed. Then, Shawn jumped up to spike the ball, his bottom half breaking the surface of the water again. Sapphire and I both cringed, immediately looking anywhere else. "Well, it's hard but not impossible."

We both laughed.

"How are things going with your new friend?" She asked out

of nowhere.

I was tempted to tell Sapphire the truth, that Jax and I hadn't actually slept together. Yet, I couldn't do so and be confident that it wouldn't get repeated back to Dustin. I definitely still wanted him to believe the lie. So, I said, "Very good. We've planned to meet up again tonight."

She looked excited to hear that. "Oh? Are you two going to the glow party tonight?"

"That's the plan," I nodded.

"Justin and I are planning to go too. We should all go together. I'd like to meet this guy you're galivanting around with."

Alarm bells rang in my brain. The woman had seen one too many episodes of *To Catch a Predator*. She was fully convinced that most people were inherently out to kill me until they passed her rigorous screening process. To be fair, my personality was the type to evoke strong reactions from people. So, homicide was a genuine possibility, but I was not as concerned.

"First of all, good word choice," I applauded, genuinely impressed by Sapphire's use of the underappreciated word. "Second of all, I'm not sure that's a good idea. It's a vacation fling. I don't want to scare him off by introducing him to the gatekeeper."

"Gatekeeper?"

I nodded, then pointed a finger. "You."

"Me? That hardly sounds like an accurate description of me."

I laughed. "Are you serious? It's a perfect description of you. You may as well be standing outside my bedroom with a giant walking stick yelling, *you shall not pass!* to potential suitors."

"Don't be so dramatic."

"I'm accurate." Sapphire always made it her mission to vet the people I was seeing, to make sure they were worthy of my, and, by extension, her time.

"What are you babbling about? I've set you up with at least a dozen men, but you never reciprocate their interest."

"That's because all you ever set me up with are freaks."

"What freaks?"

"Derek," I spoke his name like it hurt my lips to do so.

"Oh, come on. Derek was not a freak."

"He asked me to braid his hair," I recounted.

Sapphire looked extremely confused. "Derek was bald."

"Not on his back, he wasn't.

We both shuddered.

Then, realizing I couldn't dodge Sapphire's request to meet Jax, I decided it was best to agree to meet up with her and Justin later that evening. Sometimes it was easier to give Sapphire the illusion of control, even though I was a grown man. It was a tiny manipulative tactic that Ruby and I had both mastered.

"Alright, fine. I'll introduce you tonight. Just promise you won't do anything to scare Jax away."

"You have my word. I will be on my best behavior."

I wasn't sure I believed her, but I was going to have to chance it. Our conversation fell away, and we went back to basking in the heat, watching the others play volleyball. After some time, Ruby reappeared, looking pleased with herself. "Guess what," she said, crouching down on the velvet sand next to my chair.

"Prince Something of Somesuch Country proposed, and you're finally going to realize your dream of becoming a Disney Princess?"

"Honey, I am no Princess. I am a Queen."

"Noted."

"Seriously, though," she continued. "Don't look, but the guy with the neck tattoo," automatically, I looked. "I said don't look," Ruby scolded.

"What about him?"

"He says there's a cave on the island, with ancient tribe paintings that he wants to show me. It's supposed to be beautiful. Wanna go?"

Sapphire looked at her like she had just told us she'd been abducted by aliens. "Absolutely not. You shouldn't go either."

I gave Ruby a reproachful glare but didn't say anything. Sapphire and I knew Ruby could take care of herself in almost any situation in every conceivable way. Yet, this was irresponsible and dangerous even for her.

"Why not?"

"Because you don't know anything about him, for starters," Sapphire declared in her distinct big sister tone.

"And?"

"And nothing," Sapphire scolded. "He's a complete stranger that you met on a foreign beach twenty minutes ago. That would be a large enough red flag for most sensible people."

"Duh. That's why I don't want to go alone," Ruby's tone mimicked that of a seventeen-year-old valley girl. "You'll come with me, won't you, Kyle?"

"He most certainly will not," Sapphire responded for me before the words *hell no* could be formed in my larynx. "This is how people end up mugged and murdered in foreign countries. Or worse, sold into the sex trade."

"No one would sell Kyle into the sex-trade," Ruby dismissed.

"Of course they wouldn't want Kyle," Sapphire agreed far too quickly. "Look at him."

"I am right here," I reminded them. I felt the sting of insult before remembering that becoming a human trafficking victim was not something I aspired to.

Ruby and Sapphire stared blankly at me for a lingering beat before turning back to each other. "He would end up in the mugged and murdered category for sure," Sapphire decided.

Neither of those options truly appealed to me. I sat back, smiling to myself. It was the typical scenario that played out before me. Sapphire's specialty was talking people out of a poor choice, while Ruby's thing was attempting to talk people into one.

"Sorry, hon. I have to side with Sapphire on this. My people aren't notoriously lucky when it comes to taking rides with straight male strangers."

She looked visibly disappointed. "Look at him. He's so hot."

I glanced over just in time to see him hock a loogie directly onto the beach. I gagged a little bit. "Oh yes, he seems darling."

Ruby gave me a look. "Alright, so he's not perfect, but look at those abs."

"Sorry, hon. I can't appreciate his abs when I literally saw him spit snot out of his mouth."

"Great! Now you've ruined it! Thank you very much," Ruby stood up, suddenly angry. She marched over to her lounger then collapsed on it, pouting. "This is why you're single."

I laughed incredulously. "I'm single because the men you're

attracted to don't know how to use a Kleenex?"

"No, you're too picky. You see a flaw, and you can't look past it."

"I know where this is going, and I'm not having this conversation again. It's ok to have certain standards about who I allow to stick their dick inside me."

"Maybe you should lower them," Ruby flung.

"Maybe you should have some at all," I flung back.

We refused to look at each other for all of two minutes before the anger melted away like snow in the rain, then we resumed our happy banter. "I think you deserve better than a tryst with some random islander who literally has the manners of a prepubescent boy, that's all. Even you are classier than that."

Ruby seemed genuinely flattered. "Why, thank you. That might be the nicest thing you've said to me."

"Don't get used to it."

We spent the next hour or so in pleasant silence. The boys eventually rejoined us, declaring Cody and Dustin the winners of the game. That was probably for the best since Dustin would have been cranky the rest of the day if he'd lost to his brother.

My stomach rumbled, and I checked my watch. It was almost dinner time. I knew Sapphire's alarm would go off any moment, indicating it was time to slowly make our way back to the ship.

"What do you guys say we get some dinner before we head back?" Dustin asked, reading my mind. I imagined he and the other men had worked up quite an appetite. "We passed a beachside pub on the way in. We should check it out."

Sapphire seemed less than excited about the suggestion, but she agreed with the group consensus. We packed up our belongings then stopped at the restrooms so that the boys could change into something dryer. Fortunately, the outfit Shawn changed into was much more conservative than his swimwear.

A barrage of noise hit us as soon as we opened the restaurant's door, and the air smelled heavily of seafood. Since it was the dinner rush, the restaurant was crowded. Yet, they managed to get us in rather quickly. I surmised that our group's size made dollar signs fly out their eyes, which was why they'd scurried us to the front of the line.

The pub was diving themed. Scuba gear and plastic replicas

of assorted marine life lined the walls and hung from the ceiling. I was sure they meant for it to seem enchanting and fun for tourists. Still, there was something profoundly unsettling about dining under a ten-foot-long replica of a great white shark.

As expected, the menu was mostly seafood inspired. There were fish burgers, seafood tacos, fish and chips, fish stew, and even an all-day seafood buffet with a wide selection of shellfish and assorted seafood salads. I walked up to the buffet line to check out the spread. There was a questionable yet distinct odor hovering around the table that suggested to me that multiple offerings had likely turned.

"That doesn't seem sanitary," Sapphire said, sliding up to me. I agreed, and we both decided on chicken fingers instead. Shawn seemed unconcerned and ordered the buffet, even after we attempted to explain to him that clams shouldn't smell like cat pee.

I gave one last friendly warning. "Seriously, dude. Something smells funky on that table. I wouldn't chance it if I were you."

"It'll be fine," he assured me. "They wouldn't serve rotten food." His confidence was endearing, although I feared it was entirely misplaced. "Besides, I have a stomach of steel. Nothing makes me sick."

I shrugged, abandoning my concern. Shawn was a grown-up, mostly. It wasn't my place to babysit him. If Dustin wasn't concerned about his child-bride devouring a plate of potentially poisonous cuisine, why should I be?

The rest of our meals arrived without incident. Sapphire and I shared a bemused look when our chicken strips came shaped like sharks. Had we ordered off the kids' menu without realizing it? Justin and Dustin both ordered fish tacos, Cody had fish and chips. In contrast, Ruby, who had sworn off all carbs to fit into her dental floss-inspired bikini, dined on a salad, which was virtually just a plate of kale. She looked visibly distressed over her choice.

She leaned over to Cody. "I'll flash you a tit if you share your fries with me."

"That's not much of an incentive. I can practically see both already," Cody teased, gesturing to Ruby's upper half. "Maybe you should sweeten the pot."

Gross. "What are you suggesting?" I demanded. "That she blows you for a French fry?"

"It's perfectly ok," Ruby assured me. "It wouldn't be the first time I blew a man for dinner."

Sapphire clapped her hands in an attempt to silence us, her eyes blazing. "Do you people mind? This is not an appropriate dinner conversation."

Ruby shoved a forkful of kale into her mouth then grunted, "Sorry, *mom*," into her salad.

After dinner, we split up into two different cabs to return to the port. Sapphire, Justin, Ruby and Cody piled into one, while I got shafted with Dustin and Shawn in the other. The car reeked of cigar smoke, all musky and woodsy, and the seats and floor were covered in a thick layer of protective plastic. I was also alarmed to discover my seatbelt sliced in half. As though someone had been cut out of it at one point.

Dustin and I each took a window seat, happy to be as far away from each other as possible, while Shawn slid in between us. He was starting to look a little grey around the gills, so I mentioned it.

"I am feeling a little queasy," he admitted. Part of me wanted to say I told him so, relishing in the victory of being right. However, one glance at him told me that he wasn't kidding about feeling ill. He was starting to look green.

"Do you want to switch seats?" I offered. "So you can have the window?"

He shook his head once before laying it down on Dustin's lap. Several moments later, the cab turned left, then right, then swerved to miss multiple potholes. Shawn let out a single groan and immediately hurled his steel-stomach guts out. He retched over and over again, on the floor of the cab.

If it were happening in a movie, it would have been comically gross, but happening right in front of us, it was disgusting. Dustin and I both started to scream the shrill, emasculating cries of two terrified queers. I lifted my feet, hugging them close to my knees as vomit started to coat most of the floor. The putrid stink of bile quickly filled up the air around us.

"Open a window!" I shrieked as I attempted the power

window button on my side of the car.

"I'm trying! It won't open," Dustin squealed.

"Mine won't either!" I started to bang on the plexiglass partition that separated the driver from the rear passengers. "Excuse me, sir! Could you please roll down the windows?"

"So sorry. Broken." That was the only response he gave us. Shawn was destroying the backseat of his car, and the driver seemed utterly unalarmed. If it were happening back home, the driver would have already pulled over and thrown our disgusting asses out. It occurred to me that it was probably not the first time a tourist had projectile vomited in the backseat of his car. Suddenly the protective plastic made perfect sense.

I looked at Shawn in horror as he continued his retching. "Why are you still puking? How much did you eat?"

"Don't yell at him," Dustin ordered. "It's not his fault."

"Whose fault is it then?" I screeched. "I told him not to eat from that blasted buffet!" I had one vice-like grip on the door's handle and my other hand over my heart.

"This is not the time to say I told you so, Kyle!"

"It is, and I did!"

Dustin's brow rose. His face filled with anger at my snappish response. "You're such an ass!" He growled.

I grunted in Dustin's direction before pulling the collar of my shirt up over my nose. I felt like I was going to pass out from the stench.

Beside me, Shawn moaned painfully in between heaves. "Don't fight."

"Oh shut up, Linda Blair!" I snapped.

Suddenly, the driver swerved out of traffic, changing lanes then merging again. My grip on the door handle tightened as I tried to keep from sliding into one of the many pools of vomit. Sadly, the turn was too sharp, and my grip was not secure enough. The centrifugal force caused me to collide with Shawn painfully and disgustingly, who was in the throes of another series of retches.

Vomit. All. Over. Me.

I screamed incoherently even as I clawed my way back to my side of the car. I didn't think I'd ever be able to look at Shawn the same way again. Dustin pressed his head against his window while Shawn continued to puke, and I continued to scream.

The car drove on.

The sun had almost set by the time we made it back onto the ship. Dustin and I had to practically drag Shawn on board, one on either side of him, helping to hold him upright. Contrary to how handsome he typically was, he looked like death warmed over, especially with the yellowish vomit stains down the front of his shirt and the acidic odor that lingered around us.

I didn't look or smell much better. Of course, Dustin had emerged relatively unscathed, but Shawn had successfully saturated me with bile. As we cleared security, we garnered several concerned looks from other guests and staff. It occurred to me that, to spectators, I looked like I had been hurling my guts out as well.

I helped Dustin get Shawn to their suite then carry him into the bathroom. Shawn collapsed on the floor, the feeling of the tile nice and cool against his warm cheeks. "I want to die," he murmured, hugging the toilet like a long-lost lover.

Stepping out of the bathroom, I gave Dustin a private moment to tend to his boyfriend. I stood awkwardly in the center of the suite, afraid to move or touch anything. The stench of vomit continued to burn my eyes. I feared a single shower wouldn't be enough to dilute the scent.

Dustin stepped out of the bathroom, closing the door behind him with a solid click, leaving Shawn to moan in private. He flung off his sandals, walking barefoot across the carpet to open the balcony door to air out the room. Even with the door shut, I had been able to hear the sound of the water crashing against the ship as it pulled away from shore. With the doors opened, the entire room was filled with the sound.

"I want you to know," I told him as he turned his back to me, looking out at the water. "and I'm sure I've said this to you before, but that was by far the worst experience of my life."

Even with his back turned to me, I could sense his smile. "Well, you've made me want to puke for years. I didn't expect you to have the same effect on poor Shawn."

"Oh yes. Poor Shawn," I echoed, giving a tiny apologetic wince.

"Thank you for your help," Dustin said with sincerity.

"Of course." Like there had been any other choice. Part of me had wanted to leave them to fend for themselves, but I would have felt guilty. "I'm sorry for how I reacted in the car. I shouldn't have yelled like that."

He shrugged. "It's ok, it was disgusting. If it were your boyfriend puking all over me, I probably would have reacted the same way."

Or worse, I thought to myself. I was sure if someone had puked on Dustin, he would have reacted with much more than colorful words. I had seen Dustin react nuclearly to minor grossities in the past. The guy had stepped in dog shit one time and acted as though his whole foot would have to be amputated because of it.

"How is he?" I asked, tilting my head towards the closed bathroom door.

Dustin gave me what I recognized immediately as a fake smile. "He'll be ok."

I smiled back, though the gesture didn't feel entirely appropriate or kind. "That's good. I'm glad."

"Are you, really?" Dustin's tone was nearly accusatory. I suppose I understood why. I hadn't been remarkably tolerant of Shawn in the last two days.

I cleared my throat. "Look, I'm only going to say this once. If you ever repeat it, I swear to God I will kill you—but I like him." I realized I really did, just as I said it.

"You do?" Dustin was understandably skeptical.

"I'm trying not to," I admitted. "Shawn is so sweet and innocent, it makes it hard." Dustin grinned. "Don't misunderstand me," I said, holding up a finger. "I still feel like I'm babysitting when I'm around him, but he's not a bad guy."

"He's a great guy," Dustin assured me. "He doesn't think he'll be better by tomorrow, though. By the look of him, I'm inclined to agree."

"That's too bad. I hope you didn't have big plans for the next island."

"Unfortunately, we do. I've booked an excursion at some swanky resort."

"Oh?"

"Yeah. It was supposed to be a fun afternoon of sightseeing and stuff, but I don't think Shawn is going to be up for it."

"Yeah," I agreed. "I'm afraid the only sightseeing Shawn will be doing in the next twenty-four hours is the distance between the bathroom and bed."

Dustin nodded. "Which sucks because the excursion wasn't cheap."

"Refund?" I suggested simply.

"No. It's non-transferable and non-refundable."

"Shitty," I offered flippantly. "Well, I'm going to head back to my room for a shower. I'll probably have to wash my hair at least three times to remove the smell of bile."

"You should throw those clothes directly in the wash," Dustin suggested.

"Oh no. I have no time for laundry tonight. These," I moved my hands up and down, singling my ensemble, "are going straight in the trash."

"No time?" Dustin asked. "Why? You have plans or something?"

Dammit, I cursed internally. Dustin had finally managed to go a full five minutes without finding something to pester me about, and there I went, letting it slip that I had plans. Not plans. A date. A second date with Jax. "Yes, I do," I replied ambiguously.

"With your Kiwi friend?"

"That is none of your business," I replied, smiling at his nosiness. "And for the record, he's from Australia, not New Zealand." I turned towards the door.

"You know," Dustin started after me, treading lightly. "Shawn suggested something in the bathroom that is probably a terrible idea."

Oh no. "What was that?" I asked, turning back around to face him, dread gathering in the pit of my stomach.

"He had the idea that, maybe, you and I should go on tomorrow's excursion."

I looked at him like he suggested we go on a murder spree. "Together?" I gulped.

"Yes," Dustin nodded, trying to look breezy about it.

I doubled over in a guffaw of laughter, but when Dustin rolled his eyes, it hit me. I stood at attention, finding the situation immediately less funny. "Oh, you're serious."

"The excursion is for two people," He explained, making a

gesture back and forth between himself and the bathroom, where we could hear Shawn let out another painful groan. "Since my preferred date isn't going to make it, Shawn and I thought maybe you'd like to go instead."

Holy shit. It was both incredibly generous and incredibly fucking stupid. I waved my hands in front of myself to indicate how preposterous I thought the suggestion was. "Why would I want that?"

"It's an all-expense paid afternoon on a beautiful island. Why wouldn't you want that?"

"The company?" I asked, raising my eyebrows.

I expected him to roll his eyes or snark back, but he surprised me. "Honestly, I wouldn't blame you if you didn't want to come, but if you did, you'd really be doing Shawn and I a solid. Otherwise, that's a good two-hundred-dollars down the drain."

"Why me, though? Why not your brother?"

"Well," that careful tone reappeared. "It's technically a couple's retreat. Whoever I bring would have to be comfortable pretending to be my other half. So, showing up with my twin brother wouldn't be convincing."

"What about Cody? Or even Ruby?"

"They already have Shawn's name on the itinerary. So showing up with a woman wouldn't work. Cody is pretty open mined, but I don't think he's pretend-to-my-gay-lover open-minded."

"You think I am?" Dustin scolded me with his eyes, and I sighed deeply. "Wouldn't you rather take the loss? How much fun could we really have? We don't even like each other."

"That's not true," Dustin disputed. "I don't dislike you."

I said the first thing that came to mind. "Are you drunk? We both know that's a lie."

"No, it's not. Honestly, I like you fine. It's just that you're my ex. I enjoy going toe to toe with you. There's a certain victory that comes with getting under your skin." I looked at him skeptically. "We called a truce, remember? Consider this an olive branch of sorts." I threw another hesitant expression his way. "It'll be fun, I promise."

In the silence that followed, I had to bite down ridiculously hard on my tongue to suppress the urge to laugh hysterically again. I knew the guarantee of fun was one Dustin couldn't ensure, but I considered his offer, nonetheless.

"Where did you say we'd be going after sightseeing?"

"I didn't."

"Do you plan to?"

"Will knowing help you to say yes?"

"Quite possibly. There's a fifty percent chance."

"Where's your sense of surprise, Kyle?"

"You've given me enough surprises to last a lifetime, Dusty."

Nothing tickled me more than razzing him, but he didn't take the bait. Instead, he rolled his eyes at me again. "A park and spa, ok?"

"I do love a good facial."

Dustin raised an eyebrow. "Do you ever think before you speak?"

"Obviously not."

"You should probably start."

"Indeed."

"So, what do you say? You'll come with?"

A spa would be lovely. Very lovely, actually. He had also mentioned the words *swanky resort* in the conversation, but did I want to spend more time with Dustin? Time alone with him?

The immediate response was a resounding, hell no. Yet, that afternoon hadn't been excruciating. Parts of it had actually been enjoyable. Somewhere, in the gentle lapping of the waves and the scorching heat of the sun, we had successfully left our complicated anger behind, meeting in the middle. So would one day of sightseeing and relaxing with Dustin be that horrible? No, but having to pretend to be his boyfriend would be practically unbearable.

"Please?" He spoke softly. He wasn't yet begging, but I could tell he was on the cusp.

Standing awkwardly next to Dustin, while covered in his boyfriend's vomit, somehow made the idea of spending the afternoon alone with Dustin feel relatively benign. I should have known that was a flawed assessment. Individually Dustin and I were above-average intelligent people. Yet together, we were foolish. This thought popped into my head, even as I agreed to take Shawn's place.

It was definitely a terrible idea, but it would be fine, right?

TWELVE
JAX

After Kyle agreed to drinks and dancing, I sprinted to my cabin in a panic, to try on every article of clothing I brought with me. It was a glow party, and I honestly couldn't remember if I had packed anything white. Fortunately, I had. I opted to dress in head-to-toe-white, but then, for fun, I added some cheap colorful sunglasses I'd picked up at the gift-shop.

I had been thrilled when Kyle agreed to join me, considering he fully admitted to not enjoy dancing. Having seen some of his moves on the eve of embarkation, I fully understood why. At first, I didn't expect him to say yes at all. Even after he did, a part of me expected him to cancel after his long day with his friends. Still, he said he would meet me at the Havana Bar, a Cuban inspired watering hole on the ship, so I held onto faith that he would.

I sat in a plush wingback chair at one of the tables in direct line of vision from the door. I watched it periodically, hoping to see his adorable face glide through. Every time the door opened, I sat a little straighter in my chair, prepared to wave. Each time, I was disappointed when it wasn't him. I checked my watch. Kyle was already fifteen minutes late, but I refused to jump to conclusions. I could wait another forty-five minutes before entering stood-up territory.

Then I saw him.

He was wearing white denim shorts, a smoky blue breathable collar shirt, and grey sneakers. He looked preppy and casually delicious, with his ginger hair styled to a perfect comb-over-fade. He walked through the revolving door, then glanced around.

I waved what was supposed to be a nonchalant hand. Still, I immediately feared it came across as more enthusiastic than necessary. Our eyes quickly met each other, and the tiny upward quirk of Kyle's lips gave me hope.

I stood, gesturing to the chair adjacent to me as he approached with confident strides. "I was starting to worry," I told him honestly. "I thought maybe you were too tired after

159

your adventures on the island today."

"I am tired," he said, sitting down. "I wouldn't cancel on you, though."

I smiled. "We have some time to waste before the party starts. Have you eaten?"

Kyle nodded. "We ate at some dive-bar on our way back to the ship."

"It was kind of a seedy place, huh?"

"No. It was literally a diving themed bar. There were snorkels and scuba gear everywhere."

I chuckled. "Sounds tacky."

"It was, and the food was questionable at best."

I leaned back, thumbing the stitching on the armrest of the chair. "Are you a foodie?"

"If by foodie you mean adventurous, then no, but I know what I like. I didn't particularly enjoy my food."

"Why's that?"

"My chicken strips were shaped like sharks."

"That sounds festive!"

"Sure, if you're six." He bobbed his head for effect. "At my age, they were more embarrassing than exciting. Honestly, though, they were probably the safest thing on the menu."

I raised an eyebrow.

"Let's just say, there was an all-day seafood buffet that had a distinctive cat-food-esque odour to it."

I barked out a laugh. I thought Kyle was joking. When I realized he wasn't, I made an unmistakable gross face. "I hope nobody ate any of that."

He waved a hand dismissively. "Nobody important."

I wasn't sure what that meant, so I tilted my head to the side, considering. The waitress came to our table to take a drink order, interrupting our conversation. I ordered a martini while Kyle ordered something far too colourful with far too much sugar.

"So what did you get up to today?" He asked me.

"I explored Oranjestad. It's quite a beautiful city." It really, really was. Even though I had been exploring it alone, I had thoroughly enjoyed the adventure.

"I started at the Fort Zoutman Historical Museum, where I climbed the old clock tower. It has a stunning view of downtown Aruba. I took at least a dozen photos there alone." Kyle smiled, listening intently. "Afterwards, I ventured to Wilhelmina Park, snapping pictures of the iguanas as they scampered amongst the palm trees." Kyle had made a face then, and I gathered from the expression that he wasn't all that fond of lizards. "Then, I hopped on to the streetcar, climbing on and off at will, checking out the shops along the main strip. Finally, I had lunch the Coco Plum, a French Mediterranean restaurant. There I read for a bit while nibbling on something called pan bati—which was the sweetest, most delicious bread I had ever tasted."

"Sounds like you had a perfect day," Kyle said, smiling.

"I did," I nodded. "Even more perfect now that I have your company," I said, leaning in closer.

"I'm happy to be spending time with you too," He blushed. "I think this is precisely what I need after the day I had." He picked up his drink, sliding the straw into his mouth. It was far too suggestive, and it made me imagine what he would look like with my dick in his mouth instead.

"Did you not enjoy yourself today?"

"No, I did. It was just taxing, considering some of the company."

"Oh yes. The ex." Kyle nodded. "That must have been cozy." Kyle nodded again. "You two were well behaved, I assume. No additional baked goods met their end?"

"I was on my best behaviour," he said, crossing his heart with his finger. "Perhaps too well behaved."

"Meaning?"

"Dustin wants us to hang out tomorrow."

"Hang out?"

Kyle nodded. "Sightseeing and whatnot. We are going to a spa afterwards, so that part I can look forward to at least. Dustin's paying, so I intend to get the works done; massage, facial, mani-pedi—the whole shebang."

"A massage sounds nice, but I'm not so sure about the rest of it."

"Being pampered isn't your thing?"

"I haven't had much luck with spas in the past. I got a fungal infection from a pedicure once and had an allergic reaction to a Brazilian wax."

He grimaced. "That last one sounds painful."

"It bloody-well was. I developed these awful bumps all over my doodle. I looked like I had herpes for a week."

Kyle laughed heartedly at that, and I did so too in return. When the moment passed, we both exhaled heavily. "I trust that has since cleared up?" He asked.

I laughed again, louder, lighter, and the smile reached my eyes, causing them to crinkle up in the corners. "Yes, I am all good in that department."

"I'm happy to hear that." I was sure he hadn't meant it to sound suggestive, but it absolutely did. My cock jumped in response.

I decided to let the innuendo, intentional or not, go unaddressed. "That's good that you and Dustin are trying to be friends. Sometimes it's important to keep the peace."

"More important than my dignity?"

"That depends who you ask, I suppose." I took a drink. "Was Dustin your last relationship?"

"My last real one, yes. I've dated a few different guys since, but nothing serious."

"You're not still hung up on him, are you?" I asked the question, completely void of any thought to how Kyle would take it and hated myself for it immediately. I hoped he would see it as a casual inquiry between two new acquaintances, but his expression looked insulted.

His answer was short both in words and temperament. "No."

I was a dipstick and instantly regretted saying it. Thankfully, my idiocy coincided with the waiter coming to take another drink order, so by the time the conversation resumed, Kyle seemed ready to forget the offence.

"All in all," he said, switching back to the original topic, "it was actually a good day. My friend Sapphire has a way of ensuring the most well-planned, organized outings. She considers every detail."

"Every detail except food, obviously."

"To be fair, the food was an afterthought. Sapphire assumed we'd all want to eat back here on the ship."

"Probably would have been safer."

"Cheaper too. I paid twenty-five dollars for four shark-shaped chicken strips and cold fries."

"You poor thing. You make it sound so traumatic."

"It was life-altering," Kyle said dryly. "I'll never be the same.

"How was the beach?"

"Magnificent," he beamed. "I didn't go in the water, but just being there, looking out at it, was breathtaking."

"Why didn't you go in?"

"Honestly? I was intimidated."

"By the beach?"

He rolled his eyes playfully. "By the company I keep." My interest peaked, and I repositioned myself in my chair. "All of the guys in my group are rocking six-packs, bubble butts and shoulders that would make Michelangelo's David envious." My eyes bore into him. I suspected I knew where he was going with his confession, but I waited for him to say it. Finally, he did. "I'm the dad-bod in the group. I didn't want to take my shirt off and be compared to them."

"Who would have compared you?"

"Me," he admitted, candidly, his smile a wholesome concoction of self-deprecation and sweetness.

I wanted to tell him it was silly, but I didn't want to discount his feelings. Our eyes met, and not for the first time, I had a perfect look at his face. He was art, from the line of his elegant nose to the set of his lips, to the squared angles of his long face. His eyes were a shade of green, so spectacular, they reminded me of something you would see in the land of Oz. They dazzled like emeralds in the soft light of the candles and halogen torches around the Havana Bar. I felt a definite surge inside me, imagining how they would look closed in ecstasy.

I could feel my cock twitch again. My body did all kinds of traitorous things, imagining Kyle as a lover. I wanted him. That much was certain. The way he could seamlessly transition from delightful and cheery directly into clever witticisms served as an aphrodisiac. Intelligence was sexy, and it took smarts to be funny.

We settled into easy conversation. Kyle told me nearly everything about his life. He had wanted to attend Harvard but lacked the grades or the courage to go to school out of his home state. So, even though he would have much rather worked for a New York Publishing house, Pegasus Press was the only house to offer him an interview. Kyle assumed that was because his resume lacked an Ivy League education. He had started as an assistant, working his way up for a decade. He talked about his favourite people, his favourite restaurants, his favourite causes and his favourite ways to pass the time. On the outside, I was totally calm, nodding and following along while Kyle spoke. Inwardly, I was cataloguing all of the information.

"She wants to hang out with us tonight," Kyle announced suddenly, and for a moment, I wasn't sure to whom he was referring. Then, of course, I realized… "Sapphire." He said her name as it popped into my consciousness. "I mean, as long as you're comfortable with that. I know we're only hanging out, but she wants to make sure you're not a serial killer."

The notion of hanging out with Sapphire unnerved me slightly, but not enough to deter me. "I'm sure it will be fun."

"I wish I were as confident. You will likely feel like you're being interrogated at some point. It's not personal, I assure you. Sapphire's protective and territorial. Kind of like a chihuahua. I'm surprised she hasn't tried peeing on me, to be honest."

I leaned back in my chair as though trying to distance myself from him. "Is that something you're into?"

Kyle nearly spat out his mouthful of alcohol. "Absolutely not!" He said, wrinkling his nose. "That's on the never-will-I-ever list, right between fisting and sex with food."

I laughed robustly. "That's a relief! To each their own, I suppose, but I've never understood the attraction."

"Me neither!" Kyle agreed enthusiastically. "And the sheets! What about the sheets?"

"I suspect that if someone is willing to have their partner piss and shit all over them, they're probably not overly concerned with the state of their linens," I mused.

"You're probably right," Kyle agreed.

"I'm so glad we both agree that is off the table."

"I didn't realize you were interested in visiting the restaurant," Kyle chuckled, the innuendo returning to his voice.

I let out a husky laugh. "I thought I made that fairly obvious last night."

He laughed, leaning back, apparently gobsmacked yet charmed by my forthrightness. "That was just kissing. You could have been bored, for all I know."

"Have you been known to make out with people because you're bored?"

"Not usually, but it has happened. Typically while under the influence of obscene amounts of liquor." This time, he smiled broadly, and I felt a surge of adrenaline go through me.

"Is that what happened last night? "I asked, my mouth tugged into a smile. "Were you bored?"

Kyle leaned back in his chair, scratching his chin, making it seem like he had to contemplate the question, and I absolutely loved it. It was a rare show of confidence that was in such contrast to the way he had engaged with me since we'd met. Then Kyle laughed. "I plead the fifth," he winked. I grinned at him, altogether seeing through his façade. "Next question," he said.

I lifted my chin to him. "First kiss?"

"My thoughts on ours? Or did you mean, in general?"

"I meant your first kiss ever. What was it like? Although now I also wouldn't mind hearing your thoughts on ours."

"It was painful and disappointing."

Unable to decipher which kiss he was referencing, ours or one from his childhood, I raised a brow, unsure if I should be offended. Kyle must have realized his lack of clarity because he quickly added;

"I was eleven. I had read in a magazine that teenage girls should practice kissing each other. So, naturally, I thought it would only make sense that boys practice on each other too."

"That must have made you bloody popular on the playground," I said dryly.

"One would think, but no. Instead, it made me the target of some very colourful nicknames."

"I bet."

"Anyway, one of my friends, Brendan, wasn't as opposed to the idea as all the others. So, we decided to practice on each other."

"And? How was it?" I inquired with a smirk, sitting my chin on my hand, thoroughly hooked on the conversation.

"Terrible. I had this weird worry about our noses hitting, so I opened my mouth and spun my tongue around a few times. Half-way through the experience, Brendan must have changed his mind because he bit down on my tongue—hard. Then he gave me a black eye."

I scowled, imagining the pain. "Sounds awful."

"Believe me, it was. In retrospect, if Brendan were trying to shove his tongue down my throat like an overzealous eel, I probably would have bitten him too."

"Thank God, you practised. Your kissing has bloody improved," I winked, intentionally trying to fluster him.

It worked. Kyle's face turned crimson, and he darted his gaze back to the floor. The expression only lasted a second before he found the sarcastic confidence that I'd already come to expect from him. "You know," he said. "That might be the first time I've ever heard someone thank God for man-on-man action."

"I thank him for that, every day," I quipped. "So, your first kiss was with a bloke? Have you ever been with a woman?"

Kyle narrowed his eyes at me, playfully. "Do you want a complete rundown of my sexual history?"

"Maybe a bit later," I laughed. "I'm just trying to get to know you better."

"In that case, no, I have never been with a woman," Kyle said, swallowing another large sip of his cocktail. "Have you?"

I nodded. "Like a lot of us, I explored the idea of heterosexuality. I quickly realized it wasn't for me. Kissing a woman felt nice but lacked passion. I didn't feel that fire I knew I was supposed to feel. It felt empty and sterile. Not at all the way it felt kissing you the other night." Kyle seemed visibly nervous by my declaration, and I stared at him, thoroughly enjoying the spot of red that painted his cheeks. I loved how easily he blushed, his natural pigment making any colour change stand out like dog's balls. "I plan on doing it again."

He opened his mouth to say something, and for a beat, it felt like a revelation was going to pour down over me, but Kyle snapped his mouth shut again without breathing a word. Then, he wrenched his gaze away from me before he got too awkward.

A meaningful hush fell over us. It wasn't an uncomfortable silence. Instead, it was erotic and seductive, as it gave our imaginations time to wander and reflect back on our kissing from the previous night. Although words were not being exchanged, the looks we gave each other from across the small table spoke volumes. Kyle bit his lower lip at one point. At that moment, I imagined those lips doing a significant number of things.

"Maybe I'll let you," he said finally, coyly, his mouth curling into a delighted grin. At his short words, any intelligent thought fell away. I was wiped clean of any reaction except lust.

I glanced at my watch and was gobsmacked by the time. Two hours of talking and laughing had felt like minutes in Kyle's presence. Yet, beneath the joy of his company, I felt a stirring of worry. I liked him. Heaps. Too much for this early in the game.

I knew we had ought to head to the glow party, but the notion of sharing him with his friends didn't interest me as much as it did Kyle. Yet, he had said we would meet them, and I had agreed, so I announced it was time for us to go.

He seemed equally disappointed to call an end to our intimate evening. "If we must," he conceded. I extended my hand to him, and he used it to hoist himself up from his chair. We stood dangerously close to each other, both of us silently daring the other to move. Kyle broke first, and when he finally did move, it wasn't in the direction I had hoped. He blinked, turning away.

I followed him, assuming he would make his way to the stairwell since the party was only two flights up. Instead, he led me to the elevator, and I didn't object. We chatted idly while we waited for the doors to open. When they did, I was thrilled to discover it vacant. As soon as the doors closed and we were alone, I pressed Kyle against the elevator wall, his eyes widened, but he didn't push me away. Instead, he slipped his arms around my neck, kissing me back.

That was all the encouragement I needed. To Kyle's surprise, I took his hands in mine, confining them above his head. Kyle's eyes fluttered in excitement as I leaned closer, my lips brushing over his. We kissed deeply; our bodies pressed together. Sadly and all too soon, the elevator came to a stop, and the doors behind us opened.

It had taken every ounce of willpower not to yank Kyle back into the elevator and press the emergency stop button. Which I found poetically ironic since the last thing I wanted to do was stop.

THIRTEEN
KYLE

The ship's lobby looked like the inside of a hallucinogenic episode. Large panels of white fabric cloaked every wall and hung from the ceiling in bubbling waves. A combination of neon and black lights illuminated the material with kaleidoscopic beams.

Stewards and bartenders were both dressed in combinations of white and neon. They glowed against the black light, dancing and bopping while they supervised the guests or slung drinks to the thirsty dancers. One of the bartenders was wearing fluorescent pink nail polish and dark eyeliner. He usually was in uniform, but that night was an opportunity to express his individuality. I had noticed him a few days earlier, immediately suspecting that he was also a friend of Dorothy. That night, seeing him come alive, in clothes of his choosing, totally comfortable and uninhibited, it was far more apparent.

The DJ was spinning music that was right up my alley. A fun blend of modern pop and classics from the eighties and nineties. Sapphire and Justin were already standing at the bar as Bruce Springsteen's "Born in the USA" blasted on the sound system.

Sapphire was as poised and beautiful as always. She was wearing a simple white sundress, her black hair cascading down her back in inky waves. Sapphire turned, meeting my eyes with no surprise as if already knowing I was there. She immediately raised her brow, inquiring about the handsome gentleman that stood to my left. Knowing each other as we did, I knew what the look meant. I nodded, indicating that yes, he was the man that was keeping me entertained on the ship. She then enthusiastically waved us over.

Like Sapphire, Jax was also dressed all in white except for a cheap pair of pink plastic-framed novelty sunglasses hanging from the neckline of his sleeveless button-up shirt. Justin was in black knee-length shorts and a red sleeveless top. Apparently, he had decided not to participate in the glow party in the same way the rest of us had. Guests were encouraged to wear white or fluorescent so that we would glow in the strategic lighting. I was in white and blue, so I lit-up relatively bright. The only part of Justin's attire that was illuminated was the small white particles on the front of his shorts; lint. It was ordinarily invisible to the naked eye, but the black light drew attention to it.

When Jax and I joined Sapphire and Justin, the bartender was already lining up three colorful shots on the bar in front of them. Justin handed the bartender his sailor's card, and the bartender swiped it across a black card-reader.

"Sapphire, Justin, this is my friend Jax," I introduced and Jax, like the mature gentlemen he was, extended his hand to Justin.

Justin shook it, offering a polite but entirely indifferent, "Hey." Sapphire examined Jax with a little more scrutiny.

"You look out of breath," she said, eyeing me with suspicion.

"We had some fun in the elevator," I admitted, blushing.

Sapphire raised her hand to stop me. "Please don't elaborate." She then turned her attention to the handsome man beside me. "So, Jacks?" She shook his hand, repeating his name like one would a word they had heard for the first time. "Is that with an X or an S?"

"An X."

"Is that short for Jaxson?"

Why hadn't it occurred to me to ask that? Jax nodded. "It was. Not anymore, though. Nobody's called me that in decades."

"Why not?"

What the hell is with the third degree, I wondered. If she was going to interrogate him over something as simple as his name, it was bound to be a long evening. I threw Sapphire a look that urged her to knock it off, and, tentatively, she obliged.

"I come from a long line of Jacksons. Technically, I'm Jaxson Abernathy, the third. My oldies were kind enough to spell my name differently than my father and grandfather, but it's still confusing when we're all in the same room. My grandfather was Jackson, my dad is Jack, and I'm just Jax."

Sapphire nodded understanding, and, as subliminally requested by me, asked Jax no further questions.

"These shots aren't going to drink themselves," Justin chimed in, gesturing to the cluster of glasses on the ledge in front of him.

"Oh, dear," I stepped forward, peering down at the bright green liquid. "What's in these? Rum?"

"Something like that," Justin replied evasively. "They're called Mexican Samurais."

"Hey, we're missing one," I said, pointing that there were only three glasses on the counter.

"No-no," Sapphire waved a hand. "No shots for me, thank you. I'd like to remember in the morning."

The remaining three of us each picked up a glass, clinking them together somewhat sloppily. "To the newlyweds!" Jax declared before we swallowed them down.

They were not vodka.

"That was disgusting," I complained, making a sour face.

"You're disgusting," Justin teased back. "If you're going to do shots, tequila is the only way to go."

"Gross," I scowled

Jax nudged me with his muscular shoulder. "Not a fan of tequila?"

"I haven't drunk tequila since college. It tends to make me—"

"Flamboyant?" Sapphire offered.

"Fun?" Justin suggested.

I faked insult. "Excuse me, I am always fun."

"And flamboyant," Justin said, then Sapphire slapped him playfully against his chest.

I turned to Jax. "Please ignore these people. I've never met them before in my life. I thought you'd like me more if I had friends, so I hired them. I regret that now."

Justin flagged down the bartender. "Can we get another round of these, please?"

"Not for me, thank you," I declined.

"Don't be a wuss," Justin taunted, handing me a new shot glass of green fluid.

"You never finished your thought earlier," Jax reminded me. "About tequila. What does it do to you?"

I found myself enthralled by how the simple question curled into his accent. Velvety and delectable like soft-serve ice cream. I had never considered the Australian accent sexy before. Thanks to Jax, I would no longer consider it any other way. I blushed, and he misinterpreted my coloring.

"Oh! I see," Jax winked. "Tequila makes you randy, does it?" No, tequila didn't. Any randiness I was feeling was all thanks to Jax Abernathy and our brief but insanely hot make-out session in the elevator.

"He wishes," Sapphire laughed. "Kyle is super cute, but he's the biggest prude."

"I am not."

"Oh, honey," she placed a hand on my forearm. "Yes, you are. I swear you must have had copies of *Vogue* under your mattress, instead of dirty magazines, as a kid."

I folded my arms, pouting.

"So what does tequila do to you then?" Jax asked again.

"It usually makes him blow chunks," Sapphire answered for me.

"Well then," Jax said, carefully taking the full glass from my fingers. "Let's keep this out of your reach, shall we?" He swallowed back both shots, then hailed the barkeep. "Can we get two more? Maybe something a little more delicate for the gentleman?"

Gentleman? I was reasonably confident I had never been called one of those before. "Cheers," Jax said as the bartender placed two more shots in front of us.

I didn't know what they were, but they smelled sweet like melons. I slid one towards Jax, but he slid it back to me. "No-no. I'm already a shot ahead of you. You've got some catching up to do."

"Then I'll be ahead of you," I pointed out.

"Perfect," he grinned, gesturing to both glasses.

I did as he urged, slamming both drinks back quickly. They were tasty and definitely not tequila. The three shots in the short period made my chest feel warm and my head happy.

After that, each of us ordered a real beverage. Jax ordered a martini, Justin a beer, and Sapphire looked to be drinking soda water, but I was sure there was vodka or something mixed in. I opted for that evening's featured beverage. Something called a Tidal Wave.

If you wanted to get as drunk as possible for as little as

possible, a Tidal Wave seemed like a fancy way to do it. When the waitress delivered the monstrous drink, I looked at it with equal parts thrill and horror. It was a potent concoction of vodka, rum, blue curacao, melon liquor, lime slush and an upside-down bottle of Caribbean beer. And, to make it even more fun, they served it in a souvenir fishbowl. It tasted delicious, and it glowed a bright teal color under the black lights. Still, I knew immediately that no good decision would be made after its consumption.

Sapphire led us to a nearby, sticky booth. We tumbled in, already feeling the effects of the three consecutive shots. The lights were low except for the black light that cast each of us in a hazy blue-ish tint.

Jax and I sat side-by-side, but far enough away to remain casual. I couldn't help but notice Jax's immaculate bone structure and how the unusual lighting hollowed out his face, making the sharp angles even more intense. His arm was draped across the back of the booth, and if I leaned back, even slightly, I could feel his fingers brush the curve of my shoulder. Each time we made contact, tiny flicks of fire ignited my flesh. I tried my hardest not to lean back at all, lest I burst into flame.

Already on the dancefloor, Ruby gyrated suggestively against the lap of a stranger. She made eye contact with our table. I was sure it was with one of us specifically, but I couldn't tell with whom at a distance. She furled her finger in our direction, beckoning us to accompany her on the floor. Sapphire was the first to join her sister just as "Vacation" by The Go-Go's began playing on the sound system.

That left only the three of us men at the table. I loved Justin, I considered him family, but we honestly had little in common. Sapphire was usually the buffer between us. So, to avoid awkward small talk, Justin ordered three more rounds of shots.

In honor of the song playing, we raised a toast to our vacation. After the first two shots, my eyes bulged. Technically they were my fourth and fifth shot in a half hour. By the sixth, my equilibrium started to teeter.

Whitney Houston's "How Will I Know" replaced The Go-Go's and Sapphire launched herself back towards our table. "Baby," she pulled at Justin's t-shirt. "Dance with me."

He smiled, the same annoying charming smile as his twin. I

loved him like a brother, but at that moment, I cringed. "You know I hate dancing," he told his wife.

"It's *Whitney*," she whined.

I looked over endearingly at the couple, who laughed together, then Justin shrugged in my direction. "I can't argue with Whitney," he shouted over the noise before succumbing to Sapphires pleading. They disappeared onto the dancefloor together.

I watched the entire exchange with an ear-to-ear grin. I leaned over to Jax and drunkenly yelled, "In the fifteen years that I've known them, I've only seen them dance together three times."

"Let me guess," Jax yelled back. "Only to Whitney?"

"Always. Whitney's her diva. You can't deny a girl her diva." I watched her and Justin on the dancefloor. Her dark hair was flying as she nailed every word of the song.

"Who's your diva?" Jax asked me, drawing my attention back to him.

I groaned, sounding embarrassed before I even revealed the answer. "Cher."

Jax cackled, nodding appreciatively, "I enjoy Cher on occasion."

I went on like an embarrassing schoolboy. "Her version of "Walking in Memphis" is so much better than the original. Don't you think?"

"I can't say that I've ever heard it."

Anyone who liked Cher knew her version. I arced a brow over at him. "You don't actually like Cher, do you?"

Jax's mouth fell open, pretending to be insulted. "Would I lie about Cher to you?"

"Probably," I nodded. "Especially if you're trying to get lucky."

Jax flashed me a megawatt smile that shined bright in the black-lit room. He then leaned back into the booth, making a show of raising his muscular arms then clasping his hands behind his head. "What makes you think I'd need to try? What makes you think I'm even interested?

"You're not interested in me?" I challenged. "Well then, you're making a mistake. I'm very interesting." I was pleasantly impressed by how confident I sounded. It probably helped that I knew, beyond a doubt, that he was interested in me, regardless of what he claimed at that moment.

"Yes, you are. Intriguing, one might say." He shot me a wink.

I positively melted then quickly attempted to calm my growing nervousness. I couldn't believe the anxiety that grew within me with only a smile or a flex of Jax's biceps. I felt like a schoolboy, feeling the excitement and fear of his first crush.

"Who's your diva?" I asked, realizing I hadn't done so earlier.

He thought for a moment. "That's a tossup between Kylie and Olivia."

"Olivia?"

He looked pained. "Newton-John."

"The woman from *Grease*?"

"You uncultured swine," he choked, falling forward onto the table laughing. "How dare you reduce Olivia to just the woman from grease. She is an icon, and don't you forget it."

I laughed. "I will try not to." He smiled, and maybe it was the fact that half my blood was booze by that point, but I was suddenly reminded that the first thing I had noticed about Jax was his smile.

"Have you ever seen *Sordid Lives*?" He asked.

"No, but I live a sordid life. Does that count?"

"Not really, no." At least he was honest. "If you have a chance, you really should watch it. I think you'd really like it."

"Maybe I'll rent it when I get home."

"Rent it? Are you going to hop into your time machine and pick it up at a Blockbuster Video?"

I held down a laugh that I suspected was much larger than his joke actually deserved. "Maybe. You don't know what kind of car I drive," I teased, referring to the DeLorean from *Back to the Future*.

Cindy Lauper's "Girls Just Want to Have Fun" blared through the sound system.

"If you do go back in time, please find the fifteen-year-old-me and tell him that a blue faux hawk is not a wise fashion choice."

"Blue?"

He nodded. "It was my do-anything-to-piss-off-my-oldies

phase."

"Oh?"

"I was already a moody teen, and their divorce put me over the edge. Let's just say blue hair didn't accomplish anything except to make me look like a Smurf my entire sophomore year."

"The blue didn't bother them?" I asked, lifting my glass and taking a deep suck through my straw.

"I'm sure it would have if they had noticed. I was boarding at Barker, and when I came home on the weekends, they were seldom around." I felt a pang of pity for him. "Don't worry, though. My grades were something they couldn't ignore. They were so bad, it made up for the total lack of effect the blue hair had on them." I smiled warmly. "What about you? Were you a troublemaker growing up?"

I laughed at the very thought. "Hardly. I was a typical brown-nosing know-it-all. I was usually buried so deep in a book, there wasn't time for teenage mischief."

"You were a bit unpopular, were you?"

"Not at all." The comment didn't offend me, but it wasn't an accurate assessment. "My older brother was the golden boy in high school. Everybody loved him. Girls knew the easiest way to get close to him was to be friends with me, so I was actually quite popular."

Jax studied me for several long seconds. "It sounds like you lived a little in his shadow."

I contemplated for a moment. "Maybe a little bit, but I never really felt that way. Clark had a way of taking every watt of the spotlight then redirecting it back to others. He was such a generous person in every way."

"Was?"

"He died a few years ago. Brain aneurysm. He would have turned forty-two this year."

"That's awful," Jax offered. "I'm sorry."

"It's ok," I said out of habit, then added, "It's taken a long time for me to be able to say that. It's ok. When Clark died, I thought the world would end. He was my big brother. I had never known a world without him in it. It was hard to imagine one could exist."

"It sounds like you were very close."

"Inseparable. Clark was my protector and my confidant. He made the world make sense to me." I paused. "Sapphire helped me pick up the pieces when he passed. She and Dustin held me together and forced me to carry on."

"Let's have a toast to your brother, shall we?" Jax suggested, flagging down a server.

Fifteen minutes and two more shots later, I reached the bottom of my drink, sucking in watery air loudly. "Alright," Jax said, taking the empty glass from my hands and putting it on the table in front of us. At first, I thought he was going to order me another Tidal Wave. That terrified me because I was quite sure my stomach couldn't tolerate any more booze. Then, he said something that scared me even more. "Get up. We're dancing." Then he grabbed my hand, dragging me to the dancefloor.

We joined Sapphire and Justin as Diana Ross's "I'm Coming Out" started its unmistakable notes. The dancefloor was packed full of clammy bodies, all jumping and flailing and spilling their margaritas and daiquiris all over the floor, and occasionally themselves. Several people had dark spots on their glowing white t-shirts and dresses. Ruby had vanished, so had the handsome stranger she had been grinding up against earlier. I could imagine exactly what they were doing at that moment, but I tried not to.

Jax had some serious moves. They were an amalgamation of intense, hard lines and hip action. The intensity of his presence was so powerful on the dancefloor, he seemed to shimmer, drawing in the light, the air, and the sound. He pulsated, gyrated and flicked in perfect beat to the music.

I wasn't accustomed to dancing. I rarely did it, and I wasn't particularly good at it either. My body lacked the rhythm and grace that people like Sapphire and Jax made look so effortless. If not for the influence of alcohol, I likely would have been too self-conscious to even try.

An hour of dancing and several drinks later, I was almost ready to take a break when Cher's "If I Could Turn Back Time" boomed loudly through the speakers. I considered it serendipitous and decided to dance through my growing exhaustion. Beads of sweat gathered at my temples.

"If I could reach the stars, I'd give them all to you!" Sapphire and I sang in unison, spinning around each other like battling tops. Then we took turns belting out the final words of the chorus.

"Then you'd love me..."

"Love me!" Sapphire echoed.

"Like you used to do. Aaaah!" We finished together. Then I grabbed her hand, spinning her in a ballerina twirl before we started giggling like children. I couldn't remember the last time I'd laughed that purely.

My eyes, hot and dizzy from spinning, locked with Jax's. Somewhere under the haze of liquor, I could see myself reflected in his vision. In that reflection, I saw myself in a way I hadn't in a long time; sweaty, joyous, silly and handsome, and I couldn't help but smile broadly at him. He returned it in equal measure. I was surprised by how much more special I felt in his company.

In a babel of off-key singing, cheering and flashing lights, the song blasted into its bridge, and there wasn't a single person in the room not singing along. It was loud, sweaty and wonderful.

Just like that, the fact that Shawn had vomited all over me was momentarily forgotten. I couldn't recall when I had last experienced such sparkling, easy joy or when I had felt so bright or infectiously alive. However, all good things came to an end, and soon Cher gave way to Prince, and it was a less than pleasant-sounding transition. As much as I loved "Little Red Corvette," I needed to catch my breath.

I was very, very drunk, and the music was very, very loud, and I could feel my balance starting to teeter slightly. Jax entwined his fingers around mine, looking down at me with a sweet smile and soft, adoring eyes. I could feel an immediate electricity course through me, something completely separate from the liquor and the music. "I could use some air," he said, holding me still, burning his remarkable eyes deep into me. "Wanna go for a walk?"

Simply by holding my hand, he sent my heart into palpitations and my stomach somersaulting. I nodded, then he led me through the tangle of dancing bodies then off the dancefloor. In the hall, we passed Sapphire, who was on her way back from the restroom.

"Don't do anything Ruby would do," she said with a

glimmer of mischief in her eyes.

"Don't worry, I'll keep a close eye on him," Jax assured her with a wink.

"I'm sure you will," she said to Jax before quickly kissed me on the cheek. "Have fun," she whispered to me before vanishing around the corner.

Jax led me up a run of stairs, then through a long corridor that opened up suddenly onto the outdoor deck and into the crisp ocean air. The wind was mighty but warm. I could feel my red hair tousling, and my t-shirt, damp with sweat, clung to my torso. I noticed, with excitement, that Jax's shirt was doing the same. Except, where mine revealed a less than perfect frame, Jax's shirt hugged washboard abs and hard muscle. I pulled at my shirt, self-conscious.

It was late already, past midnight, and all around us, blackness loomed. The ocean looked like a deep and endless pool of oil, and the ebony sky equally vast. If not for the stars and moon that speckled the tapestry above us, one would not have been able to tell where the water ceased and the sky began.

That far away from the loud music and dancers, the ocean's heavy silence was nearly deafening. Not at all peaceful like I thought it would be. The waves lapped up against the ship as it traveled, and all you could hear was the violent collision of water hitting sturdy steel. It was a reminder that, at night, at that speed, that far out on the water, we were floating on liquid death.

For a moment, I stood, transfixed by the sight of the moon reflecting off the black water. I'd seen the ocean before. Several times, actually. I'd visited the island of Vancouver, Canada, and walked on the beaches of Cancun and Puerto Vallarta. I'd even paid tribute to the shores of Pearl Harbour. I'd stood on the line where entire nations ended, but I had never been so far out on the water before. Where technically, I was in no country. No territory. No continent. I was in international waters. The land was a distant memory, and I was nowhere yet everywhere all at once.

Jax stood quietly, hands on the railing, looking up at the brilliant stars. He looked transformed in the moonlight. It cast him in half shadow, softening the sharp angles of his statuesque face. I didn't know him well enough to gauge his sobriety, but he'd had at least as much to drink as I had, so I wagered his body was feeling equally rubbery.

I trudged up to stand next to him. "It's so dark out," I stated foolishly. Of course it was dark. It was night.

"Look," Jax said, pointing his left index finger outward and upward. "That's Canis Major."

"Major who?" I queried, looking up into the cloudless sky. I recognized a slight slur in my words.

Jax grinned. "Canis Major. It's a constellation. It's sometimes called The Greater Dog."

"I've never heard of it."

"It's not one of the more popular ones. See that bright star there?" He asked, pointing. I leaned in closer to him, trying to follow the direction of his finger. That close to him, I could feel his breath against my face, the scent of tequila still lingering on it. I could also smell the arctic-ice fragrance of his deodorant. Sure enough, I found a bold shimmering star aligned with his fingertip. "That's Sirius, the brightest star in the night sky."

"I thought that the brightest was the North Star."

"Common mistake. Polaris isn't even in the top ten of brightest stars."

"Polaris?"

"The North Star," he clarified. "It's actually ranked fiftieth, I think, in terms of brilliance." I hummed. "It's said that Canis Major represents the dog Laelaps, a gift from Zeus to his lover Europa. The dog was so famous for its speed that Zeus elevated it to the sky."

"That's an interesting story."

"It's only one of many," he admitted, raking a hand through his hair. "Some consider Canis Major to represent one of Orion's hunting dogs, helping Orion fight Taurus the bull. It's a more violent story, so I prefer the first."

"How do you know all this?" There was the cursed slur again. I hoped the sound of the waves lapping against the side of the ship somewhat drowned it out.

He pulled back on the railing, almost as if he were going to launch himself forward, but of course, he didn't. He hung onto the bar with his well-toned arms, leaning back on his heels, which flexed his equally muscular calves. The sheer beauty of him set off a small set of fireworks in my chest. I kept myself still, schooling my sudden reaction to him, knowing it was foolish and unwarranted. He was only stretching. It shouldn't have invited such a dramatic response. Yet, it did—everything Jax did set me on fire. "It was in an astronomy course I took," he explained, but I was so distracted by ogling him that I had forgotten I'd even asked a question.

I nodded, making a note that the Australian hottie was a little bit of a space-nerd. Some part of my brain that was likely soaked in Caribbean rum automatically registered that characteristic as something strange. As though someone as beautiful as Jax couldn't have interests outside of working-out, tanning and preening. I realized immediately that it was an ignorant thought, so I pushed the bias from my mind.

"Impressive," I said, and if possible, Jax stood taller, proud.

"You thought I was just a pretty face, didn't you?"

Immediately, I dispelled his bogus accusation. Although, honestly, I wasn't sure what I thought. I considered all the additional interests Jax had yet to disclose. Obviously, there was more to him than his perfect face and body. I wondered about the layers behind the beautiful surface. I was curious about his home in Australia, the years that shaped him, and how he ultimately ended up the smart, sensitive and talented man who stood before me.

I examined his features in the moonlight; the crook of his nose, his square jaw, and the dozens of freckles that speckled his bare, sun-kissed shoulders. They very much reminded me of the stars above us. I suddenly felt the desire to connect those freckles and name the constellations they would create.

Jax's eyes darted from the stars to my face then back again. "What's on your mind? You seem distracted suddenly."

My breath caught, and I cleared my throat. "I was thinking that you're an enigma."

"Am I?"

"Well, we've hung out on this vessel for a few days now, and I still don't know much about you."

"To be fair, you haven't asked much. We've talked mostly about you." It was a truth I had hoped he wouldn't point out.

I made an expression full of guilt and embarrassment. "Yeah, I have a tendency to do that. I'm sorry."

"That wasn't meant as a dig," he assured me, noticing my

change in demeanor. "You've been dealing with some drama during the last few days. I understand."

That I was, but my tendency to make all situations and conversations about myself was not isolated to just that trip or that drama, and I told him as much.

"So, what you're telling me is, you're a bit of a narcissist?"

"Don't narcissists think irrationally high of themselves? If so, that is definitely not me."

"So you have issues with self-esteem?" He raised his eyebrows meaningfully.

"Doesn't everybody? At least a little?"

"Not me."

"Well then, maybe you're the narcissist?" I teased.

He laugh-groaned. "Touché."

"I dunno," I went on, shrugging. "I've never struggled with confidence, but I've never really thought too highly of myself either. I like to think I have a healthy, realistic disposition. I'm a never-ending work in progress. There's always something else for me to learn or different ways to grow. Sometimes other people catch on to those things faster than I do, which keeps me humble...and I realize that I'm doing it again."

"Doing what?"

"Talking about myself, when I was supposed to be getting to know you."

"It's quite alright, I promise."

"No, it isn't," I said with certainty. "I want to get to know you."

"I'm sure you do."

"I'm serious! It's my turn to ask you some questions."

"Some sounds too infinite. I'll give you three."

"Only three?"

"For now."

"Well then, I better make them good," Jax bobbed his head in wait while I considered what to ask. "Ok," I stood up straighter. "Why did you leave Australia?"

"I haven't. Not technically. My official address is still Hornsby, although I haven't been back in nearly four years."

"That's a long time to be away from home."

He shrugged. "As a photographer, it's important that I accumulate a portfolio that is more than roos and opera houses."

"Where are you living now?"

He shrugged. "Everywhere and nowhere. Technically, I've been in America for over a decade off and on. I've lived in San Diego, New York, and Baltimore. I seldom stay in one place too long. I like to travel."

"Do you mind if I ask how a photographer has the means to travel so frequently?"

"Are you sure you want that to be your second question?"

If he was indeed going to hold me to three questions only, I wasn't sure I wanted to spend one inquiring about his financial state. Wouldn't that make me seem superficial and shallow? I decided that yes, it likely would. So I asked something else instead.

"What was your last relationship like?"

He seemed surprised by the question. "I thought it was inappropriate to discuss past relationships while on a date?"

Did it really count as a date if you knew you'd never see each other again in a week? I calmed my pondering mind and responded, "You already know all of the sordid details of my last relationship," I reminded him. "A little tit-for-tat is perfectly acceptable."

"Tit?" He drawled. "Is that your way of asking me to take my shirt off?"

The vision of Jax standing shirtless and gorgeous popped into my mind. Immediately and involuntarily, I began to giggle like a nervous Disney hyena. I quickly clapped my hand over my mouth, mortified by the sound.

He laughed heartily at my expense. "Should I take that as a yes?"

"No…yes…maybe…I don't know."

He raised both brows, surprised. "Am I making you nervous again?"

"No," I lied.

"Yes?" Jax challenged

"Maybe."

"I don't know," he taunted, playing with the collar of his button-up shirt. I noticed that only the three middle buttons were fastened. "I think I turn you on."

He undid one lower button, and I caught an eyeful of his happy trail, soft against his hard, flat abs. Immediately bashful,

I laughed and looked away.

"No?" He pouted; bottom lip extended.

"Yes," I said.

Wait. I meant yes, he does turn me on. What if he thinks I mean yes to his assessment of no?

"Maybe?" Jax asked.

Maybe? Maybe what? Which one?

It felt like the room was spinning. "I don't know," I said, honestly unsure. I was confused into a tizzy.

He refastened his button.

Fuck. The opportunity came and went, like something being pulled out of my hand right before I could grasp it. I tried to hide my devastating disappointment by returning to the original topic. "Don't think I didn't notice you changing the subject," I judged. "You haven't answered my question."

"I don't know what you're talking about," he said coyly. "What question was that?"

"Your last relationship," I reminded him, knowing very well that he hadn't forgotten. "If you don't want to talk about it, it's ok. I can ask something else."

"There's not much to tell," he assured me. "His name was Josh. We dated long-distance for little over a year," he started, staring out onto the water. "Some people can handle long term relationships. Others can't."

"Which one are you?"

"Someone who can." He grinned, giving me a brilliant smile.

"I assume Josh was not?"

He nodded. "The trick with long-distance relationships is there has to be complete trust. Josh was a jealous person, so the relationship was doomed from the start. It wasn't his fault. Some people are just wired that way."

"Did it end amicably?"

"There was no reason for it not to. We both realized it wasn't working, and it was hurting us both too much to keep trying."

I shrugged, stifling a yawn. "That sounds like a pretty reasonable reason to break up to me."

"Yes, reasonable," he agreed. "Still, it makes for dreadfully boring conversation."

Oops.

"Sorry, I wasn't yawning at you, I promise."

"I know," he assured me. "I just feel relationships are like books. There's no sense discussing the ones you didn't like. I prefer to close the cover and move on to another. Hopefully one with a better ending than the last."

His use of literature as a metaphor for relationships sent my inner book-nerd into a fever.

"Last question," he commanded, clearly finished with the current topic.

I dwelled for several seconds. Since I had tainted the air around us with the last question, I wanted to be sure that my next inquiry added some levity. "If you could have dinner with any four individuals, living or dead, who would they be?"

"Wow. You're delving deep, aren't you? Next, you'll be asking if I were a tree, what tree would I be."

"Call me Barbara Walters," I said with a wiggle of my brows.

"Well then, Barbara, let me think." He swayed forward, then back against the railing. "My grandfather, for one. As dull as that may sound. He died last year, and I wouldn't pass up the chance to see him again."

"Were you two close?"

Jax nodded. "My oldies weren't the most attentive. They were both too wrapped up in their own lives, especially after the divorce. I didn't have siblings to turn to, so my grandfather became the one I could count on. He was my confidant, my sounding board, my mate. Some of my favorite memories are roaming the bush with him. Just him, me and our shotguns."

A silence fell as my brain went down a sudden and crazy tunnel. I never understood hunting or the people that did it for sport. I had never encountered a beautiful, majestic creature and thought to myself, *man, I want to kill that*. Images of buffalo heads mounted on his wall or taxidermic dingoes sparked into my brain. Or worse, a kangaroo or a koala.

I pulled in a lungful of hair, pushing the thoughts away. I was doing what I always did. I had caught a whiff of a tiny, almost-flaw, and I immediately imagined it as much more significant and disastrous than it really was. So what if Jax was a hunter? Big deal. Maybe they only carried guns for protection. It was the outback, after all.

"I'm sorry you lost him," I offered sincerely, ignoring the

flashes of animal carcasses that still lingered in my mind's eye.

"Thank you," he smiled sadly. "I didn't really lose him, though. He's everywhere now. His energy still exists as part of the universe."

His lines were long and lean in the moonlight, and his skin glowed soft and blue. I felt terrible ogling him while he was discussing the heartache of losing his grandfather, but I couldn't help it. He looked sincere, adorable and intelligent, talking about him.

"That's a nice way to think about it," I said, almost in a whisper. "It makes sense that you'd want him to be your first guest."

He shrugged. "Yes, but he's not an exciting choice. Not like Queen Elizabeth or Jesus."

"You have three other guests yet to invite," I reminded him. "You could still invite Jesus. I'm sure he'd appreciate the invitation, considering how awful his last dinner party went."

He laughed, flashing his megawatt smile. "Cheeky bugger!"

"Guilty," I admitted, shrugging. "So, who else would you invite?"

"Marilyn Monroe."

I raised an eyebrow. "Marilyn? Why?"

"I have a theory," he replied, turning around to lean his back on the railing. "People think she was some air-headed sex-pot. I think she was the smartest Sheila in the room. She wanted to be a star. She knew what she had to do and who she had to be to achieve it. That's smart."

"You're right. That does sound smart." It actually sounded like Ruby to me, but I kept that to myself. "You still have two more guests."

"Brassaï," he said simply.

My brows came together. "I'm sorry, I don't know who that is."

"He was a Hungarian photographer. He died before I was born," Jax explained, fan-boy excitement spreading across his features. "He was a master of composition. His black and white street photography was amazing."

"He's an idol of yours, obviously?"

He glanced down at himself, then smiled. "More than that. He's the entire reason I wanted to pursue photography. My dad had one of Brassaï's pieces in his study, and it mesmerized me from the moment I saw it. Every day I would look at it and tell myself, one day, I would capture something just as striking."

I smiled at his memory. "I'll have to look him up."

"If you're going to, make sure you look up "The Stairs of Montmartre." It's my favorite piece."

"I will," I said, genuinely meaning it. Anything that had Jax gushing like that was definitely worth investigating. I did my absolute best to stifle the yawn I felt bubbling to the surface. Yet, despite my best effort, it slipped free.

"Am I boring you?" Jax asked with a grin.

"Gosh no!" I assured him, clasping my hand on his forearm. "I'm sorry. I think it's the ocean air."

"Well, it is late," he said. "We should probably start our way back."

"Hey! That's not fair. You still have one more guest to invite."

"Oh! Well, that one is easy." I waited for him to reveal his final response. "You."

The simple word bounced around my cranium before it absorbed. When it did, I felt the blood rush to the surface of my face, turning my cheeks red. My gaze met his. "Me?" I asked, suddenly chilled, and not from the night air.

"You," Jax repeated, leaning closer. This time his tone was suggestive and titillating. He made eye contact with me, so intense that the memory of his eyes alone would keep me satisfied for months to come, on lonely nights of self-pleasure. He didn't break eye contact. Not even to breathe. Then I felt goosebumps dance across my flesh as he laid a few short, exploratory kisses upon my lips. He tasted like cheap alcohol and sunlight, which caused tiny sounds of delight to build in my throat.

I didn't know what happened next. All that registered was my stomach erupting into flames, consuming my entire body. I lost awareness of my surroundings and myself until I was but a hollow shell filled with desire. Jax's lips captured mine perfectly, moved roughly against them, his hand snaking around me and pulling me into his hard chest. It was more heated than the kiss we had shared the night before. It was more urgent than our brief make-out session in the elevator. It was filled with pent-up hunger, neither of us capable nor willing to contain it any longer. His kiss made me come undone. I wanted his arms around me, his lips on mine, and the rest of the world to fall away.

I moaned loudly and was almost embarrassed that I fell so quickly into unrestrained pleasure, but then he responded to me equally. Swiftly and without warning, he spun me against the railing, my back leaning awkwardly over the bars, and continued to kiss me with increased intensity. That sent my heart rate racing. I had anticipated the kiss, but I definitely hadn't expected the hungry, urgent way his lips tasted me. His kisses weren't sloppy or frantic. They were deliberate, precise and determined, like a skillful explorer mapping the territory of my mouth.

I was on fire. Pure, unhindered flames scorched my body, stoked by the swipe of Jax's tongue against mine. His teeth captured my lip while his hands ran along the sides of my body. If felt so good, I thought I might die from the pleasure.

"Wait," I said, my throat dry and breathless. I swallowed, trying to moisten my tongue, which felt like cotton.

Jax looked at me, wild-eyed. His face flushed and transfixed, his lips parted and swollen. He was so pretty, it almost hurt to look at him. Still, I *was* looking at him, and he was looking right back. "Why?" he drawled. "Did I misread the signals?"

Signals? Was I sending signals? If so, I needed to know exactly what I did, so I could easily do it repeatedly for the rest of the trip.

"No," I replied emphatically. "I mean, should we, like, slow down? It's late, and I'm drunk." Even as I spoke the words, I cringed. Inside myself, I heard something scream, *shut up, you moron!* I was reasonably sure the sound was coming from my cock and not my brain. Kissing Jax was like having a single bite of something delicious. I immediately wanted to go back for more but didn't trust myself not to devour him completely.

"Too drunk to kiss me?" He waited for me to respond, but my tongue was suddenly fat and useless in my mouth. "Don't overthink it. Just do what feels good," he grinned, leaning in to resume our kiss. As soon as our lips reunited, whatever I had been planning to say dissolved into thin air, and I opened up to him like a flower did the sun. We kissed deep and lingering, and

I lost all concept of time. It felt like hours. It felt like minutes. It felt like an eternity, and it felt too good to stop.

All that passion, all that longing, it exploded within me. It felt as if I had been given a glass of refreshing cold water after not drinking anything for days. It had me wrapping my arms around Jax's neck, running my fingers through his hair. It had me kissing back just as hard as if I couldn't get any closer. Every thought fled my mind instantly, and I was left with only one blaring conclusion: I needed him. Now.

My hands started traveling downward on instinct, lower and lower, ready to massage the front of Jax's shorts until he reached down to stop me. Then the reality of where we were came rushing back like a bucket of icy water. I pulled back slowly and attempted to step away from him, but Jax held me firm.

"Not here," he whispered into my ear.

Heat washed over my face when his words registered. I bit down on a sound that tried to escape my mouth and rasped instead a simple, "Ok." It was quite evident that we both wanted to take it further, but he was right. There, in the middle of the promenade, was not the place. We needed to disappear into a room where clothes could come off, and our bodies could come together.

Jax chose that moment to kiss down my neck; the column of my throat, the knob of my Adam's apple, the hollow at my collarbone. I trembled beneath his travels. In response, I slid my hand up to the side of his jaw, ghosting over his cheek with one finger. Then it was his turn to break away.

I stared into his eyes, trying to read him. He was watching me in return, and for the life of me, I couldn't look away. I could feel the heat of his gaze, a shifting, molten shadow behind his stormy eyes that felt like both a warning and a welcome. He held me captive, and for a second, I could have sworn he could read my thoughts—my unbidden, sexual fantasies.

Even through the barrier of clothes, I could feel the heat of his body against my stomach. A moment of silence lingered, heavy with desire. Jax bit his lip, visibly searching for the right words, and he eventually came to a decision. He leaned in, his breath warm against my ear. His voice was low and hot, and it burned right through me when he spoke next. "I need you naked. Now."

All the air was sucked out of my lungs, and I was speechless. I expected Jax to say something flirty, not something that would send my libido spiraling out of control. "Come back to my cabin." His voice was nothing but a whisper that held so much more than his words.

It wasn't a question, and who was I to argue with such a command?

FOURTEEN
KYLE

In one wild motion, Jax pulled me in by my shirt collar, slamming my back up against the closet door. Then, his mouth was on mine.

The first kiss was so hot it practically seared me, then it was followed by another equally as spicy, then another. We had kissed all the way back to his cabin. Stopping in every quiet corridor or corner we could find. At one point, he had pushed me behind a row of giant potted plants, and I thought, for a moment, that he was going to take me right there among the fiddlehead ficus trees.

Eventually, we did find our way back to his cabin. It may have taken minutes, it might have taken hours, I had no idea, and I didn't care. I had lost all awareness of the world around me and any concept of time. The ship, the wind, and the ocean were probably still making sounds, somewhere. Yet, it all faded into silence as my senses became otherwise occupied.

Jax's mouth was warm and delicious. It was nothing like kissing Dustin. It was nothing like kissing anyone I'd ever kissed in my life. It felt as vast and formidable as the ocean we floated on, knocking the wind out of my lungs, encompassing every part of me. I suddenly couldn't fathom why we hadn't been doing this since the first afternoon we'd met. Why had we gone through the pretense of getting to know each other when we knew our time was limited? Kissing would have been a much more productive use of our time.

With unbridled frenzy, we tore at each other's shirts. For some reason, my blue button-up shirt was much easier to disrobe than Jax's tight sleeveless one. If we weren't frantically attempting to undress each other simultaneously, the task might have been more successful. Jax started to unlatch my shirt buttons with surgeon-like precision until impatience won out, and he pulled it off over my head instead. I struggled to get even a single one of his buttons unlatched, which was even more frustrating since only three of them were done-up in the first place. I growled at the annoying fabric covering the hard muscle of his body.

Noticing my dilemma, Jax took one small step back, laughing. It was a brilliantly sexy sound that caused a volcano of passion to erupt within me. Then, in one swift motion across his chest, Jax tore his shirt right down the center, popping buttons off in several directions. Then, he tossed the torn fabric behind him with gusto. It was white-hot, and I felt it light me up from the inside.

When Jax returned to the crevice between my legs, I hooked one knee around the back of his calf to keep him from escaping again. I ran my hands over his sculpted chest. All that smooth, warm, tanned skin under my hands made me feverish. Jax sucked in a breath as I grazed a finger over his nipple. Then, my hands dipped lower and lower until I found his inner thigh and the rousing appendage pulsing there.

I could not express how much I liked intense, about-to-get-laid Jax. I saw pure lust in his eyes, and it made my toes curl. "Do you see what you do to me?" he asked breathlessly.

I very pointedly looked down at the growing tightness in his white shorts. "Yes, I do."

Jax took a few unsteady steps backward before hooking his fingers in my shorts' waistband then pulling me towards the bed. I tried not to think too hard about what would happen once we got there. I hadn't been intimate with anyone in almost a year, but I was confident that I remembered what to do. While I wasn't typically interested in casual hook-ups, I was more than willing to make an exception in Jax's case. I wanted desperately to follow through on all the disgustingly beautiful things that had been playing out in elaborate detail in my mind for the past few days.

As we traveled toward the bed, I exhaled slowly, eyes on Jax's exquisite features. I let myself stare. Yes, the package in its entirety was gorgeous. Anyone with eyes could see that right away. Yet, I had never taken time to really examine each of his features and appreciate how they fit together to create such a portrait of perfection. I noted his happy, deep-set eyes and the charming way they crinkled in the corners when he smiled his wide, dimpled grin. I took in his firm, chiseled jaw and masculine nose, which reminded me of Michelangelo and his statue. I pondered his adorable ears, which were, by most standards, a little too round and stuck out a little too far. However, that only served as proof that even the most gorgeous person was still imperfect. All simple features, that when examined independently, were pleasant, but nothing extraordinary. Yet, when pieced together, they became art.

"You're beautiful," the words slipped out of me without intent.

An unguarded and infectious grin took over Jax's entire face for a moment before he leaned in, our noses brushing. His soft lips hovered close to mine, not yet touching, deliberately toying with my desire. When they finally connected again, I could have sworn I felt a shock, like static, jolt between us.

Feeling the bed contact the back of his knees, Jax lowered himself to the mattress. He slid back to prop himself up on his elbows, his legs opening so that I could nestle myself between his thighs. Still kissing me, he leaned back, pulling my weight on top of him. We laid there together, kissing tenderly. Our naked torsos pressed together; the warmth of our bodies caused an even greater heat to surge within us.

There was a tenderness in the way his lips feathered across mine. Desire often caused movement to become rough and hastened, but Jax remained slow and measured. He wasn't merely giving in to the heat of the moment. He was giving the moment room to breathe. Allowing time for the heat to become an ember, that ember to grow into a flame and that flame to swell into a bonfire that consumed us.

My breath hitched when, with an impressive display of agility, we rolled together, reversing our positions. My head fell back onto the pillow, and I closed my eyes, feeling the air sweetly pressed out of my lungs, with the smooth slide of Jax's body over mine. He lingered above me, looking down at me with his endearing eyes and swollen mouth. I could feel something alive and potentially dangerous between us. Still, I had no intention of stopping the trajectory we were headed. I looked up at him, waiting, eager, hungry for more.

He bent down, grazing his lips over my left collarbone, then he lent into the crook of my neck, dragging his lips over the sensitive skin behind my ear. I held my breath while Jax nuzzled there and moaned a little when he bit down lightly on the side of my neck. I knew it would probably leave a mark, but I didn't care. Then, with small flicks of his tongue, he followed my pulse back across my neck towards my waiting mouth.

One of my palms flattened over his hip, and Jax inhaled sharply at my touch. I pulled him closer so that he was straddling me, one knee on either side. He ground down into my lap, grunting as he was met with the length of me, already half-hard under him. The sound that escaped me was virile and primitive.

That's when the kisses turned messy, graceless, and demanding. I kissed Jax until it felt like I couldn't breathe. I kissed him until my lips burned from friction, and my tongue felt sore from doing acrobats in his mouth.

As Jax's body settled over me, with a warm, steady weight, I pushed my hands into his thick hair, and it was lush and soft as I imagined it would be. We made eye contact, deep and intimate before I tugged him down into another all-consuming kiss. In all my years, I had never been kissed like that. As though my lips were oxygen and Jax needed them for survival.

He pulled down the waistband of my shorts, then traced a fingertip along the line of my underwear. Before I knew it, his hands were wrapped around me, stroking with methodical rhythm. Suddenly my mind went all wavy. There was no thought at all, only a pleasurable haze that nothing could penetrate.

"Stop," I warned after several minutes, clenching my fists. I was so close to erupting that I worried I might overflow and drown us both.

Immediately, Jax teased me. "Already?" He laughed, leaning forward to kiss my stomach.

My breath caught. "I'm sorry, it's been a while," I admitted, embarrassingly recalling the veritable wasteland my sex life had become.

"Is that so?" He asked, grinning wide. I couldn't help but notice that he did not stop stroking. He did, however, reduce speed. "Why has it been so long?"

"I don't know," I lied. "I'm picky, I guess." That much was true. Jax didn't need to know that I was closed-off, pigheaded and bitter. It was not the right time to reveal those qualities. Maybe when I wasn't laying naked on his bed, with my cock in his hands, it would be a more appropriate time to share.

"I'm flattered I make the grade then," he said, then I was breathless as he kissed a string of heat across my inner thigh and beyond. When he returned to my eye level, he said. "I'm going to take my shorts off now. If that's ok with you?"

"Oh, yes," I giggled, dizzily. "That's totally fine with me."

He slipped out of his shorts, and I was surprised and excited to see that he wasn't wearing underwear, and he was already hard. At least seven inches long and as thick as a pepper mill, it throbbed in all the right places. I tried to hide the excitement I felt merely looking at his veiny shaft and perfectly proportional uncircumcised head. Jax returned to the bed, connecting our bodies at our hard cruxes. We both groaned as we ground into each other.

Jax moved his lips down to my chest, and under his mouth, I felt my heartbeat fall out of rhythm. The building excitement of what was to come made my whole body feel like it was drowning in elation. It took nearly all my focus to keep my head afloat.

With my lips parted and my fingers loosely tangled in his hair, Jax moved across my body like an eclipse. He tasted my collar bones, nipples, solar plexus, and stomach; he left no region unexplored. He blazed heat into me with the press of his mouth over my pulse points until he stopped suddenly, then looked to me with tense, dark eyes.

"I'm on PrEP," he said. Somehow even preventative medication sounded sexy and hypnotic rolling off his tongue. "Although," he added, "I also have condoms if that makes you more comfortable."

"Please," I said simply, stroking his hair. Jax reached over to the bedside table, fumbling blindly through a small travel kit. He revealed a bottle of lube and a condom and tore the small silver packet open with his teeth. "Let me," I said, taking the sheath from him. Our eye contact never wavering, I slowly, methodically rolled it down over the extent of him. Then, like the rolling sun, his warmth moved across every inch of my body.

He flung my one leg over his left shoulder, sliding his aching base into my warmth. Any doubts I may have had about Jax's sexual prowess were quelled immediately. With the first thrust,

I was in heaven. My eyes shot wide, mouth agape, the world disappearing before my eyes until there was nothing more than the ecstasy coursing throughout my body. It numbed my mind and invigorated my senses. He hooked his arms around my leg, testing out speeds and angles, and we let out unified moans of pleasure as he pumped in and out. We locked eyes while my body molded beneath him, a gasp escaping me each time he filled me with his massive length.

"You feel amazing." He tasted my bottom lip, sucking a little.

The only response I could muster was a moan. It had been so long that it was like discovering pleasure for the first time. My body responded in ways I had forgotten possible. My back arched up off the mattress, and a litany of profanities escaped my lips. Words that would have made me blush under any other circumstances were flung casually.

I couldn't believe what I was doing. It wasn't like me to hop into bed with a man I just met, but I couldn't contain myself. My increasing lack of control only fuelled Jax's determination. He greedily scooped me up against his chest, as if he were trying to touch all of me at once, and I clung to him in return, feeling our sweat mingle.

He began thrusting with a ferocity and purpose that brought me closer and closer to insanity. He relished every second, knowing I was coming more and more undone. Deeper and deeper, faster and faster, until we were locked in an unbreakable rhythm, moving together like two souls entwined. The music of our union was hypnotic. The soft grunting that escaped him with every thrust, my bursting exhales, the tender moans of pleasure that hummed from both of us at different intervals. If I could have recorded it and streamed it on iTunes, I would have.

Without suspending thrusts, Jax leaned in as far as he could, and I strained to meet him the rest of the way. Then we kissed hungrily, aggressively, devouring as much of each other as we could. I held on to his body, wanting more of him, and he gladly gave me everything I wanted. Soon, the sheer momentum of his thrusts caused me to collapse back down on the mattress—the sheet tangled beneath my body as I writhed in ecstasy.

Jax also appeared to be reeling in pleasure. His eyes were closed, his mouth stuck someplace between a grin and a grimace. Beads of sweat gathered at his temples, and there was an intoxicating beauty in the way he seemed to be literally lost in me.

In one swift movement, his strong hands flipped me onto my stomach. Leaning over me from behind, he found my hollow again. I could feel his broad shoulders against my back as he pinned me tightly to his chest, pounding me from behind. It felt better than anything I'd felt before. Messy, chaotic and rough, but so close to actual bliss. As my eyes rolled back in my head, I made a mental note to ask him where he learned to rub the prostate with such precision.

Suddenly, I felt something quiver inside him. That quiver became a pulsation, and that pulsation became an eruption. With every phase of his climax, his grunting became louder and thrusting more intense. His crescendo brought me to my own, and soon we were singing together in a chorus of orgasm.

Afterward, I came back into my body in increments. We collapsed on the bed, me on the mattress, laying in the wet spot I'd created, Jax on top of me, panting. Both of us shaking, boneless and wrecked, floating in a haze of afterglow. We stayed like that several minutes before he pressed a sticky kiss between my shoulder blades, then shifted up to lay next to me on the mattress. I turned to my side to greet him.

Jax nuzzled his face into the crook of my neck, and I placed my arm around his waist in approval. We breathed in the scent of each other. Sweaty and sweet, ripe with the moment we had just shared. I wanted to take a picture of him at that moment. His soft hair brushing against my collarbone, his eyes closed in recovery.

"That was fun," I said, poking him in the ribs. "Thanks for making an honest man out of me." I teased, referring to the lie I had told days earlier.

"Hmmm," Jax hummed, the tip of his nose catching mine. "I've wanted to do that since I first saw you, drunk and covered in cake," He admitted, pressing a kiss to my temple. He then rested his head on the pillow, trying to catch his breath.

The memory of that meeting seemed more distant than three days. I couldn't fathom why Jax would have found me even remotely attractive, stinking of cheap champagne and covered in buttercream. I must have looked like a lunatic. I laughed into

Jax's mouth, instantly entertained and horrified by the image conjured in my mind.

Jax rolled over onto his back, staring up at the ceiling. My automatic response was to do the same, but I fought that urge. Instead, I stayed on my side, propping my head on my bent elbow. My vision was still blurry from pleasure, my mind still trying to comprehend what had happened between us.

"We should do this again, sometime," I cringed as soon as I uttered the phrase. It was so cliché and awkward.

"I'm here all week," he replied, in a tone that I couldn't quite gauge. His hair was messy and slightly damp with sweat, and exertion still painted his cheeks.

I covered my eyes with one hand, already regretting the words that I felt bubbling to the surface. "If you don't want to, that's ok too. I'm sure you do this kind of thing all the time."

I meant it to sound nonchalant and casual. Instead, Jax looked at me like I had called him a dirty, raging nymphomaniac. "What kind of thing is that?"

I tried to backtrack quickly. "I just mean, I'm sure you hook up often." I realized immediately that it didn't sound any better. I tried a third attempt. "I mean, look at you," my eyes flickered across Jax's naked body, "You're gorgeous. You must get people throwing themselves at you all the time."

I wouldn't have thought it possible, but Jax blushed. "Just because people throw themselves doesn't mean I automatically catch them. Besides, I could say the same about you."

Modesty immediately kicked in. "Please don't compare us. Look at you. You have zero percent body fat and abs that would make Superman jealous. It's not even fair," I said, pulling the cotton sheet over my exposed bits.

Jax briskly yanked the sheet back down. "No," he said, almost sternly. "Look at *you*. You're crazy hot, even without the perfect body."

I felt simultaneously flattered and insulted.

"All those things you listed about me are superficial nonsense. They don't really mean anything. Sexy is about what's in here," Jax tapped me at the temples. "And in here," he placed his large palm against my chest.

Part of my brain found it strange, and strangely wonderful, how down to earth and humble Jax seemed to be. Mature. The other part was reasonably confident he was full of shit. There was an unarguable and blatant distinction between the two of us. He was an Adonis, whereas I was a dad-bod, sans children. I doubted the content of my brain or my heart could compensate.

Sensing my doubt, Jax leaned across, pressing a soft kiss to my mouth, his fingers lightly caressing my jaw. His touch was tender and romantic, and I had to remind myself not to get attached to such gestures.

"You know, I'm not usually this type of person," I drawled.

"What sort of person would that be?" He sat up. Our legs were still entangled, and Jax reached out with his hand, running a lazy finger up and down my arm in steady trails.

"The sort that sleeps with a complete stranger."

"I wouldn't say we're complete strangers. We've known each other a few days now."

"You know what I mean. I'm usually much more sexually reserved."

"Timid?"

I nodded. "Some have even dared to call me frigid."

"Those bastards." Mirth nipped at his words, making me chuckle. "Does that mean I'm special?"

"No," I answered without thought.

"Ouch."

"You're different, that's all. I feel comfortable with you, which is nice but highly unusual. I don't know. Maybe that does mean you're special."

"I knew it! Tell me more about how special I am."

I laughed again. "I think I've inflated your ego enough for one night."

"Keep talking sweet to me like that, and you'll inflate more than my ego."

My lips twitched, but I held back the smile. "How do you do that?"

"Do what?"

"Be so charming all the time, so effortlessly. If I said half of what you do, I'd come across cocky or arrogant."

"It's the accent," he stroked up and down my arm. "People go bonkers for the accent." He then kissed my shoulder before breaking away.

He fished his white shorts from the foot of the bed, pulling them back on. Of course, it made perfect sense to get dressed and go about our evening. We weren't going to spoon all night and wake up in each other's arms. It was a mutually satisfying sexual experience, and I was mature enough to recognize that. Still, I was disappointed to no longer have visual access to his perfect physique. Following his lead, I too began to redress.

"I really should head to bed," he said, handing me my shirt from a corner of the room. "I was going to scout a few locations tomorrow when we dock," Our next port was Bonaire. "There are several places I really want to photograph. I'd love for you to join me if you're free."

"I can't," I frowned. "I have to go to that spa thing with Dustin."

"Blow him off," he suggested. "You'll have more fun with me anyway."

"So confident," I mused. "Unfortunately, I made a commitment. So as much as I would prefer to bail and hang out with you, I would feel bad."

"I suppose that's fair," he relented. "What about the day after? We're porting in Grand Turk. We can make a whole day of it."

"I don't know. I'll have to check with Sapphire first." I said, attempting to fix my hair.

"Why?" He came up behind me, looking over my shoulder, meeting my eyes in the mirror. "Does she have you on a leash?"

"Don't tease. Sapphire would probably put me on one if she could," I turned around to look at him. "It's just that this is technically her trip. So I should make sure she hasn't already planned something for us to do."

"Look at you being all considerate."

"I try, sometimes."

He grinned. "Well, it's a standing offer."

"You don't have to feel obligated to entertain me," I said, walking toward the door to put on my shoes. I hadn't meant the comment in any negative way. I wanted him to know that I wasn't expecting to be his tag-along the entire trip, just because we'd slept together, but my comment unsettled him.

"Stop," he ordered, following me to the door. "I don't feel obligated. I want to spend time with you."

"You do?" I asked as Jax took several steps so that we were nearly chest to chest again.

He didn't laugh at my obtuseness. He didn't even give a hint of a smile. "Only a galah would not want to spend every single minute with you." The words fell off his lips easily, and even though I wasn't sure what a galah was, they hit me right in the stomach. I could only nod, a sappy smile stretching across my lips. At the sight, Jax grinned, then tousled my still messy hair.

"Alright then," I nodded. "I'll let you know." I stood awkwardly in the doorway, not quite ready to end the evening. My eyes fell to his lips. He licked them, no doubt knowing the effect that it would have on me.

"Can I kiss you goodnight?" He asked.

I found the question a little odd. Especially since we had shared at least a hundred kisses in the last hour, but Jax stood, looking at me, waiting for my consent. I looked back at him, moistening my lips, my mouth slightly open, sending him a clear message. He received it without issue. Leaning down, he kissed me one more time, passionately and fiercely, then I did my best to strut out of the room with jellified insides and shaky knees.

Twenty minutes later, I could still taste him on my lips.

FIFTEEN
KYLE

It was one of those crisp, clear mornings that I knew would eventually give way to sweltering heat. The ship had docked before sunrise, and I emerged that morning feeling equal parts nausea and dread. I felt sick from the low-grade hangover I had fallen out of bed with, and I felt anxious from the lapse in judgment that had caused me to agree to spend all day with Dustin. The two of us spending the day together spelled disaster. I knew it would be like charging right into a dragon's lair.

"You're late," Dustin said in greeting. "I told you the bus left promptly at eight am,"

"It's still here, isn't it?"

"That's not the point." Then Dustin registered my appearance. "You look tired."

I most definitely was. Unfortunately, Dustin did not look tired or hungover. He looked fresh-faced and relaxed, in a sleeveless tank and soft grey linen shorts. Obviously, he had gone to bed early. Likely lulled to sleep by the sounds of Shawn's retching.

"You're damn lucky I agreed to come with you in the first place, so you get this, or you get nothing." I was such an asshole and realized it the second the words left my mouth.

"Rough morning?" Dustin laughed at my surliness.

"Late night."

"With your Aussie?"

"If you must know, yes." I gave him a smarmy brow then pushed past him towards the bus.

Calling it a bus was very liberal use of the word. In reality, it was a hollowed-out van, in kidnapper white, with questionably installed seating. A big and tall island local in a floral button-up collared shirt stood outside the vehicle to welcome us. He asked the name our reservation was under, and once he confirmed we were on the list, he waved us on. The moment I climbed in, that sense of dread returned with a vengeance. This was a mistake. I felt Dustin tap on my shoulder.

"Are you planning on sitting any time soon? You're blocking the way."

I pushed down the snarky voice in my head. "I swear I've seen this van in a made for TV movie."

"And?"

"And the person inside was raped then hogtied while the van was set ablaze."

"Sounds more entertaining than your speech from the other night," Dustin said dryly.

I turned around, murdering him with eyeball daggers before smiling and facing forward again. "Would you like to sit in the back, dear?" I emphasized the final word in such a way that it sounded surprisingly like dipshit. Pretending to be a couple on the excursion was going to be a test of my patience and self-restraint.

"Those seats are as good as any," Dustin's voice sounded vaguely annoyed by my hesitation.

Two other couples were seated in the van already—both looking far too eager for eight in the morning. The first couple looked to be in their early twenties, tanned, toned and bohemian chic with their matching straw cowboy hats and her corn-colored hair in dreads. The second couple was a little older and pudgier. Typical tourists in every way, both in khaki shorts and floral shirts you could tell they had never worn before and had purchased specifically for this vacation. The gentleman's green ball cap said "Minnesota Wild," and I immediately imagined their thick Minnesotan accents.

I chose the last row of seats on the left, settling in by the window. As expected, it felt much like sitting on rocks. Dustin nestled in beside me, then glanced over me and out at the street. I kept my elbows carefully tucked into my sides, out of his space.

"Would you like the window?" The excursion was on his dime, so I felt only obligated to offer. He didn't answer. For someone who practically begged me to take his boyfriend's place on the adventure, he sure was acting less than appreciative. Maybe he was regretting that decision. "Are you sure you still want me to come? There's still time to change your mind."

"Non-refundable, remember?" Of course I did. It was the only reason I had begrudgingly agreed to go on the grand adventure in the first place. Subsequently forced to turn down another date with the handsome, magnetic Jax just to do it.

The driver closed the van door, giving us all a thumbs-up through the window, indicating we were ready to head out. Once he was in the driver's seat, he made a distorted announcement through the cheap P.A system. "Good morning, lovers! I'm your guide for today's adventure, Jose, but you can call me Cupid."

I turned my attention out the window, trying not to roll my eyes too obviously at his lameness.

"Today's excursion is all about combining your three favorite things," Cupid continued. "Adrenaline, exercise and the person next to you."

I turned to look at Dustin. None of those were on my list of favorites.

"We're going to start with a tour of breathtaking Bonaire," Cupid went on, pulling the van away from the curb. "The tour will ultimately lead to the adventure park. There, you will engage in snorkeling, archery, wall climbing, zip-lining and trust-building exercises, specifically catered to you and your relationship goals."

I glared at Dustin, "That driver had better be joking."

"Just remember this adventure was supposed to be for Shawn, not for you. He likes this type of thing."

I groaned. "This is going to be torture."

Dustin laughed at my expense as the driver continued his welcome. "Sit back and relax because we're getting this party started right now!" Cupid was far too aggressively cheerful.

To our right, the Minnesota Wilds sat eagerly soaking up Cupid's message. Mrs. Minnesota pulled a sunscreen bottle from her bag and liberally coated both arms and then her legs. Immediately, the powerful scent of chemicals disguised as coconut wafted over us. How much sun did she seriously think she was going to be exposed to in the van? When she finished, she handed the bottle to Mr. Minnesota, who was flipping through a tourism guide he'd picked up from the cubby strapped to the back of the seat in front of him.

Dustin interrupted the sunscreen pass with the precision of a star quarterback. "Can you please not put that on in here?" He asked with gentle but unmistakable authority. "The windows don't open, and Kyle is allergic to perfumes."

I most certainly was not, but if the lie would save us further exposure to the overwhelming scent, I was happy to be thrown under the bus. Or, in this case, van.

Mrs. Minnesota flashed us an embarrassed, but understanding smile then tucked the bottle back in her bag. "Uff-da, I am so sorry," she offered. Her jaw was locked, the corners of her mouth barely moving, making all her vowel sounds rise an octave.

"You two are such a handsome couple," Mrs. Minnesota mused.

I wanted to shout that Dustin and I hadn't been a couple for a long time. Still, it was a couples retreat, so instead, I smiled at her with as much insincerity I could muster then said thank you.

"We've never met a same-sex couple before," she admitted, and by the way she said same-sex in a hushed tone, I believed her. "We love Ellen, though. Philip even bought an Elton John CD once, doncha know?"

Beside her, Phillip nodded.

"That's fabulous," I cranked my gayness up to eleven by way of forced jazz hands.

"It's so nice that you all can get married now," Mrs. Minnesota blathered on.

"Isn't it?" I humored her.

"You betcha. We never understood what all the fuss was about, ain't that right, Phillip?" Beside her, Phillip nodded again. "How long have you been together?"

Dustin and I exchanged an uncomfortable glance.

"We've been together fifteen years," Dustin cut in. It was the truth. She didn't need to know all the messy details of what happened since then.

"Wow! Congratulations. That's quite the accomplishment for your people, isn't it?"

There it was. The inevitable, benign ignorance that lived within most heterosexuals, no matter how accepting or tolerant they considered themselves. *Our people?* I decided to address her ignorance with humor since she hadn't meant her comment maliciously. "Well, most of our relationships do seem to expire faster than milk."

She and Phillip laughed. Dustin did not.

After picking up several other couples along the way, the van pulled up to the tour's first stop. As the group of us stepped out from the vehicle, I attempted to weave myself as far away from Mrs. Minnesota and Phillip as possible. Yet, like a puppy dog, she followed me.

"Aren't these something?" She marveled at the row of old, clay buildings before us. They were simple, small and windowless. They reminded me more of large dog houses than homes, so I couldn't fathom what had her so entranced.

"These huts are preserved from when slaves worked the salt flats," Cupid told the group of us. "Don't let the idyllic setting fool you. Life was once quite harsh for the people of Bonaire. These huts serve as a reminder of the slavery that existed in these salt flats."

A flock of gulls passed overhead, and I looked up to the sky. "Man, it is so beautiful out here."

Next to me, Dustin replied quietly. "It really is, but could you imagine having to live in one of these?"

"I don't know," I hummed, looking out at the idyllic setting as another lone seagull flew overhead, trying to keep up with its brethren. True, the huts were basically prison cells, but they were conveniently located on the coastline. Sleeping on the beach and waking up to the sun rising above the surf didn't sound so bad. Then, I remembered they were slaves, forced to work at the salt mines, and I immediately felt guilty for disrespecting the place's history.

Back in the van, en route to the next location, Phillip, who appeared to be a man of few words, squinted out the window, directly into the sun. "It's a nice day."

I waited, assuming he would say something more. He didn't. The first and only words out of his mouth, and he chose to talk about the weather. How droll. I hoped my boredom wasn't written all over my face.

The blessed silence stretched on for a moment until Mrs. Minnesota felt the need to end it. "Since we were all picked up at the pier, I assume you are also traveling on Lollipop?"

"Yep," I nodded, hoping my crisp replies would send her a clear message. It didn't.

"We love cruising. We've traveled on Lollipop three times now."

"Three times?" I hummed, only half listening.

"Oh sure, we've been on other ships, but Lollipop is the best, 'cause it's the biggest." So Mrs. Minnesota was a size queen, I quipped in my head.

More silence.

"We should all have drinks together one of these evenings," she continued. "Perhaps see one of the shows."

Mrs. Minnesota seemed way too eager, but Phillip seemed less excited by the dinner invitation. I sided with Phillip. An hour in a van with her, and I was already bored. I couldn't imagine an entire evening of drinks and entertainment. Dustin also looked like he was going to vehemently protest the suggestion.

After an hour more sightseeing, churches, relics, parliament buildings and cemeteries, the van detoured down a narrow dirt road that weaved into a valley of sorts. At the base of it, we drove through a large, rusted metal gate. Finally, the van came to a stop in front of a red, barn-looking building with a large overhanging sign that read, Island Adventure Park.

I had never been to an adventure park before. Still, the image I had concocted in my mind was surprisingly accurate. Parts of it looked like a farm, with horses for riding corralled to the south. To the north, there was a large climbing wall, at least fifty feet high. A stone walkway led west down to a beach that looked more rocks and coral than sand. In a forest of Brazilwoods and Divi Divi trees behind the barn, I could barely make out the plethora of wires and ladders of the zip lining course. It looked like fun if thrill-seeking was your idea of entertainment. It was not mine. I once again found myself wondering why I agreed to take Shawn's place. Right, because Dustin had practically begged, and I lacked the spine to stand him up.

When I left the air-conditioned van, a blast of early afternoon sun immediately caused sweat to gather in all the various crevices of my body. Looking down at the beach path, I welcomed the notion of submerging myself in the water. As if reading my mind, Dustin interrupted my thoughts. "We didn't sign-up for snorkeling. Sorry to disappoint you."

"Of course not. Why would the one thing I want to do ever be on the itinerary?" I pondered rhetorically.

"You can swim with the fishies some other time, and, on your own dime."

I supposed that was fair. "So, what is on the agenda for today?"

"First, the sky-coaster followed by the climbing wall, just for a warmup."

"A *warmup*?" If I sounded terrified, it was because I was. "Then what?"

He paused, a slow grin taking over his face. "Just a five-mile hike."

I practically shrieked. "*Just* five miles? *Only* five miles? Why not a marathon?"

"It should only take an hour," he assured me rolling his eyes. "Relax."

"I'd love to!" I replied in an angry whisper. "That is actually what I would prefer to do. Yet, for some reason, you and your child bride insist on vacationing incorrectly."

He laughed. "After the hike, we're also booked for a massage. Will that get you to stop whining?"

I almost smiled. "Not completely, but at least it's something I'll enjoy."

Cupid handed us off to our personal director, at least that's what he called the thin, over-tanned woman who shook our hands, introducing herself. Sandrine was to guide us through the whole experience. Her hair was sun-streaked, and her teeth unnaturally white. She looked the part of an island woman, but something about her didn't feel genuine to the paradise around us. I suspected her birth certificate read Piedmont South Dakota or someplace equally less exciting.

"By the end of today, you'll be a stronger couple. Both physically and emotionally," Sandrine promised us. It took an extreme amount of discipline for me not to laugh in her face.

As if on cue, Mrs. Minnesota, whose name I still didn't know and had little desire to inquire about, materialized beside me, followed closely by her husband.

"Ohmygod. Isn't it exciting?" She asked.

"So exciting." I hid my annoyed expression by pretending to enthusiastically agree. Dustin looked over at me, amused.

"We hope you two have a good time today. You should meet up with us, back on the ship," Mrs. Minnesota winked. "We know how to have fun."

Eventually, she and Phillip were ushered away by their own personal director and led down a path towards the beach. I was grateful for small mercies and that we no longer had to attempt conversation with the couple. They seemed genuinely nice, in a small-town sort of way, but I had no desire to play a role in their grand adventure on the good ship Lollipop. I could already see them returning to their book clubs or bowling leagues, regaling their group with the story of their evening spent with *the gays*. They'd feel unjustly cultured and enlightened, and I wanted no part of it.

Dustin leaned into me, whispering, "What do you think she meant by *fun*?"

"Probably something innocent, like wine tasting or canasta. They look like canasta people."

"Ok. I can deal with that."

"Or," I continued. "They could be swingers, hoping for a little group action."

Dustin turned to me slowly, wearing a puzzled expression. "We're *gay*."

I shrugged. "Maybe Phillip is into ass play. Maybe she likes to watch?"

Dustin's eyes widened in alarm, and he reddened a little. The signs of his discomfort gave me life.

Sandrine led us to a small table then handed each of us a clipboard with several waivers. Nothing made me feel safer than a dozen legal forms absolving the park of any responsibility in the event of my death—not.

Dustin could see the reservation and fear spread across my features, like a shadow. "What's wrong? You afraid?"

"No," I lied. Heights, at the best of times, made me uneasy. When accompanied by that level of paperwork, it made me feel sick to my stomach. Of course, now that Dustin had called me out on my fear, I couldn't very well give in to it. I felt very much like I was risking my life to prove a point, which was a circumstance I found myself in often. It was foolish but familiar territory.

"Are you sure?" He asked, reading my mind, my face or both. "You look pretty scared."

I inhaled slowly, shaking my head. "Don't make this more painful than it already is." I gave one last sigh of resignation before signing my name several times on the stack of pages.

"You don't have to do this if you don't want to," Dustin said sagely.

"It's already done." I handed the clipboard back to Sandrine. "Besides, I know you're going to judge me if I don't."

He chuckled, handing his clipboard back to Sandrine also. "I'm going to judge you anyway. You know that."

I did.

Sandrine clapped her hands. "Alright, let's get you settled in for the afternoon." She led us down a cobblestone walkway toward a row of wood cabanas. "You're in cabin three. Feel free to leave your belongings in one of the lockers. Once we're finished with the activities, we'll come back here for your massage." She looked at her watch. "We're a little ahead of schedule, so I'll give you a few minutes to get settled. This room is yours for the day, so feel free to do anything your bodies are inspired to do." She winked suggestively.

My body was suddenly inspired to hurl.

"When you're ready, please meet me up the hill, by the sky coaster." Then she was gone.

When we were out from under the blazing sun, Dustin gave me one more opportunity to flee. "You're sure you want to do this?"

I placed my cellphone and wallet in the locker then took the sunscreen out of my backpack before locking it up. "Shut up and put this on," I ordered, passing Dustin the SPF60. He looked at the bottle as though I may have laced it with ebola. "I know how easily you burn. Put it on. Don't be stubborn."

He did as I instructed, then he turned around so I could get his back. The sensation of my hands upon his sinewy muscles felt familiar and uncomfortably sensual. The last time my hands had moved across him in that way, they had left passionate marks in their wake. By sheer force of will, I pushed the memory from my mind. When I was finished with his back, he returned the favor. I thought my skin would crawl under his

209

touch. To my horror and confusion, it did not.

Once the sunscreen was adequately applied, we retreated to our respective corners. Then, from a safe distance, we exchanged deodorant and bug spray by tossing them back and forth. It was a silent routine we had done a thousand times when we were a couple. The knowledge that we had not been a couple for quite some time, yet slipped back into the routine so naturally caused a feeling of nostalgia to grow in my chest. I pushed it back down to the pits of my stomach.

The hill Sandrine spoke of was really more like a mountain. Yes, it had concrete stairs all the way up, but they were steep, and the sun was blistering. By the time we finally made it to the base of the sky coaster, my t-shirt was already dripping sweat, and my thighs were terribly angry with me. To think I still had a real hike to go on afterward.

"Dustin, Shawn," Sandrine greeted us.

"Actually, my name is Kyle," I corrected her, breathlessly. I really had to increase my cardio.

Sandrine seemed wounded. She glanced at Dustin then back to me. "I'm so sorry, my itinerary says Shawn."

"Perhaps, but the dozen forms you had me sign my life away on, say Kyle."

"Very well," she smiled, but I could tell I had ticked her off. I made a note to blame my bitchiness on the heat. "All of the activities here are designed to build trust, cooperation and unity between couples," she said with gusto. "Our goal is that you will leave here today not only feeling physically charged, but emotionally as well."

I tried not to roll my eyes.

"The sky-coaster is one of our lowest stamina activities, but also one of our most challenging," Sandrine explained, gesturing to the car. I was fairly sure that wasn't the right word to describe the contraption. It looked like a piece of equipment you'd find at the gym. A metal frame, entirely open on both sides, two low seats, both with five-point harnesses and pedals like a bicycle. "In this activity, you will be forced to work as a unit. You will have to pedal together, entirely in-sync, or the bike will lock up. Then you'll have to wait to continue."

I glared at Dustin with the heat of a thousand suns.

"Please, take your seats," Sandrine instructed with a gigantic hand gesture. She was laying the drama on a little thick.

Carefully, I lowered myself into one of the bucket seats, slipping my feet into the pedal grips. Dustin settled in next to me, doing the same. Sandrine attended to us one at a time. First, she got uncomfortably close to my crotch. She secured the harness, tightening a fail-safe carabiner, then pulled the straps at my feet before moving over to Dustin. I recalled that the last time I was in a harness and straps, it was an entirely different type of activity.

As if reading my mind, Dustin whispered to me, smiling. "Reminds me of San Francisco."

A few years before our relationship entirely imploded, we had taken a brief vacation to California. Actually, it was really a business trip for Dustin, and I tagged along. Our romance had already begun its slow spiral down the toilet, but we were hoping a change of scenery could help ignite some much-needed fire.

Towards the end of our trip, Dustin had suggested we try something new and hit-up a sex club. To my terror and Dustin's sheer delight, it ended up being an S&M themed sex club. As you could imagine, that was far out of my comfort zone. So much so that he may as well have asked if he could set me on fire and stomp on my scrotum. Which, for all I knew, could very well have been something S&M people were into.

Desperately wanting to salvage our relationship, I begrudgingly agreed to stay and try out some of the equipment. Dustin waited until I was strapped in, naked, except for an intricate leather harness, studded for god knows what reason. Then, he revealed the ball-gag he wanted to shove in my mouth and the giant twelve-inch dildo he intended to fuck me with.

My safe-word was I-think-the-fuck-not.

After I successfully escaped the sex swing, with the grace and dignity of a drunk giraffe, we left San Francisco. We didn't speak of the incident again. I never quite recovered. Since then, the sight of leather of any kind made me incredibly uneasy. Looking at a belt made me blush.

Once Sandrine was confident we were secure, she gave directions. "The total length of the track is three miles. You'll start here, then up through the treeline, then over a breathtaking ravine. We encourage you to pause there and really take it in."

211

She wanted us to hover over a giant cliff, suspended by thin little cables? The phrase, I-think-the-fuck-not, once again seemed appropriate.

"Remember," Sandrine called out as our car began to rise, "this exercise only works as long as your minds and bodies are in-sync."

I made eye contact with Dustin, and we shared a brief what-the-hell-did-we-get-ourselves-into moment. Soon, we were suspended from a track at least seventy-five feet in the air. Ahead of us, a digital clock counted down the seconds. Next to it were two circular lights, one red and one green. At that moment, the red light blazed.

10...9...

"Why does this entire thing feel like couples therapy?" I asked Dustin while we waited.

"Shut up."

8...7...

"I didn't think you two had been together long enough to need therapy."

"We don't."

6...5...

I gestured to the world around us with a raised eyebrow. Dustin sighed a deep, weary sigh. "It was a Groupon."

4...3...

"Obviously, somebody didn't read the fine print."

He scowled.

2...1...

The light finally turned green, and I immediately tried to pedal. We remained motionless. Dustin looked at me like I was daft.

"We have to do it in unison. Weren't you listening?"

I grunted, frustrated.

"That attitude isn't going to get us to the end of this track any faster.

He wasn't wrong. I groaned. "On the count of three?"

He nodded and began counting. When we reached three, Dustin attempted to set a pace by chanting out loud.

"And now."

We peddled one full rotation.

"And now."

We did so again.

By the third rotation, we had developed a rhythm and were able to achieve some real distance. Ultimately, we got too comfortable and stopped paying attention, which caused us to fall out of sync again. The coaster stalled.

"This is ridiculous," I fumed. "How is this considered fun?"

"It's not supposed to be fun. It's supposed to be exercise."

"How is it even that?" I exclaimed. "We've traveled twenty feet in ten minutes. "

"Ok, let's try again," Dustin suggested, and we did.

Slowly, we found our rhythm, and when comfortable, we increased our pace. Dustin pointed to things he saw around us, and occasionally I did the same. There was no bickering or verbal jabs. Surprisingly, I also had no desire to smack him or poke his eyes out. There was only the confusing truth that I was enjoying his company.

Soon we were on the precipice of the ravine. The sun was high in the sky when the treetops finally opened up to reveal the deep valley below us. The gorge was steep and narrow, and the hillsides were thick with the lush umbrella of trees we had emerged from. From that height, in the open space above the ravine, I could see the island's southern perimeter and the seemingly endless ocean that lay beyond it. I usually hated heights, but at that moment, I had honestly never felt more weightless or, to my surprise, calmer. It was a beautiful view, and Sandrine had been right to encourage us to appreciate it.

Dustin also seemed enthralled with the experience, and there, for a single breath, we forgot how much we disliked each other. Instead, we leaned into a lovely moment of appreciation. Even though I wasn't looking at him, I knew the exact moment Dustin's eyes fell on me. Almost like a chemical reaction. I glanced back in his direction, but he quickly turned away.

"What?" I demanded, instantly suspicious.

Our eyes met, and whatever he was planning to say died in his throat. Instead, he shrugged, "It's nothing." I didn't buy it, so I glared at him in wait. "It's just nice to see you not thinking for a change," he admitted.

"I'm always thinking."

"Not then, you weren't. You were lost in the moment, enjoying the view like I was. I could tell. You looked handsome."

"Yes, and your opinion of how I look is *so* important to me," I shifted, wondering why I was suddenly so uncomfortable. It was a compliment. It shouldn't have felt so ominous.

Squinting into the sun, he asked, "Does your sarcasm have an off switch?"

"We spent fifteen years together, Dusty. If you haven't found it by now, it probably doesn't exist."

Dustin gave a genuine smile. Brilliant and contagious.

"The air smells beautiful up here," I commented.

"It's clean. Away from all the pollution."

"What was skydiving like?" The question came out of nowhere, but it occurred to me that I hadn't asked before. "Was it like this?" I gestured to the ground far below us.

"It was..." he searched for the right word. "Windy and blurry."

"Did you like it?"

"I liked how alive it made me feel."

"As opposed to how dead you normally feel?" I said, unable to help myself.

He chuckled. "No. It was like my mind and my body was disconnected. Like my brain was still in the airplane, looking down at the ground while my body was already in freefall. Every sense was in hyperdrive. My brain couldn't keep up."

"That sounds terrifying."

"It was. On my way up, I became very aware of the reality of my decision. I knew that death was a possibility, albeit an extremely rare one, but I didn't care. I didn't want the fear of death to stop me from living." He paused, and I sat silent, transfixed by his words. "Consider the wire that we're suspended from right now. It's just a wire, man-made, imperfect, fallible. It could snap at any moment. Then what?"

"We'd fall to our fucking deaths," I said as I looked to the thick copper wire above us to make sure it was still there.

He shrugged, smiling. "You're probably right, but does that mean we should have avoided the ride? Missed this view? All because we were afraid of something that could happen but likely never would?"

"So you enjoyed skydiving because it could have killed you?"

"No," he shook his head, gazing out at the gorge. "I enjoyed skydiving because I trusted that it *wouldn't* kill me." He turned to me. "Haven't you ever experienced that adrenaline rush that makes your entire body come alive and makes any fears you had totally worth it?"

We fell into a contemplative silence. We were so close; I could smell Dustin's cologne mixed with the scent of sunscreen. I could see the tiny beads of sweat gathering at his temples from the tropical heat, and both of us felt clammy where our thighs touched.

"Is it weird that I don't find you as vile today as I normally do?"

He smiled at me. "I was thinking the same thing about you."

Imagine that. We agreed on something.

"I still don't like you," I told him, pushing my hand through my red mop of hair.

"I'm not sure I believe you."

The fact was, I didn't fully believe it anymore either.

SIXTEEN
KYLE

Once we made the full circle back to the track's start, Sandrine escorted us to the climbing wall. That experience was far less exciting and admittedly more embarrassing.

The climbing wall was essentially a vertical skating rink with multiple inclines and a hundred colorful man-made holds. I had no experience and practically no upper-body strength. So, my turn on the wall was spent mostly slipping and hanging from the lead rope, which would bunch up painfully against my groin each time I lost my grip. I'd sway back and forth for several mortifying seconds before attempting again. Eventually, I made it to the top. Dustin, of course, had zero issues making it to the top in his first attempt. My distaste for him bubbled to the surface again.

After our hike, which was clearly not meant for a beginner like me, we returned to the cabana. I felt sore, breathless and broken while Dustin, annoyingly, seemed unaffected by the physical activity.

"That was fun," I said dryly once we were back in the cabana. I reached into my bag, retrieving my deodorant, which I desperately needed. I put on a heavy layer before tossing it over to Dustin. He caught it with ease, then peeled off his shirt, which was damp with afternoon sweat. I tried not to appreciate his six-pack abs but faltered. He caught me.

"You can look if you want," he said, bending down to rummage in his bag. I fought to repel his charm as hard as I could. "It's nothing you haven't seen before."

I shot an arsenal of harmful thoughts in his direction. "I wasn't looking," I said, my cheeks warming. He gave me a wicked grin because we both knew it was a lie. Then he started to pull down his shorts, and I experienced a moment of pure terror. The last thing I needed or wanted was a totally naked Dustin in front of me. "What are you doing?" My voice came out panicked.

"Getting ready for our massage." He said, slipping out of his shorts then tugging at the waistband of his underwear.

I was so tired and sore that I had completely forgotten the couple part of a couple's massage. We would have to be naked and oiled up in the same room. Together.

That thought startled me as much as the tap that came at the door, suddenly. "Gentlemen," Sandrines's too-sweet-to-be-genuine voice called. "There are silk robes in the closet to the left of the mirror. Please remove all clothing then put on the robes. When your ready, I'll lead you to the tub. Shall I return in five minutes?"

"Yes, please," Dustin called back to her as he stepped out of his underwear, standing naked before me. There was so much tan skin to take in, it sent my pulse skyrocketing. His eyes never left me, his smile never fading.

"Stop looking at me like that," I barked, turning my face away from him bashfully. "I am not getting naked in front of you."

"You've already been naked in front of me this week," Dustin reminded.

My head flung back towards him, and I clutched my imaginary pearls. "How dare you bring that up. I am trying desperately to forget that whole ordeal." I tried my absolute best to keep my eyes on his face.

"Are you truly incapable of not arguing?"

"I'm not arguing," I said matter-of-factly. The room suddenly felt about half as big as it did when we arrived. I was sure that was simply because clothes were coming off. "I'm just not doing it."

"What's the big deal? You knew we were having a massage."

"Yes, but you conveniently left out the naked hot tub experience."

"So?"

"So, I thought we'd head straight for the massage tables. I thought, at worst, we'd endure a few moments of awkward maneuvering while we slipped under our respective sheets. It didn't occur to me that we'd be stewing in each other's naked filth beforehand."

"Gross. How dirty *are* you?"

217

"I am not—that is not the point."

"What is your point?" I could see him fighting a smile.

"My point is, I am not doing it."

Ten minutes later, I *was* doing it. The hot tub gurgled between us, air bubbles breaking the surface, like a pot of boiling water.

"Can't you ever do one thing without having to be so goddamn extra about it?" Dustin demanded, taking note of my extreme agitation. "I can't even see anything."

I fully recognized that I was being dramatic. Reluctantly, I looked down towards my lap to see for myself, then across the basin to see precisely how much, if anything, I could see of Dustin. I saw shoulders, clavicles, chest, and when he stretched or stood up, I could see several inches of abs below his nipples. Ultimately, he was right. The water was too deep, and the bubbles made seeing anything below the waterline pretty much impossible.

Dustin leaned his head back, stretching his arms across the sides, sighing theatrically. "Doesn't this feel great?"

I was sure it would have felt amazing if I allowed myself to relax, but I was still uncomfortable. I wasn't wholly convinced that Dustin didn't have some supersonic powers of perception. Something that gave him the ability to see through the water and directly to my nether regions, like a naval sonar device for cock. I had only agreed to the soak because Sandrine made it abundantly clear that I would get no massage unless I did so. For a skinny young thing, she was a little bossy. She had practically ordered me into the tub or off the property.

"Our therapists work only on freshly soaked bodies," she had told me. "It makes the body more pliable and able to experience the full benefit of their work. I strongly encourage you to participate, but if you'd like to wait back on the bus, you can."

The van was likely as hot as an oven under the tropical sun. I had no desire to cook inside it without open windows or water like a neglected poodle, so I gave into the little tyrant.

I had to admit, the water and the steam engulfing my skin did feel nice. The water was blissfully warm, and the jets pulsating against my shoulders, my back and my feet soothed my tired body. That, combined with the scent of lavender, almost made me forget that I was naked as a jaybird, a mere three feet from my lover-turned-nemesis. If two weeks ago, someone had shown me a photograph of us at that moment, I probably would have died of shock.

I sank into the tub as best I could, trying to relax my head back against the ledge of the tub like Dustin had, but it felt awkward and unnatural to me. Instead, I lowered myself further down into the basin until only my head was exposed.

Of course, Dustin misinterpreted my new position as an attempt to hide. "You're ridiculous. We've been naked together thousands of times. Even if we could see anything through the water, would it really be the end of the world?"

I concentrated on keeping my face neutral. "Yes."

"I already saw you naked once this trip," he reminded me again. "You look fine."

Fine? I was about to make a retort until I realized it wasn't intended as a jab. He had meant it as a compliment.

"Thank you." Whether or not Dustin had meant the comment sincerely was irrelevant. I suddenly felt a little more comfortable in the jacuzzi.

"Maybe you're worried that you still like what you see?" He teased, tucking his hands behind his head, flexing his biceps distractingly.

Just like that, the comfort was gone.

"Get over yourself," I flung at him. As far as comebacks went, it was embarrassingly limp. Especially given that Dustin did look rather impressive naked and wet. He looked effortlessly sexy and casually smoldering. It irritated me, and he knew it.

"I think it's *you* who needs to get over me," he teased again.

I scrunched up my face, profoundly suffering for something I must have done in a previous life. "I just vomited a little."

Dustin must have been warm because he moved to a different bench inside the hot tub, one that was a little higher, leaving more skin exposed to the air. He rose like a siren out of the water. My eyes followed his movement, appreciating how his muscles contracted then lengthened, the way droplets of water traveled down his skin. I hated myself for even noticing. A weird silence followed. Strange, because we both knew I saw his every attractive quality. It was impossible not to when he was naked in front of me.

Neither of us spoke or moved for several minutes. Slowly, a new kind of unease trickled through me as I felt the gentle pressure of a foot over mine. I thought I'd imagined it at first. Perhaps it was air currents caused by the jets. When I felt it a second time, I looked to Dustin, whose eyes were closed, head tilted back, seemingly relaxing.

I chose to give him the benefit of the doubt. It was a small tub, and if either of us stretched out, of course, we would make contact. This was one reason I stayed bunched up into a ball on my side of the basin. Yet, the third time I felt it, it was absolutely not an accident. I felt his foot inch higher up my leg. I examined Dustin more closely to confirm what I'd already suspected. Sure enough, I caught him open one eye, peek at me with a stifled grin, then go back to pretending to be innocently relaxing.

Meanwhile, his foot continued to travel. I felt my cock twitch involuntarily as he inched closer to my upper thigh. I clasped my hand over his foot, panicked. "What the hell are you doing?"

"Calm down, Kyle." I ignored the tingle in my spine at the way he said my name. "I'm teasing you. I wouldn't have made contact."

"I am not amused," I warned him, seeing the mischief hidden behind his small smile.

"What else is new? You're never amused. You've always been wound too tight."

"That is not true."

"Yes, it is, and you know it. Everyone knows it. You can't ever take a joke."

His words held more weight than they should have. I gaped, offended. "Excuse me, you dark stain on humanity! I am hilarious. Everyone says so. Why would you even say that?"

"Do you want the short answer?"

I nodded. "That would be ideal, yes."

"You are funny, I'll give you that. Your specialty is one-liners, back-handed compliments, the occasional knock-knock joke, but that's where it ends. You don't like pranks, you hate adventure as much as you hate complications, and you detest anything spontaneous." I wanted to be insulted, but it did sound like me. "It's why I was so surprised when you said you slept with that Australian. It's so unlike you. If it weren't for that ugly hickey you're sporting, I still wouldn't believe it."

I immediately brought my hand to my neck. I had done my best to cover the hickey with a concealer that morning and thought I had done so successfully. Between the afternoon sweating and the hot tub, the camouflage must have washed away.

"I can't believe you let him give you a hickey. What are you guys, teenagers?"

"This from the man who is actually dating one."

"That may be," Dustin shrugged. "Yet, even Shawn knows not to brand me."

"I hope Shawn is doing alright," I offered, proud of myself for my sincerity and for how swiftly I changed the subject.

"He'll be fine," Dustin replied. His tone was a little sour, and before I could comment, Dustin chose that moment to randomly dunk his entire head beneath the waterline. When he surfaced, he spat out water, sending a splash in my direction.

I couldn't help but smile. "Speaking of acting our ages, maybe you should try it, instead of acting your shoe size."

"I've got big feet," Dustin replied, "and you know what they say about that."

The things I must endure, I told myself, rolling my eyes. "I am not discussing your penis," I said. "Not now. Not ever. Especially not while we're naked in a pool together. Which, by the way, we will never speak of to anyone."

"Not even to Sapphire? She would get such a kick out of this."

"Did I stutter? I said no one."

"I have to tell Shawn at least."

"Oh yeah," I nodded facetiously. "That's exactly what your boyfriend needs to hear. How while he was puking his guts out, you were enjoying a relaxing, romantic adventure with your ex."

"You call this romantic?"

"With the right person, yes."

Dustin waved a wet hand dismissively. "You worry too much. Besides, it was Shawn's idea to have you take his place."

"I still don't understand why he did that." The confusion in my voice was palpable.

"Honestly, I'm not sure. Maybe Shawn thought it would be a good opportunity for us to build trust or even a friendship." He paused. "Or at the very least, get over wanting to murder each other."

"Did he realize we'd be naked when he made that suggestion?" The look on Dustin's face told me Shawn hadn't known. I nodded in finality. "Like I said, we will never speak of this again. To anyone."

"Ok fine." Dustin relented.

Another lull in the conversation settled, giving me a moment to reflect on what Dustin had said. Was I on the verge of becoming an old stick-in-the-mud? Too tightly wound to really let go? I wasn't the most adventurous person. I never had been. I had always preferred to play everything safe, follow the rules, don't break the law, don't do drugs. I didn't even speed.

"I wonder if maybe you're right," I broke the quiet.

Dustin opened one eye. "You'll have to narrow it down a little. I'm right all the time."

"About me being no fun to be around."

The unmistakable look of satisfaction on his face made way for a more compassionate expression. "I didn't say you weren't fun. You're just stuffy and a little judgy."

"*I'm* judgy?" My voice shot up an octave.

"Yes," he nodded sharply. "I'm glad we agree."

Static filled my bloodstream, and I was about to go off on him until Dustin blurted out a laugh. "Oh, calm down. This isn't anything you haven't heard before." He was right. Sapphire had made a similar comment a few days earlier when we were by the pool.

"Do you think that's why I haven't had a boyfriend in two years? Do men hate me because I'm a big, old fun-sucking stick-in-the-mud? Is that why I'm still single?

"I prefer to think that it's because all men pale in comparison to me, and you can't bring yourself to settle."

I guffawed. "I'm trying to ask you a real question."

"It's a stupid question, so I thought it warranted a stupid answer." His face softened, his eyes glinting. "Men don't hate you. Honestly, you're impossible to hate." That made me feel a little better, but then he went on. "I'm pretty sure they fear you, though."

"Fear me? Why would anyone be afraid of me."

"Maybe not afraid, but definitely intimidated. You're a smart guy. You're well-read and well connected. You use big words, have high expectations and a low tolerance for bullshit. It's a lot." He shrugged. "I would say, you're probably single because most men don't feel good enough for you."

"Did I make you feel that way?"

Dustin's mouth slowly turned into a frown. "I think we made each other feel that way." There was a heaviness in his words that should have been entirely normal, yet it sparked a thread of sorrow deep within me. Right in front of me, naked, was the man I was sure, at one point, I would spend the rest of my life with. It felt familiar and intimate but also dangerous and inappropriate.

Dustin ran his strong hands through his damp hair, away from his face. Droplets of water slowly cascaded down his thick neck, broad shoulders and chest before disappearing into the water from whence they came. He noticed me, noticing him again, and he returned my stare with one of his own, just as a drop of water rolled down his perfect nose and disappeared into his pouty mouth. Then he bit back a grin. "If your eyes linger any longer, I'll have to charge you rent."

I bit my lips closed, glaring up at him. He knew exactly what he was doing. *What a monster.* "I don't know what you're talking about." I lied.

"You can admit it, it's ok," he assured me, letting out a breathy laugh. "I know I look good. You can admit that you still want me."

I wanted to drown him. I sighed, the sound heavy and prolonged. I knew I should respond to his comment in some smart-ass way, but my brain had become a solid brick of Styrofoam. So instead of resorting to violence, I submerged myself, hoping I'd conveniently die.

At this, Dustin let out a bursting laugh. I reached out, attempting to punt him, but the water's resistance slowed the force of my kick, making it more of a gentle nudge than an outright boot. Underwater, in the small ceramic tub with my leg extended, the force of the jets caused me to lose my balance. Surprised, I flailed, only slightly, but in my panic, I felt my foot collide, hard, with something soft and squishy.

Oh god.

Even underwater and splashing, I could hear Dustin grunt in agony. Then I found my footing, emerging from the water, just in time to see Dustin's grim face go under. Even through the bubbles, I could see him cupping his groin where my foot had kicked him.

I tried not to smile even as I was overcome with the desire to celebrate the cruel victory.

SEVENTEEN
KYLE

Being around Dustin and enjoying his company was like falling down the rabbit hole. The world looked familiar but also wrong in a fundamental way. Like everything was upside down or inside out.

The afternoon had been undeniably easy. Yes, we had bickered several times, but it had been mostly lighthearted banter. Dustin had managed to be charming most of the day, which had me reconsidering my belief that he was, in fact, the devil incarnate. His ability to be entirely evil one moment then Prince Charming the next was a magic trick I couldn't figure out. Yet somehow, in twelve hours, we had started to build more good moments than bad. That was utterly mystifying.

What was even more bewildering was I was starting to like it. I realized that staying firmly on team I-Hate-Dustin was going to be more difficult than I anticipated. That realization made me more uneasy than I could describe.

After our expedition at the adventure park, which was really more of a couple's ranch, we explored a small market in the town's center. There I happened upon some adorable trinkets at low prices. Then we settled on a beach-side patio for dinner. The restaurant itself was elegant but dated, with leaded glass candle holders and wicker lanterns that made the space glow. The tiny square tables on the patio were slightly too intimate for comfort. Still, the food smelled incredible, and the view of the setting sun against the white-sand beach of Bonaire almost took my breath away.

"Thank you for coming with me today," Dustin said in between mouthfuls of his tilapia.

"Thank you for the invitation," I replied sincerely. "It's not something I would have elected to do on my own, but it was fun."

"It wouldn't normally be my type of thing either," he shrugged. "Shawn is young and impulsive and far more adventurous than I am. He makes me less boring."

I took a bite of my steak and was pleased to see him cringe when I spoke with my mouth full. "You were never boring,

Dusty."

He raised a brow. "Are you having a stroke?"

"Excuse me?" I asked, setting down my wine glass, taking a deep breath. I resisted the urge to reach across the table and poke him in the eye.

"You actually said something nice to me."

"Oh. That. Well, I wouldn't call that nice. I only said you weren't boring. The fact that you're an unfaithful, lying wretch went without saying."

His eyes twinkled as he laughed along with me. "Of course, that's obvious. Thank you for yelling that across the restaurant, by the way."

"Anytime." My smile unfurled before I sliced again into my sirloin.

"I can't believe you're surrounded by the freshest selection of seafood in the world, and you ordered a steak."

"Your boyfriend is literally hurling his guts out, as we speak, because of some bad clams," I reminded him. "I'm comfortable with my choice."

"You always were the one to play it smart," he mulled.

"Smart?" I repeated the word to see if it fit right. I wasn't confident that it did. "I wouldn't say that. Safe perhaps, but not smart."

"Is there a difference?"

"Of course," I said simply, covering my mouth with my napkin to hide the half-masticated piece of cow that was rolling inside. I swallowed. "Playing it safe is choosing to do what you know is easy. Playing it smart is choosing to do what you know is right."

He nodded understanding, then polished off his third Mai Tai before flagging down the waitress for a fourth. "I guess I've never been really good at either. I tend to do whatever feels good at the time."

"I know."

My simple words landed with a heavy thud. In the soft glow of the golden hour, I could see Dustin's smile fall and darkness settle behind his eyes. He retreated into his neck, shoulders hunched, face ashen. He blinked down to his plate. "Yes, I know you do. You know me better than almost anyone, except Justin, of course."

That went without saying, but I made a note that he chose to say it anyway. "That's bound to be true. We spent more than a decade getting to know every little thing about each other." Then I added for good measure, "I'm sure Shawn will know you that well too, one day."

Then, as though I had pushed a button somewhere on his back, Dustin stiffened. "Don't."

"Don't what?" I questioned, confused.

He chewed then swallowed before speaking. "Start a fight. We've had a fun day. I don't want to argue with you now."

"I'm not starting a fight," I said almost defensively. "I'm making perfectly civilized conversation."

"For now," he countered. "When it comes to Shawn, you tend to go straight for the jugular."

"That's not true," I started before taking stock of the fact that evidence proved otherwise. Then I reconsidered. "Ok, it's not entirely untrue either. I don't mean to, but—"

"But what?" He challenged, and everything went tight between us in anticipation of what I'd say next.

"It still stings," I admitted, choosing my words carefully. "Even after all this time."

"We weren't in a good place back then, and I was looking for something."

"Not the cheating, genius. I've gotten over that, for the most part. Although it does not spark joy."

"Then what?" He asked, prodding at his plate before zeroing in on my face.

"Seeing you and Shawn together. Well, not Shawn specifically. Seeing you with anyone stings a little."

"Oh, really?" he tried to hide a handsome smile over his newly delivered beverage.

"Don't get smug," I warned, sharply. "I'm having a fleeting moment of honesty with you. Please don't make me regret it." I already did. My admission was a sign of weakness. One I feared he would exploit.

He gave a coy little pout, and it was impossible to ignore the cute way his full bottom lip quivered as it jutted out. "You wound me. I am never smug."

"I know you better than anyone, remember? We both know smug is your default setting."

227

He agreed with a hearty smile. "And yours is sarcastic and condescending."

"More stubborn and pigheaded as of late, but typically yes," I nodded, giving a cheesy thumbs-up.

We paid the check, split evenly, of course, and rather than head back through the street entrance, we left the restaurant via the patio, making our way down the shoreline. The sun hadn't entirely vanished beneath the horizon, and a soft glow settled over us, engulfing the beach in an amber fire. As we walked, the soft sand sifted over my sandals, between my toes, feeling warm against my skin.

Considering the flat terrain, my steps felt surprisingly unsteady. I chalked it up to the combination of red wine and heat, so I promised myself I would switch to water once back on-board the ship. Vacation or not, I had been drinking too much, even by my own standards.

"So tell me more about this jealousy you feel," Dustin pressed. It sounded so ludicrous to me that I actually barked out a laugh.

"Jealous? No." I tried to be as straightforward as possible. "I just don't like seeing you with someone else."

"That sounds like jealousy to me."

I decided on a subject change, no longer confident that jealousy wasn't the appropriate word to describe how I felt. "It's nice to see your parents again."

"They miss you," he admitted. "They've never said anything to me, but I know that they do."

"How do you know?

"Little things," he explained. "They talk about movies they think you would like. Sometimes they think they see you in theatres or malls."

"That all sounds normal," I assured him.

"My parents sometimes mention you in front of Shawn, and I can tell it makes him uncomfortable."

"I'm sure they don't mean to upset him."

"Try telling Shawn that," Dustin said with a frustrated shrug.

"He's not so understanding, I take it?"

"Shawn's young," he said it like I had somehow forgotten that I had neckties older than his boyfriend. "He's never had a long-term relationship before. He doesn't understand that it was more than just *our* relationship that ended when you and I broke up."

"That makes sense, I suppose." I wasn't sure how else to respond. "Your parents will mention me less frequently, with time."

A moment of silence passed, then I saw a frown slowly crease Dustin's brow. With a little trepidation, He pressed on. "Honestly, I'm not sure how much time we have left."

His admission caught me off guard. I tried to mask my surprise by pinching my mouth into a strange little hole. "Oh? That sucks. You guys seem so happy." It wasn't a lie. They really had seemed annoyingly happy.

He hesitated for a moment, then when he finally answered, his voice came out hollow. "We're not unhappy, but this entire trip has been very eye-opening to me."

"How so?" I asked. It sounded a little breathy to me, and I was sure it was because I overate at dinner and was a bit winded from the walk.

"One on one, we're ok, but when we're hanging out with the group, it's hard to ignore how little we have in common." Dustin's frustration manifested into a series of long strides I had to work to keep up with. Then he stopped so suddenly that I collided with his muscular back. I caught my balance quickly while he spun around to face me. "He doesn't get our jokes or social references. He feels lost and unintelligent because he doesn't have the same life experiences or knowledge. Then he gets down on himself or angry at me because I put him in a situation where he feels inadequate."

"I have to admit to feeling partly responsible for that. I certainly haven't been shy about poking fun at your age difference."

"No, it isn't that," he assured me, lowering himself to sit on the beach. "Shawn knows our age difference makes us a target for harmless teasing." He leaned back on his arms, stretching his legs out in front of him, crossing them at the ankle.

Not wanting to hover over him rudely, I chose a patch of sand to his right and sat with my knees to the side. I said nothing. I simply sat, listening. I knew it was something Dustin must have needed off his chest. Especially if he was willing to confide in me of all people.

"It's incredibly frustrating," He continued, chewing his lip, thinking. "And it's not only awkward when he's with our group. It's equally challenging when I'm hanging out with his friends. They're good kids, but I hate spending time with them."

I pretended not to notice his use of the word *kids*.

"Their conversations lack substance," Dustin went on. "I can't talk to them about art or history, or even politics. Half of them don't even know who their Senator is. Yet, they can easily have an hour-long discussion about whether or not Shawn Mendes is a closet case."

I allowed a reluctant, sad smile to slip free.

"It has reaffirmed that there is a fundamental issue with us as a couple," Dustin drawled, staring out at the ocean. In the distance, I could see our ship anchored in the port. "When we first got together, he made me feel so young, but now…" He trailed off, reaching up to smooth a piece of hair that was rustling in the breeze. I could tell the motion came from a place of vulnerability caused by his admission and not vanity. That moment of vulnerability, as brief as it was, created a tiny fracture in his role as my nemesis. A real enemy wouldn't have shown the kinks in his armor so freely.

"Now what?"

"When I'm with him, I feel like the oldest person in the room."

With that one single sentence, my heart gave an aching jab against my breastbone. Dustin's response was so honest and real that I couldn't bring myself to tease him. I also related to his profession more than I could say. Being single those last two years myself, trying to find a Prince Charming in a smorgasbord of inappropriate or broken men, made me feel older than ever. Dating was a young person's game, and I was quickly running out of the energy it took to play.

Because I could relate to his vulnerability, I responded with compassion. "There's nothing wrong with getting older, Dustin. It happens to all of us. Besides, even for an old guy, you're still cute."

Half of his mouth turned up, and I knew what was coming, "You still think I'm cute?"

"In a way," I said on an exhale. Then I stopped short, instantly regretting the admission.

Dustin smiled wider. "What way is that?"

"An annoying one," I teased.

We both chuckled briefly before Dustin returned to the topic at hand. "Shawn and I don't seem to fit in the real world. Not the way you and I do."

I chose not to respond to the comparison. It was a weird cognitive dissonance, Dustin of the present and Dustin of the past. In my memory, he was arrogant and selfish. He moved through life effortlessly, never taking anything or anyone too seriously and always making people laugh at other people's expense. He did what he wanted when he wanted. Yet, the Dustin that sat beside me now was thoughtful, remorseful and sad. It left me feeling dizzy and restless.

"Thank you for letting me talk about that."

"Of course," I told him. "It's my good karma deed for the day."

The wind blew his blonde hair all over his head as he squinted out at the surf. "Look at that," he gestured to the enormous body of water that surrounded us. The ocean was calm that evening, barely a wave to be seen—only the gentle curling of the water as it broke against the shore.

"Breathtaking," I nodded solemnly.

"Reminds you how small and insignificant we are, in the grand scheme of things, doesn't it?" I was surprised by the seriousness of his tone.

"Are we having a philosophical conversation?"

"Not at all," he half-smiled. "I only thought we should take it in. Something this glorious deserves to be appreciated."

I breathed in the ocean air, clean and invigorating, while Dustin blinked out to the water.

"I never really appreciated you, did I?" *Wow.* That came out of left field. If I hadn't already been sitting, I might have fallen over.

I tried to contain my instant discomfort with the sudden direction the conversation was taking. "I don't give it much thought anymore," I lied.

"I do," he admitted. "I've thought about it more often than I should. Especially in the last few days."

My mouth unsuccessfully attempted several sentences before settling on, "I think that's normal. This was the first time we've seen each other since then."

A brief silence settled. "Well," Dustin said when he finally spoke. "I can't very well change what I did. I can tell you, though, there was no excuse. You didn't deserve that. I am sorry."

"Wow," I was taken back. "That's quite a different tune from a few days ago. I clearly recall you suggesting it was my fault."

"I am fully aware of what an asshole I was during the wedding. I blame it on pride."

Surprisingly, the fact that he looked absolutely miserable, reflecting back on his mistakes, didn't fill me with the joy I had expected. Quite the opposite, I felt terrible for him. "I haven't behaved well either," I admitted graciously.

"I understand exactly what you were saying earlier," Dustin detoured suddenly. "About seeing me with someone else. I've felt the same way seeing you with that guy the last few days."

I hadn't even considered that seeing Jax and I together would have the same impact on Dustin that seeing him and Shawn together had on me. He gazed out at the shoreline, looking like he was fighting the urge to sprint down the beach and drown himself in the surf. "It's not easy seeing someone you care about with somebody else."

I felt the tires come to a screeching halt inside my brain, trying to comprehend what I heard. In my answering silence, Dustin must have sensed my panic because he followed up with, "I've missed you. I hadn't realized how much until recently."

A laugh shot out of me in a surprised snort. "Are you serious? All we do is argue."

"It's fun for me," he said simply.

There was a long pause before I said, "You might need therapy."

He chuckled. "Indeed, I might."

"I'm serious. This may come as a shock to you, but it's taken every ounce of my self-control not to poison you these past few days."

"Poison me? I always thought you'd kill me in a much more personal way."

"Trust me, I've considered every possible scenario. Poison is the one least likely to be traced back to me."

"Ha. Well..."

"Don't act like you haven't also been plotting my demise. Truth be told, I was fairly confident your invitation to the adventure park today was part of an elaborate plan to murder me. I thought you'd make it look like an accident."

"I was going to, initially, but when I saw how many people were with us, I realized I hadn't thought it through," he shrugged. "I'll come up with a Plan B before the trip is over." His lips twitched up in one corner.

"I'll wait with bated breath," I replied, giving him a rare, genuine smile in return. I was surprised by how comfortable and civilized our conversation could be when we both wanted it. I found myself enjoying the quick rhythm of our banter. Against my better judgment, I liked his company.

A comfortable silence fell between us while we sat side by side on the warm sand. I examined Dustin's face in profile, glowing in the rays of the setting sun. I followed the smooth line of his nose and the gentle dip at the center of his lower lip. Usually, where I was concerned, there was something about his expression that was friendly but distant. Yet, at that moment, his face looked different, engaged, guarded and nervous, but with an underlying tenderness.

"I think there's a fine line between love and hate," Dustin said, shifting his position, nudging our shoulders together.

I stared at him for several quiet beats. "I don't hate you, Dustin."

"You love me, then?"

A tiny bud of sympathy bloomed in my chest. I bit my lip and wondered how to phrase my response. "In my own way," I edged carefully. "I suppose a part of me always will."

There was so much truth embedded in my words that I was surprised when he laughed, a single, breathy chuckle. "In your own way," he repeated, and I nodded. I caught something cascade across his face. A muscle in his jaw moved, and something soft tugged at his lips. "Do you ever miss me?"

The question didn't surprise me, given the direction our conversation had swerved. I considered for a moment while Dustin studiously avoided looking at me. I could still see him, however. There was a vulnerability in his expression. Seeing it caused the bloom of sympathy to return. "Sometimes," I said, feeling no need to be dishonest. "We were together for a long time. We loved each other. Those feelings don't simply disappear."

Dustin shook his head ruefully, and I suspected I'd answered a question far beyond the one he asked. "No, they don't. Mine certainly haven't."

I gave a nervous laugh. Dustin suddenly seemed full of confessions. I don't know what made me compare him to a sad child. It could have been the orange light of sunset or the way the ocean breeze caused his hair to dance. It could have been the words or the way he said them. Whatever it was, it made the look in his eyes deep, acute with something I couldn't quite name, and it filled me with a tender nostalgia I wasn't prepared for. Seeing him vulnerable, even for a second, was disorienting. It made me remember a time when I could look at his face and not hate it. I didn't know how to respond to his honesty, so I said as much.

Dustin bit his lip, then waited for a beat. "Do you feel it too?" he asked, turning his body toward me. He kept looking at me, holding my gaze for two seconds too long.

"Please don't look at me like that," I said, almost breathlessly.

"Why?"

"Because it makes me uncomfortable."

"Why?"

"Because it feels too familiar."

He stared at me for a couple of loaded seconds before asking, "Familiar, in a bad way?"

"Familiar, in a confusing way."

Dustin inched closer. I knew him well and recognized his expression immediately, eyelids half-open, his mouth twitching. "Confusing because it feels right?"

It *did* feel right, in its own unexpected way. Then I remembered Shawn, and it felt very, very wrong again. I inched away from him and the kiss that almost was. "Dustin, you have a boyfriend."

"What if I didn't?" He asked, rubbing one hand on the underside of his jaw.

"You do."

Determination rose in his voice, and he stuck out his chin in that stubborn way he sometimes did. "What if I didn't?"

"What's the point in discussing hypotheticals?"

"Humour me," Dustin pleaded, his eyes making an adoring circuit of my face. "If we were here, on this trip, together, and we were both single, what would happen?"

"That depends. If you were acting like a total jerk, like you were at the beginning of this trip, probably nothing."

"What if I wasn't? What if every day was like today?"

I considered it for a moment. The day *had* been surprisingly wonderful and had gone by with impressive ease. He had been notably sweet most of the day. If every day was like that... The thought trailed off in my mind, and in that absence of immediate response, Dustin found his window and smashed it wide open. He grabbed my face in both hands, then, before I even realized what was happening, our lips connected.

I froze, registering the familiar pressure of Dustin's lips, the coarseness of his five o'clock shadow scratching against my jaw. The world became static, and my brain struggled to battle through the haze. I attempted to make a quick calculation of all the tiny moments that led to that event. I could not deny that I didn't really mind Dustin's lips against mine. In fact, a growing part of me actually liked it. Liked it a lot. That realization nearly caused my brain to short circuit.

His mouth was warm, lips smooth and firm. He still looked really nice that close up. Maybe even better than he did from a distance. His eyes were so insanely blue, his lashes were long to the point of absurdity, and he was warm. So warm.

I tried to hate it and failed. Losing myself, I leaned into the kiss, my mouth sliding open. Dustin brushed his tongue against mine while one of his hands pushed into my hair. Like electricity, it jolted me back to the reality of our situation and life in general.

As suddenly as the kiss began, I detangled myself from his embrace. Immediately, I rose to my feet in unbalanced urgency. "What was...hell...that?" I stumbled over my own tongue in a frazzled rush.

"In English?"

"What the fuck was that?" I demanded, eyes wide as I scrubbed a hand across my face.

"If you don't recognize a kiss, I'd wager your Australian isn't doing it right."

"Of course I recognize it, Dusty," I flung back at him. I was in no mood for banter. I wasn't sure what I was in the mood for anymore. At that moment, my temperament straddled someplace between rage and raging desire. "Why would you do that?"

"Because I wanted to," he said simply. "And I could tell you were waiting for me to do it."

I was taken back. "I most certainly was not!"

"Yes, you were. I could tell."

I wanted to scream ugly profanities at him but couldn't because he was right in this particular situation. I *had* seen the signs. I'd registered the lingering glances, how he purposely inched closer and closer until our shoulders were touching, the way he had licked his lips in preparation. I had seen the signs and ignored them. Not because I wanted him to kiss me. I ignored the warnings because I had wondered if he would follow through, and more so, how it would feel if he did.

"I thought I was over you. Over us," Dustin rolled on like he hadn't said something completely shocking. "Being here with you, like this, I can't deny that I still love you."

"Dustin…" my voice trailed off. He stared at me as I purposely looked anywhere else. He knew that I knew he was staring. I sensed it like a doe felt a predator. He could also tell that, just like a deer, I was about to run.

"You feel it too. I know you do. It's why we fight the way that we do."

"No," I shook my head. "We fight because we're both too stubborn and proud to admit when we're unreasonable."

It took him a moment to say anything further, his gaze heavy on me. "We were happy before. We could be happy again."

"Were we happy?" I challenged. "If we were really happy, you wouldn't have been cheating, and I would have noticed that you were a lot sooner than I did."

Dustin huffed out an incredulous breath through his nose. Even when I looked away, I could tell he was trying to get my eyes back on his face. When Dustin spoke again, it was soft, as if he were trying not to break the spell. "I want you back, Kyle."

I said nothing, but inside, I was screaming like a woman chased with a chainsaw in a horror movie.

He was looking at me so intently, he didn't even seem to

notice the blast of warm wind that came at us from the ocean waves, ruffling the front of his hair.

Finally, I said, "Everything about you and me looks better in the rear-view mirror, Dustin. It might be best to leave it there."

"That's the thing about rear-view mirrors, though," he said whimsically. "It's never too late to turn the car around."

There was a beat of silence.

Then another.

In that time, it took us much longer than it should have to wrench our gazes away from each other.

"Promise me, you'll think about it," Dustin nearly begged.

I could guarantee I would be thinking about it. Whether I wanted to or not.

EIGHTEEN
KYLE

I woke up the next morning, a sense of dread filling me. The conversation with Dustin had been playing on a loop in my head all night. It was very frustrating.

Even more aggravating, I couldn't stop thinking about the kiss. I tried. Really, I had. Yet Dustin's lips felt so familiar and surprisingly comfortable pressed against mine that it left me contemplating everything I thought I knew.

I was a classic over-thinker. My brain moved fast and in many different directions at once. I tried to remind myself of the reasons we broke up in the first place. Still, they couldn't quell the resurgence of affection and desire that were slowly stirring inside me. Not even twelve hours and countless cocktails, alone in my cabin, had scrubbed the feeling from my mind. If anything, those cocktails had left me sleepless and incapable of sober reflection.

Beneath all the rational lies I told myself, the situation was far more primitive. Dustin was still gorgeous, I was still attracted to him, and kissing him still felt good. Wrong, but good.

I was distracted by his broad shoulders, long legs and narrow waist, and the way they caused blood to pulsate within me. Although the memory felt like another lifetime, I could still recall how Dustin's voice sounded low in my ear during pillow talk at three in the morning. The thought of it ignited a flame in the pit of my stomach. I tried to persuade myself that it was loneliness and fear pulling me back towards Dustin after all this time, but my loins were not as convinced.

I hadn't told anyone, not even Sapphire. I had no idea if she would react with applause or with scorn, and I was honestly in no mood for either. I wasn't sure if I wanted her to know at all. Ever.

I had successfully avoided everyone for the last twelve hours. Pent-up in my cabin with only my guilt and my confusing thoughts to keep me company. I felt shame because I allowed Dustin to kiss me. Dustin, who had a boyfriend.

Shawn was a sweet guy, albeit a little child-like, but he didn't deserve to be cheated on, and the guilt was three-fold because I knew too well what that felt like.

Merely being around Dustin had clouded my judgment. I had managed to avoid him successfully for two years. Then came the cruise. In the few short days, Dustin proved that he was still the best sparring partner. He had also been entirely charming on several occasions and frequently shirtless. With Justin and Sapphire's marriage, it would become increasingly difficult not to share space with him periodically. Was sharing space really all that bad? We had an attraction. Neither one of us could deny it. The kiss had solidified any doubts I may have had. My affection for him still lingered, somewhere under all my sarcasm and vitriol.

Realistically, I knew my initial behavior when seeing Dustin again for the first time had been reactionary and defensive. Most importantly, it hadn't been attractive. So logically, that meant there must have been some truth to what Dustin had said. He claimed to love me, even though I had been treating him like garbage. That either meant his feelings were real or that he was a masochist. Maybe both.

Then there was Jax, sweet, charming, heartthrob Jax. I wasn't sure what was going on between us. Yet, I could easily remember the way my fingers felt as they trailed that place where his square jaw met his neck and the place his neck met his broad shoulders and the tendon that stretched the length between them. I recalled, in surround sound clarity, how his hands felt against my skin, his thumbs bracing against my temples as he feathered me with kisses. How his firm hands roamed other places with a precision far beyond my wildest dreams. I couldn't forget Jax's mouth and what he did with it.

The way he made me feel meant something. When I thought about him, something twisted in my chest, like a combination of heartache and hope. He was so easy to be with. Fun. I enjoyed his sense of humor, and of course, his interest in me was flattering to my ego, which was still a little bruised. I was tempted to let myself fall for him, but everything was happening too quickly.

It had only been three days, and we'd only slept together once. It was far too soon to schedule a U-Haul, I reminded myself. Jax was a temporary amusement. In a little more than a week, he would automatically become a non-issue. The cruise would be over, then we'd retreat to our respective parts of the country.

All I really needed to know where Jax was concerned was that we had plans that day. I was meeting him for breakfast, then we were going to enjoy the island of Grand Turk together. My primary mission was to stop thinking about the kiss with Dustin long enough to enjoy it.

I was in a prison of my own creation. Exhaling, I tried to let the anxiety seep out of me. I needed to review what I knew. So, I compiled a list in my head.

One. I was attracted to both Dustin and Jax. If I was frank, Jax had a slight advantage in that department. He was still shiny and new, making me feel excited in a way Dustin, after all our years together, couldn't.

Two. Jax had no long-term potential. We'd met by chance on a luxury cruise liner, and when the ship made its final dock, we'd likely never see each other again. Best case scenario, we'd exchange numbers and addresses, maybe hooking-up once a year if and when he traveled through town. That would get stale after a while, even with mind-blowing sex.

Three. Dustin may have been more accessible, but our history proved him to also be unreliable. While I subscribed to the belief that people could change, I hadn't seen any evidence that he had. If anything, him kissing me on the beach only reinforced that he hadn't.

After having been a sexual pariah for the last two years, having two gorgeous men wanting me, should have been somewhat satisfying, but it wasn't. Nothing about it felt good. Confusing, terrifying, exhausting, but not good.

"Open up, whore!" Ruby's voice was muffled by the thick wood of my door, but I recognized it immediately. I hoisted myself up out of bed to answer the door.

"I really wish you would come up with a different greeting," I said, opening the door. I turned back toward the bed, but I didn't sit.

Ruby followed me inside, perching her perfectly shaped ass on the edge of the desk. She was in a yellow sundress, accented with teal jewelry. "I wish Idris Elba would fall from the sky and directly into my vagina, but that is also unlikely to happen."

"Theoretically, depending on the circumstances, the angle of your pelvis and the trajectory—"

Ruby held up her hand. "Stop. Only you could make a perfect sexual fantasy sound like a physics lesson."

"I hate you sometimes," I told her, rolling my eyes.

She blew me a kiss. "You love me."

"I do, but I can't be social today. I'm supposed to be meeting Jax in an hour. You'll have to find someone else to pester."

"Rude! You owe me for standing me up at dinner last night."

"I'm sorry I didn't realize we had plans."

"Honey, it's a standing arrangement," She sighed, placing her hands on her hips. "You're my wingman, and I'm yours. Was this not explained to you?"

"Not officially, no."

"It's fine. It gave me a chance to grease a few gears."

I lowered my glasses to the tip of my nose. "Gears? What gears?"

"Cody."

"As in Justin's best friend, Cody?" I narrowed my eyes at her. "Please tell me you didn't sleep with him."

"I did not, but I will."

"Why?" I bordered on whining. "He's such a cretin."

"You're not wrong, but he has abs like Zac Efron, so I'm willing to overlook it."

"Well, good luck with your mission."

"From your lips to God's ears," she said. "Believe it or not, the guy is a bit of a prude. He didn't fall for any of my usual tricks."

"Tricks?"

"Yes, Kyle, tricks. Honestly, sometimes you are so naïve."

"I'm not naïve. I just don't see the point of trying to trick a man into sleeping with you."

"Oh, honey, that's what makes you naïve. Women outnumber men two-to-one. So we have to be smarter than you."

I gave her a look.

"Not *you*. I meant *real* men."

I exhaled tightly. "I'm a real…never mind," I decided to let it go.

"The greatest lie women have ever told was when we led men to believe that they had all the power. In truth, we call all the shots and men, straight men that is, haven't got a clue. They think they're choosing us, but really, we choose them. We have a whole bag of tricks to make them choose us in return."

"You've got to be kidding me," I replied, except I could totally picture it.

"It's true. Women are sly creatures."

"I refuse to believe that all women are that manipulative."

She slanted a look at me. "It's not manipulation. It's seduction," she clarified. "How do you think I know how to get what I want from men? Seduction is the most important skill a woman can have."

"What about survival skills?"

"It *is* a survival skill. You'd be surprised by the things I could teach you."

"Surprised, or terrified?"

"Maybe both," she chuckled. "Trust me, I know what I'm talking about. I help my girlfriends land men all the time."

"Oh yes, I'm sure dozens of lives have been enriched by your wisdom."

"Maybe if you took my advice, your dating life would be a swimming pool rather than a dried-up well."

That seemed like the perfect opening to discuss what was on my mind. "It's funny you say that because right now, my dating life is a little too wet for comfort."

"You can never be too moist," she said through a Cheshire grin. "It hurts otherwise."

I laughed. "How are we friends?"

"Opposites attract?

"Yes, well, vaginal lubricants aside, there is such a thing as too much."

"Oh? I'm intrigued. Tell me more."

"So, uh," I attempted. "Remember when Dustin and I dated?"

Ruby answered dryly. "You never let anyone forget. Why?"

"Well," I said, feeling inexplicable, traitorous warmth flash up the back of my neck. "Well, he…um…I mean…that is…we…"

"Spit it out or shove it back in. I've had Brazilian waxes less

242

painful than this."

"Yeah. Well..." I coughed. "Weird thing happened. We went out for dinner the other night, because...like...Shawn was sick. And...well...he kind of ... kissed me?"

That threw Ruby for a brief loop before she cocked her head to the side and spoke. "Are you asking me or telling me?"

"Telling you, of course."

"Hmmm," Ruby nodded contemplatively. "Was it a I'm-so-glad-we-put-our-bullshit-behind-us-and-can-finally-be-friends, kiss? Or was it a I've-missed-you-so-much-I-want-to-stick-my-dick-inside-you-right-now, kiss?"

"Definitely the second one."

"Are you sure?"

"I realize this may come as a surprise to you, but I know when someone else's tongue is in my mouth."

She didn't even flinch at my snarky comeback. She shrugged like my confession was already common knowledge. "That took longer than I thought it would."

I stared at her. "You're not surprised?"

She shrugged. "You were together a lifetime, and you do fight like two people who want to rip each other's clothes off."

I stiffened. "Wait. I did not want to do that. I mean, I don't. Still don't. I think."

"Whatever you say," She waved her hands dismissively. "Was it a good kiss? Was there tongue? Did you get hard?"

I shook my head doglike as if it could disperse the topic from the room. "Never mind. Forget I mentioned it."

"Don't be like that," Ruby demanded, but when she saw that I wasn't going to give her any details about the kiss, she moved on with a heavy sigh. "Did you like it? That's at least a question you should be comfortable answering."

"I did," I admitted, hiding my face behind the crook of my elbow.

"I knew it," she said. "You two will fuck before the trip is up."

"Stop," I groaned. "We will not."

She threw her head back, cackling. "Kyle, I thought you were supposed to be smart."

"I am! Except when it comes to dating stuff. When it comes to this, I'm very, very stupid."

"Yes, you are," she agreed. "How is it possible that you didn't know Dustin was still into you?"

"I don't know. Maybe the fact that Dustin has his own bubble-butt boyfriend?"

"Yes, because he would be the first person to ever date somebody simply to fill the void," Ruby said as if it was the most obvious thing in the world.

"Do you think that's what he's doing?" I was aware that I was rocking anxiously on my heels, but I couldn't seem to stop.

Ruby looked annoyed. "Of course, that's what he's doing! Seriously Kyle, he called you every day for three months, then sent you a long-winded letter, begging for you to take him back. A man doesn't try that hard to get your attention if he's just going to move on."

I let that sink in for half a second, then remembered the other part of my dilemma. "Dustin wants us to get back together."

"That's nice for him, but what do *you* want?"

A pause.

"I…" I started hesitantly. "… don't know. I'm not sure."

"You better get sure. That's a big decision to make."

I glared at her. "Thank you, I didn't already know that."

"Whatever happened with the sexy Aussie? What's the deal there?"

"There's no deal. Jax is a person I met. We're having fun. That's all."

"Sure," Ruby nodded, clearly not buying it. "I've seen the way he looks at you."

"How does Jax look at me?"

"The same way people look at an all-you-can-eat buffet."

I arched an eyebrow. "With caution and mild disgust?"

Ruby chuckled. "Like he can't decide what to put in his mouth first."

I rolled my eyes. "Even if that were true, I'm not sure Jax matters much in this scenario."

"Oh no," Ruby scowled. "Did you scare him away like all the others?"

"No," I said, mildly offended. "It's just, Jax is vacation fun. A temporary amusement. It's too complicated to ever be anything serious."

"Oh, I get it. You found a flaw," Ruby said, nodding. "I

knew there had to be something wrong with him. Nothing good comes in a package that pretty," she said with a flip of her hair, then she took a breath. "What's wrong with him? Sociopath? Compulsive gambler? Escaped convict?"

I raised an eyebrow at the last one.

"Don't look at me like that," she scolded. "It could happen."

I waved the ridiculous suggestion away. "There's nothing wrong with Jax, exactly. At least not technically. There's an obstacle, that's all."

"Such as?" I couldn't tell if she was genuinely interested or humoring me.

"I don't know," I said slowly, then regretted saying it. I had already said that too many times in the span of our conversation. So I tried again. "You'll think it's stupid."

Ruby nodded. "Probably, but tell me anyway."

So I did. When I was finished, I waited for Ruby's take on things.

"You're an ass," she declared.

"That doesn't sound very objective."

"Objectively, you're an ass. Is that better?"

"Not really, no."

"What else did you expect me to say?" She challenged. "You're considering closing the door on a perfectly nice guy, who also happens to be gorgeous, by the way, just because you don't live in the same city?

I shrugged. "I don't do long-distance."

She shook her head, "You don't do *any* complications. Unless it comes wrapped in a neat little package with a perfect, sparkly bow, you don't want any part of it."

"That's not true."

"It *is* true, and this situation proves it."

"Shit," I said, collapsing backward on the bed, smothering my face with a pillow. "I need someone to tell me what to do."

"You're barking up the wrong tree, sunshine. Telling people what to do is more Sapphire's territory." Then she asked, "Who do you have the most chemistry with?"

"Chemistry?" I repeated the word like it was the first time I'd ever heard it. I knew I should have paid attention in science class instead of ogling Ray Semenyna, the cute volleyball player with the cleft in his chin. "I'm not sure. I think it's pretty even."

"You could always date them both," was somehow Ruby's idea of a comforting suggestion. "These days, throuples are a valid relationship choice."

I looked at her like she had lost her mind. "Not for me, thank you."

"Oh, come on," Ruby whined. "Imagine being the meat between that sandwich." She bit her bottom lip as the image took form in her mind. "If it happens, all I ask is that you take photos."

"Never going to happen," I said definitively.

"Well, if the choice is between Dustin or the Australian, I would choose the Aussie."

"Why?"

"Have you seen that man's ass? You could bounce a quarter off that thing."

Objectively, it was a fantastic ass. My mind flashed to the smooth lines of Jax's body, and even more so, the way his flesh felt, warm and powerful against my naked skin. At the sheer thought, my stomach did some embarrassing acrobatics I would never admit to anyone, ever. Not even to Ruby.

"Aren't we getting a tad ahead of ourselves?" I asked. "I've known Jax for three days. What if he isn't even interested in seeing me after this vacation?"

"You should probably ask him."

"It's been three dates. I can't ask Jax about our future after three dates. It's way too *Fatal Attraction.*"

"We're on vacation time," she shrugged. "Things work differently."

"I'm not sure that's true."

"Look," she sighed. "You know I'm not good at the whole tactful emotional communication thing, but since Sapphire's not here, I'll give it a try." She pressed on. "Jax obviously likes you, and you obviously like him. Currently, your romance has an expiration date. When the vacation ends, so likely will your affair to remember. So ask him if he wants to keep in touch and see what he says."

"But—"

"Shut up. I'm trying to be sensitive, and it's easier if you don't interrupt me," Ruby said, rolling her eyes, exasperated.

"You like this guy. I mean, really really like him. So stop being a little bitch and ask him what's up."

I tossed my head back, laughing. She was like Sapphire sometimes, in that she could cut right down to the truth of things. While Sapphire's tactics were more heartfelt and tender, Ruby's approach was more matter of fact and direct. Sometimes, her razor's edge was exactly what I needed. She watched me, grinning but still judging. She had a point. I did, against all odds, really like Jax. Yet my residual feelings for Dustin still lingered, muddling that realization.

"No one can tell you what to do or how to feel," she continued. "Only you can decide how you feel about either of them."

She was absolutely right, and it pained me to admit it. "Thank you for listening. You've given me a lot to think about."

"I know everybody thinks I'm just a dumb slut, but I see things. I see people."

"I don't think that."

"Yes, you do. Everyone does, and that's ok. I'm comfortable with the role I play."

I sat up at attention. "If I have ever made you feel that way, I'm so sorry."

"You have," she said simply, and she recognized my immediate regret. "It's ok, though. I've reached a point where I kind of enjoy it now."

"Ruby, honestly, you've been my best friend on this boat. It's Sapphire's honeymoon so—"

"So I've been a good substitute," she interrupted. "I get it."

"No! Not a substitute!" I assured her. "I've really enjoyed getting to spend time with you on this trip. You've been great."

"I know I'm great," she said with confidence. "Everyone says so," then she took a breath. "I just wish, sometimes, people treated me like I was good enough."

A stab of guilt immediately hit me, and I swore to myself that I'd try to do better.

NINETEEN
JAX

I leaned against the palm tree, watching Kyle as he made his way into the water surrounding Grand Turk.

I had met him at the lido brekkie buffet, as agreed. The minute I saw him hovering near the crêpe-station, all coherent thought slipped out of my head. Even from across the room, there was something almost magnetic about him. Beachy and casual in robin's egg blue swim trunks and a white polo shirt., he looked cut from the pages of a preppy catalogue. I was tempted to mount him, right there next to the fruit compote.

"G'day there," I drawled, sneaking up behind him, whispering the greeting in his ear.

Kyle turned quickly, and it was blatantly apparent that he hadn't known it was me behind him. Once it registered, he answered my smile.

He looked incredibly handsome; his ginger hair perfectly combed except for a stubborn cowlick on his crown that reminded me of Alfalfa from The Little Rascals. Standing that close to him, I could smell his cologne, and I almost took in a large whiff.

"Good morning, Jax," Kyle greeted back. I liked the way my name sounded on the wind of his voice.

"You look nice." Kyle didn't have a ton of muscle, but he was well-shaped with broad shoulders, and the clothes complimented him well.

"Thank you." His smile remained as he stepped around me, out of the way of people wanting to order food.

"How was your sleep?"

"Could have been better, actually. I tossed and turned a lot."

"I'm sorry to hear that. I thought for sure you'd sleep well after your adventure with Dustin."

"What?" Kyle seemed instantly uncomfortable. "What do you mean?"

I looked at him, puzzled. "Didn't Dustin take you sightseeing and whatnot all day yesterday?"

"Oh. Right. Yes, he did," Kyle nodded. "Sightseeing and

hiking. Nothing exciting."

"Did you enjoy it?"

He shrugged awkwardly, making a strange puffing sound with his lips. "It was fine."

Just fine? He didn't much seem in the mood to discuss his day spent with his ex. So I decided to focus on our day instead. "I can't promise today will be any more exciting. There's not much to do on the island, but I can think of a few things I could do to excite you," I winked.

That simple sentence lit the space between us with such sexual energy I saw his breath catch in his throat. Kyle gave a sudden nervous chuckle. I didn't understand his anxious reaction to my sexual innuendo. The time for being nervous around me had theoretically passed. I'd been inside him. It no longer made sense for him to be shy.

"Do you want brekkie before we go?"

He shook his head. "I already had a granola bar, but if you're hungry, we can eat first."

"No, that's ok. We don't have much time on this island. Only a few hours. I'd like to enjoy every minute we can before we're forced back onto this floating city."

The ship was already docked at the two-hundred-foot-long pier. We disembarked quickly, making a short and easy walk through the cruise centre to one of the most beautiful beaches.

Widely believed to be Christopher Columbus' first landfall in the Americas, Grand Turk was a small island in the British territory of Turks and Caicos. Only seven miles long, and maybe a mile at its widest, the island had a population of fewer than five thousand people. So when a cruise ship the size of Lollipop arrived, the island's population was quickly doubled.

Since the island was so small, there weren't heaps of tourist attractions. So, the only thing to do on the island was to enjoy the sun, the surf and the sand. For that reason alone, the cruise company didn't allow much time on the island. Only four hours. Only long enough for the ship to refuel and the tourists to support the island restaurants and market vendors. Sure, one could hit up Margaritaville, but at ten in the morning, tequila wasn't calling my name quite yet.

I wanted to explore with Kyle. I wanted to see the various expressions cross his face as he took in the island architecture or the ancient landmarks. Or to see that spark of recognition when he realized we were exploring the same land as Francis Drake and swimming in the same water Blackbeard sailed on. That was going to have to wait until the next island. For now, I had to be content with seeing Kyle in a bathing suit and watching him splash around.

The water was so crystal clear that you could actually see an eel or two swim by, utterly uninterested in the tourists that frolicked there. Kyle had squealed when he saw the first one, and not in delight either. It had been a shrill, panicked cry, and he swam back up to the shore with more speed than I thought possible. It took several minutes before he decided to venture back in.

The water lapped around his waist, a bright smile lighting up his features as he waded in the surf. He moved like he knew I was watching him, with purpose and confidence. I wondered if he knew how under his spell I was. After the other night, I was in deep trouble. I felt like a teenager with emotions I didn't know how to control. Which was absurd because I was an adult with a job. I had no business acting like a galah with a crush.

I hadn't intended to let things with Kyle go so far so quickly. Sex tended to muddle things, and the last thing I wanted was to upset our situation's delicate balance. Yet too many shots mixed with my undeniable attraction, and I had been unable to control myself.

When I saw Kyle dance so carefree and spirited, something he claimed to never do, I knew I wanted him. I had already accepted that I was attracted to him. Still, at that moment, on that dancefloor, while he laughed and twirled his best mate around to that classic Cher song, I also knew that I wanted him with an all-consuming desire. I had to have him, taste him, and fill him. I needed to make him scream my name until his voice was hoarse and our bodies trembled together.

I'd had many lovers over the years, men more muscular, more chiselled, more rugged and definitely more masculine than Kyle. Not that he was overtly feminine. He was just quite obviously gay. It wasn't a bad thing at all, but it wasn't what I was usually drawn to. Yet the other night had felt like something clicking into place. Our bodies knew each other instantly, as though recognizing each other from a previous existence. It had been the most natural and comfortable first sexual experience I'd ever had with anyone. In his company, I felt the blessed feeling of something that had eluded me for far too long, possibility.

He glanced up at me. It was fascinating how many emotions I could see run over his face, then saw the genuine effort he put into schooling his features. He was such an open book. I suppressed a smile. "Aren't you coming in?" he asked, spinning slowly as waves lapped up against him. "The water is so warm."

As much as I enjoyed watching him, I couldn't say no to that smile. I jogged down the beach, peeling off my shirt as I approached the waterline. I tossed it aside, running into the water, my knees high, just as a swell breached the shore. The force of the incoming wave caused me to stagger, and I fell back on my ass as the water crested.

Kyle laughed heartily at my expense. "Are you ok?" He giggled, reaching out both arms to help me back to my feet.

"The only thing wounded is my pride," I laughed as he gripped both my hands with his, ready to hoist me to my feet. I had another idea. As Kyle took hold, I used my exponential strength to pull him down into the water with me. We fell back together, like clumsy ankle-biters, laughing and splashing. Another wave came just as Kyle rolled over, and he pressed his face to my wet shoulder to shield himself from the impact.

I couldn't remember the last time I'd had so much fun. We frolicked in the surf for nearly an hour, like we were brats again until we were both tired from laughter. Periodically I would attempt to lead Kyle further out into the water. Still, he would reach a certain point then suddenly stop. No matter what I did or how I coaxed him, he wouldn't swim any further out into the ocean. There was definitely a story attached to his behaviour, and I intended to ask about it later.

By the time we dragged our tired, wet bodies back to the beach, we were adequately pruney. We laid on the sand, sunbathing, our towels soaking up the remains of ocean water and drying almost instantly in the harsh sun of Cockburn Town. We chatted lazily about all manner of things. We started with simple things like pop-culture and salacious celebrity gossip before moving on to more serious topics, like politics and religion.

We had so much in common, yet enough differences to keep the conversation interesting. We both detested most country music, yet Kyle had an appreciation for Dolly and Reba that even he couldn't explain. I could agree that they both had great voices for their time, but neither would ever make it on my playlist. We both loved Sandra Bullock. Kyle thought she had deserved an Oscar for Gravity. I considered Bullock's performance to be lacklustre and self-indulgent. We both believed there was life on other planets, but I believed in UFOs while Kyle thought there had to be a more logical explanation. Neither of us believed in ghosts, but we were both open to the possibility.

Conversation with Kyle flowed like wine, and I felt pickled off it and off him. Yet, beneath the joy of his company, I tried to be rational. Perhaps it wasn't Kyle at all that had me feeling that way. Maybe it was spending all day in the water and sun, without anything to eat, that had me feeling so weak in the knees.

"Are you hungry?" I asked, turning my neck to look at him while keeping my back flat on my towel.

He mirrored my position. "I could eat."

"Jack's Shack is up the shoreline. A woman on the ship told me that I absolutely had to give it a burl while on the island. Want to check it out?"

"Sure," he shrugged.

We pulled our shirts back on, gathered our belongings, tucking everything into our backpacks. The restaurant wasn't far. It was a large tiki hut with a spacious deck and mostly bar service but a few select tables.

Kyle looked less ravenous than I felt, but he hadn't eaten much all day either, so I knew he must have been as starving from frolicking in saltwater and sun as I was. Jack's menu was an aromatic selection of traditional Caribbean dishes. Everything smelled so good, I couldn't decide what to order. Kyle must have been having the same dilemma because he turned to me and asked, "Do you want to each order something different, then share?"

That's precisely what we did. I ordered the cracked conch plate with peas and rice, while Kyle decided on jerk chook and a salad. We gathered our Styrofoam plates, the smell of deliciousness filling the air and took them to one of the tables, where we could sit across from each other.

I instantly picked up my fork, digging into the rice, mixing it with a bit of the sauce before putting it in my mouth. "Dig in," I encouraged, after swallowing. Kyle did. He scooped up a forkful of his chook and shoved it in his mouth. He hummed dramatically when it hit his tastebuds. "Is it good?"

Kyle's saucer wide eyes fell on me as he nodded. "It might be the best chicken I've ever had," he declared, placing another fork full on his tongue. "Did you grab napkins?" He asked, covering his mouth with his hand as he chewed. I nodded, handing him one of the paper napkins I had rested underneath my plate. A second later, he was sagging with a sigh. "It's so good. A little spicier than I expected, but really wonderful."

I sampled a bit of my conch. The meat was perfectly prepared, soft, although a little rubbery. I expected it to smell fishy, but it didn't. It had a unique flavour, like an unexpected combination of crab and salmon. I let out a groan of euphoria. "Try the conch," I suggested.

Kyle was more than willing to oblige. He dug his plastic fork into the seafood, tearing off a piece. "Wow," he said, not caring that his mouth was full. "I've never had conch before. It has an unusual texture."

"Unusual bad?"

"I haven't decided yet," he admitted, taking another bite. "It's definitely an acquired taste. What is conch exactly?"

"It's a giant sea snail."

Kyle's face turned green almost immediately, and he grimaced, scraping his tongue with his upper teeth. I laughed at his reaction. For a moment, I thought he might throw his fork dramatically, or worse, puke right there at the table. "Not a fan?"

"Sorry," He said, slowly regaining his composure. "I know it's completely psychosomatic, but I can't eat that."

"It's not that bad," I assured him, amused. "Think of it as escargot."

"I won't eat that either."

I kept my eyes on him as he returned to his chook dish. "You're strictly a boring steak and potatoes kind of bloke, aren't you?"

Kyle stiffened. I enjoyed seeing him blink at me, clearly not knowing what to say in response. "No. I'm not that boring. I've tried a few unusual dishes over the years."

"Such as?"

Kyle lifted his chin. "Shark fin soup, alligator," he ummed as he searched his memory. "Camel."

"You've eaten camel?"

He nodded, shoving another forkful of chook in his mouth. "At a Somalian wedding. It's not like I would have ever walked into a restaurant and voluntarily order it."

"I doubt many restaurants could afford to serve it. It's a rather expensive cut of meat. Did you like it?"

Kyle shrugged. "I'd eat it again. It tasted like beef. Do they eat camel in Australia?"

"Why would we bother?" I laughed. "There are much tastier proteins on the continent. Seafood, obviously, but also, arguably the best open range beef and lamb on the planet." I took a bite of my meal. "If you are keen on the camels, I suggest you go get them. There are thousands of them running feral in the bush ready for the taking."

"That doesn't make sense to me. If there are so many camels, why not hunt them like deer?"

I laughed heartily at that. "Some people do. Some of us consider them pests. Not unlike wild dogs or rats. In some cultures, people eat cats, but I don't ask why you're not out there hunting strays, do I?"

Kyle laughed along with me. "What about kangaroo?" He asked between giggles. "Do you eat them?"

"Of course."

"Aren't they also considered pests? So what's the difference?"

"I don't know," I stumbled. "How dare you use logic against me." I pouted, then took another forkful of his chook. I decided to shift gears. "So, tell me more about your brother. What was he like?"

Kyle took a breath. I realized the question came out of the left field, so I gave him a moment to gather his thoughts. "We were a lot alike, actually, but he was smarter, more handsome and generally better at everything. Imagine a more perfect version of me."

"I don't think there could possibly be a more perfect version of you."

He looked away, flattered and embarrassed in equal measure. "He was older than me by two years. Graduated med school at the top of his class. Then, if that wasn't enough, he went on to become an amazing surgeon. He was basically a prodigy. Definitely the star of the family."

"You make it seem like you haven't accomplished anything of your own."

He laughed, though it sounded raw to my ears. "Nothing compared to him. I'm successful enough. I am, but really, my job is making money off of other people's successful work. He saved lives. He was the clear winner."

"Was it a competition?"

"Not between us, but I think our parents always hoped his success would light a fire under me."

I didn't respond to his confession. Instead, I asked, "Do you have any other siblings?"

"No, it was always just us two. Although, Sapphire is like a sister to me, and by extension, Ruby. The three of us couldn't be more different, but something about us fits together, like puzzle pieces. Apart, we're incomplete."

"You're lucky to have that. Heaps of friendships have shelf-lives. They fade or die once everyone starts leading separate ways."

"Speaking from experience?"

"I still talk to several of my mates from back home, but nowadays, those conversations feel like awkward encounters with acquaintances I hardly know. It's too easy to forget the years we spent picking each other up or holding each other steady. It sometimes feels like memories of someone else's life."

"I suppose the distance doesn't help?"

"Indeed," I agreed with a sad smile. "The Pacific Ocean does present some logistical obstacles. It makes getting together for birthdays and holidays much more complicated."

"I can imagine."

This time, I laughed. "I'm not sure you can. Unless you've experienced that kind of social isolation for yourself. For instance, I have a goddaughter. She's three-years-old, and I've yet to meet her. I've seen pictures and have seen her over video chat, but I'm not sure that counts. It's not the same."

"What's her name?"

"Lilian," I grinned wide. "She's already a spit-fire from what I can tell. My mate is going to have his hands full with that one."

"Why don't you go visit them?"

"Have you looked at the cost of airfare to Oz? It's a thousand dollars, one-way, and that's with a seat-sale."

"Wow. That is a lot of cash," he agreed. "You could always save up. If you skipped this cruise, you could have been half-way there."

"Maybe," I shrugged. Then I added with charm, "Still, then we wouldn't have met, and that wouldn't be fair to you."

"Wow. Cocky."

"And charming?"

Kyle cocked his head, considering it. "A little."

We both smiled, gazing a little too intently into each other's eyes. My vision drifted to Kyle's lips. They looked so inviting, I couldn't take my eyes off of them. The memory of my own lips and how they felt travelling across his body like eager explorers returned, causing heat to grow in the depths of my core. I wanted to kiss him again, at that moment. I looked away before I hurled myself across the table, giving in to my wayward thoughts. It felt like minutes had passed before I could gather my bearings.

When the moment was over, Kyle said suddenly. "We have about a half-hour before the ship is scheduled to leave port. We should get back."

I verified the time on my watch. "Good call."

As smooth as butter, Kyle straightened, gesturing to my Styrofoam plate. "You finished?" I nodded, and he scooped up both dishes and our napkins then deposited them in a nearby trash receptacle.

We started our walk back.

"Tomorrow we dock in St. Thomas," I announced, weaving past a small group of playing ankle-biters who were running down the beach with a kite. "There's heaps more to do on that island. I hope you don't mind, but I've arranged the entire day for us.

Kyle quirked a brow. "Did you? Since when did you become

256

the events coordinator?"

I laughed. "To be completely honest, it was all stuff I was already planning to do anyway with or without you. I'd much rather do it with you if you're available. Or do you need to check with your group first?"

He contemplated a second before smiling slyly. "No. I think they've monopolized enough of my time. What did you have planned?"

"Some good, old fashioned exploring. You'll enjoy it, I promise."

Kyle furrowed his brows, and I realized, not for the first time, how expressive his face was. "So confident. I'm not sure you know me well enough yet to know what I would or would not enjoy."

"Well, I can think of a few ways I can get to know you better this afternoon."

"Such as?"

A rakish grin spread across my face, and I could see Kyle inwardly chastise himself for even asking such a drongo question. We both knew what the afternoon would entail. Then, his grin mirrored mine.

We practically ran back to the ship.

TWENTY
KYLE

We hurried back to my cabin. Once inside, the passion that consumed us was alive and tangible. We grappled at each other, tearing at clothes like rabid animals. There was no hesitation. No seduction. No long teasing. We simply wanted each other immediately and primally. I playfully pushed Jax towards the bed. He staggered backward, pulling me with him as he fell. It was a clumsy, sideways tumble, each of us grabbing greedy handfuls of the other. Jax bounced when his back hit the mattress, and I straddled over him for several breaths, staring.

"C'mere," Jax ordered, pressing his hand against the back of my neck, bringing his smile close to mine.

I laughed hoarsely at his command but did as he instructed. I leaned down to kiss his eager mouth. Then my eyes fluttered shut, and our lips were reunited. His kiss was passionate from the start, his tongue exploring my mouth while his hands explored my body. It was full of heat and passion, garnished with an urgency I hadn't anticipated. Feeling a sound tear itself from my throat, I began kissing him blindly. I pushed him deep into the mattress, riding a continuous wave of his body as it wiggled and bucked beneath my weight. He brought his pelvis forward, pressing the hard parts of his body against the equally hard parts of mine.

Jax moved his kisses. He traveled along my jaw then buried his face in the collar of my shirt. I loved how smooth and full his lips felt. Seconds later, he bared his teeth on my neck, sucking at my shoulder, sliding his warm palm up my legs, to my waist, then under my shirt and back down again. He touched me with such tenderness and familiarity, like every part of me was worth something immeasurable. It gave me as strong a rush as the sensation of his kiss. I loved how he spread his hands wide while he explored me. Almost like he was trying to feel as much of my flesh as possible.

I pressed myself tighter into him. Touching him, feeling him, taking in the scent of him as our lips danced with each other, tongues tangling slowly until we were both breathless.

Growling, Jax started to lift my shirt up. Recognizing his silent cues, I put my arms above my head, then he pulled my shirt up and off with ease. He discarded it quickly before bringing his lips back to mine, and the touch sent a hundred emotions sizzling through me.

Jax moved lower, down my neck and further until he was dropping open-mouthed kisses between my pectorals. He wasted little time capturing my right nipple in his mouth. I gasped in a breath, twisting my fingers in his hair as I arched into the touch. I couldn't contain the moans of pleasure that rose within me. Each sound I made seemed to echo through the room.

He moved on to the other nipple, using his free hand to fondle the first. Jax pinched and rolled it between his fingers while he bit the other, licking while he twisted. He tantalized my nerves with an overload of sensation, keeping me in a constant state of heightened pleasure.

Fuelled by need, I pulled him over me and with mystifying speed, he managed to remove his own shirt before my back even hit the mattress. I hooked a finger under the waistband of his shorts, feeling the warm skin of his navel, tugging him even closer to me.

I edged in to kiss him again, but he pushed my head back with the palm of his hand. The next thing I knew, he was pulling down my swim trunks. The length of me sprung out, engorged to the tip. I let out a moan when he wrapped his lips around the head and drank all of me down.

My eyes rolled to the back of my head, and I mumbled profanities as I got into it. He worked me over with such intensity that I couldn't think of any word to adequately describe the pleasure. My body bucked under the expertise of Jax's tongue, swirling around, up and down my shaft. My left hand was lost within the sheets, and my right cupped Jax's neck gently, guiding his mouth until he came up for air suddenly. With a smile, his mouth came back over mine while he continued to stroke me with his slippery hands.

Once more, I teased the elastic waistband of his swim shorts. He swatted my hand away playfully. "Do you want something?" He asked, his mouth twisting into the sexiest smirk

I'd ever seen.

I bit my lower lip as he continued to stroke me. "You know I do."

His smile widened. "Tell me. Tell me what you want."

"You." My voice was hoarse with desire. "I want you."

"Be more specific," he urged, maintaining the rhythmic stroking of my cock. "What do you want?"

I swallowed hard. "I want you to take your shorts off."

He almost laughed. "I figured as much. Then what?"

I searched for the right words, struggling to find any that weren't ugly or vulgar. I finally settled on, "I want you inside me."

He grinned. "And then what? What do you want me to do once I'm there?" His game was both frustrating and incredibly hot. I was equally embarrassed and turned on. "Tell me," he whispered before flicking the head of my cock with his tongue.

"Fuck me," I practically moaned.

"How?" Jax questioned further. "Tell me exactly how you want me to fuck you."

I gulped, thinking for a beat. "Slowly, at first."

"Why?"

"Because I want to feel every inch of you while you enter me," I said, finally catching on to precisely the sort of things he wanted me to say. From beneath his swim shorts, I could see his cock hard and pulsing against the fabric.

"What position?"

"On my back," I said, breathless as he whispered his next question in my ear.

"Why?"

"Because I want to kiss you while you fuck me." I slid the waistband of his shorts down, exposing his mushroom head. This time he didn't swat my hand away.

"Then what?" He asked as I started to stroke the underside of his sensitive knob.

"Then faster. Picking up speed with every thrust."

"Yeah?" He growled.

"Yes," I moaned back, exposing his erection fully.

"Then what?"

"Flip me over," I said, stroking up and down his shaft as he continued to do the same to mine. "Take me from behind."

"Hard?"

"Yes."

We stroked each other harder.

"Fast?"

"Yes."

We stroked each other faster.

"Deep?"

"Oh my god, yes." I vibrated with need.

In a breathless flurry of movement, Jax removed his shorts, grabbed the necessary supplies, then did as I'd described. He slid into me slowly, inch by inch, filling me. Then rocked his hips harder, driving himself into me faster. He impaled me deeply, staring down at me the entire time.

Sweat pooled in the hollows of my collarbone, down the center of my chest to where our bodies met. Jax kept thrusting, hard and fast until I was so close to orgasm; he could sense it in the air the way dogs could an earthquake. His face was flushed with the exertion of holding back, and I could tell he was so close to breaking. His mouth fell open, his eyes glowing deep with pure lust.

I could feel something start to pool at the bottom of my stomach. Right before I came, Jax took my hand into his own, lacing our fingers together. Then we both spasmed in an explosion of pyrotechnics that would have made the Fourth of July envious. I cried out, biting down on the pillow while he burrowed his face into my neck with his release. By the end of it, we collapsed, exhausted and euphoric, our bodies shuddering. I was a boneless, soft weight in his shaking arms. I probably couldn't remember my own name if asked.

"You are amazing," he said breathlessly.

"I didn't do anything," I laughed. My stomach was slick and sticky, my hands twisted up in Jax's sweaty surfer hair, stroking it gently. He still smelled terrific, even with the layer of sweat over his body. "I just laid there."

"You don't give yourself enough credit," he said, tapping me on the nose. "You did plenty." I closed my eyes to keep from rolling them. "Still, if you want a chance to be a more active participant, give me ten minutes, then we can go again."

I did. Then, as Jax had set a timer, precisely at the ten-minute mark, we started round two.

The next morning, I woke up alone.

I couldn't remember when Jax left, but when I thought back on all the energy we had spent on each other, I wasn't surprised he had needed to crash in his own bed.

Despite our best intentions for an early bedtime, the man had kept me up for several hours with his hands, and mouth, and a shockingly large vocabulary of dirty words. We had gone four rounds, and round four had been particularly enthusiastic. My last memory was screaming incoherently while Jax thrust behind me, and I passed out soon after returning to orbit.

A week ago, would I have believed the look on my face? The giddy, sex-sated grin I couldn't seem to wipe clean? I hadn't felt like that before; intense, free-falling happiness that didn't carry with it any unease or uncertainty. I'd never adored or felt adored by someone with such heated abandon, and something told me Jax felt the same.

I remembered, as if from a million miles away, Jax telling me once not to overthink what was happening between us, so I reminded myself to heed the suggestion. I was there to have some much-needed fun. That was it. If I enjoyed Jax's presence, there was no harm having him around for the next several days, was there? After that, we would go our separate ways, and I would probably never see him again. I wouldn't get attached. Or rather, I would try not to get more attached than I already was.

The pounding on my door came before I was equipped to handle loud noises. There was a sharpness to it I recognized instantly as Ruby before she even called her trademark greeting.

"Open up whore!"

I dragged myself out of sleep with intense effort, blinking. The room was in disarray. The blankets were piled on the floor, the sheets were barely clinging to the mattress. One of the pillows was discarded by the open balcony door, where the shining sun glared through the spotless glass, curtains wafting gently in the breeze that whispered in. It took some work to sit up and get my feet under me. A thick sex fog still hovered in my brain, and my body felt strained and bruised. It was glorious.

"Girl!" she hollered, banging once more. "I know you're in there."

I rolled my eyes even though she could not see me and quickly slipped on one of the two complimentary white robes in the closet before opening the door. Ruby rolled in like a summer storm. Her hair was let loose, dark ringlets curling past her bare shoulders, leading down to a breezy dress that looked both sexy and comfortable.

"Do I look rested?" she asked, doing a one-eighty-degree turn in the middle of the room.

"I'm sorry?" I asked, stunned. I was tired, not yet caffeinated, and positively sure it showed.

"Do I look like someone who received an adequate amount of beauty sleep last night?"

I hesitated. "Is this a trick question?"

She sat her perfectly shaped ass on the edge of my bed, crossing her legs. "You're very loud."

"Excuse me?" I instinctively tightened the robe around me.

"Kyle, we share a wall." She smiled, her full lips stretched with knowing. "I heard sounds coming from this room last night that made me blush. I'm Black. That doesn't happen easily."

"Oh, God." It occurred to me then that for an atheist, I resorted to theological references rather often.

Her eyes lit up with scandal. "What was this spot you kept asking him to hit over and over again? I wouldn't normally ask, but I heard so much about it, I feel invested." She paused. "By the way, you're bossy in bed."

"Stop talking."

"See what I'm saying? Bossy," she said curtly, then she continued her teasing. "Honestly, I felt like such a part of the action, I considered putting in my diaphragm."

I wanted to die.

"I love how offended *you* look, considering what I had to listen to last night." She teased. "I hope you both stopped to hydrate yourself because—" She whistled.

My cheeks flushed so hard, they almost hurt, and my eyes darted around the room, suddenly too mortified to look at her directly. I hoped she wouldn't see my enflamed cheeks. I knew she hadn't missed it, though. Those eyes didn't miss much.

"Calm down," Ruby rolled her eyes, then scooted back on

the bed, propping her back on the one remaining pillow. She seemed to be taking far too much joy from my embarrassment. "You should be proud. What I heard was rather impressive."

I was torn between needing to change the subject entirely and wanting to extract more information to learn precisely how much she had heard. The latter won out. "Impressive? How?"

"Linguistically," she grinned. "It was like Shakespeare. You were shouting words I had to google."

Just thinking about it, my body washed in embarrassment. "Please stop."

She smirked playfully at me. "Now, where's the fun in that?"

"You could do it to be merciful."

Ruby laughed. "I am not drunk enough for that yet."

"Ruby, it's like ten in the morning."

She wheeled on me. "He who sounds like he's re-enacting a scene from *The Exorcist* when he orgasms should not pass judgment."

Holding up my hands in defense, I told her, "Fine, sorry."

She sprang up excitedly, then hankered down onto her knees, pressing her elbows into the bed, then plopping her head onto the palms of her hands. "So, tell me the deets."

"Deets?" I repeated condescendingly.

"Whatever," she rolled her eyes again. "Details. Tell me. What is he like? It certainly sounded like he rocked your world."

"He did," I admitted blushing.

Silence gathered.

"That's all I get?" Ruby demanded. "I told you when Tommy Leer stuck it up my butt without asking."

I held up a finger. "To be fair, I didn't ask for that information."

Her eyes turned scornful. "Spill it and be poetic. I want the details to give me goosebumps."

"He is amazing," I said honestly, and her expression urged me to continue, so I did. "The way he touches me, it's like he knows exactly what I need. It's like we have been together thousands of times before. I can't even find all the words to describe it."

"Magnificent? Beautiful? You could use amazing again if you want."

"Have you ever been with somebody who makes you feel more attractive than you really are?"

"Of course not. Look at me, that's not really possible, but I can understand how *you* could feel that way."

My mouth went into a thin line. "Was there something else you needed?" I demanded, annoyed. "Or did you only pop by to insult and shame me?"

"I came here to applaud you, not shame you. Also, to tell you that if you intend on a repeat performance tonight, do us both a favor and stay in *his* room." My face flushed again. "Do you have plans today?" She asked, promptly changing the subject. "Sapphire wants to drag us to some godawful pirate museum, and I could really use someone to do something else with."

I made a face. "Pirate museum? That doesn't sound like Sapphire."

Ruby groaned. "I'm fairly sure it's Justin who wants to go. I'm not sure why he gets any say about what we do."

"Maybe because it's his honeymoon?"

"Whatever," Ruby groaned again. "So what do you say? Be my knight in shining armor and rescue me from a day of boredom?"

"I can't. I have plans with Jax."

She groaned once more. "Again? Doesn't your ass need a rest? I'm surprised you can even walk this morning."

I felt my face flush again. "Sorry." I really wasn't. "Maybe Cody will keep you company?"

She groaned a fourth time. When caused by someone else's sexual escapades, it seemed lack of sleep really made her cranky. "That man either has erectile dysfunction, or he's gay."

"Excuse me? Cody is not gay."

"Well then, you explain to me why he ignores all my advances."

"Maybe Cody simply isn't interested."

"Impossible. Any straight man with a working penis wants to put it in me."

I stifled a laugh. Ruby's confidence really was mind-boggling. "Maybe he's not interested in a casual hook-up with his best friend's sister-in-law?"

"Interesting theory. I'll give it some thought."

"You do that."

"Well, since you're abandoning me in my hour of need, I suppose I should find Sapphire and get this boring show on the road," She said, raising herself off the bed. "Enjoy your Australian."

I smiled. "I will. Thank you."

As if on cue, a knock sounded, and excitement flickered across her features. "Is that him?"

I shrugged. "It could be. Jax didn't say what time he'd stop by."

"You owe me an apology for keeping me up all night with your sexual prowess," Ruby said as she opened the door.

Jax stood there, looking like the picture of perfection. "Pardon me?" He asked in his thick accent.

"Never mind her," I assured him, stepping forward, kissing him on the cheek in greeting. "She was leaving."

"She was not," Ruby retorted. "So Jax, have you ever been with a woman?"

"Ruby!" I snarled. "If you don't behave yourself, I'm going to get you spayed."

She pouted, clamping her lips, suddenly silent. That allowed Jax the opportunity to see the state I was in.

"You're not ready?" He sighed, but his eyes remained fond.

I grimaced. "I'm sorry. Give me ten minutes. I'm going to quickly shower."

He whispered under his breath, "I could join you."

I heard him loud and clear but whispered back. "I'd love that, but that would take much longer, and you have the entire day planned." He nodded. "Ruby, can you refrain from acting like a nymphomaniac long enough to keep Jax company while I get ready?"

She looked mischievous. "I'll try, but I can't make any promises."

I turned to Jax, "I'll be quick, I assure you. If she asks you anything about your penis, you have my full permission to push her off the balcony. No one will miss her."

Ruby looked offended. "Oh, relax. I'm sure we can find something else to talk about."

As I disappeared into the bathroom with a collection of clothing under my arm. I had no doubt in my mind that the something else Ruby would talk about would be me.

TWENTY-ONE
KYLE

Dinghy's Beach Bar and Grill was a colorful and eclectic outdoor hang-out on Water Island, one of the five islands of the Virgin cluster. It had been a ten-minute water-taxi ride from the larger island of St. Thomas into Druif Bay. The restaurant was right on the surf of Honeymoon Beach. So close to the ocean that the water lapped up against our feet while we ate.

It looked like a busy evening, by my standards. Every table was in use, and there was a line-up of people waiting to get one. Those people sat in an area of lounge chairs that were set up on the adjacent beach. One could order their food to eat out there, but most people preferred a table, so most people chose to wait. We had waited an hour ourselves before a table had opened up. Yet, the bartender assured us that the wait was typically much longer.

The menu focused mostly on sandwiches and salads. There were also a few larger main dishes to choose from if you were feeling extra hungry. The prices were average, but the portions were large, and the aromas were delightful. We hadn't even placed our orders, and my mouth was already watering.

The day had comprised mostly of sightseeing. We started by exploring the island's rugged shoreline, enjoying several coral-strewn points with crystalline aquamarine water. After we stumbled across some spectacular blowholes, we investigated numerous historical sights, like Fort Christian and Bluebeard's Castle. At every junction, Jax took photos.

He didn't just snap a picture. He methodically planned each and every shot. He considered shadows, the sun's position, even the direction of the wind. He would spend several minutes at each location, playing with his camera settings and determining how best to take the photo. Sometimes he would climb to a higher vantage point. Other times, he would lay as flat on the ground as possible. It was time-consuming but intriguing to watch. Whenever he got a photo he was happy with, his entire face would ignite with a grin so wide I could count his teeth.

In the process, Jax taught me more about photography. He was practically euphoric, merely talking about it. I tried to follow along, offering generous choruses of "neat" and "cool" at all the proper intervals, but a lot of it was technical jargon that I didn't wholly comprehend. I understood some phrases like composition and aspect ratio. Still, he dropped other terms like aperture, bokeh and bracketing so quickly that by the time I attempted to ask what they meant, he'd already moved on from them.

As it turned out, some of his photos had been featured in several publications, including *Reader's Digest* and *Travel and Leisure*. Landscape photography mostly. All of his pictures had been freelance submissions, and none of them had paid particularly well. We compared notes on the trials and tribulations of working in publishing, although from entirely different perspectives.

In college, I had a reputation for being rather cultured. Mostly because I was a voracious reader with a love of political science and cultural studies. My parents had raised me on a healthy mix of bluegrass, Motown, Beatles and the Rolling Stones, so I had an intimate understanding of eclecticism from an early age. Jax had a compilation of experiences and interests equally wide-ranging, yet unique entirely to him.

I learned that Jax was obsessed with classical music and could rattle off the names of every master composer, from Amadeus to Verdi. His favorite was Tchaikovsky, which was a name I had heard of before but couldn't spell when I quickly tried to google him. Jax was also a giant fan of old westerns. The type of films that gave life to everyday expressions like, *Go ahead, make my day,* and *Do you feel lucky, punk?*

When we finally took our seats at the restaurant, all female eyes turned to us, ranging over Jax hungrily. I couldn't blame them. I had spent the bulk of the afternoon doing that myself. I was reasonably confident my eyes had burned permanent markings into his pecs and biceps.

Knowing how amazing he looked naked didn't help matters. My imagination had been nowhere near accurate enough. Sitting across from him, even at that moment, I stared at him and worked at not allowing my jaw to fall open. Flashes of him naked periodically popped into my mind, making my heart race and my cheeks rouge.

I recalled in vivid detail the way his sinewy muscles had enveloped me, so strong and secure. The warmth of his flesh pressed against mine. The salty taste of him as my tongue traveled across every last inch of his body.

I felt a twitching in my shorts and immediately tried to think of anything else.

I ordered the seafood salad, Jax ordered a burger, and the young waitress flirted shamelessly with Jax as she jotted both down on her pad. She was a pretty thing, with a sweet face, and I tried to control the irrational jealousy that her innocent flirting sparked within me.

"So," Jax started. "Did you always want to work in publishing?"

"For a brief time, I wanted to be a fireman. Then, I learned to read."

"So you always wanted to work with books?"

"No, not books specifically. I fell in love with the written word in all forms. I was infatuated with the power of words. At an early age, I knew that, no matter what I decided to do, it would revolve around words. Honestly, I considered journalism for a while, but the news depresses me. So, I knew that wouldn't be a good fit."

"Really? The news depresses you?"

"How could it not? We live in a culture of 'if it bleeds, it leads'. We seldom report on good things. Violence, assault, murder, natural disasters, car accidents — these are the things modern news thrives on. I would imagine it takes a powerful person to come face-to-face with the ugliness every day and not let it destroy you."

"So journalism was out," he said, nodding. "What made you settle on publishing?"

"I didn't settle," I could hear the defensiveness rising in my voice, even though I knew Jax meant no offense. I paused when the waitress brought our drinks, took a sip of my gin and soda, then continued. "Do you want to know what my favorite part of my job is?"

"Yes, please."

"The burn pile," I said simply, and Jax looked bewildered. "Most of the books that get published are done so because the right authors have the right agents who get the right people to read their book. Also, that book has the right plot and the right theme for the time. It's not chance or fate. It's more like a mathematical equation; A plus B plus C multiplied by D equals success."

I took another sip of my gin.

"The burn pile is all the unsolicited submissions by writers who didn't have those connections. Stories that normally wouldn't see the light of day. Whenever I have time, I like to take a manuscript from somewhere in the pile and see if I can't find a hidden treasure."

"So you're the *Indiana Jones* of literature," Jax joked, bringing his draught beer to his lips.

"Exactly," I said with a laugh. "Most of the time, manuscripts from the burn pile don't measure up. They're amateur, with cliché plot points or underdeveloped characters. Sometimes though..." I smiled, thinking about it. "Sometimes, I find a diamond in the rough."

"Then what?"

"Then, I have the opportunity to change someone's life by giving an undiscovered author a chance to share their voice. It's rewarding."

"I'm sure it is," he replied, smiling. "Still, don't you sometimes wish you were the one creating something?"

"I *do* create something," I said, my eyes wide. "I create books. They may not be my words, but I help bring those words to the world. That's just as special."

"I've never thought of it like that. I hope I didn't offend you. I certainly didn't mean to."

"It's ok. The writers get most of the glory, and I understand why. It's their art. Still, there's an entire team of people that help bring that art to the world. Do you think JK Rowling became famous simply because her stories about a young wizard were entertaining? No. It took editors, publishers, marketing strategists and publicists to make that happen. People bought her books because we told them to. Of course, now we know she's transphobic and rightfully canceled, so she may not be the best example." We both laughed, although the sound felt awkward in light of how defensive I had been. "Sorry, I get a little passionate about my work."

"Don't apologize. It's refreshing to see someone be so passionate about a job they love. Too often, people treat their jobs like something they *have* to do, instead of something they *want* to do." He paused. "Have you ever considered writing a book of your own?"

I took in a breath, considering how much to tell him. "I would like to. One day."

"Why one day? What's stopping you?"

I shrugged my shoulders. "Technically, nothing."

"So?"

"So," I considered carefully. "I know how competitive the industry is."

"And?"

"And..." I shrugged again. "I guess I'm afraid that my book would end up in the burn pile."

Jax nodded, understanding. It was one thing to rescue an author from the burn pile, but it was something else entirely to be one of those authors discarded there.

The waitress brought us our food, and we both dug in. I automatically helped myself to one of Jax's fries. He smiled, taking a forkful of my salad in exchange. Then he cut his burger down the center in case I wanted half, which was tempting. It smelled wonderful, but red meat and intercourse was a dangerous combination for a bottom. I decided I wanted Jax's cock again, more than I could ever want any burger. So I showed restraint and dived into my salad.

After a beat, I decided it was my turn to ask a probing question. "Roots or wings?"

Jax shrugged. "I don't really understand the question."

"I have a theory. I think there are two types of people in the world: those who want roots and those who want wings." Jax dipped a fry into ketchup, waiting for me to continue. "Root people crave stability. They want a home, a family and a relatively drama-free existence. They thrive on responsibility and enjoy the quiet suburban life. People like my friend Sapphire."

"And wing people want to fly free?" He guessed.

"Exactly. They thrive on excitement. They don't want to be tied down by commitments or responsibilities. They want the freedom to experience the world, even if they have to do it alone. People like my friend Ruby."

Jax tilted his head. "Can someone ever be both?"

"I think most people *are* a little of both. Ultimately though, I think there comes the point when one side wins out over the other. Or someone is forced to choose."

"Forced to?"

"Yeah," I nodded. "Let's say you're a heterosexual wing-man. You're out sowing your oats or spreading your seed, or—"

"Am I also a cockie in this scenario?"

"I don't know," I laughed. "What is a cockie?"

It was his turn to laugh. "A farmer."

"No, I'm not calling you a farmer. Why would you think that?"

"Sowing my oats, spreading my seed, plowing the fields," Jax teased, finding my unintentional theme and running with it.

I laughed harder at that, my eyes crinkling up in the corners. "Stop."

"Milking the cows," he teased again, adding a hilarious moo sound for effect.

I giggled almost incoherently. "Seriously. Stop." I placed my hand on his forearm. "You're too funny."

"*I'm* funny? You're the one who had me working the fields like it was *The Grapes of Bloody Wrath*."

"I meant, imagine you were straight and having a lot of sex."

"When did farm work become synonymous with intercourse? Is that why there's that stigma about farmhands and sheep? If you mean sex, then say sex."

"I was trying to be polite."

He leaned in close to me and whispered, "I've been inside you. We should be able to talk about sex without the use of ridiculous metaphors."

"I meant, trying to be polite to everyone else," I laughed again before taking a bite of my salad.

He looked surprised. "Why? Have they also been inside you?"

I nearly choked. "What? No. Of course not."

"Then why do they matter?" he asked with a sly grin and a wink. He had a point. Why *did* they matter? Because being gay was frowned upon on the island, I reminded myself. Then I reminded him of that fact also.

"Frowned on, but not illegal," Jax clarified. Then, he stood dramatically. "Attention, everyone!" He called. Everyone in the restaurant paused their respective dining, turning in our direction. "My date here is a little nervous, so I'm going to kiss him now to get it over with. If that bothers any of you, I'm sure you'll get over it eventually."

Then he kissed me. It was quick but poignant. Some patrons in the room cheered and applauded. Others sneered or groaned, but ultimately, he was right. They didn't matter.

I shook my head, equally embarrassed and in awe of him. "You're crazy, do you know that?"

"Why? Because I refuse to worry about how other people might react?"

I nodded. "Yes. It's a dangerous world."

"True, but it's also a short life. Too short to spend it worrying about people who don't matter." Then he kissed me again.

"Can I please get back to my original point?"

He shrugged. "If you wish. Where were you?" He didn't wait for my response. "Oh yes, I was frolicking in the pastures. Please continue."

"Anyway," I drawled, only slightly irritated. "Let's say you were a wing-man, and you got some woman pregnant. You would have to choose between starting roots or keeping your wings."

"Ah, I see." He shoved a fry into his mouth then chewed.

"A true wing-man would choose wings no matter what. While some people who think they're wing-men would actually choose roots."

"So, which one are you? Roots or wings?"

"That's not fair. I asked you first." He waited, staring at me with his ridiculously gorgeous bedroom eyes. I gave in. "I would choose roots. Always roots. There's nothing more important than family; chosen or otherwise."

Jax took a long drink of his beer. I watched him swallow several times. "I'd choose wings." I tried not to frown, and he caught it instantly. "You don't like my answer."

I tried to shrug it off. "What? No. I think your answer is fine."

He laughed. "No, you don't. You think I'm one of those

pricks who would impregnate some poor girl then fuck off, don't you?"

"Of course not," but I struggled with sincerity.

"You're a horrible liar," he wasn't wrong. I was, and I knew it. "Let me clarify. I, too, would choose family."

"You just said..."

"I know what I said," he assured me. "However, there's a fundamental problem with your theory."

"What's that?"

He popped another fry in his mouth. "Birds fall in love too. Choosing wings doesn't automatically mean you're a rogue. In fact, I would argue that love is the most fantastic adventure of all. You can have both stability and adventure if you want it."

"To stability and adventure then," I said, raising my glass. Jax clinked his beer mug against my tumbler, then we drank. When we were finished drinking, I asked. "What kind of adventure do you hope for?"

"I'm open to everything and anything," he proclaimed proudly. "Whatever it ends up being, I hope it includes more of this."

I grinned flirtatiously. "That's presumptuous of you. What makes you think I'm even available for future adventures?"

He smiled, equally flirty. "I was referring to drinks and good conversation, in general, but if you happened to be there, I wouldn't complain." He then held out a fry to me. I bit into it, playfully.

We finished our meals, then after another drink each, we paid the tab.

With still a few hours to kill before we had to be back on board the Lollipop, we decided to walk to the pier and wait for the next ferry to take us back to the larger island. We left the restaurant, starting down a cobblestone sidewalk that ran alongside the beach. Usually, I would have preferred to walk barefoot along the shoreline, but the blistering sun had transitioned into an overcast sky, and I knew my feet wouldn't dry. Wet feet and sneakers irked me as much as socks and sandals did.

"So, are you dating anyone back home?" Jax asked me.

"It's a little late to be asking that, don't you think?"

"Maybe, but you haven't answered the question."

I laughed. "If I was dating someone, do you honestly think I would have slept with you?"

He grinned. "Probably. I am pretty hot."

I laughed again. "And cocky."

"What about my cock?"

I laughed harder, but the gleam in his eyes sent a jolt of lust right to my nether regions, which jumped at the memory of his naked body. "What about you?" I tried to soothe my raging hormones. "Do you have a different man waiting in every port?"

He eyed me, amused. "Two, in some ports." Then, as though an omen, a strong wind blew. For a moment, I thought he was serious, and he could tell by my lack of laughter. "Honestly, I don't typically hook-up at all while on vacation."

I wasn't sure if I believed him, but I entertained the thought. "Why is that?"

"It doesn't feel right, most of the time. Some people get attached quickly, so it's easier not to risk anyone getting hurt."

"So, I'm special?" Another gust of wind.

"You could say that," he said, biting his bottom lip in a very sexy way. "Honestly, I felt immediately comfortable with you, like I already knew you. Even when you looked like a crazy person, covered in cake. I knew right away; you were someone I could have a good time with, and it wouldn't be complicated."

I guessed that was a good thing, although I wasn't sure exactly what he meant. A guy covered in champaign and frosting, harboring a bitter feud against his ex, screamed complicated to me. The fact that he didn't normally hook-up, or at least claimed not to, made him appear even more attractive to me. If that were possible.

The cobblestone walkway came to a fork. "So you and your mate Sapphire are pretty close, huh?" Jax asked, leading me to the left, downhill, toward a large park area.

I nodded. "Best friends since the day we met. More like siblings, actually. We do everything together."

"Everything?" He questioned with a suggestive tone.

I reconsidered. "Well, no, not *everything*, but most things."

"Such as?"

"Dinners, parties, birthdays," I listed. "We haven't even taken separate vacations since at least our early twenties."

He seemed surprised. "Really? You don't ever get crook of each other?"

I shook my head. "Never. In fact, this vacation, we've spent hardly any time together at all, and I've missed her."

"Justin doesn't mind you monopolizing so much of his wife's time?"

"If he does, he's never said anything. Besides, Sapphire's a lot to take sometimes. She's a strong personality. It's probably good for their relationship that I take her off his hands so often."

"You don't ever disagree about where to go or what to do?"

"No. I let Sapphire choose the destinations. I'm usually pretty happy with her selections. She gets me to go places and do things I wouldn't normally choose for myself."

"Such as?" He asked again.

"Well," I considered. "One time, Sapphire convinced me to try surfing."

"Oh? How did that go?"

"Terrible!" I nearly screamed. "It was one of the worst experiences of my life."

"Oh? Tell me."

"Spring break, our sophomore year in college," I began, "Sapphire wanted nothing more in life than to go to Hawaii and learn to surf. I'm quite sure she got the idea from a movie and had romanticized the shit out of it. What college student has enough money to go to Hawaii?"

"I bloody-well didn't."

"We could have learned to surf in Southern California, for much less, but Sapphire was determined. When she gets an idea in her head, there's no talking her out of it. So, of course, I put the entire trip on my line of credit. Which is what you do when you're twenty-years-old and don't give a shit."

"Of course."

"So, our second day there, she dragged me out of bed at five-in-the-morning because she read somewhere that the best time for surfing was sunrise. So there we were Sapphire, the instructor and me. Who by-the-way, looked like he was about a hundred-years-old." I paused to take a breath. "No one warned me about marine life."

"Why would someone have to warn you? It was the ocean."

"Look," I said, bobbing my head with attitude. "I was born

and raised in Chicago. The only thing we have in Lake Michigan is garbage and bass. No one told me I had to watch out for jellyfish."

"Oh no!"

"Oh yes!" I hissed. "We were coming back into shallow water, and I had just hopped off the surfboard when I felt an excruciating pain on the inside of my left thigh."

Jax contorted like he had experienced that pain himself. Growing up in Australia, he likely had.

"I immediately screamed bloody murder, abandoning the surfboard and running onto the beach. When I got out of the water, my entire leg felt like someone had doused it in battery acid, and it was eating through to my bones. I thought I was going to die."

Jax gaped at me. "What did you do?" I made an expression that signified something repulsive was to follow. "Oh no."

"Oh yes!" I hissed again.

His eyes went wide. "You're not actually supposed to—"

"I didn't know that! Neither did our so-called instructor. Which goes to show how unreliable an instructor he really was." I used air quotes around the word instructor. "Anyway, there I was, laying on one of the most beautiful beaches in the world, in agony, while a hundred-year-old-looking surfer dude peed on me."

Jax laughed incredulously. "How intimate. I hope he bought you brekkie afterward."

"Very funny," I replied dryly.

Composing himself, Jax said. "So even after all that, you still trust Sapphire's judgment?"

"With my life."

He lifted his chin to me. "That's awesome. I'm glad to hear that. She and her husband seem like good people."

"They are," I assured him. "Justin is a little quiet, even a little stand-offish from time to time, but he'd take a bullet for me if I needed him to."

"Let us hope you never need him to. Correct me if I'm wrong, but he and your ex are twins?"

"Unfortunately," I replied sardonically.

"How's that going?"

"How's what going?" I asked, suddenly panicked. "Things

with Dustin?" Jax nodded. For a moment, I was tempted to be honest and tell him about Dustin's proposition but quickly decided against it. Jax and I only had a few more days together. I didn't want to taint the time we had left. "It's going alright. Things started off pretty rocky, as you know, but we agreed to an armistice. It seems to be holding."

"That's big of you."

"Don't go awarding me the peace prize quite yet," I said with a laugh. "There's still a lot of vacation left. Anything could still happen."

"I bloody-well don't envy you. I don't know if I could do it."

"It actually hasn't been that bad. It helps to have a handsome distraction," I leaned in closer, bumping Jax with my shoulder. "Honestly, I've actually found myself enjoying it once or twice."

"You have?" He raised a brow. "Should I be jealous?"

His question landed with a heavy thud, like a boulder crushing my spine. We had only known each other a week. I didn't owe him the feeling of guilt that suddenly festered within me. After all, there was no long-term possibility between us. When the cruise was over, we'd likely never see each other again. Jax didn't need to know the complicated triangle taking shape between Dustin and me.

"Of course not," I laughed. "I mean, Dustin is still the devil." Was he, though? I was no longer sure. "Besides," I added, "the vacation fling can't get jealous, can he?"

"I guess that's true," Jax's expression revealed nothing, but his tone suggested he was leaving something unsaid.

We *were* just having a vacation fling, weren't we? I flinched a little when I felt the first light, cool sprinkle hit my forehead. "It's raining," I said, wiping the droplet of water from my skin.

Jax looked skyward. "I don't feel anything." Then, as if on cue, the skies opened up and began to pour. Not merely a light summer shower. No. It was a torrential tropical storm that had the old walkway immediately flooding where it dipped lower on the terrain. We looked around for the closest shelter, but there were no storefronts or restaurants nearby.

Thunder rumbled, and lightning flashed across the sky.

We were both already drenched. Our clothes clung to us tightly, Jax's white shirt made nearly sheer from the downpour.

He grabbed my hand as we scurried hastily down the hill towards a large gazebo. Sheets of rain and gusts of wind whipped up as we ran. In our haste, I skidded on a slippery patch of mud, toppling forward, chest first into the muck. My hand was holding onto Jax's tightly, which pulled him down into the sludge with me. We tumbled and rolled together down the hill. I reached the bottom first, then Jax landed on top of me with a solid mass. If there was pain, neither of us registered it.

Jax looked down at me, and I tensed, worried he might have been angry that I had pulled him down into the mud. Instead of a frown, he was actually fighting a giggle. Immediately I relaxed, and we broke into laughter together.

He hovered over me, wet and muddy but still gorgeous. Beads of rainwater trickled down his face and onto mine. I walked some flirty fingers up his chest, feeling the veritable wall of muscle under his wet t-shirt. In turn, Jax brought his hands up to gently hold my face in both palms, tracing my cheekbones with the wet pads of his thumbs.

The rain was still falling hard, but we didn't care.

I reached out, carefully sweeping several strands of wet hair across his forehead. Jax looked down at me with such intensity that I froze with my fingers near his temple. He licked his lips, and fire erupted in my belly. I felt like I could barely get enough oxygen. The rapid rise and fall of his chest told me his breathing was accelerated as well.

His hands still cradling my face, Jax drew his mouth up to a breath away from mine. I could hear him swallow, and I wanted to follow the sound. Then he tilted my chin, kissing me once, slowly.

I gave in to it utterly. My eyes fell closed with a soft moan, and for a moment, we forgot the rain entirely. The kiss felt completely different from the kiss at the restaurant. It even felt different from the ones that came the night before. It was tender and light, like feathers moving slowly, gently across my mouth. Dancing against and tickling my lip. It felt intimate and affectionate, and it left me wanting more. Another low moan vibrated in the marrow of my bones.

I felt him pull away. When I opened my eyes, I found him standing before me, his arm outstretched. I took it, then he pulled me to my feet with ease.

"There is an incredibly long list of naughty things I want to do to you," he said, pulling me into a deep embrace. His arms came around my waist, pulling me into the heat of his chest. A shiver of thrill traveled down my spine.

His mouth moved up my neck, sucking. His hand slid beneath my shirt, coming to a warm stop over my belly button. "Do you feel adventurous?" he asked, whispering into my ear.

Heat engulfed whatever words should have been in my head. All I could manage was a simple nod of agreement. The idea of Jax doing extensive, hot things to my body laced with the thrill of potentially being caught made everything inside me turn to mud.

"Come with me," he ordered, taking my hand. I allowed him to without any hesitation like it was the most natural thing in the world. He led me slowly to the gazebo. We were already soaking and muddy, so there was little need to run any longer.

When we stepped inside the covered area, the scent of damp oak overpowered my senses. The gazebo was large and solid with high walls that came up to half the building's height on all but one side. The storm had frightened off all of the tourists, and the park was entirely vacant. We'd have more than enough privacy. A jolt of desire sped through my body.

We didn't speak. Jax pulled me close, kissing me deep and passionate. He pressed his body against mine, and I could feel his erection already hard against my belly. I closed my eyes, letting everything happen, turning off that little voice inside my head that told me that the behavior was dangerous or wrong.

I didn't care that someone could have interrupted us at any moment. I only knew that we wanted each other and that our bodies felt perfect together. Jax knelt on both knees, then pulled me gently down to him, his hands expertly removing my shirt as he did so.

He removed his own shirt then pulled me closer, pressing our wet, naked torsos together. He kissed me, his lips moving down my chin, my neck and my chest, before finding my right nipple and taking it in between his teeth. I gripped his shoulders, biting my lip while he sucked at it, the sensations making me squirm with delight.

His hand roamed down to my waist, then even lower, cupping my manhood through my shorts, rubbing firmly. Up, down and around, his palm moved, causing my erection to grow and pulsate beneath his touch. My eyes closed in satisfaction as he moved to the other nipple with his lips and his tongue tugged at it as urgently as he did the first.

I moaned hungrily.

We slid out of the remainder of our damp clothes, discarding them haphazardly around us. When we were both fully naked, we laid together, both on our sides, holding each other, enjoying the tenderness of our kissing.

I moved my hand down between us, where his beautiful cock was long, thick and ready. Needing to taste him, I broke away from his embrace, inching my way down his body. In anticipation of what was to come, Jax rolled onto his back. I took his thick cock into my fist and lapped the head, glancing up at him to catch his eye. I watched him, watching me take the head into my mouth. The look of sheer pleasure that crossed his features like a sunrise made me want to do it again and again.

So I did.

I stroked his shaft while I tongued the head of his cock, swirling it around the rim. Then I took him fully, deep inside my wet, cavernous mouth. Up and down, I moved as far and as fast as I could take him. With his hand on my head to guide me, I found a rhythm with no trouble at all. Jax helped me keep it by pumping his hips forward each time my mouth moved downward.

Eventually, he pulled me up by my shoulders. He kissed me deep and fervently before pushing me backward against the hardwood of the gazebo floor. When his mouth found my pulsating erection, a vibration of rapture hummed through me. He was still sucking my cock when he slipped one finger inside me, then another. I nearly cried out. I gasped at the sensation of his index and middle fingers preparing me for what I hoped was to come next.

He rose up, leaning over me. Gazing into my eyes, he kissed me, tenderly cradling my chin with one hand while reaching into his back pocket with the other. I couldn't stifle the chuckle that escaped me when he revealed the silver Trojan.

"You came prepared." I giggled.

"The first rule of scouting, always be prepared."

"You were a Boy Scout?"

He nodded but didn't answer the question outright. Instead, he kissed me again. I could tell his desire by the ravenous way his mouth devoured mine.

When he finally slid his length inside me, I was more than ready. We never broke eye contact, while slowly, inch by inch, he filled me. When he was fully submerged in my hollow, my eyes squeezed shut. I focussed on the sensation of him filling me. It felt so good, I couldn't help but groan as he started to pump slowly in and out of my body.

While he thrust, slowly, deliberately, his hand slipped down between my thighs to play with my scrotum. I writhed beneath him, knowing it wouldn't take long for me to reach orgasm. He slammed into me, thrusting harder, faster, and I knew he was almost there as well.

"I'm going to," I said, breathless, the pleasure rising, sending me close to the edge.

Jax leaned in, pressing his finger against my lips to stop me from speaking. "Just enjoy it. Enjoy me inside you."

I tried not to say a word, but the pleasure grew to an incredible peak. With Jax inside of me, I orgasmed hard, the pleasure almost blinding me. Ecstasy shuddered through my body from my core down my legs and up into my chest.

The spasms of my body around his cock, sent Jax over the edge as well. I felt him twitch inside me, then he too was in the throes of orgasm. His thrusts slowed while he groaned, grunting through the pleasure. Then he collapsed against me, his arms on either side of my shoulders, his face close to mine. With my face nestled against his shoulder, I could smell his hair. The distinct fragrance of citrus conditioner blended with the sweet smell of fresh rain and the musk of our union.

We laid there, spent, longer than we probably should have, listening to the pitter-patter of raindrops colliding with the rafters that sheltered us. I could have laid there for an eternity, lulled to sleep by the symphony of the tropical storm mixed with Jax's breathing.

I was surprised and pleased with myself. I had never done anything quite that adventurous before. I was reasonably sure I wouldn't have done so either, with anyone other than Jax. He brought out something in me that I had no idea existed. A sexual appetite that demanded gratification.

Eventually, the euphoria wore off, and we remembered where we were. We redressed, our clothes no dryer than they were when we'd discarded them. When we were dressed and ready, Jax took my hand in his, bringing it to his lips in a gesture I'd only seen in old movies. Then we made our way back up the hill and to the cobblestone walkway.

The rain had started to slow, and tourists had begun to emerge from where they had sought shelter. Some people stared as we walked by, some smiled, some even scowled or whispered under their breath. We didn't care. We walked on.

We walked hand-in-hand all the way back to the pier.

Through the rain.

TWENTY-TWO
KYLE

The next two days were spent at sea, and they became a whirlwind of room service and orgasms. We secluded ourselves in Jax's room, far enough from Ruby's eavesdropping and Dustin's disconcerting presence. Usually, I was terrified at the notion of spending the night with a new romantic interest. I mean, what if he had to go to the bathroom? What if he farted in his sleep? Or worse. What if I did? Surprisingly, those fears never reared their ugly heads.

The one fear that did present itself was the fear that we were far too loud. I was positive Jax's neighbors could hear every enthusiastic chorus of the songs, *Yes! Fuck me harder!* and *I'm coming!* that we played on repeat. We paused periodically, only to refuel and shower our tired bodies. Still, the latter felt like a fruitless venture since we resumed our passionate, sweat-inducing marathon immediately afterward. We spent hours upon hours with his naked body connected to mine, punctuated by stretches of easy conversation and remarkably intimate silence.

On Friday, we thought we'd save time by showering together. That was already a challenging feat in a space the size of an airplane lavatory. Yet, once that glass shower door closed and our bodies were confined together in that two-square-feet of space, the last thing either of us wanted to do was bathe.

The moment I turned the showerhead on, Jax's lips connected with mine like a bolt of lightning. His tongue slipping into my mouth to tangle with mine. Like ivy, I wound around him in response. My arms twined around his neck, my fingers twisting in his hair, my body curving into his.

A low moan rumbled up his throat as his body arched over me—one hand on the curve of my neck, the other crushing me to him. Demand burned from Jax, searing me everywhere we touched. Slowly, his hand drifted down my hip, down my thigh, trailing fire in the wake of his fingertips until he swept his hand around the hard rod between my legs.

A jolt burst through me from the point of contact to every

limb, and I gasped into his mouth, but he didn't relent. My sharp breath melted into a groan as he began to stroke the length of me. My body felt completely at Jax's command, and I braced my back against the fiberglass wall. His hand worked me over, slick and frictionless with the help of the cascading water. I breathed deep and loud through my nose, the air hot and steamy from the shower, filling my lungs.

All the while, his lips devoured mine until I broke away with a sheer need to look at him fully. He was so beautiful, the fullness of his lips, the sweetness of him on my tongue. When he thumbed my bottom lip, I felt the gesture deep in my chest.

"God, you're gorgeous," I breathed, my chest tight with desire.

I reached out my hand to grasp his cock the way he held mine, but he swatted my hand away. "No," he whispered against my collarbone, his hand keeping pace as he jacked me. "This is all about you. We can take care of me later." My body sang with his every word.

Since he wouldn't let me grab his dick, I reached my arms around him, caressing the curves of his hot ass, squeezing and kneading the meaty flesh. "Please," I gasped, not knowing what I was begging for but knowing he was the only one who could give it to me.

Jax pressed the weight of his body against me. His own member hard against my thigh as he tightened his grip on mine. "Come," he whispered, stroking me with more pressure and intent.

Heat surged through me as my body responded to his command like a recruit would a drill sergeant. Every molecule in my body flexed and spasmed, and I exploded in a hot rush of milk. Then my body went limp, though my heart still galloped in my chest.

Destroyed, I slumped forward, lowering my forehead to the curve where his shoulder met his neck, my breath nothing more than punctuated gasps. He stroked my wet hair briefly before tilting my head upwards to kiss him once, twice, three times more.

Afterward, we changed back into shorts, but no shirts, and laid a blanket and some pillows out on the balcony. Jax leaned back against my bare chest, my arms wrapped around him, and we engaged in intimate chatter while watching the sunset.

"We could go to the comedy club tonight," I suggested.

"We could," he agreed, trailing a lazy finger up and down my arm, which held him. There was something about his tone that suggested that as much as he would have been willing to do it, it wasn't at the top of his list of desires.

"Or?"

"Or I could take you to the bed right now and have my way with you."

All of my internal organs turned to goo at his words. I shook my head at him as warmth bloomed in my chest. "Already? I only just dried off from our shower expedition."

He playfully bopped me on the nose with his pointer finger. "What can I say? It left me wanting more."

Before I could even form words to respond, Jax's hands were suddenly buried in my tight red locks. His lips on mine again demanded and took every bit of me he wanted, unable to control his hunger. I reciprocated his urgency, as consumed by desire as he seemingly was. Kissing him like I'd been starved for him all my life, my lips trailed down his neck, my teeth grazing his flesh, and Jax couldn't contain the soft moan that broke free. He angled his neck to receive more of my biting kisses, and I gladly fulfilled his tacit plea.

We couldn't get close enough, our torsos twisting awkwardly from our positions on the balcony. Jax purred into my mouth, the sound triggering a succession of firing nerves from my lips to my crotch. We slowly began to rise up off the balcony floor and made our way back inside, but we never stopped kissing or touching. We tumbled jointly onto the soft mattress, laughing together. Then we quickly removed our thin layer of clothing and rolled into place before resuming our emphatic kissing.

My lips rained down on his skin, inching their way down his jaw to the crook of his neck. They suckled there for only a few seconds, but when they moved on, they left a small cluster of purple dots in their wake.

I pushed him onto his back, straddling him like a cowboy would a stallion. My palms moved down his hard chest and abs. He flexed and released under my touch—his body at my complete disposal. My fingertips explored his body, committing every curve, every line to memory as though he were an ancient map to a cache of solid gold. He smiled up at me, his lips already swollen from our kissing, his body hard and long underneath me. If I knew it would be my last vision, I would have given up my eyesight happily.

Scooting lower on the bed until I was no longer straddling him, I urged his legs apart with the subtle pressure of my hands. I took a comfortable kneeling position in the V of his open legs, then licked down his abs. My movement was slow and tantalizing, my tongue leaving a wet trail behind, before placing several delicate kisses over the soft flesh of his lower stomach. Jax rose his hips in offering, and I buried my face in the sweetness of his meat. I licked up and down his shaft, sucked on his perfect head, even nibbled playfully on his scrotum.

I wanted to feast on his flesh, devour him whole, take my pleasure by giving him pleasure. Jax didn't have to speak. He didn't have to tell me he liked it or ask me to keep going. He hummed, gasped and muttered sweet words of profanity under his breath, which only fuelled me on. It sent a spiraling tremor down my spine and directly to the deep throb between my legs.

His hips rolled against me, but I didn't relent. I fucked the hard length of him with the warmth of my mouth. His hands tangled in my hair, clutching my short strands like reins. His grip tightened each time I took him entirely in my mouth and swirled my tongue around his submerged shaft. I didn't want to stop. I took him deeper until my lips pressed solidly against his scrotum. I moved up and down the length of him harder, faster, drawing the orgasm out of him.

"I want you inside me," he moaned, and it took me by surprise. I had topped only a handful of times in my life. Typically the men I dated preferred to be the ones doing the pounding. So it took a moment to register his request.

"Are you sure?" I asked. "I don't do it very often. What if I'm not good at it?"

"Practice makes perfect," he drawled low and sexy. "Fuck me, Kyle," he whispered. I found his eagerness and vulnerability intoxicating.

Dustin had refused to let me fuck him. Ever. He was a total top, and even the suggestion of a role reversal was instantly laughed away as preposterous. It took a long time to realize that his dismissal was never about me or my sexual prowess. It was a matter of trust. Now, Jax laid before me, ready to accept me into him, with a level of confidence I wasn't sure I deserved, but I wanted to be worthy of it. I wanted to be worthy of him.

With a nervous growl, I hooked my arm around him and twisted, guiding him onto his stomach. The mattress jostled from the movement, and he laughed at my unexpected display of masculinity.

My cock ached. I stroked it once before guiding it to Jax's waiting passage, teasing him several moments, sliding it up and down the thin line where his cheeks met. Then, I explored his cavern with my fingertips—one finger at first, then a second. I plunged into the warmth of his cavity, and it welcomed my fingers freely, opening up and stretching around my digits. While my fingers explored him in more depth, I leaned in to drag the width of my tongue up the line of his spine, and the sweat of his body tingled against my tastebuds. Jax released a hiss of pleasure.

Reaching for the condom with one hand, I grabbed his ass and spread it with the other. I throbbed almost painfully as I rolled the latex sheath down my rod. Jax complied wordlessly when I kicked his legs further apart with my knee. Holding his cheeks apart with my one hand and holding my cock in the other, I brought the tip of me to his hollow, pressing until my crown slowly slipped inside. My body shook from his tightness as he stretched and formed, then finally relaxed around my girth. With my palm low on his back, I anchored myself. Once I was steady, I brought my hands to his waist, gripping tight and holding fast.

My eyes locked on the point where our bodies met as I flexed my hips, pulled his, then felt the heat of him swallow me whole. My breath became hot and ragged as I thrust deep into him. Slowly at first, until I found a pace and a rhythm we were both happy with.

"Fuck! That feels so fucking good!" The words sizzled in my ears and seemed to echo in my mind until I realized the words were coming from me. I groaned, pulling out once, then slamming back into him.

His shoulders pressed into the mattress. When I thrust again, I leaned into the motion, reaching down, clamping my hand around his shaft. I began stroking.

"Oh fuck yeah," Jax moaned.

I stroked him and pounded simultaneously, pleasuring him from both ends. Beads of sweat started to gather at my temples.

"Harder!" Jax commanded.

As requested, I pulled out, then hammered into him with so much power, the smack of our skin making contact echoed through the room. I did so again and again and again. Until I felt that glorious tingle edging its way from the bottom of me. It was too soon for my shaft to throb and swell that way, too soon to come, too soon to lose control, so I reduced my speed.

I slid in and out in a steady slow wave that was meant to buy me time, but control was already too far out of my grasp to reign back in. I could feel my mounting orgasm encroaching whether I want it to arrive or not. Jax's ass muscles flexed around me, and my cock pulsed in answer. His hands twisted in the sheets as I jacked his staff and pumped into him simultaneously.

Bursts of color flashed in my mind with every sensation. Jax buried his head in the pillow, stifling a groan. Lowering my chest to him, my hips hammered as I pressed tender kisses to the back of his neck and shoulder blades.

"Come," I whispered, stroking him harder. I refused to climax until we could do so together. Jax gasped, his fingers gripping the sheets with more urgency. "Come," I commanded again, slamming my throbbing cock deep into him while stroking his faster. "I want you to come with me."

Then he did with a masculine grunt. His body flexed, his mouth twisted, his lungs seized, his shoulders trembled, and then his cream rushed forth in three intense pulses. I took that as an invitation to let go and enjoy my own release. I thrust a few more times, deep and determined. Once. Twice. Three times. Then a hot, throbbing surge rushed through me, and I came with an intensity I'd seldom felt before.

I collapsed on his back, and we both fell to the mattress. My lips grazed his shoulders and his neck before I found my own section of the bed, then we rolled to face each other. He tucked into my chest, kissed my throat, sighed his contentment, our arms entangling together in a mutual embrace.

Our bodies fit perfectly, like the joining of two magnets. One of Jax's legs rested between my thighs, our chests pressed together, our mouths mere inches away from each other. We kissed, the sweet, tender kisses of afterglow. Holding Jax, looking into his eyes, I felt a flickering flame ignite in my heart. I tried to ignore it as we fell asleep, cradled in each other's arms.

Saturday was a repeat of Friday. We woke up to the sun's blazing warmth, made-out lazily for an hour or so, ate breakfast, then fucked. We stopped long enough for me to have lunch with Sapphire, where I nibbled on lettuce cups, and she regaled me with tales of honeymoon bliss. I'd invited Jax to come with, of course, but he had elected to spend the hour taking photos on the promenade deck instead. Before I returned to Jax's suite, I made a pitstop at my own, to gather a change of clothes—not that I had any intention of wearing them.

When I returned to our den of iniquity, Jax was already there waiting for me. Hard. So, of course, we fucked again. Afterward, we played cards on the balcony for an hour. I blew him right before we ordered dinner, then after dessert, we fucked for the third time before taking a nap.

When I woke, the room was dark. The sun had set, and we had quite literally screwed the day away. I'd never had sex like that before, with an insatiable hunger that couldn't be sautéed. Although it was really no surprise. Jax knew precisely how to fill me with desire. He knew what he wanted and, even more importantly, what *I* wanted. Out of the ether, he pulled my most secret desires, knowing what would please me better than I did.

I opened my eyes and blinked, noticing the open balcony doors and the curtains flowing in the wind. Then I rolled over to confirm what I already sensed. Jax was still sleeping soundly, curled up on his side, facing away from me. I liked waking up next to somebody. More specifically, I really enjoyed waking up next to Jax. It felt remarkably natural. Merely being in proximity to him brought a smile to my face. Reaching out, I followed the jagged line of his spine with my fingers. I trailed up and down the ridges as though they were a braille map of his body.

Vaguely, I remembered telling myself that I wasn't going to build an attachment. Yet, watching Jax sleep, I felt the stirring of something in the hollows of my chest. The small act of watching him, a man I had barely known a week, felt much more intimate than it should have.

I knew, objectively, that I should check myself. Nip whatever I thought I was feeling in the bud before it had a chance to smother me like a weed did a garden. It was only physical, wasn't it? I was no longer sure.

There were so many things about Jax I found adorable, admirable and irresistible. Like the way he bit his lower lip when he was thinking. Or the way he always seemed so calm and confident. The way he knew how attractive he was but still remained humble. The way he held open doors for people and knelt down to talk directly to children instead of hovering over them. The way his strong hands and elegant fingers caressed me with hunger and tenderness in equal measure. The way he wasn't afraid to be himself, openly and without fear. Of course, I loved the way he could make me feel like the most important person in the room with simply a glance and a smile. Lastly, I had to admit, I was kind of obsessed with the way he chuckled right after climaxing.

Turning back to my side of the bed, I decided not to overthink it, or more accurately, *try* not to. My movement must have jostled Jax awake because he pressed his aroused body against my back a few moments later. I pretended to notice at first, but when Jax reached around to fondle me, it became increasingly difficult to fake. I pressed my ass against his erection, and with that invitation, Jax started grinding against me.

Like teenagers, we dry-humped for several erotic minutes until he pulled me on top of him. I straddled his hips, my knees on either side of his, and I leaned down to kiss him, looking into his eyes. I could feel him smiling against my lips.

I moved my mouth lower, pressing it against his well-developed pecs, his washboard abs, then even further down. His cock was already hard and dripping. I licked him from base to tip before taking the head into my mouth.

"Hmm, Kyle, that feels so good." I smiled inside, thoroughly enjoying that I could please him so well.

Jax pulled me up from his lap, so we could kiss once more. I cupped his jaw, running my fingers through his hair while our tongues explored each other. The kiss seemed endless, and my body grew more aroused with every second.

His hand groped me, taking my left nipple between his

thumb and forefinger. In turn, I slid mine around his cock, pressing it against my opening, my lust growing as I teased his body. He reached over to his shaving bag on the other side of the bed, pulling out a condom, then handing it to me. I opened the package, then he leaned back on his hands as I unrolled it over his thick member.

"Ride me," he said in a husky voice.

I moved up, positioning myself over him. Jax held his erection in one hand, and I lowered down onto him, gasping as he filled me up, inch by glorious inch. I steadied myself, enjoying the sensation of this hard thickness filling me up so completely. He pushed his hips up, filling me even more deeply. Then he took my member in his hand and began to stroke. A jolt of pleasure coursed through me.

"I won't take long," I gasped. I was so ready. I knew that if Jax continued to stroke me as I rode him, I'd quickly go over the edge.

"Neither will I," he admitted, stroking me faster as I rose up and down on his throbbing post. Already the pleasure was so great, I closed my eyes, biting my lip.

"Open your eyes," he said, his voice demanding. "I want to see you see me."

I did as he instructed. Our gazes burned deep into each other as I moved on him. Jax continued to stroke me, matching his pace to the rise and fall of my ass. Each second drove me closer to orgasm. I rode him faster. Harder. Our joined bodies bounced on the mattress like it was a trampoline. His hand moved up and down on my shaft while he moved in and out of my hole. Our breaths quickened, but we never broke eye contact.

I gasped as the pleasure built inside of me. "I'm going to," I said, my eyes closing despite my best attempt to keep them open. "I'm going to—"

My body tensed as my orgasm started. Waves of pleasure spread up into my belly and down my thighs, making me shudder.

"Don't stop," he ordered. He brought his hands around to cup my ass cheeks, then took control of my movement. With his help, I continued to rise and fall on him. I placed my hands on his chest, inches away from the mess I'd made on his stomach. Soon he grunted in pleasure while his own orgasm began.

"Oh fuck," he groaned, his body quivering. He willed his eyes to stay open to meet mine. When our bodies had quit spasming, he laid back, and I collapsed on top of him, practically fluttering inside.

We laid there, swathed in the bliss of having climaxed together.

I wasn't usually a swooner. When it came to men, I was more than often indifferent, border lining on frigid. Jax was different. I came alive under him, on top of him, and inside him.

When Jax smiled, it was worse, or better, depending on how I thought of it. My entire body felt bathed in the glow of him. Like a blinding, warm light emanated from his pores. The feeling reminded me of Christian paintings of virgins and saints and the shining crowns worn by those religious figures. That was fitting, since several times, during the height of our passion, Jax had me screaming the name of God so loudly, the entire room felt consecrated.

After we cleaned up, we returned to the bed. Snuggling close, we watched a few black and white films playing on one of the ship's limited satellite stations. *It Happened One Night*, immediately followed by *The Philadelphia Story*. To some, staying inside, watching television may have seemed like a complete waste of a fabulous vacation. Especially considering the many activities the ship had to offer. To me, it felt like doing anything else would have been a charade—a pointless waste of time.

Going out, meeting up with Sapphire or Ruby, laughing it up, dancing and getting slightly drunk, all paled in comparison to what I was doing at that exact moment. I was entirely, inescapably caught up in Jax, and I wanted to enjoy every single moment of him that I could, while I could. Why would I need liquor when Jax was more intoxicating? Why would I need to dance when our bodies were capable of much more pleasurable forms of expression?

I felt like an addict, obsessed with the high, with the lightness I felt. I wanted to stay forever, sailing aimlessly across the aqua blue waters of the Caribbean. To lay in bed with Jax for eternity, listening to the ocean while we fell asleep, cradled in each other's arms. I wanted to escape into the world of sunshine and romance until the end of time. Who needed to work? I could sublet my apartment and live on the open water. Did I really need to see my parents again? Sure, I'd miss them, but I could send postcards. I could write, couldn't I? I knew it was a silly fantasy, but it was one of the more tempting ones.

"Do you think we could stay here forever?" I asked Jax, speaking my fantasies aloud.

His one hand rested on the pillow while the other trailed gently across my back. "We can try, but we may need to eat or use the bathroom at some point."

I chuckled lightly. "I don't mean here in bed, silly. I mean here, on vacation. I don't ever want to go back to real life."

"What's so wrong with real life?" He asked, turning to grab his camera off the nightstand. When he returned to his position on the bed, he started playing with the switches.

I rested my head on his chest, listening to the steady thrum of his heartbeat, playing with the wisps of hair that lived there. "For starters, it's not eternally eighty-seven degrees." I could feel his chest rise and fall beneath me, and something inside me uncoiled. It felt so natural with him like I could say or share anything.

It was unlike any relationship I'd experienced before. New relationships, even flings, were notoriously stressful, exhausting, and uncertain. Things with Jax were easy, fun, effortless and comfortable. Still, with that comfort came the awareness of how fast everything was evolving. It was almost dizzying. I heard words bubbling up and out of my throat, ones I couldn't believe I was saying out loud. "I'm going to miss you."

I felt immediately vulnerable and instantly regretted it, but Jax leaned in to kiss me. When he was only half an inch away, he said, "I'm right here."

"I know," I replied almost in a whisper. "Still, when the ship docks, we might never see each other again."

"Well," Jax breathed. "I've meant to tell you something." I stiffened, automatically shifting into defense mode. "I've lined up some work in Chicago."

A mixture of alarm and excitement went off in my head like fireworks. If he had taken a job in Chicago just for me, after knowing me a week, that would have been a little too serial killer, stalker-esque for comfort. Jax must have sensed my sudden trepidation. He was far more intuitive than anyone I'd met before.

He kissed my nose. "Don't panic. I already had things set in motion before I met you and just received word this afternoon that the job got the green light. I didn't mention it before because you didn't strike me as the type to believe in coincidence."

He was absolutely right. I didn't believe in coincidence as a rule, but I tried to contain my natural cynicism. "So you and I will actually be living in the same city?" My heart took off at a gallop as the reality of that prospect settled in.

He kissed me again, moving his mouth to my cheek, my jaw, then my neck. "For as long as the work holds out." The sheer awesomeness of his words was enough to set off a flare gun of joy over my head.

"How long would that be?"

"Hard to say. It could be a while," Jax kissed me again.

"Then what?"

"Then I'd probably go wherever there's work."

My heart sank a little. Where would that leave me? I wanted to ask, but I swallowed the words. It was not the time nor the place. It likely never would be. I had no claim to him after only ten days, and I knew that. If the work dried up, he would go where it could be found, and we would go our separate ways. That had always been the original plan. Was continuing to see each other even wise given that truth? Was it only prolonging the inevitable ending? The questions caused a pang in my chest, and I tried to ignore it. It was an emotion I didn't want to allow myself to feel.

"Would you go back to Australia?"

He wasn't fazed by the question. "Maybe, at some point. Have you ever been?"

"I've never wanted to," I said, in a complete knee-jerk response. Jax frowned, then looked back toward his camera. "It's just," I explained, pulling his face back to mine, "I've seen the pictures of all those strange and deadly creatures you have there. Giant spiders and enormous bats. Essentially everything on that continent is gargantuan and trying to kill you."

He laughed heartedly, bringing his arms up around my

shoulders to squeeze me to his chest. "You exaggerate. It's perfectly safe."

I grunted, unconvinced.

His face was soft and amused. "One day, I'll prove it to you. We'll go there, and you'll love it."

Elation filled my chest, making me feel as buoyant as the ship we were on. Jax spoke with such certainty. Like there wasn't a single doubt in his mind that we would continue to explore what was happening between us once we hit the mainland. Like there wasn't a single hesitation that we would be together long enough to plan another vacation.

Jax must not have realized the implications of what he had said because a brief but distinct expression of uncertainty flashed across his features. "That was presumptuous of me," he said slowly. "I suppose I should start by asking if you would even be interested in continuing to see me once we get back to real life."

I tried not to grin because the idea made me incredibly happy. The notion of us becoming a real couple sent a surge of excitement through me. I tried to contain it by responding sardonically. "I thought we were just a vacation fling. I'm not sure if I want anything more permanent."

"You're a wanker," he said, playfully spanking my ass.

"Hey!" I giggled, getting even by poking him in the ribcage.

When Dustin and I first broke up, I had dreams of meeting a gorgeous man. Someone ambitious, funny, and fabulous in bed. Someone who would sweep me off my feet, making me forget the hurt and anger I felt. Needless to say, my knight in shining armor never came. I stumbled across a few idiots in tin foil, but they always fell short.

Jax, on the other hand, was no idiot. He wasn't even a knight. Jax was a Prince. Charming, ambitious, gorgeous, and absolutely sweeping me off my feet in many ways. My body said yes, my heart said yes, but my brain kept saying things I didn't want to hear, like;

Slow down.

Stop.

He's too pretty.

He's out of your league.

You've only known each other for a week.

I had spent the last two years feeling insignificant, undesirable, even worthless—residual damage from Dustin's betrayal. That feeling had been reinforced by a procession of bad dates and rejections. All of a sudden, thanks to Jax, my heart was reminded that I was significant and desired. My brain, however, still didn't quite know how to process that information. It wasn't ready to believe.

No matter how natural it all felt to my heart, my head worried that I was in for a rough crash landing when we did return to the real world. Who people were when on vacation was often quite different than who they were when the stresses and obligations of real-life resumed. Still, at that moment, everything felt so good, I forced myself to set those fears aside for now.

"So, is that something you'd be interested in?" he asked again. The words were spoken into the sensitive skin behind my ear. The feeling of his breath tickling my lobe was soft and seductive.

My brain was a blender all of a sudden. I tried to unscramble my thoughts and put them into words. I wanted to squeal out loud repeatedly, like a crazed Harry Styles fan, but I feared that would come across too eager. So instead, I attempted to play it cool.

"Possibly," I shrugged. I instantly cringed because somehow, I made playing it cool sound like complete indifference.

He inclined his head, sheepish. "Oh, ok."

Seeing him suddenly nervous had a bizarre effect on me. It made me want to coddle him and put him at ease. I undercut my comment by leaning up to kiss him gently, then intensely, long, slow and heated. I felt Jax's body shifting beneath me. He liked it. So did I.

I pushed him back down on the mattress before he got too rowdy, laying my head back down on his chest. I took a deep breath like I was about to jump off a cliff into a pool of dark water. "What I mean is, if you wanted to keep seeing each other once we're home, I wouldn't be totally opposed."

I knew, if I turned to look at his face, he'd be smiling. I could feel it in the way his arm tightened around me.

"I'm happy to hear that," he squeezed me a little tighter.

"This trip is almost over, and I haven't been looking forward to saying goodbye."

My heart went gooey at his admission. "There are still two days left. It's too bad they're both at sea, on the way back to Miami. There's not much to do."

"There is one thing we could do."

Immediately I looked him in the eye. "As amazing as sex with you is, I need to leave this room at some point. This is starting to feel like Stockholm syndrome," I teased, and he laughed. "Seriously, I feel like I've been sold into human bondage. We don't even stop fucking long enough for me to comb my hair. I barely have time to brush my teeth between orgasms. I have abandoned all grooming. I must look like a street urchin."

He laughed deep. "You always look adorable. As far as I'm concerned, you never have to groom again." He ran his nose along the curve of my jaw before straightening again. "Ok, except the teeth brushing part. Please continue to prioritize that."

"Noted," I said, eyes closing when his fingers trailed lower, tracing my hip bone. I felt the way he smiled against my chin, along the column of my throat. I pulled away slightly. "Seriously though, as amazing as sex with you is, I need to leave this room. Sapphire is going to send a search party any moment."

"Luckily, what I was going to suggest involves doing precisely that."

"Oh?"

"Tomorrow night, they're throwing a themed party in the auditorium. It'll probably be terribly cheesy, but it's going to be the last big event before we dock, so I thought you'd like to go."

My mind cycled back to the itinerary we'd all been giving upon boarding, and I remembered exactly what the theme of the party was scheduled to be. Jax was right. It was probably going to be very cheesy. Still, Sapphire had already told us, weeks ago, that we were all expected to attend together. It was to be our last big hurrah on the open water. I'd bought a cute outfit and everything. "Are you asking me to the prom?" My tone was teasing, but inside I was practically dancing.

He nodded. "I am."

"I don't know," I shrugged noncommittally. "I always imagined a much more extravagant promposal."

He laughed. "What do you want? Doves? A flash mob? Should I jump out of a cake?"

I got really excited by that last suggestion. "Oh! Can you? It would fit considering the circumstances under which we met."

He laughed again. "So is that a yes?"

"Of course it's a yes! It will be quite refreshing to have a date for this prom. I didn't for my last one."

"You went to your prom alone?" The way he said it, it almost sounded like an accusation.

"I did not go alone," I assured him. "I just didn't have a date. There's a difference. I went with friends."

"I didn't go at all."

That surprised me. "Why not? Prom is a right of passage. Everyone should go."

"We don't really have a prom in Oz. We have a year twelve formal, but it doesn't carry the same symbolism or pressures as your North American prom. Ours is only an excuse to get dressed up and dance badly."

"Sounds exactly like prom to me."

He smiled. "Maybe so, but I couldn't be bothered to go."

"Then why do you want to go to this one?"

"Maybe I've grown up and seen the errors of my youth."

"Or?" I queried, not buying that excuse for a second.

"I know how delicious you look in a suit and thought it could be fun."

That definitely sounded more accurate. My mouth spread into a slow smile, and I kissed Jax before saying, "Sapphire wants all of us to go together. She wants to make an entire day of it, with Ruby and I starting with brunch, then spa treatments, then dinner, then the dance. You should come."

"Brunch?" He asked, his expression odd.

"It's Sunday. We always brunch on Sundays."

He laughed. "I've never really understood brunch."

"What's to understand?" I asked playfully. "It's lunch, only with breakfast foods."

He laughed, then took my hand and began playing absent-mindedly with my fingers. "That's precisely my point. Call it lunch, and order eggs."

"Are you sure you're gay?" I asked, looking up at him.

He grinned, nuzzling his nose behind my ear. "It bloody-well seems that way, doesn't it? Or do I need to fuck you again to prove myself?"

Even in the dark of the room, I could feel myself blush. "Tempting as that is," and it was, "I'm beat." Also, quite honestly, my ass needed a reprieve. "So, what do you say? Should I ask Sapphire if it's ok for you to come?

"No," he waved his hand. "I don't want to be the tag-along. You go. Have fun with your friends. We can meet up at the dance." I was disappointed, but I knew it was probably the better choice. Ruby and Sapphire would have likely spent the entire day interrogating him anyway.

The conversation fell away, and we went back to the television's soft black and white glow. A third movie had started, *The Wizard of Oz*. I smiled. It had always been one of my favorites. I only wished it hadn't started so late. It was already midnight. I couldn't possibly stay up to watch it all and still be bright-eyed and bushy-tailed when I met Sapphire at ten the next morning. I decided I could watch it for a bit.

The Wizard of Oz had always resonated with me. Four misfits journeying down the yellow brick road felt like a metaphor for my circle of friends and our lives together. Each of us searching for the one thing we lacked and leaning on each other until we found it.

The film had also taught me to treasure the people who help you along your journey. Like Ruby, who was the most provocative Dorothy I'd ever seen, and Sapphire, who I long ago decided was my Glinda. She was stoic and beautiful and usually right.

Then, for the first time, it struck me that if Ruby was my Dorothy and Sapphire was my Glinda, maybe I had my own wizard too. Someone to remind me that I wasn't broken or missing pieces. I was complete and perfectly flawed, just as I was. Maybe it wasn't the Wizard of Oz I had been meant to find. Perhaps, it was the Wizard of Aus.

Lost in the movie and in my thoughts, I realized Jax hadn't spoken in almost an hour. I muted the television, and in that newfound silence, I heard Jax's breath slow and heavy. The sound of sleep. I shifted in the bed beside him, taking the expensive camera from his resting hands. I placed it on the nightstand on my side of his bed. Then, I pulled the sheet over us.

"I'm crazy about you."

I heard Jax's words come out like mumbles. I waited. My heart was in my throat, clawing its way up. Jax's eyes were closed, his breath still deep. He was asleep, I told myself. This wasn't a thing he was saying. He was talking in his sleep. It didn't mean he was crazy about me. In his dreams, he could have been talking to anyone. He could have been mad about Chris Hemsworth. Honestly, who wasn't?

Yet, my heart swelled watching him. I wanted him all the time—every minute of the day. I wanted to spend the rest of our time together, making love and getting to know each other more. There may have been no place like home, but there was also no one like Jax Abernathy.

I was falling hard. The thought both scared and excited me. That fear was likely going to win though, I knew it even as I tried to battle it.

I reached up, touching a thumb to Jax's cheekbone, holding my breath. Knowing he couldn't hear me through his slumber gave me the confidence I needed to quietly admit, "I'm crazy about you, too."

I rolled onto my back as one solitary tear slipped free. Whether it was a tear of joy or fear, it was too soon to tell. I could already feel my heart being taken by him, which was an interesting development since I'd started to wonder if, maybe, I was the Tin Man.

TWENTY-THREE
KYLE

"I don't want to risk sounding like your sister or anything," I knocked on the cabin door, frowning down at my watch, "but you need to hurry up. It's almost six o'clock. You're going to make us late."

"I know," Ruby called back from her room.

"You know that you're going to make us late, or you know how to tell time?"

"Both! Now kindly fuck off. I don't need Sapphire 2.0."

"Sorry," I shouted. "I just know what Sapphire is going to say if we're late."

"Girl, keep your panties on," Ruby shouted back. "You cannot rush perfection."

I rolled my eyes. "Your confidence is exhausting, and please, don't call me girl."

The door opened. "Quit whining. I could call you much worse if I wanted."

"Could and have."

"Not this trip," she flashed a toothy grin then turned around, lifting her dark hair up above her right shoulder. "Zip me?"

I moved the clasp up, closing the seam on her red sequinned dress. She turned around, tousling her hair back over both shoulders. "How do I look?"

Like most of her clothing, the dress was short and tight, but the sequins and high neck added a level of sophistication that most of her wardrobe lacked. The six-inch, gold, come-fuck-me-heels were a little extra. Then again, so was Ruby. "You look good," I nodded, hardly caring.

Ruby lurched back, cocking her hip, "Good?" She echoed, clearly not flattered by my choice of words, "Good? Is that the best you can do?"

"Stunning, ravishing, breathtaking," I listed synonyms in an attempt to appease her. "No woman has ever or will ever look more beautiful than you do right now." That last part was a little thick, but she loved it. She twirled happily at the sound of my praise, insincere or not.

"Much better," she nodded, pleased.

Every sail, towards the end of the run, the cruise had a formal evening. It was a grand opportunity for the entire ship to doll themselves up, guests in black-tie splendor and the crew in their official officer's uniforms. It was really only an excuse to dress pretentiously and have professional photos taken. Photos the cruise line would then try to sell you at twenty dollars per image. It was a sneaky money-making opportunity disguised as prom. Participation wasn't technically mandatory. However, no guest was permitted in the dining room or in the Liquid Lounge auditorium that evening without theme-appropriate attire. So it was in every guest's best interest to participate.

To make it interesting for the crew, every formal evening had a different theme. According to one of the chambermaids I had spoken to, the last theme had been the roaring twenties. I would have much preferred that over the one we were stuck with. I was sure Jax would have looked amazing as a 1920's gangster, and I could pull off a fedora like nobody's business, but no. We got stuck with a prom.

"Do I look stupid?" I asked Ruby.

She raised a perfectly tweezed brow. "Define stupid."

I turned away from her, no longer interested in her opinion. "Wait," she placed her claw-like fingers on my shoulder, urging me back around.

"Well?" I pressed impatiently.

"You look..." She contemplated, examining me with the scrutiny of Sherlock Holmes. "Like Liberace and Elton John had a love child, and that child grew up to be obsessed with Diana Ross."

I sighed, defeated. "That's it. I'm not going."

"What possessed you to buy a sequinned blazer in the first place?"

"The cruising guide said, an enchanted evening on the sea. Formal attire only. Sequins encouraged."

"The sequinned part might have been gender-specific."

"Fuck gender norms," I declared proudly.

Ruby nodded her approval. "I can get on board with that, but why pink?"

"I like pink."

"You look like shiny Pepto-Bismol."

"You look like a sparkly used tampon," I sneered at her.

"You look like you're attending a gay breast cancer gala."

"You look like you're attending a reunion of retired sex-workers."

"Jokes on you," she shrugged. "That was the look I was going for." Then she began to sashay down the hall. I followed her like a glittering pink usher.

"Have you decided what you're going to do?" She asked me.

She didn't have to clarify. I knew precisely what she was referring to. Dustin and Jax. The first, the man of my past, with whom I shared the bulk of my adult years. A man who knew me, really knew me, in ways I didn't even know myself. The second, a man who was brand new and exciting. Stimulating in ways that thrilled and terrified me simultaneously. The first had broken my heart once but had recently promised never to do so again. The second, I feared, had the potential to destroy my heart worse than Dustin ever had.

"I think I have," I told her honestly. "It's just hard because I have a history with Dustin. There's a strange sense of loyalty there."

"Loyalty isn't the same as love," she pointed out astutely.

"I know that," I nodded. "Yet the feelings are so similar. It's still a little confusing."

"It shouldn't be *that* confusing," Ruby said sardonically, and I sent her a look that urged her to continue. "The man is a cheater. He cheated on you two years ago, and he's cheating on Shawn now. You may not have slept together, but he kissed you and is pursuing you, while his boyfriend is literally ten feet away. Betrayal starts in the brain, not the bedroom."

"I know, you're right."

"Ok," she accepted. "So, does that mean you're choosing Jax?"

"That's the way I'm leaning."

"Leaning?" She repeated the word like it was entirely foreign to her. "What does that even mean?"

"It means I'm not totally sure if I'm going to pursue that either. Jax is so wonderful." He really, really was. "It's also very new. What if we start dating, for real, and a week from now, it all falls to shit?"

"What if it doesn't?" she challenged.

"It will," I stated definitively. "It always does."

"Snap out of it!" She slapped me. She actually hit me. I stared at her with utter disbelief, cupping my throbbing face. The woman was stronger than she seemed. "What?" She questioned obtusely. "I thought you'd enjoy the Cher reference." She wasn't wrong, but my cheek hurt, and that made it hard to appreciate.

"I am not very good at dating," I admitted. "I have only been in two relationships in the last twenty years. I'm completely out of my depth."

"I've been in twenty relationships in the last two years, so I assure you, so am I." Maybe I was barking up the wrong tree. "Do you love Jax?"

"Can you fall in love in ten days?" I wasn't convinced that it was even possible.

"I don't know," she shrugged. "I've been known to fall in love in a single night."

"Yes, but that's a very specific kind of love. A love that usually requires the morning after pill."

For a moment, I thought she might slap me again, so I ducked. Instead, she laughed. "It's funny because it's true." Then she asked me, "Does it *feel* like love?"

"Maybe." I couldn't deny that I did feel something. Jax filled me with excitement. He made me come alive, and that made me feel good. Good about myself and in general. He was charming, sexy and a decent human being. Which was almost an impossible combination. I couldn't deny my attraction to him, but I also couldn't deny my fear.

"Do you trust him?" Ruby asked suddenly.

"He hasn't really given me any reason not to."

"That's good."

"Although I also haven't known him long enough for him to earn it," I added.

"Fair enough." She paused, pondering. "What does Sapphire think about all this?"

"I haven't talked to her about it."

Ruby looked at me like I had revealed her favorite singer had died. "So, you're actually coming to me, and only me, for advice?" Her tone suggested underlying panic at that notion.

"She's been busy. She's on her honeymoon, and someone

told me to stop making things about me."

Ruby smiled. "So, you do listen."

My lip curled. "Sometimes. When the advice is good."

"I'm probably the last person who should be giving anyone relationship advice. My dating record reads more like a prison rap sheet."

"I think that makes you the perfect person to ask. You have triple the experience that Sapphire has."

"That's true," she preened, summoning the elevator. As we waited, I examined myself in the reflection of the stainless-steel elevator doors. Immediately, I was reminded of the supreme cruelty of fluorescent lighting. Ruby still managed to look stunning, as usual. Somehow, even the horrendous overhead lighting of the hallway stood no match against her natural features. I was not so lucky. Ruby was right; I did look like Pepto-Bismol. I groaned internally.

"The only person who knows what you want to do is you," Ruby said, tossing her hair. "Although if I were you, I wouldn't be so quick to run away, scared. At least not until he gives you a reason to."

A few moments later, the elevator dinged open, and we stepped inside. I pressed the button for the main deck before realizing it was already lit up. Then I noticed we weren't alone. A pudgy, balding gentleman in a cheap brown suit stood in the corner with his wife. She looked like she had stripped a thrift store mannequin before dousing herself in vanilla fields perfume.

Then I took a closer look. *Shit.* It was the same woman I had flashed in the hall the morning I'd woken up in the laundry room. I cleared my throat. "Good evening," I nodded politely while trying desperately to ignore the fact that the woman had seen me butt-ass naked only a few days earlier.

She obviously had trouble ignoring that fact also. Colour splashed across her cheekbones as she moved closer to her husband, refusing to connect her gaze with mine. She looked like she wished the cables would snap, and we would all fall to our deaths. Clearly, I made her as uncomfortable as a sexual predator would. I couldn't even be angered by her reaction. She *had* caught me banging on random doors in the wee hours of the morning, stark naked and sweaty.

Automatically I was conflicted between apologizing for our awkward encounter or purposely saying or doing something equally embarrassing to get another entertaining reaction from her. The floors counted slower than I thought possible, making the journey uncomfortable enough for both of us, so I decided to spare her.

The elevator dinged once more, and the doors opened onto the mezzanine floor. The older couple stepped off first, the woman quite eager to be away from me. Ruby and I followed casually, then we veered away from them, descending a small staircase to Horizon's Restaurant.

Soft piano music echoed through the air as we made our way to the restaurant's double doors. A photographer stood at the entrance, waiting to snap pictures of the guests as they arrived in their formal attire. This was wise since many of them would likely spill red wine or creamy sauces on themselves during dinner.

"All right, pose," Ruby instructed over her shoulder. I did as she requested, crossing my arms in faux masculinity, while she perched one hand on my shoulder, the other on her hip. I hated having my picture taken, but I knew it would have been pointless to argue with her demand.

When the photographer was finished, the hostess, dressed in all black except for matching red belt and stilettos, greeted us with a bright smile, recognizing us immediately. She motioned for us to follow her down the teal carpeting, and we happily obliged.

Our table was the same one it had been the entire week. A long square table in the back of the room, adjacent to a rear wall of windows, looking out onto the water and the setting sun. By this point, I could have found it without being ushered. Still, the restaurant had an undeniable air of sophistication that would have been less poignant had we simply been allowed to seat ourselves.

The table was set for fifteen, in glittering white and gold. The majority of our group was already seated. Dr. and Mrs. Johnson were sitting in the middle of the long table, Sapphire and Justin sat directly to their left and Dustin's parents were across from them. Dustin and Shawn were noticeably absent. A few other friends and relatives were peppered around the table, leaving only a few chairs vacant. One of those chairs was beside Cody. Ruby swooped in, taking that chair before I even had time to blink, which shouldn't have surprised me.

I glanced down at the end of the table where three vacant chairs sat side by side. I supposed any of them would do perfectly well, but Sapphire's aunt Lorraine sat closest to the empty cluster. Being right-handed, there were few things in life more annoying to me than sitting to the left of a left-handed person during dinner. Constantly bumping elbows and water glasses, each of us silently fighting for dominance at the table. I took the chair at the very end to avoid this, which no one seemed insulted by.

"There they are!" Justin crowed, nodding to his brother as Dustin and Shawn sauntered up to the table. "I was starting to wonder if we had to send a search party."

The couple made their way to the end of the table, to the two remaining vacant chairs. Right. Beside. Me. I shouldn't have been surprised since they were the only two chairs left, but I braced myself for impact anyway.

They were both dressed in theme. Shawn wore a skinny-cut burgundy suit and black bowtie, tapered pants clinging tightly to his legs and ass and...well...other regions. I had to look away before he caught me gawking. He reminded me of Kevin Bacon in *Footloose*. Dustin's suit was black, smooth, elegant and sexy. Very very sexy.

Shock and horror ricocheted through me, and I wanted to rub Purell on my brain. I shouldn't have been thinking of Dustin in that way. I shouldn't have been thinking about Dustin at all.

Like a gentleman, he pulled out the empty chair closest to Aunt Lorraine, then Shawn found his perch, smiling. Dustin took the last remaining chair between Shawn and me. Watching Shawn and Dustin interact, all coupley, caused a moment of hope to bloom in me.

Perhaps Dustin's proposition had been nothing more than a drunk confession. It wasn't like we'd spoken about it since. I'd purposely been avoiding him. Maybe he'd forgotten all about it. That would certainly make things easier.

"Sorry, we would have been here sooner," Dustin flashed a dazzling, handsome smile at his brother. "We had some business to attend to. So..." He trailed off, then winked. The implications were enough to eliminate any doubts. They'd had sex.

I wish I could explain the tiny jealous monster that reared up inside my chest. The rational part of my brain knew that I had no claim to the feeling. Shawn was his boyfriend. It was pretty straightforward. I mean, I had spent the last three days having unbelievable sex of my own. What right did I have to be jealous? Hadn't I just told Ruby that I didn't even want Dustin anyway?

"Dustin," Shawn laughed innocently. "Your family doesn't want to know everything."

I certainly didn't. I took in a deep, cleansing breath.

Dustin maintained his perfect smile, draping his arm across the back of Shawn's chair, leaning in. "There's no need to be embarrassed."

"I don't think he's embarrassed, Dustin," I chimed in. "I think he's just trying to keep the rest of us from losing our appetites."

Dustin glanced at me then, like he had suddenly noticed I was there at all. "Kyle," he nodded. "You look colorful."

"Thank you," I replied crisply. "You look—"

"Behave, you two," Sapphire warned before I could complete my sentence. "It's one of our last nights together. I don't want you to ruin it by fighting."

"Yeah," Ruby jabbed at us. "You two should kiss and make up." I immediately shot daggers in her direction. Dustin didn't miss it either.

Shawn seemed oblivious to Ruby's tone. He chuckled, giving Dustin an adoring look. "You can make up, but I'm the only one who gets to kiss you."

If only he knew.

"You sure about that?" Ruby asked with a sly grin. The rest of the table laughed, assuming, of course, that she was joking. Dustin and I were not as amused.

God damn it, Ruby. It served me right for trusting her with one too many details. I folded my arms across my chest briefly before changing my mind and brushing my hand nervously through my hair instead.

Sapphire caught it immediately. "Why are you suddenly so fidgety?" She asked me.

"I'm…not," I stuttered lamely. "I'm merely disgusted by the suggestion of Dustin and I making out."

Dr. Johnson, empowered by one too many pina coladas, barked out a laugh, hitting the table. "I've seen you two make out before."

Awkward. I tried to change the subject. "My gosh, I'm hungry."

As if on cue, the server appeared and began to take everyone's order, starting at the end then rotating clockwise. When the server came to me, I picked up the menu card, glancing at the evening's limited, albeit delicious offerings. Each night of the cruise, the restaurant offered hungry sailors different appetizers, entrées and desserts. Four of each category to choose from, that cycled through to provide a diverse selection each evening. That night, I had a choice of spaghetti carbonara, seared striped bass, broiled mane lobster tail, or the featured vegetarian dish. I ordered the bass and a bottle of Pinot Grigio, which the server incorrectly assumed was to share.

Soon after the server departed with our orders, the conversation drifted to more comfortable territory, and we stayed there for most of the dinner. We chatted about a variety of benign topics. The stunning sights we'd seen all week, where we'd each like to vacation to next, and of course, entertaining stories from our various pasts. Everything was going delightfully smooth until suddenly Mrs. Johnson asked, "So Dustin, when do you and Shawn think you'll take that next step?"

My ears perked up, and I nearly dropped my fork. Sapphire noticed. "What's with you? It's like you've never seen flatware before."

"Too much caffeine today," I lied quickly, turning my attention back to Dustin to see how he would react to Mrs. Johnson's inquiry. He seemed entirely unfazed by her question.

"We are enjoying taking it one day at a time," he said.

At the other end of the table, Dustin's mother put down her knife. "Well, you're not getting any younger," she pointed out. "I'd like to see you settled down before I die."

Dusting grabbed Shawn's hand, bringing it to his lips. "We're not in any rush," he assured everyone, the corner of his mouth twitching upward. "Shawn still has a few years of school left. After that, maybe we'll talk about it more seriously."

I blinked, carefully cutting my fish and shifting in my seat uncomfortably. I could barely keep my jaw from hitting the floor. A few years? A few days ago, he had told me he wanted to end things with Shawn when we got back on solid ground. How quickly his tune had changed.

"What about you, Kyle?" Mrs. Salinger pressed. Each glass of wine making her more and more chatty.

I took a sip of my beverage. I really didn't like where the conversation was going. "What about me?"

"Are you going to settle down any time soon?"

"Not likely. It usually helps to be dating someone first," I shrugged. Then I thought about Jax, wondering if maybe I already was.

Mrs. Salinger nodded like she understood. "You're such a good boy," she said. I supposed it would never matter how old I got; I was still a child to her. "Anybody would be so lucky to have you. I was really disappointed when things didn't work out between you and our Dustin."

That was a sweet yet highly inappropriate declaration, considering Dustin and his new boyfriend were literally in front of her. Suddenly realizing her error, she added, "That's all in the past, though. I just want you to be happy."

"Thank you, Kathy. I am happy. I'll settle down sooner or later."

"Of course you will," Dustin agreed. "Your adventures in online dating are bound to pay off eventually."

I'd signed up for several dating sights over the last year-and-a-half. All of them time-consuming, and none of them successful. *Match.com* and I were not compatible. *eHarmony* had been a symphony of egocentrics and perverts. I caught crabs from *Plenty of Fish*, literally. Ten days later, after I used all the ointment and shaved myself to look like a prepubescent boy, I decided to try one last website. Still, when I received an unsolicited dick-pic from OnMyKnees4Jesus69, I decided that *Christian Mingle* was also not for me.

I turned to Dustin, surprised. "How do you know about that?"

"Sapphire told me," he lied so quickly. I knew it was a lie because I had been so wholly mortified by the entire experience that I never breathed a word of my online escapades to anyone. Not even to Sapphire. I decided to let the lie hang between us. "For a moment, I thought you might have stalked me online."

"Not at all," he claimed. Then he added, "I especially enjoyed your *OkCupid* profile. Not at all desperate."

My jaw tightened, and I felt a storm build in my chest. Anger was good. I could be angry at Dustin. It was preferable to being smitten. I laughed a casual ha-ha-ha-oh-you-rascal laugh then stomped on his foot beneath the table. Dustin gritted his teeth.

"I don't know how you kids do that, online dating," Dr. Johnson said, in between bites of his lava cake. "Dating was intimidating enough, in my day, without FaceShop and PhotoTune. You all look like supermodels on your FaceGrams and Insta-snaps." Several of us smiled at his flubbing of the app names. "What happens when you're expecting Michelle Pfeiffer, but a troll with bad breath and foot fungus shows up at your door, instead?"

The entire table burst into laughter, I included. It was my first real laugh since I sat at the table. Dr. Johnson was a podiatrist, so naturally, all of his anecdotes somehow seemed to involve feet.

"Typically, you don't tell them where you live until after you're sure they're not a troll," I explained, draining the last of my wine. "If a troll did show up, though, I'd have a nice drink with him before directing him to the nearest bridge. I'm not completely shallow."

Dr. Johnson didn't seem totally satisfied with my reply. "I don't know. That computer dating doesn't seem natural. Swiping left, right, up and down. Too impersonal. It sounds more like shopping than dating."

"That's exactly what it is," I agreed. "You're shopping for a prospective mate. It's really pretty simple."

Mrs. Salinger didn't seem convinced. "It certainly doesn't sound simple. In my day, we actually went out and met people. Dances, blind dates, drinks. For God's sake, you could be talking to a serial killer online."

"That's true," I agreed. "There are usually red flags, though. The most difficult thing to master is reading people and their non-verbal cues."

"What do you mean?" Mrs. Salinger asked.

"Well, if you're not used to it, it's a little like navigating a foreign country. There's an entire language you need to learn."

"What kind of language?" Sapphire's mom inquired further.

"Things to look out for, hidden meanings, things to avoid doing. That kind of thing."

"Such as?"

"For starters, you need to be incredibly careful with the types of pictures you post online. You want to avoid posting any picture that makes you look too attractive."

Mr. Salinger tilted his drunk head. "Isn't that the whole point of a profile photo? To look attractive to others?"

"True, but you don't want to look too attractive, or people will start to assume you're a catfish."

"Catfish?" Mrs. Salinger queried.

"A scam artist," I clarified. "Someone pretending to be someone else."

"Why would someone do that?" She questioned further.

I shrugged. "Sometimes monetary gain or sometimes it's a real person you know or rejected, and they're trying to get even."

"Sometimes they're gay guys, pretending to be chicks, just to get off," Cody volunteered. I glared at him, but he wasn't technically wrong.

"That sounds awful," Mrs. Johnson gasped. "Whatever happened to meeting someone organically? Whatever happened to romance?"

"These days, sex comes before romance," I said dryly. "People have busy lives. They don't want to waste time on someone they're not compatible with sexually."

"It's true," Ruby nodded from her perch next to Cody. "Sex has become a greeting. Almost like a handshake."

"A handshake? Really? How dreadful," Mrs. Salinger carefully dabbed at her mouth with a napkin. "You're not like that, though. Are you, Kyle?"

"Not usually, no."

"That's good," she nodded approvingly. "You're a good boy," she repeated. "You'll meet somebody amazing. I know it."

"Thank you," I nodded. "Actually, I might have met someone already." My mind wandered again to Jax, and I couldn't help but smile. Suddenly I felt a light flicker against my thigh. I looked down slowly to find Dustin's well-manicured fingers trailing up my pant leg. He had casually dipped his left hand below the sightline of the table. I had been generally annoyed when he and Shawn so casually alluded to their fuck-fest. Now, with Dustin's hand upon my thigh, I was suddenly very singularly pissed.

Mrs. Salinger leaned forward, intrigued. "Might have? I'm not sure I understand. Either you've met someone, or you haven't."

Dustin was still fondling my thigh. I tenderly placed my right hand atop of his, entwining our fingers together. His hand was warm, healthy, and held me tight. It felt so familiar.

"I *have* met someone," I explained to Mrs. Salinger. "It's too soon to tell where it's going, though."

My fingers were still laced with Dustin's. I sensed his calm confidence. Then I saw his face morph into an expression of surprised agony when I attempted to break his fingers by bending them backward with force. I heard several of his knuckles crack, and I felt victorious.

Dustin coughed, his eyes watering. He looked pissed for about two seconds before panic wiped it away, then he looked towards Shawn to see if he noticed the violent yet brief exchange between us. Shawn seemed oblivious. He looked up, only long enough to learn where the groan had come from, before returning to his lobster bisque as if it were the most fascinating soup ever created.

I glared at Dustin while he nursed his wounds. Who the fuck did Dustin think he was? The man had professed his feelings for me, kissed me, made me question everything, then paraded his current boyfriend in front of me like no conversation was ever had between us at all. I had been willing to overlook it when I thought, maybe, he had come to his senses and decided to forget the entire ordeal. Clearly, by the way he had touched my thigh, so intimately, that hadn't been the case. What had me even more seething was that he had the nerve to touch me, at all, that close to his boyfriend, like I was some common home-wrecking whore.

Not today, Satan!

I inhaled, then exhaled, reeling in my temper. How stupid

was Dustin? Worse yet, how stupid was I? How could I have even entertained the idea of getting back together with him. I must have temporarily lost my mind.

"Justin, have you and your new wife talked about kids at all?" Cody asked from his end of the table. The rest of the group drifted their attention. It always boggled my mind that people felt brazen enough to ask personal questions like they were somehow entitled to the information. They weren't. It was actually rather rude to ask. Still, they did. Always.

"Cody, that's not an appropriate question," I piped up.

"It's not any different than asking about your dating habits," he replied. Ruby had her flattened palms clasped over Cody's broad shoulders, marking her territory. Obviously, she'd decided on her escort for the evening.

"I beg to differ. There is a difference between asking, *are you dating anyone?* and *are you planning to impregnate someone?* Big difference. The first is a casual inquiry, the other penetrates deep."

Cody scowled. "Leave it to a gay guy to work penetration into the conversation."

The entire table groaned at his response.

"What?" He seemed genuinely mystified by the reaction. "It was a joke. It was funny."

A moment of awkwardness consumed the table, but we could always count on Sapphire to slice through it. She hated silence, awkward or otherwise. "To answer your question, Cody, we will be starting a family very soon."

Mrs. Johnson's ears perked up at her daughter's words. "Soon? How soon?"

Sapphire smiled sheepishly, and panic exploded in the pit of my stomach. I knew what she was about to say before her mouth even began to form words. There had been clues, but I had been too wrapped up in Dustin and Jax chaos to notice. I hadn't seen her with a single drink the entire trip, even on her wedding night.

"In about five months," Sapphire gleamed proudly. The entire table cheered and applauded while Mrs. Johnson squealed, an ear-shattering scream of joy, rushing over to Sapphires' side of the table to embrace her.

"This is splendid news!" Mrs. Johnson beamed, then she

turned to her husband. "James, you should say a few words."

We all swung our eyes to Dr. Johnson, who looked at his wife like she suggested he stand up and break-dance for us. To be fair, Sapphire's father was not the most gifted orator. He was much better with planters warts and bunions. "Sure. Uh, a new baby is one of life's greatest gifts. I'm sure you'll be fine parents."

"They'll be *amazing* parents," I corrected with a grin.

Sapphire's dad lifted his wineglass to me in thanks. "Yes, of course. And... let's hope he, or she—"

"They," Sapphire bit her lower lip. "We're having twins!"

I suddenly felt faint.

"I can't believe I'm going to be an aunt," Ruby said in mild disbelief.

"This is amazing!" Dustin grinned widely. "I'm going to be an uncle!"

And I was going to be...

Nothing.

The thought crept in without warning. All of a sudden, my anger at Dustin gave way to make room for sadness and fear. I was going to be nothing. This blessed event had nothing to do with me. Not really. Not in any way that mattered. I was a spectator. Dustin's earlier warning echoed in my mind.

One of us is going to be left behind, and it won't be me.

Needing a break, I pushed myself back from the table, dropping my napkin on my empty plate. "If you'll all excuse me. Call of nature," I nodded to the group politely before finding my way to the restroom. I didn't need to go. I only needed an exit.

Once there, I stood at the mirror for a little too long, staring at myself a little too hard. My reflection gazed back; my brow furrowed, lips turned down at the corners, expression a mixture of terrified, bewildered, and hurt. Sapphire was my best friend. We were supposed to tell each other everything. Why wouldn't Sapphire have told me she was pregnant months ago? Then I reminded myself that I hadn't been entirely upfront with her as of late either. Maybe that was a sign that our relationship was already changing.

I turned on the faucet, splashing cold water on my face as though it could somehow wash away the dark thoughts. It cooled down my skin, but it didn't help clear out the haze or help me think. The restroom door opened behind me. Automatically, I turned on the faucet again, pretending to wash my hands rather than look aimlessly in the mirror.

"Nice jacket," I recognized the voice immediately.

"You hate this jacket," I told Dustin as he came to stand beside me at the counter. I didn't turn to look at him. Instead, we made eye contact through the mirror. "You have always hated anything with sequins or glitter, and you definitely have never liked pink."

"Yeah, but you make it look good."

"Oh pah-lease," I rolled my eyes, and he smiled his sly, sexy smile. "Shawn looks like he's fully recovered from his food poisoning." My tone was short and aggressive. Dustin caught it right away.

"Yeah, for a few days now."

"That's great."

"Are you pissed about something?" he asked, and a dry, sardonic laugh exploded out of me.

"Am I pissed about something? Are you serious?"

He took a deep breath, blowing his cheeks out as he exhaled. "Yeah, you seem angry."

"Do I?" I took a deep breath, pulling myself to my full height. "What would I possibly be angry about?" Maybe the fact that he was trying to feel me up at the dinner table. I decided not to say anything. Instead, I simply hummed. "I'm fine."

He watched me for a moment, then he crossed his arms. "There is a land of passive-aggressive people, and you are their king," he quipped. "Seriously, are you sure you're ok? You look nasty."

"Nasty? Wow. So flattering. Why don't you tell me I look tired or haggard?"

"Because you don't," he said matter-of-factly. "You do look nasty, angry and pissed." I moved past him, heading towards the door. He grabbed my wrist, spinning me back around to face him. My palm was itching to smack him. "Shawn and I didn't have sex," he told me, unprompted.

"I didn't ask," I said, shaking him loose.

"I know. I also know that's what you are assuming. I just want you to know that we didn't."

317

"That's not any of my business."

Dustin looked wounded. "Maybe not, but I wanted you to know anyway.

"You certainly implied that you two had sex."

"We did other things, but we didn't fuck. I'm not going to do that with Shawn until you..." he trailed off.

"Until I what?" I eyed him suspiciously.

"Until you decide if you still want me as much as I still want you."

"Dustin, stop." I looked away from him. "This is not the time to have this conversation."

"Why not?"

I couldn't tell if he was purposely obtuse or not. An inspection of his expression didn't clear it up for me either. "We're in a public washroom," I said vexed, gesturing to the room around us. "Having someone proclaim their undying love for me while surrounded by urinals is not my idea of romance."

"I recall a time when urinals didn't phase you," he said, a suggestive tone settling over his words. He leaned closer to me. "In fact, I remember several bathroom stalls we made very romantic."

I placed my hand against his chest, pushing him back before he got too close. "That wasn't romance. That was hormones and lots of vodka."

He looked me squarely in the eye. "Yeah, but it was fun."

"Perhaps," I accepted. "Still, my days of being pounded from behind while bent over a public toilet are over."

He chuckled at the imagery. "Pity. You were so good at it. There are other positions, though."

"Keep dreaming. My legs are closed to you." I moved an additional foot away from him and decided on a swift change in the subject. "You're going to be an uncle. You must be excited."

"I'm thrilled," he beamed. Dustin always loved children, although neither of us had any desire to have one of our own. Throughout our relationship, we had known several friends who hopped onto the baby train. Unfortunately, many of those friendships dissolved eventually, since the baby train frequently led our friends further and further away from where we were.

Sapphire having a baby would be different, though. At least

for Dustin. Uncle Dustin. Uncle by blood.

For me, I suspected it would be a rerun of previous friendships I'd had. Sapphire and I would try in the beginning. We really would. Sooner or later, though, lunch dates would be exchanged for playdates. Our book club would dissolve to make room for parenting groups. Fancy Saturday night dinners at five-star restaurants would be replaced by family-friendly dinner parties. There, Sapphire and her new parent friends would try in-vain to have an adult conversation over a chorus of screaming children. Curse words would be taboo, and baby talk would be encouraged. Phrases like, *no, don't touch that!* or *don't make me count to three* would become daily mantras. Eventually, I would go from that trusted best friend who always had her back to that childless acquaintance who couldn't understand. Finally, our friendship would be reduced to Christmas cards, and Facebook likes. If I were lucky, the occasional invitation to a child's birthday party would arrive in the mail. I saw it as clearly as my reflection in the bathroom mirror.

Dustin waved his hand in front of my face. I had zoned out in my thoughts. "You don't look as excited."

I snapped back to reality, like waking from hypnosis. "I'm thrilled for Justin and Sapphire. Really." I was. There was a lingering but in the air, and Dustin gave me the eye, waiting for it to land. "It just means things will change, that's all."

"What's wrong with that? The only constant in life is change. Adapt, and change. It's what we're designed to do." He examined my face, reading my thoughts correctly like he always could. "Sapphire is going to be a mom. Her life has to change. That means your friendship has to change too. If you don't want it to end, then it has to evolve."

"Wow," I spoke with a small laugh. "That was actually intelligent."

"You seem surprised."

"Honestly, from you, it is kind of surprising. It suggests that you aren't the sex-crazed scoundrel you pretend to be. That under all that bravado and ego, you're still the sensitive, intelligent boy I fell in love with so long ago."

"Wow," Dustin said, his deep laugh bouncing off the acoustics. "That might be the third nice thing you've said to me this whole trip. It's certainly the only thing you've said to me in the last few days."

I gave him a compassionate look. It had clearly not gone unnoticed that I had been avoiding him. "Sorry. I've been busy."

"With your Australian?"

I didn't answer. Instead, I said, "You know, I'm surprised to hear you give me that advice about Sapphire. Considering only a few days ago, you seemed fully convinced that she was ready to toss me away if you and I couldn't get along."

Dustin frowned, his brows knitting together. "That was a week ago," he pointed out. "I'm no longer of the mindset that she has to make a choice. I think we've proven we can play nice," he moved closer to me again. "*Very* nice. Our kind of chemistry doesn't go away."

I pursed my lips, biting down on my cheek as a solemn pause settled over us. His demeanor had softened, and a sensual tone had infiltrated his voice again. It did something to my stomach, something between butterflies and nausea. The feeling distracted me for two microseconds. Long enough for Dustin to bridge the gap between us.

"Have you given any thought to our conversation?" His hand moved closer, curling around mine, warm and encompassing. My reflex was to jerk away, but he held me steady.

"Yes," I admitted. "I'm afraid you're not going to like the conclusion I've come to."

"You don't want to be with me?" He stepped closer.

I pressed my hand against his chest again, a lame attempt to keep him at bay. "No, I don't. I'm sorry."

"I don't believe you," he said, sliding his gaze over my features, clearly unconvinced.

I wanted to push him back, but my body would not respond to my brain. Thankfully, my voice hadn't entirely forsaken me. "I'm not going to let you kiss me again," I told him bluntly.

Unfazed, he inched even closer, backing me up until I was pressed against the stall door. It swung inward upon impact, banging loudly against the interior walls of the cubicle. It caught me by surprise, and I gave an embarrassing startled shriek.

"I think you will," he leaned in, closer than before. He

smelled unbelievably good, like expensive cologne, champagne and a distinct Dustin smell. A scent that hadn't changed in our two years apart. It immediately brought back every single memory of our fifteen years together.

Suddenly, I wished we were surrounded by people because I couldn't trust myself without an audience. I mustered what was left of my resolve and raised my chin defiantly. "I would rather give a rim-job to Jabba the Hutt than have your mouth on mine again."

"I've seen pictures of the guys you dated after me. I'd say you've been there and done that."

I couldn't help but laugh. As I did, Dustin leaned in, bringing his lips dangerously close to mine.

"No!" I managed, breathless yet firm. Thwacking him on the nose like a misbehaving puppy.

"What the hell, Kyle?" he cursed, cupping his nose with the palm of his hand, but he did not move to let me out of the bathroom stall.

"We can't do this. I won't," I said, pushing past Dustin. I turned to face him. He did the same. We changed positions exactly, and we did so like a well-rehearsed dance routine. "You have a boyfriend."

"I miss you," he whined.

"You keep saying that like it matters. It doesn't." I paced backward, hands on my hips. "We were together fifteen years, Dustin. I am not a random someone you secretly make out with in a dirty bathroom."

"I know that. It wouldn't be that way."

Before I could think of a response, there was the soft sound of footsteps from the other side of the bathroom door, followed by the sound of squeaky hinges opening. In a panic, Dustin's eyes met mine. In lightning speed, his demeanor went from one of lust to one of pure dread. The next thing I knew, I was being pulled sideways by my jacket, and Dustin was pinning me hard against the wall. He slammed the stall door behind us, sealing us both inside the bathroom cubicle.

"What the hell are you doing?" I whispered as Dustin shoved me into the tiny crevice between the wall and the toilet, hiding my feet. He pressed his finger to my lips, silently telling me to shut-the-fuck-up. My automatic reaction was to create distance between us, which I tried to do, but only managed to bang my head painfully against the tile wall behind me.

"Dustin?" It was Shawn. "Are you still in here, babe?" He called into the room.

"Yep. Sorry," Dustin replied from the stall. "That cream brûlée is not agreeing with me."

I narrowed my eyes at him, judging hard. He tilted his head in angst, holding me tighter to the wall. I bucked my hips, trying to shake him off, but he was taller, tougher and had a fistful of my sequinned blazer.

"Poor baby," Shawn came further into the room, closing the bathroom door behind him. "I told you not to order it. You know how dairy affects your bowel."

"I know," Dustin agreed. "I should have listened. You head back up the room. I'll be up as soon as I can."

I shifted uncomfortably against Dustin, and he accidentally elbowed me in the rib when trying to push me back. I let out a muffled yelp. Dustin attempted to mask my sounds by making some of his own. Nasty, grunting noises. The sounds of defecation. Gross. The last thing I wanted, while being held captive against my will, next to a toilet, was to imagine my captor taking a shit.

"Ok, babe," Shawn sounded so concerned. "Do you want me to stop at the pharmacy and pick you up some Lactaid?"

Dustin grunted more. He was laying it on a little thick, I thought. "No, that's ok. I think I'll be fine once it works its way out. Pretty sure I'm almost done here."

"Ok, sweets. I'll see you upstairs."

"Ok, hon, sounds good!" Dustin said, a little louder than warranted, trying to mask his rising panic of being found out. "See you in a bit."

A few seconds later, the door opened, then closed. Shawn was gone. We waited for several counts before moving, just to be sure. Dustin peered over the top of the stall wall. Once he had visual confirmation that we were alone in the room, he opened the door, allowing me to escape.

"That was close," he said, his breath haggard.

I emerged from the stall, looking wobbly. My dress shirt was disheveled and wrinkly, and my hair was a mess. I tried to pat it back into place. "This is exactly what I imagined it would be like. You and I cowering in a bathroom stall, your elbow inside my rib cage," I sniped. My head throbbed from where I clocked it against the wall.

He didn't say anything. He looked down at the bathroom floor, guilty.

Thankfully, the personal space bubble was back. Now that I wasn't as distracted, I was able to focus my message more clearly. "You can't corner me like this, Dustin. You have a boyfriend. A boyfriend who, at this moment, is probably getting you indigestion pills, even though you told him not to. That's how much he cares about you." I made a move towards the door.

"Kyle," Dustin hissed, grabbing me by the wrist.

"No, Dusty," I shook him loose. "This is ridiculous."

"Us being together is ridiculous?"

"Yes," I felt exhausted. Everything about the conversation was emotionally and physically draining. "We couldn't even stand each other a week ago."

"We like each other now."

"You cheated on me!" I nearly yelled it. The words ricocheted off the walls, echoing in our ears. I waited for the acoustics to settle before I continued. "Now you're cheating on Shawn."

"This is different," he said, grabbing me by the stupid lapel of my stupid blazer and kissing my foolish mouth.

"No," I groaned in exasperation, shoving Dustin backward by the shoulders, making a show of looking him up and down, disgusted. "It isn't any different!" The room echoed again, and I paused to gather my composure. "Shawn is a good guy. As much as I try not to like him, I do. He doesn't deserve this."

Dustin went totally silent, totally still, before whispering an impassioned, "He's not you."

"No, he isn't," I agreed. "He's sweet, young, impressionable and just starting to figure out where he fits in the world. Having someone betray him, like this, could break him. I know because it nearly broke me, and I wasn't nearly as innocent as he is."

Dustin stared at me, trying to process what I'd said.

"Look," I continued. "A few nights ago, right before you kissed me, you sat on that beach, telling me how much you've changed. You told me how much you regret how you treated me." He looked down at the floor again, unable to meet my disapproving gaze. "Then tonight, you sat at that dinner table and had the nerve to talk about marriage and a future with him, while the whole time you were feeling up my leg under the table." I let that sink in before moving on. "Dustin, you're not acting like a changed person. You're acting like the same lying ass I caught banging a nineteen-year-old in our bed. Do you really think I'd want to make-out with that person?"

"You and I—"

"No," I put my hand up in front of his face, shutting him down flatly. "There is no *you and I*. This has nothing to do with me. Not anymore. This is about you and Shawn. Do whatever you want, but leave me out of it." I attempted to smooth out my wrinkled shirt.

"You're still attracted to me. I know you are."

"Of course I am!" I yelled. "I have eyes! You're a good-looking guy. You've always been a good-looking guy, you'll probably die a good-looking guy, and I will likely always be attracted to you, on some level, but I'm not in love with you, Dusty. I barely even like you."

I hadn't been thinking the words. They had simply come out. When I heard them, I knew, without any doubt, that truer words had never been spoken. It was suddenly so clear, just as Ruby said it should have been all along. I wasn't in love with Dustin. Hadn't been for a long while. I barely liked him. He was still family. Indeed, that feeling hadn't gone away, but my affection for him was no more than I would have felt for an annoying cousin.

We had a history, and honestly, there was still comfort there. Dustin was like a worn-out pair of blue jeans. They no longer looked flattering, stretched out in the ass with holes in the knees and crotch. You know you should throw them out without a second thought, but you don't because you can't imagine any other pair of jeans feeling so comfortable. Even though they're ugly, even though you're embarrassed to be seen in public wearing them, even though you know you can and should do better, you keep them. You've been wearing them so long, they're basically an appendage, and you feel more like yourself with them than without. Yet, suddenly, I didn't want them anymore. I was prepared to throw them away. I was ready to let them go. Ready to let Dustin go.

I attempted to smooth out my wrinkled jacket as I watched Dustin's face fall. I felt terrible but also relieved. The words had to be said because otherwise, he would have continued his exhausting, unhealthy pursuit of me.

"Now, I have to go. I have a date with an absolutely amazing, gorgeous guy who, for some reason, I can't completely understand yet, really likes me." I swung open the bathroom door with gusto. "Please leave me alone, Dustin. I've moved on."

For the first time, I realized with happy clarity that I really, honestly had

TWENTY-FOUR
KYLE

T he prom was already in full swing. The music could be heard through the thick double doors of the ship's auditorium and into The Liquid Lounge. Three levels of tables led down to a stage that spanned the ship's entire width. It had a massive dancefloor leading out from it, and it was already packed. The party's noise nearly rivaled the music's boom, but still, people were piling in. Each one of them in their finest, flashiest or most elegant prom attire.

My eyes were wide as I took it all in. It looked nothing like my high school prom had, but it did look like every over-the-top prom I'd ever seen in movies or on television. Colors seemed muted under the soft overhead lighting. Still, it was enough illumination to make every gem, every sequin, every piece of jewelry sparkle and twinkle like night stars. Blue, pink and green drapes hung in long panels in strategic places throughout the room, and white streamers fluttered from the ceiling. Giant clear helium balloons, secured by white ribbons, floated in several areas with glittering flecks of silver glitter dancing inside them. It looked magical, and like it would be a bitch to clean at the end of the night.

Justin and Sapphire had gone back to their room to change into their prom ensemble because Sapphire claimed it was too hideous to wear to dinner. She hadn't lied. They met me in the lobby, Sapphire wearing one of the tackiest eighties-inspired prom dressed I'd ever seen. It was teal, poufy and short, with a giant bow on the ass, and it matched Justin's powder blue tuxedo perfectly. They looked ridiculous, and I loved it. It made me feel slightly more confident about my pink sequin blazer.

"Let's get some photos first," Sapphire commanded, gesturing to a corner of the room where the cruise ship photographer had set up a picture station. Thankfully, the backdrop wasn't as hideous as the one I'd had at my prom twenty-some years ago. There were no fake Greek columns accented by helium balloons. Instead, the backdrop was a simple night scene. It looked like the ship's top deck, white railing in front of a dark ocean while a large moon and star-filled night sky shone above, reflecting in the water below. It occurred to me that we could have simply gone to the upper deck to take the same photo without using a tacky backing screen. However, that would have meant limiting access to the lido deck to only those in prom attire. This way, the illusion of a high school prom was maintained without interfering with those guests who chose not to participate.

The line-up for photos was still small. I wagered it would only get busier as the night went on, and people became more intoxicated and more inclined to want their pictures taken. I'd always found that ironic since the more people drank, the less photogenic they typically were. The photographer waved Sapphire and Justin forward, leaving me next in line. Sapphire, true to form, was quick to tell the photographer precisely what she wanted.

"I want several photos with my husband and me," she said. I pretended not to notice that she had almost entirely stopped referring to Justin by name since the wedding. Whenever she referred to him, it was only as her husband, like she got a certain level of pleasure by saying the word. "Then, I want a few with my friend and me, then a few more with all three of us." She turned to me. "Do you want any by yourself?"

"God no," I shook my head, horrified by the mere suggestion.

The photographer was patient as Sapphire rattled off a list of things and poses she was not interested in. "I don't want any photos of us kissing. They're tacky, and I have enough of those from the wedding. Nothing with him holding me from behind either. I'm pregnant and starting to feel a little self-conscious about my stomach. I don't want anything to draw attention to it." The woman was crazy. Her stomach was still ridiculously flat. My tummy looked rounder after a heavy meal than her's did after one trimester. "And for the love of Christ," she went on. "No props!"

When we were finished posing, Justin, who had been clearly bored by the entire photoshoot, clapped his hands, rubbing them together in anticipation. "Alright!" he exclaimed. "Let's party!"

Without looking back at me, he held Sapphire's hand as they bounded off. I followed them to the bar where Justin was already ordering us drinks. Sapphire sipped on a Shirley Temple while Justin passed me the featured drink, prom punch, which was basically fruit punch with an obscene amount of rum.

As if on cue, Matt, the ridiculously handsome cruise director, took the microphone. "Happy prom, everybody!" he screamed in his thick British accent. "This is our last big party before we head back to the mainland, and we're making it the best one yet!" The crowd roared.

Among that crowd, I could see Ruby, already on the ballroom floor, dancing provocatively. She was surrounded by a group of four guys, one of them Cody. He had changed into a grey houndstooth blazer and black slacks. As expected, he looked handsome. A short distance away, a group of cookie-cutter bottled blonde women eyed Ruby up and down. From the looks on their faces, it was easy to decipher that they were deep in conversation about the beautiful dark-skinned woman dominating all the single men's attention. They were clearly unimpressed by her. I could tell they were likely using words like *trash* and *slut* to describe her in their conversation.

Either unaware or unfazed, Ruby waved to me. I watched as she moved her bottom round and round, grinding it on the men who took turns standing behind her, holding her waist. Her hips were magic, her curves broad and sensual. Every time the beat picked up, she would pop her booty with a force that defied gravity. I smiled, nodding in her direction while Sapphire and

Justin found an empty booth. They scooted uncomfortably into the bench seating, waiting for me to do the same.

"I'm going to find Jax," I told them, struggling to be heard over the loud music. I practically had to yell.

"Be sure to find us later," Sapphire shouted back. "I want to get some more photos with the entire group."

Of course she did. I had no doubt she would. I nodded in agreement, then began my search. I thought it best to start at the third level and work my way down. While I traveled, I kept a watchful eye out for Dustin and Shawn as well. I didn't see them. Honestly, I had no idea if they still intended to show up, especially considering Dustin's dynamic performance in *Poop Fiction*. They may have decided to stay in their cabin and nurse Dustin's non-existent bowel condition. Which was a possibility I selfishly preferred.

I had made an entire loop of the auditorium and was about to start a second when my eyes found him. My feet took root, stopping me mid-stride at the vision of him on the other side of the dancefloor.

Jax wore an elegant black suit, cut to perfection. His waist was narrow, his shoulders and his chest expansive. His thighs were so muscular I could see the shadows of definition even from across the dancefloor. For a splash of color, he had opted for a patent leather pink bow tie, which matched the pink hue of my jacket almost perfectly. It sat slightly crooked against his collar, but even with that small imperfection, he looked like a masterpiece, and I felt as if I'd conjured him from a dream. I didn't even mind the leather satchel he had slung diagonally across his chest.

He didn't see me at first through the collection of dancers that bopped and flailed between us. Then, as if by my order, the crowds parted, and our eyes met. Eyes that set a hot fire in my belly. Eyes that touched me like a caress. They whispered to me from across the crowded room how happy he was to see me, and I heard the words as if he'd spoken them aloud. Jax smiled, broad and bright, and the vision drew the breath from my lungs in a moment that stretched out between us like a rubber band.

Before I could move, he began a slow, confident saunter across the floor. I thought for sure he'd have to dodge and weave around the cluster of enthusiastic dancers. Yet, they seemed to instinctively stop and clear a path for him, as though mesmerized by the sheer power of his presence.

"I was coming to find you," he said as soon as he was close enough to be heard over the music.

"Here I am," I smiled, almost licking my lips.

"Here you are," he smiled back, and it was like a punch to the gut how much I liked his face.

"Nice tie," I said, reaching out to center it.

"Thank you. You look amazing." The compliment warmed my cheeks, even though I knew I looked like a sparkling pink flamingo.

"I don't know. Don't you think it's a little much? Look at the way it reflects the light. I'm blinding everyone within a two-mile radius."

"It is quite aggressively pink, isn't it?" Jax smirked.

I nodded. "I know. It was an impulse purchase."

"You impulsively bought a pink sequin blazer?"

"To be fair, there were pants to match, but I had the good sense to not buy those."

He chuckled, coming closer, resting his hands on my waist, washing me in the scent of his cologne. "I think you—"

I held up my hand to stop him. "Please don't say I look great in anything I wear, or I might punch you in the gut."

His amusement strengthened. "That seems highly unnecessary."

"Like this jacket?"

"Don't be ridiculous," he laughed again. "You do look great." Then he reached into his satchel, "Although it might clash with this," he said, revealing a delicate red flower in a clear plastic casing.

"You bought me a corsage?" I almost laughed, equally touched and embarrassed.

Jax shrugged, taking the wristlet out of its case. "They were selling them at the gift shop for tonight. I looked for a boutonniere, but apparently, women don't buy men flowers at prom. You don't have to wear it if you find a wrist corsage embarrassing."

"Why would I be embarrassed? A flower is a flower. What difference does it make if it's on my lapel or my wrist?"

Jax smiled at that and held the corsage out with both hands stretching the band apart with his fingers. I slid my hand through the circle, then Jax gently brought the elastics to rest against my pulse point.

"Perfect," he said, sliding the plastic case back into his satchel. When his hands came back out, his camera was in his clutches. "Let's take a picture together."

My smile faltered. "Oh no." I unconsciously shifted away, but Jax held me fast to him by placing his nimble fingers at my waist. "Sapphire already made me pose for several pictures. I'm pretty sure the glare of the flash off my jacket blinded the poor photographer."

Jax rolled his eyes playfully. "Lucky for me, I'll be on the other side of the camera with you." I still hesitated. "I'll delete it if it's bad. I promise." He gave me pouted-lip and sad puppy-dog eyes. How could I say no to that?

He wrapped his arm around me, pulling me close. I was slightly in front of him, my back pressed firmly to his muscular chest. He fiddled with a few switches on his expensive camera, then held it out in front of us, as far as his long arms would allow. He must have set a timer because without touching anything, a light on the camera blinked green once, twice, three times. Then, right before the flash went off, Jax pressed the most delicate of kisses directly to my cheek. That caused me to feel instantly giddy and manifested in an immediate giant smile.

When he broke away, he turned the camera around to show

me the image. It wasn't awful. Jax looked terrific, of course. Tanned, chiseled jaw and perfectly coiffed hair. His expensive black suit with that little pop of color looked chic and dapper. He'd snapped the photo the exact moment he'd kissed my cheek, so my face was bright and smiling. I looked ok, separately, but next to Jax, I looked bloated and pale. Except for my blazer, which was almost too bright to look at. I made a note to never again pair my red hair with anything pink. No matter how much I liked the color.

"See? You look hot," Jax smirked. If by hot, he meant sweaty, then yes, I did. "Can I keep it?" He asked.

I laughed. "Yeah, I guess you can."

"We can take another one if you don't like it."

I wasn't confident a second photo would be any better, so I told him the current one was great, but he was having none of it.

"Just one more," he claimed, and like a gullible fool, I believed him. There were actually two more photos: one of us smiling at each other in profile and a final one of us kissing. Those two photos turned out to be the most perfect things I'd ever seen in my life.

"Do you think we should dance?" I asked with trepidation.

"That's a silly question. Of course we should dance. It *is* a dance, after all." Jax didn't hesitate to take hold of my hand, pulling me toward the floor. It was already crammed with people, but he carved out space for us with ease.

The song playing had a steady tempo, which should have made it easy to find the rhythm, but I struggled as usual. I attempted to move my hips like Jax, but where his were loose and fluid while mine were stiff and rigid. So instead, I settled on a simple side-step, back and forth, as close to on beat as I could muster. I could tell I was a half-count behind, but Jax didn't seem to mind.

Several songs and two rounds of drinks later, Justin and Sapphire found us on the floor, and we formed a dance circle.

Everyone took turns spinning and twirling around, clapping in encouragement to whoever was in the center. The DJ played all of the best prom classics: *Footloose, The Rockefeller Skank, Dancing on the Ceiling*, and more. We valiantly and tirelessly shook our groove things to music I hadn't listened to in years.

The DJ played song after song, one right after the other. I didn't know how people managed to keep up, but they did. Almost two hours straight of dancing, and I was sorely spent. It was then the music turned. As if instinctively knowing that dancers needed a chance to catch their breath, the DJ transitioned to a song that was slow and romantic. Justin and Sapphire didn't miss a beat. They immediately fell into hold, her head resting comfortably on the swell of his chest.

"Well," I sighed, turning to make my way to the edge of the floor. My plan was to wait in the shadows while the couple had their moment. "I suppose no prom is complete without a few cheesy slow dances."

"Where do you think you're going?" Jax caught my wrist as I reached the precipice of where the ballroom floor and the sitting area met. "Is this not a full-service date?"

My eyebrow lifted, and I attempted to mask my smirk. "That depends what you mean by full-service," I smiled suggestively.

Jax didn't miss my tone. "That will come later," he promised. "For now, I think you can afford me the honor of a slow dance or two."

He was right. I could and would have happily. Although the reality that we would be the only same-sex couple on the dancefloor didn't go unnoticed by me. I knew it wouldn't go unnoticed by anyone else either, and that made me nervous.

As gay men, many of the small affectionate practices taken for granted by heterosexuals were denied to us. Simple things like handholding, kissing or slow dancing in public were never intimate. They became political statements or acts of rebellion. Behavior that garnered attention or judgment, sometimes applause but sometimes violence too. It rarely stayed a moment

333

shared by just two people. It became a moment shared between two people and the world. I wasn't sure I wanted to share Jax with the entire room.

"Come," Jax smiled like a vixen. He led me through the throng of drinkers and back into the center of the dancefloor, near Sapphire and Justin. The methodic tune of U2's *With or Without You* oozed from the overhead speakers, its gentle, haunting melody lulling us into a rhythm. I was apprehensive at first, but then Jax placed his one hand on my waist, the other on my shoulder, and the simple touch bolstered my confidence, and we began to sway.

I enjoyed the way Jax moved against me, the way his hands held on to me as though he alone were keeping me upright and safe.

"People are watching," I said, catching several passing glances.

He took my face in his hands, looking at me like I was a sacred relic. "Let them."

"Easier said than done."

"Nonsense. It's as easily done as said." His mouth came to a gentle landing on the side of my neck. "Focus on me." Then, as if by magic, the entire room fell away. There was no awkwardness or tentative touches. It was just us. Jax smiled at me like there was nowhere else he'd rather be, and no one else he'd rather be with. It was the same way he had smiled at me all week.

We were in our own little world where there was no fear, no people, only us together as we danced, lost in each other's eyes. The hunger I saw in Jax's gaze hit me so hard, I nearly combusted. His eyes were ablaze with such intense emotion, I wondered for a second what I did to deserve it.

I leaned into his chest, resting my head in the curve of his neck. His arm came around me and his free hand entwined with mine. Although people still surrounded us, it felt like we were in a perfect little bubble that no one else could penetrate. "I don't think I've ever thanked you for taking pity on some poor schmuck covered in cake."

"Trust me, pity was the furthest thing on my mind when I saw you sitting there." We made a slow rotation on our plot of the dancefloor. "I thought you were the most adorable bloke I'd ever seen. Even covered in royal frosting."

"Buttercream," I corrected softly. There was more I wanted to say but wasn't sure it was the time. After a moment's deliberation, I decided to let it loose anyway. "I told Dustin to fuck off."

Jax looked surprised. "Really?"

"Not in those exact words, but he got the message."

"What message was that?"

"Well," I started hesitantly. I wasn't sure how much I should tell Jax. I decided I'd already opened the can, so I might as well spill the beans. "Dustin propositioned me. He wanted us to get back together," I spat it out quickly.

To this piece of information, Jax did not appear shocked. "I see. "Should I be worried?"

I smiled, attempting to act nonchalant. "Did you miss the part about me telling Dustin to fuck off?"

"No, I did hear it," Jax smiled warmly. "I also know that couldn't have been an easy decision. I realize the history that you two have together."

"Emphasis on history," I said, returning his smile with one equally warm. Although I wasn't sure who I was trying to assure, Jax or myself. He was right, it had been a difficult decision, but he didn't need to know how hard I had wracked my brain before I had made it. When it came right down to it, though, my hesitation had been nothing but fear. So, I pushed that fear down to the pits of my bowels, hoping it would eventually work its way out of my system. Which was disgusting imagery, even if accurate.

I didn't know what the future held for Jax and me, but I would try to give the relationship every chance I could to succeed. I really enjoyed Jax: his smile, his wit, and of course, his beauty and brains. A week ago, I wouldn't have believed the calm, adoring way he looked at me. Now, when I was with him, I felt happy and safe and seen.

"Why are you telling me this?"

"I just figured, if we're going to try this in the real world, I don't want to have any secrets from you."

I expected his smile to broaden, but instead, he nodded solemnly. "Thank you. I'm glad you told me." Then, like a switch, his demeanor turned playful. "Does this mean I'm officially your boyfriend now?"

I couldn't help but laugh. "I haven't really given that much thought to titles."

"You should. I'm an excellent boyfriend. You'd be lucky to have me."

My laughter dimmed, but the smile remained fixed on my face to match his. "Ah, I was wondering when your ego would rear its head again."

"It's never too far away, Kyle," he nodded, smiling. "It's never too far away."

I groaned but kept grinning. I didn't pull away when Jax slid his hand to my hip and twirled me again, right as Bono reached the bridge of the song.

"I guess that would be ok," I said quietly as I fiddled with the edge of his suit jacket. I kept my eyes on my hands, overwhelmed by the feeling that when the dance ended, the magic would disappear along with it.

"What would be ok?" He knew exactly what I was saying but was purposely being obtuse. I could tell by his knowing smirk.

"If you wanted to call yourself my boyfriend." I felt silly, even saying it. It seemed so juvenile.

Jax met my eyes, and I felt the recognition of the moment of our hearts. Humming, he brought his lips to mine. "I like the sound of that." Then we kissed, and it was absolutely magical.

The truth of the matter was that I'd never experienced anything like the fireworks Jax provoked in me with a simple touch. Those fireworks were nothing compared to what happened when we kissed. He wound his arms around my neck, the kiss deepening. My nerves fired at the feel of his long body flush against mine from sternum to hip to thigh.

"You like when I kiss you," he hummed into my mouth with confidence.

I looked away, instantly modest. "And here I thought I was very cool about it."

"Oh, you were, but the male body has a way of betraying even our most guarded thoughts," he teased, casting his eyes down to where my semi-hard cock pressed against his thigh. What could I say? Dancing that close to Jax while dressed in a tight, well-tailored suit did not pair well with my self-control.

Sadly, and all too soon, the slow song ended, and one with a faster rhythm took its place. The real world came rushing back, along with the knowledge that we weren't alone. We stayed, embraced, even after the tempo had changed, staring intensely at each other. We both registered the emotions that were silently being communicated between us.

He kissed me again, deepening it gently, a tiny, sweet taste. When he pulled back, he ran a finger across my forehead. As if he could read my thoughts, his grin widened, and he held out his hand. "Do you think it's time to do more with our bodies than just dancing?"

I looked at his outstretched hand, then back up at his gaze, feeling the answer on the tip of my tongue before my brain even registered the question. My lips parted, eyes dropping to his mouth. "Yes. What do you think?"

"I think I'd like to have sex with my boyfriend, now that I have one."

Hearing him refer to me as such made my stomach shrink about two sizes, and my heart balloon about three, until it was a thundering beast in my chest. I placed my hand in his, then he leaned in to kiss me once. I couldn't help the sappy smile that came over my face as he led me off the dancefloor.

It felt like it took forever to get back to Jax's room. Once there, we found the mattress together, our mouths still melding in a kiss that burned slow, hot and deep. He pressed me into the bed as his hands slid down my chest, gathering the hem of my dress shirt in his fists. I had discarded my blazer at some point, but I didn't much care when or where. Jax slid my shirt up my torso, stopping when I got the hint and tugged it off the rest of the way myself.

Then, I rose to my knees, slowly unbuttoning Jax's dress shirt in return. It hung open, and I moved my hands up his exposed skin, feeling the hardness of his chest, before reaching his shoulders then sliding the fabric off of him like a peel.

No words were spoken. Less the sound of us rustling against each other, the room was quiet. The sound of Jax lowering his zipper truly cut through the silence, then before I knew it, we were both completely naked. The second his cock was free, I wrapped my long fingers around its girth, stroking gently.

We rose to meet each other, our mouths coming together like magnets. Then our hands seemed to be everywhere at once: in my hair, between Jax's legs, on my lips, his neck, my waist.

Jax used one of his hands to reach for the bag of supplies on the nightstand. He had just withdrawn a condom when I pressed my right hand on top of his. "I want to feel you," I whispered.

"Are you sure?"

I nodded. "I trust you." Lord help me, I did. "I want to feel you inside me. Skin to—"

He stifled my words with the muzzle of his lips and kissed me so profoundly, our lips stretched almost painfully. His body moved with determination and barely restrained power as he flung me back onto the bed. Without the need for instruction, I kicked my right leg up over Jax's shoulder and with a dollop of saliva and a flex of his hips, he filled my warmth with his aching rod. He slid into me slowly. I could feel every inch of hard heat as my body tightened, then eventually relaxed and formed around him. Our bodies were a seam with no space. We were joined completely.

We fucked slow and deep. It felt different than all the times before. There were no dirty words, no passionate cursing, no screaming out the names of deities neither of us believed in. There was only an epic tenderness that left both of us gasping and trembling on the ivory bedspread more than any orgasm ever had or could. We climaxed together, release ripping through us until both our bodies were numb, weak and happy. So, so happy.

Collapsing on top of me, Jax pulled me into his arms, sealing our union with a searing kiss. We laid together, hot, sticky and breathless. I didn't want to move or breathe or even bathe. I only wanted to remain locked in his tender euphoric embrace. It was there, resting in the circle of his arms, I wondered how I'd managed to find myself where I was. It was that thought that carried me off to sleep.

I woke an hour or more later, the last remnants of prom punch needing to be released from my tiny bladder. It was still night, and it was still dark. I crawled out of bed, slowly as not to wake Jax, and tiptoed to the small bathroom.

On my way back, I stared down at the marvelous sleeping man. His slow breathing, his slightly parted lips, the face that made my toes curl, were at peace. I was tempted to brush my fingers over his stubble but was afraid to wake him. Looking at him, I felt my heart fill with emotions that terrified me. The feeling of fear rushed through me so quickly that I was suddenly overwhelmed with the urge to leave.

Needing air, I opened the patio door and stepped out onto the balcony. The moon was high and bright over the raven sky, and the ocean was calm. The only wind was caused by the ship as it sliced through the water at its nautical speed. The only waves were those caused by the turmoil in my mind.

What was I doing? *Nine days*, I reminded myself. *We only met nine days ago.*

I didn't really know the beautiful man who lay asleep. At least, not in any real way. We were still strangers, no matter how much it felt like we weren't. How could I have allowed myself to get so attached? To fall for him so quickly? It was a recipe for disaster. Every fiber of my being knew it was all moving too fast, but I didn't want to stop. I felt like I had stumbled hard, deep into a pit. The opening was closing above me, trapping me in the dark. Part of me was clawing at the walls, trying to climb free, while the other part of me was fully content to let the darkness swallow me whole.

Give in to it, I heard a whisper from inside my soul. *Don't think, just feel.*

I'm scared, I whispered back. *This is all happening too fast.*

This is happiness. You're just not used to the feeling. It feels good, doesn't it?

It does, I agreed, *but it also feels too good to be true.*

Why can't it feel good and *be true?*

Because I'm not that lucky.

Even though my internal conversation was silent, the whisper of ocean air from the open door must have stirred Jax awake. "Kyle?" I heard him call from the bed. "What are you doing?"

I continued to stare out into the dark. "Did I wake you?" I resisted the urge to turn and look at him.

"Not exactly. I couldn't feel you in the bed anymore, and I got worried that you left."

He came up behind me, wrapping his arms around me, enveloping me in the sheet he wore as a cape. I snuggled into his shoulder. Feeling him there, behind me, awake and worried, made things seem a little less dark, although not any less confusing.

"I got up to use the bathroom," I said honestly. "I didn't want to crawl back into bed and risk waking you."

"Well, I'm awake now. What do you suggest we do since we're both awake?"

I glanced back at him over my shoulder. His tone said it all, and truthfully, I had been anticipating it. Already I could feel tugs of desire mounting inside me. "I have no idea," I said, feigning innocence.

At that, he growled, pulling me closer, nuzzling his face into my neck. His open mouth pressed hot breath against my skin. "I love it when you play naïve," he teased, flicking the back of my neck with his tongue. I laughed, enjoying the way it felt.

Jax pressed himself tighter against my backside, his erection poking my butt cheek under the security of our cocoon. He caught me grinning. "Like what you feel?"

"Very much so," I replied with a nod as he slid his hands down to palm at my naked ass while placing gentle kisses on the back of my neck. "I think you already know that."

"Come back to bed," he coaxed, thrusting playfully behind me. With a giggle, I allowed him to pull me back into the room and back into bed. As we both knew I would. My dark thoughts from moments earlier were suddenly drowned out by the music of our lovemaking

TWENTY-FIVE
KYLE

When I awoke, it was after dawn, and the sun poured brightly across the bed, bathing me in a hot rectangle of light. I opened my eyes, confused for a moment as to where I was. Then, the previous night's lovemaking came rushing back. It brought a smile to my face.

The last ten days had been utterly, absolutely, entirely perfect, and I was sad to see my final sunrise at sea. The following morning, we would be docked, and we would resume our regularly scheduled monotony. The sun and sand would be replaced by subways and staff meetings, but we still had one more day until then.

I rolled over to greet Jax good morning, but I collided straight into his vacant pillow instead. It smelled like him, the unlikely combination of coconut and man. The entire room did, which only made sense since I had spent the night in his cabin, as I had the last few days. So, why was his side of the bed empty?

Perhaps he was in the bathroom?

Slowly, I sat upright in his bed and called his name. I received no response. He was nowhere to be seen, yet he was everywhere in the room. I saw him in the neat row of shirts hanging in the closet. I spotted him in the bag of camera equipment on the floor by the sofa. I recognized him in the collection of shoes lined up by the balcony door. I could even feel him in the gentle rocking of the ship cutting through the water. It reminded me of the rhythmic way we had moved the night before, rocking and thrusting together until we exploded in perfect symmetry.

I climbed out of bed and, wearing only my boxer-briefs, stumbled to the coffee pot, then set it to percolate. On the desk there, I saw further signs of Jax: his watch, his wallet, the silver chain he wore around his neck, and his passport. Those things, especially his passport, should have been kept in the room's security box for safekeeping. Cabins were cleaned once a day, plus turn-down service in the evenings. As trusting as Jax may have been, housekeeping staff were people, and people were sometimes shady. I made a note to scold him when he did appear.

Alone in his room, I saw it as an opportunity to do what every self-respecting person would do. Snoop.

I peeked through the dresser drawers, thumbing his socks and underwear. I noticed a scandalous red speedo and wondered why I hadn't seen him wearing that around the pool deck. I felt myself blush as I imagined how amazing it would look on him, tight and bulbous in all the right places—the color-popping against his golden flesh.

Moving into the bathroom, I tried to calm my morning bedhead, then quickly brushed my teeth. In the event Jax wanted to pick up where we left off the night before, I needed to ensure my dragon breath didn't scare him away.

When I was done, I scoured his collection of products. I smelled his cologne, his deodorant, his tanning lotion. I felt an immediate sting of jealousy that he had the freedom to wear something other than SPF1000. Seriously, on most sunny days, I would have been safest in full body armor, and his lotion was basically scented margarine.

Leaving the washroom, I continued my rummaging. I combed through the clothes hanging in the closet. A collection of shirts and shorts, most in solid colors void of pattern or pageantry. I found a pair of grey sweatpants, which affected me much like seeing the red speedo had.

Closing the closet, I returned to the desk, where the coffee was finally brewed. I poured myself a cup then toyed with the trinkets there. I picked up the silver chain, letting the metal slide between my fingers. It was heavier than it looked. It felt expensive.

I moved on to the watch. Honestly, I was surprised Jax even had one. Most people seemed to prefer fancy step-counting gadgets as opposed to traditional analog timepieces. It too looked expensive; real leather bands in shades of blue. The blue matched the hands on the watch's silver face perfectly. It said Cartier, but I was confident it was a knock-off.

Drawing the line at rifling through someone's wallet, I skipped over it, picking up the passport instead. Flipping to the middle of the booklet, I found Jax's painfully handsome face.

Even staring expressionless into the camera, in a simple black t-shirt with somewhat messy hair, the man was striking. He could have easily graced the cover of any magazine he wanted. I wondered for the first time why such a beautiful man preferred to be behind the camera instead.

Next to the photo, I perused the specifics. Height: Six-foot-two-inches. Hair: Brown. Eyes: Hazel. No, that wasn't right. *Stunning* hazel eyes. Weight: One-hundred-ninety-three-pounds of pure muscle.

Hearing the keycard swiping in the door, I looked over, startled, and dropped the document I'd been holding. It fell to the floor, it's pages rustling in its descent.

"Good morning," I said, dropping to my knees to pick up his passport. "Where were you?"

Jax entered the room, carrying a tray of assorted fruits and bread. "I ran down to the buffet to get you brekkie and a coffee, but I see you already made a cup?"

"That sludge?" I grimaced, standing up again, his passport in hand. "I'll take the liquid gold from the coffee cart upstairs, over this garbage anytime."

He grinned, pleased with himself and handed me the cardboard cup. "One venti non-fat-no-whip-cinnamon-dolce-latte, just for you. Although, if you ask me, it sounds more like dessert. Smells more like it too."

"That is so sweet of you!" I beamed, trying not to let the fact that Jax knew how I liked my coffee go straight to my heart. "Thank you."

He placed the tray of food on the short coffee table in front of the sofa. "I couldn't have you starve. After last night, I'm sure you worked up quite an appetite."

Laughing, I set my coffee cup down on the night table. "I can't think of any better way to burn calories."

He gestured to the tray. "Fuel up because I plan on taking you for another spin very shortly." Then he chuckled softly.

"What?" I asked, tilting my head inquisitively.

"Your hair in the morning is truly a wonder to behold. Did you know that?"

I ran my fingers through my red waves. "Yes, it has a mind of its own. It takes a little patience and a lot of product to tame it. I did try, though."

"I like it. You look wild and dangerous."

I laughed dryly. "Oh yeah, that's me."

We made very deliberate eye contact. "What do you have there?" Jax asked.

I had almost forgotten I was still holding his passport. "Sorry, I was bored, and I was just—"

"You were snooping," he finished.

"Only a little, I promise." I waved his passport at him. "You know you really should keep this locked up."

"I'm not concerned," He shrugged. "If it makes you feel better, though, I can put it in the safe."

I smiled cheekily, flipping open the booklet back to his picture page. "If you really want to make me feel better, you'd get me a copy of this photo." I made a whistling sound. "Very sexy."

"You're ridiculous," he chuckled. "It's a passport photo. Everyone looks anemic in that lighting."

I took a closer look at the photo. "I don't know, you look very yummy." Grinning, he took the passport from my hand before I could drool over the image any further. He moved to put it in the safe, just as I'd told him he should.

I noticed a folded piece of paper lying on the floor where the passport had fallen. It hadn't been there earlier, so I knew it must have fallen out of the booklet.

"Hang on," I bent down to pick it up, unfolding it to make sure it wasn't garbage or an old receipt. "I think this fell out of your..." my voice trailed off when I saw what it was, a spark of warning triggering at the base of my spine.

He turned to look back at me. "What were you saying?"

I didn't respond. My brain was working overtime, trying to compute new information. Jax could tell something was suddenly off with me. He nudged me with his shoulder. "Hey, what's wrong?"

I frowned, discomfort wriggling through me like a bucket of worms. I looked up at him, my expression bewildered. Dread turning the surface of my skin cold. "What's this?" I stepped away from him, as though he suddenly had some horribly contagious disease.

"What is what?"

"This," I repeated more harshly, flapping the piece of paper in my hand. Jax seemed genuinely confused, so I clarified. "Why has Sapphire written you a check for fifteen-hundred-dollars?"

Panic rolled across his features like a storm cloud. "Um..." he didn't answer straight away. I watched him search for words that I knew would be a lie. One typically didn't have to hunt for the truth.

"The truth, please," I ordered, staring him down, trying to weed it out with my gaze. "Why would she write you a check and why for this much money?"

"You should probably ask Sapphire."

His words were like a cold shower, freezing my core. "I'm asking *you*."

He took a deep sigh. "You might want to sit down."

"I'm fine," I assured him. "Now tell me."

He hesitated for what felt like forever before finally saying, "We didn't meet by accident."

I chewed my lower lip for a few beats, nervously. "What do you mean by that?"

He tilted his head, gaze roaming my face deliberately. "I think you know."

It took a moment for his words to really sink in. When they did, the floor nearly gave way beneath me. I turned away from him, falling back on my heels like I'd been slapped. I did know. "Sapphire," I said her name like it was a curse against my lips.

He nodded, clearly miserable. "I'm here because Sapphire asked me to be."

I froze when he said it, the realization striking me with brute force. "She *paid* you to be?"

He looked sad and guilty as he answered in one single syllable word. "Yes."

My eyes widened larger. I felt like I was standing at the static center of a spinning room. "Sapphire *hired* you?" My voice rose in dramatic inflections. It sounded accusatory, like I had learned he had murdered the real Jax Abernathy and assumed his life. "You're an *escort*?"

Again, he replied in a single word. "Yes." Then he scanned my face like he was trying to gauge my reaction, which I thought by that point was fairly obvious.

The shock made me anxious, and anxiety made me angry.

"Who the hell are you?" I demanded. "Is your name even Jax?"

He leaned back against the wall. "Of course it is. You saw my passport."

"It could have been fake! Like everything else I know about you." Gone was the sweet adoration from the night before. In its place; anger and disappointment. It was painful. I felt it like a punch to my sternum. I started to pace agitatedly. "Are you even a photographer? Are you even Australian? You're probably from California. You're a fucking actor, from California, aren't you?"

"I'm not an actor. I am Australian. Yes, I am a photographer, but it doesn't always pay the bills."

"So you have sex for money to compensate your income?" I flung at him.

"That's not..." He looked at me like I was having a stroke. "Please calm down."

My eyes nearly popped out of my skull. "No! I will not calm down!" I stopped pacing long enough to emphasize my point. "This is gross!"

He flinched, and I immediately felt terrible. "Ouch," he said, genuinely hurt.

I softened momentarily. "Sorry, not *you*. You are still gorgeous, but this," I moved my hand back and forth between us. "This is wrong." He reached out to grab my hand. "No!" I shrieked, pulling my hands away from him, shaking them out at my sides. "Don't you touch me! Don't you dare touch me! You may not get to touch me ever again." Whatever sexual excitement that had been there when Jax first entered the room was decidedly dead. Murdered by my discovery.

"You're overreacting."

"Oh, I'm sorry," I drawled, sounding wretched, but with bitter defiance rising in me. "Is my reaction to the news that my best friend hired me a prostitute not meeting your standards? I'll keep that in mind the next time I find out my boyfriend is actually a paid whore!"

Jax slanted a harsh, humorless laugh at me. "You don't even know what you're talking about. If you would let me explain."

"Why? So you can tell more lies?"

"No."

"Ok then, let's hear the truth."

"Thank you."

I held up my hand abruptly. "No, I don't want some explanation you can spin. Answer me in one word. True or false, Sapphire brought you here on some secret mission to seduce me?"

He hesitated. I could tell he didn't want to answer the question. There was clearly more he wanted to say than the single word I was determined to hold him to.

"Answer me!" I demanded.

He swallowed. "True."

I nodded. "True or false," I said again. "My best friend in the world paid you fifteen hundred dollars to...to..." I growled. "I can't even say it." My best friend hired Jax to sleep with me. The same best friend who would watch nostalgic nineties movies with me every Friday night while we wore moisturizing facial masks and devoured all the junk food ever made. My best friend, who was more like a sister, was secretly a lying prostitute-renting villain who could not be trusted.

Pushing my hands into my hair, I wished I could reach into my head just as easily and shift everything around until it made sense. I started to hyperventilate. Humiliation felt like a tight band around my throat. I lost all ability to speak, think or comprehend. It felt like I was free-falling without a parachute. Needing to sit down, I perched on the edge of the bed and put my head between my knees. I felt sick.

"I'm sorry," he offered. "I'm so, so sorry. I wanted to tell you. I really did, but I couldn't."

Furious, betrayed tears stung behind my eyes. "Why not?"

He choked a little, shaking his head. After a few beats of silence, he confided, "The agency makes us sign a confidentiality contract. You were never supposed to know. Ever."

"*Agency?*" My voice rose again. "Am I really so pathetic that it took an entire team of people to help Sapphire find a date for me?"

I was mortified when I felt my throat grow tight with tears, but I would not let them fall. I would not humiliate myself further by crying. I was outside, looking down on myself. I could hear Jax telling me I was overreacting, and the rational part of me knew he was probably right. Still, my feelings were mine, and they felt justified at the moment. I couldn't ignore or contain them.

Taking a deep breath, I rose from the bed. I had somehow forgotten that I was still only wearing my underwear and I suddenly felt uncomfortably exposed. "I need to go."

He was surprised. "Really? Now? We're in the middle of something, Kyle."

"No, we're not." I slid into my shorts. "We can't do this anymore. You know why we can't."

Jax swallowed hard. "Just like that? All because I'm—"

"A hooker? Yes!" I turned away from him as my snide words hit him hard. I felt as if it should have been the most obvious truth in the world, yet something nagged at me in the back of my mind. "Do you even *like* me? Or were you just doing your job?"

"Of course I like you," he said, scuffing the heel of his foot against the floor. "If you would calm down, we can discuss this rationally."

I held up one hand, eyes closed. "Don't. There is nothing rational about this. I am not overreacting. This isn't a little white lie, like shaving a few years off your age or lying about where you're from. You were *paid* to date me!"

"I get that you're freaked out, I really do, but don't you dare pretend like what's happening between us isn't real." I wheeled around to leave, but he grabbed me by the arm. "Please, don't do this to me."

I stopped, turning very slowly, my eyes on the place where his hand clamped my wrist. For a brief moment, the prospect of my head popping off in a comical release of steam became a genuine concern.

"Don't do this to *you*?" I demanded, shaking him loose. "I'm not doing anything to you! You are not the victim in the scenario. You were paid quite well to date me. On the contrary, you were paid quite well to *fuck* me!" He winced again at my words. Attempting to tamp down my anger, I took a deep breath.

"I care about you."

"No!" I cried, unshed tears glistening behind my eyes. "You lied to me. You kept this one crucial thing from me, the truth of who you are and why we met. What has dictated every moment of…of…whatever this was between us, has been a lie."

Jax didn't appear to have much to say to that.

"Just tell me this; is fifteen-hundred and a free vacation the going rate for orgasms these days? Or did she pay you a little extra because I'm such a fucking burden to be around?"

"You're not…" Jax didn't even have the strength to finish his statement. He looked down at the floor, defeated. I'd sufficiently beaten him, but it brought me no pleasure.

Rubbing my eyes, I tried to get my brain back online. I swallowed a few times to get past the clog of emotions in my throat. The pain in my chest was acute. It felt like a hot tear in my ribs, and I knew it had the power to ruin me. "Why would she do this?" I almost sobbed.

Jax didn't speak, didn't move, didn't breathe. He wasn't even looking at me anymore. Regret and guilt tangled his ability to meet my gaze. "I'm not sure. I make it a habit not to ask questions. You would need to ask Sapphire. She's the client."

I stared at him a moment longer, then turned, making my way to the door. I felt embarrassment, confusion, anger and bile bubbling in the pit of my stomach. Client. The word sounded so clinical and professional. Not at all free-spirited, romantic and fun. Not at all like what I had thought was happening between Jax and me. Obviously, that had been only an excellent performance by a dedicated customer service agent.

I didn't look at him after that. I simply left the room. When I closed the door, the soft click of it seemed to echo throughout the ship. Ask the client, he had said. That was precisely what I intended to do.

I was furious. Shocked and furious. Embarrassed, Shocked and furious. Devastated, embarrassed, shocked and furious. There was no limit to the plethora of emotions that were indiscriminately raging through me, furious being the most important among them.

Storming through the halls of the ship, I weaved up stairwells and down corridors. My body knew exactly where it needed to go, although my mouth had no idea what it would say once it got there. My mind was a disaster, and I wasn't sure I was any more ready to confront Sapphire than I was an hour ago. I was a mess. I wasn't sure I would even be able to form words.

Conniving wasn't a word I would have used to describe Sapphire before that day. Controlling? Sometimes. Manipulative? Perhaps, but weren't we all periodically? Yet, conniving? No. Which was why it felt like such a big shock to my system. More than being angry, I felt disappointed. First, because the romance between Jax and I was utterly, painfully fabricated, but also because I didn't know Sapphire as well as I thought I did.

Disappointment was not an emotion I had ever equated with Sapphire either. She was usually the one I could call to talk me down off a ledge. The friend who forced me to have kale smoothies for breakfast each morning because she was concerned about my cholesterol. The friend who knew all the right things to say at all the right moments to make me feel powerful, strong and loved.

It felt like someone had shown me the secret behind my favorite magic trick, leaving me utterly disillusioned with magic and with life. Everything was a lie. Sapphire and Jax were both fakes. I longed for a time before I had known any of it. When I still saw the magic in the everyday. Although, I knew that was my irrational anger talking. I was far too cynical to ever honestly believe in the magic of the everyday. Yet, the last two weeks with Jax had made me open to it. Now I was slammed shut again.

I reached the door at the end of the hall faster than I thought possible. My legs carried me swiftly when fuelled by rage. It was still early in the morning, but I didn't care. I banged loudly against Sapphire's cabin door, growling her name at the top of my lungs.

Sapphire opened the door, looking dewy. She was wearing a white, fluffy bathrobe, and her hair was wet from the shower. She seemed totally unprepared for the shitstorm I was about to unleash on her. Seeing me and the state I was in, her face showed alarm. "Kyle, what's going on? You're freaking me out."

I barged past her into the room. Justin was sitting on the balcony, enjoying a cup of coffee. He called from outside. "Is everything alright, hon?"

"I don't know yet, babe," Sapphire replied apprehensively,

tossing her hair over her shoulder, flicking droplets of water onto me.

I opened my mouth to speak, but I had no idea yet what to say. So instead, I glared, hoping Sapphire could tell the scope of my anxiety and my anger. It was clearly written all over my face. After all our years together, she should have been able to read me. She definitely could. I watched her slowly realize.

"Um, darling," she called out to the balcony. "Would you mind giving Kyle and me a few minutes?"

Justin sauntered in from the balcony. "Where am I supposed to go?" As usual, he was oblivious to the tension that hovered in the room.

Shrugging, Sapphire told him, "Go down to the breakfast buffet. Have some bacon."

"I thought I wasn't allowed to have bacon?"

I rolled my eyes. Sapphire gave me a look that was half-amused, half-bewildered. "Consider it my wedding gift to you," she jibed. "Give us a half hour. Please."

Justin quickly threw a ball cap on over his matted hair, kissed his wife goodbye then left us alone.

I looked at her, practically murderous. Anger flared in me, surging through my heaving chest as I stood, my eyes blazing in her direction. "You bitch!"

That made Sapphire laugh in her disbelieving *Oh, Kyle* way. "Good morning to you too."

"This isn't funny, Sapphire!" My voice had risen in volume and pitch, my palms pressed firmly at my sides. I often lost my temper; I just didn't usually lose it with Sapphire.

She frowned, confused. "Maybe you should start by telling me what has you so insane this morning."

"Take a wild guess, Miss Matchmaker," I said, voice bitter, my hands on my hips.

Sapphire set her gaze down to the floor. "Shit."

I said nothing for a long moment. I was waiting for Sapphire to continue. "You better have more to say than just shit."

I was sure she did. The funny thing was, she didn't say much of anything. A clock ticked somewhere in the room, too loud in the awkward silence.

Rather than speaking, she made her way to the bed, letting the silence stretch in a thin thread between us before she cut it.

"So…" she began, sitting on the edge of the mattress. "What do you want to know?"

A surge of adrenaline went through my veins. "I don't know, Sapphire. Perhaps you could start by explaining to me why Jax has a personal check from you for fifteen hundred dollars?"

Saying it aloud made it real. It was mortifying. I felt dumb. So, so dumb. I wondered if it was too late to swan dive off Sapphire's balcony.

Her voice was feathery and relaxed. "Calm down, and we'll talk about it."

My back straightened. "Calm down? You hired Jax to fuck me, and you're telling me to calm down?" I thought I heard her give an exasperated sigh as I turned on my heel and started pacing the room. I clenched my hands into fists at my sides, knowing I would never hit Sapphire, knowing I would never hit any woman. Still, I couldn't help but imagine what it would be like to slam one of my fists into the wall, dangerously close to her head.

"Not to fuck you. To distract you."

Snorting out a laugh, I spun back around to face her. I felt drunk. "It's the same thing! You hired a man for me!" The distinction was a technicality, and she knew it. Sapphire's answering silence told me that she did know it but hoped I would have looked past it.

"I know how it looks," she said finally, her guilty eyes searching my face. "I didn't hire Jax for you. I hired him for me."

I flinched like I'd been physically slapped. Sapphire shifted uncomfortably on the bed. "What the hell does that mean?" I demanded.

She looked at me like I was an overly complex problem, and she could write a dissertation on all the ways I annoyed her. "You know what it means," she assured me, resting her hands on the bed beside her. "Please don't make me say it."

Silence hung in the air between us. I stared at her hollowly, feeling like my heart was caught somewhere between my tonsils. I had no idea what she was trying to tell me. When she realized I hadn't figured it out, she said, "I didn't want to have to babysit you!" She didn't yell, but her voice came out angry and frustrated. I felt instant pain like she had stabbed me with sharp, scorching steel. "You were already very vocal about how much you didn't want to come on this trip. You seemed quite determined to be miserable." I crossed my arms. "I asked Ruby to keep you company, but we both know how Ruby is."

"So you hired a prostitute!?" My anger was palpable.

Flames. On the side of my face.

My throat, my face, my everything burned with unbridled anger. I paced the room, the imaginary image of Jax and Sapphire conspiring together flashing into my mind, spurring my rage.

Sapphire was quiet, brow furrowed. She fidgeted when she was anxious, and at that moment, she was tugging on her wedding ring, absently spinning it around her finger. Eventually, she exhaled, her shoulders dropping. "He's not a prostitute."

"If you say he's an escort, I swear to God I'm going to throw something at you."

"I needed a backup plan," she said, her voice sharp. "In case Ruby got distracted, which I knew she would. Jax was here to keep you entertained, so you didn't make this entire trip about you being alone and miserable."

"That is not something I would do!"

"Yes, it is!" Sapphire laughed ruefully. "You've been doing it since I asked you to be my man of honor!" She started to list the examples. "First, you didn't even want to come to my wedding because you didn't want to see Dustin. Then, you tried to make me feel guilty on my wedding day because it made you uncomfortable that I allowed Dustin to bring his boyfriend. Then, you looked so incredibly miserable, walking down the aisle next to Dustin, that people weren't even looking at me. They were looking at you! You barked disgustingly inappropriate things at my wedding guests during your speech because you were frustrated. You destroyed my wedding cake because you were drunk, and you were angry with Dustin."

As she went down the list of my bad behavior, I was faced with reality as she saw it. I had been a problem she felt necessary to contain. This new perspective pulled me up short, and the truth of it blew through me. I felt additional anger and pain start to brew. Her words got under my skin, even though I knew there was truth to them.

"It's always about you," she went on. "I know you don't do it on purpose, but you do it all the same. I try to control where we go, what we do, and who we do it with because it's the only way I'm guaranteed that something in our friendship will be about me and what I want."

I shook my head, trying to chew on her answer.

She continued. "Jax was my insurance policy. He was my guarantee that I could have you, my best friend in the world, on this trip with me and still have this time be about me." She looked like she was about to cry.

Defensiveness pushed aside introspection, and I resorted back to anger. "So you hired some guy from, where? Google?"

Sapphire sighed, pinching the bridge of her nose. "Could you stop being an obtuse fucking asshole for, like, twenty seconds?"

"Can you stop being a manipulative cunt?" I heard myself shout before I even consciously decided to say it. To her credit, she didn't even look offended. Her face was expressionless, and she only blinked. "Seriously, Sapphire? You hired a fucking gigolo, and somehow, I'm the asshole? I can't even…" I cut the words short, rubbing my chin with aggravation.

We looked at anything but each other. Eventually, Sapphire turned her face back to me. I watched her expression flutter through something angry, then to pained before finally settling on gentle. "Jax was supposed to be a gift for both of us," She said, shaking her head sadly.

"A *gift*?" I uttered the word with a level of disdain one would usually reserve for fecal matter. "What if I didn't like him? Could I have exchanged him for a blonde? Or a caftan?"

She held up her hands in a request for a temporary cease-fire. "I wanted a little bit of a break, and I knew you needed a little romance."

I barked out a laugh, seeing her request and denying it flatly. "Romance? Do you know what they call romance you have to *pay* for?"

It was a rhetorical question, but a part of me hoped she would answer, just to hear the words *trick* or *john* come out of her mouth. Sapphire didn't answer. Briefly, I thought I'd gotten through to her from the way she closed her eyes and braced herself against the headboard. Still, when she reopened her eyes, I realized she had spent that moment searching for more reasons to explain all of it away. Her eye contact was hard and deliberate.

"First of all, it wasn't like I picked him up on the corner of Madison. He works for a legit agency. The network uses them from time to time to provide dates for our talent. It's strictly professional. Secondly, yes, I technically paid for him to hang out with you, but why does that matter? You had a good time with him, didn't you?"

Exhaling a shaky breath, I ran one hand through my hair. I started to pace back, away from the door, which I realize I'd gravitated near as some automatic fight-or-flight response. "Why does that matter? Are you fucking serious? It matters because it's fake! It matters because it's embarrassing! It matters because it's *wrong*!"

"Holy shit, Kyle," Sapphire snapped, bolting to a stand, pointing a finger at me. "You're so stubborn. Why are you like this? You have a serious moral superiority complex, you know that?" Her face was so tight.

My jaw clicked shut as I met her eyes, mine glaring, hers cold. "I do not."

"Yes, you do! You have these ridiculous ideas in your head about how things should be or how people should behave, and when people don't do things exactly how you think they should, you attack."

"I do not."

"You're doing it now!" She yelled. "Are you honestly so simultaneously self-centered and unaware of yourself that you don't even realize how self-centered you are?"

I opened my mouth then closed it again. There was no great way to answer that.

"You tend to swallow all the air in the room. You do it with people all the time. You did it with Dustin. You constantly pulled focus. It's probably one of the reasons he cheated. He was starved for attention." Ouch. That stung. "Maybe if you weren't turning into a bitter, selfish, sarcastic, narcissistic old troll, I wouldn't have to pay people to spend time with you. If you're not careful, you're going to end up completely alone."

That stung more. It felt like a physical punch to my stomach, and I took an instinctive step back. My face was hot, and I stood there blinking, mouth open, ready to respond, but absolutely nothing came out. Even if I could speak, I didn't know what to say. I was struck entirely mute. My stomach dropped through the ship's floor into the darkest depths of the ocean beneath us.

My mind was a beehive, humming, buzzing and crawling in my skull. I had gone to her room with what I thought was a clear idea of who she was. I thought I'd known who we were together, as friends, but that image was crumbling before me. Sapphire and I sometimes argued, which was bound to happen when you spent almost every moment with somebody. This, however, was new. Was that what she really thought of me? Sapphire thought I was bitter, selfish and narcissistic? She genuinely felt that I was a horrible little troll and was going to end up alone?

Finally, I spoke. "Well, since spending time with me is such a horrible experience, I'll make it easy for you. I don't ever want to see you again." I immediately wanted to sift the words out of the air and shove them back into my face.

"Kyle..." she started, sitting back on the bed, spent.

"You know," I interrupted, being too proud to take back my words, so instead, pushing forward with their sentiment. Once I decided on a course of action, there was no dissolving of my commitment. "This is actually perfect because I can't even look at you right now."

I stomped toward the door. Sapphire sat motionless, speechless.

"I'll be sure to reimburse you for your *gift* and the cruise." I snarled, pulling the door open. I paused there, in the open doorway, looking at Sapphire. She had started to cry.

Being a true best friend meant sometimes feeling responsible for the other's emotional well-being. At that moment, all I wished to do was take it back. I wanted to pretend I was joking and travel back to when I knew nothing about her scheme. Part of me wanted to stop, close the door, join her on the bed, and cry it out like we'd done for countless arguments in the past, but I couldn't. A larger, more powerful part of me wanted to make Sapphire hurt, as deeply and as thoroughly as I was hurting at that moment.

A bitter old troll, that's what she thought of me, someone who had to pay a fee for anyone to even want to spend time with him. She knew my every insecurity and had used them against me. Her words were sharper than any blade and more piercing than any bullet.

"I'm sorry, Kyle," she whispered, her voice horse against the cascading tears. "I don't know what else to say to make you believe me. You were never supposed to find out."

"A lie is more reliable than rope. No matter what you say or do, it will always catch you up, eventually."

It was something my grandmother used to say, and I had never quoted it before. Sapphire didn't seem impressed by the proverb. She looked defeated as her breathing increased, and she struggled through her tears. "I never wanted..."

"Yeah, well, you did," I interrupted coldly. My throat was getting tight. I tried to swallow but couldn't.

Sapphire was looking back at me, her mouth open, her eyes wet. "You know how much I love you."

"No!" I yelled, clenching my fists. My eyes turned to steel. "Don't you do that! Don't pretend like you give a shit about me. If you really did, you wouldn't have done this."

My hands, knees and heart shook. I turned and walked away, needing out of that room, needing to calm down, needing to remind myself that not everyone wanted to hurt me.

"You're my best friend," she called after me, between sobs.

Shaking my head, I felt my own tears pressing in from the back of my eyes. "Not anymore," I growled, storming out of the room, slamming the door behind me. For the first time in a long time, I felt truly alone.

TWENTY-SIX
KYLE

It was the worst I'd ever felt. Worse even than when I'd caught Dustin cheating. There was a hollowed-out vacancy in my heart, and it left me on the precipice of a violent fit or bursting into tears. I tried not to think on my way back to my room. If I did, I feared I might have broken down, becoming an inconsolable, blubbering mess, right there in the hall.

When I reached the door to my room, I paused, anxiety buzzing in my ear, like the tiny wings of a petulant wasp. I could feel my heart racing, beads of sweat gathering at my temples and my neckline. My breaths were coming shallow, and my hands were shaking too much to use my keycard. I recognized the signs, the low hum of an impending panic attack.

At that moment, the kaleidoscope of emotions coursing through my mind and heart were dizzying and nonsensical. Ten days. I had known Jax for ten days. The depth of deception and betrayal I felt seemed disproportionate to our time spent together.

Oh, but what a time it had been! In those ten days, I had felt more at ease and more like myself than I had in an exceptionally long time. The levels of joy and pleasure I had felt in Jax's presence, in his embrace, and in his bed were immeasurable and defied all common-sense. Our time together may have been brief, but it had also been magical.

I shook my head. No, I couldn't think about that now. It would only cloud my judgment. I needed my head to be clear so I could process everything I now knew. Thinking about the fantastic sex or how spectacular Jax had made me feel would only send me running back to his gorgeous, muscular, lying arms.

Seducing me and taking me to bed had been his plan all along. A sinking feeling grew in my chest as this thought occurred to me. As great as he had made me feel, it hadn't been real. It had been his mission. I had been a target, and the thought made my stomach roil. I clenched my fist, battling with a mixture of anger and disgust that enflamed my body.

In hindsight, it made perfect sense. Looking at the two of us side-by-side, it should have been blatantly obvious. On the hotness scale, I was a four, whereas Jax was a perfect ten. Screw that. He was more like a fifteen. Yet, like an idiot, I had been too lost in the sexual haze to think critically. I berated myself for that lapse in judgment with all my mental strength. I should have guessed he was an escort. Of course, a man that pretty would only spend time with someone like me if paid to do so.

Even though Jax hadn't technically rejected me, a feeling of rejection and shame slipped over me like a rogue wave. There was so much going through my mind. It was impossible to process it all, especially out there in the hall, so I took a deep, trembling breath then pressed the keycard against the scanner.

It beeped red.

"No-no-no-no," I begged, a stinging rush of tears nipping at the corners of my eyes. "Don't do this to me again." I scanned the card a second time. Once again, it beeped in malfunction. "Work! You mother-fucking-piece-of-god-dammed-shit!" I screamed, kicking the door violently. "Work!"

My heart thundered as I added my angry fists to the mix. The sound of my pulse was deafening, my breath ragged and aching with every draw. I punched, kicked and screamed until the screams melted into soft sobs, and my body collapsed against the door. Exhausted and broken, I pressed my forehead firmly against the peephole, wishing I could disappear.

"Kyle?" Dustin asked, poking his head out of his own room to see what the commotion was about. "What's wrong?"

When I didn't respond, he stepped fully out into the hall, coming to stand beside me. "What's wrong?" He asked again, pressing his hand gently on my shoulder.

"This fucking door!" I wailed, throwing my head upwards towards the ceiling.

"Okay," he said hesitantly. He didn't buy for one single second that the uncooperative door was the sole reason for my current state. He gingerly took the keycard from my clutch and pressed it against the reader. It scanned green for him. Of course it did. It was such a stupid machine.

Opening the door, I immediately stormed inside. Reeling, I fell onto the bed, then picked up a pillow and screamed into it.

Dustin trailed behind me, making a detour to grab the box of tissues on the writing desk before plopping down next to me on the bed. He placed the box in between us.

I could see Dustin's internal struggle. I watched him fidget awkwardly beside me, fighting the urge to wrap his arm over my shoulder to console me. "Now, what's really wrong? I don't believe that the door has you this distraught."

Grabbing a few squares of tissue, I brutally blew my nose, then tossed them to the side before grabbing a couple more and dabbing at my eyes. "It's too embarrassing to talk about." I blew and tossed again.

"More embarrassing than barging in my room stark-naked and Shawn finding us with your testicles in my face?"

I gave a small laugh through the tears. "Well, no, but equally damaging to my psyche."

He reached for my hand but didn't squeeze it in his. "I can't help you until you tell me what's wrong," he said gently. I sniffled in reply. "Is it your Australian?"

A whole new set of tears erupted. This time, Dustin made contact. He wrapped a strong arm around me, pulling me close to his shoulder. He held me there, tight to him. That close, through my tears, I could see the genuine concern in Dustin's eyes, heartfelt and real.

"Hey, it's okay," he assured me, stroking the back of my head like he used to when we were together, and I was upset. "If you don't want to tell me, I can call Sapphire."

I let out a painfully loud wail. I expected Dustin to comically cover his ears to shield himself from my banshee-esque cry. Instead, he held firm, pulling me closer. "So, uh," Dustin attempted. "I'm guessing from your response that you and Sapphire are also in a fight now?" I whimpered. He lifted my chin to meet his eyes. "You can tell me. I promise I won't be a dick about it."

"You're a dick about everything," I sobbed, almost inaudibly.

"That's mostly true," Dustin agreed with a subtle grin. "Still, you can tell me stuff. I am capable of empathy."

"I really liked him," I said once I stopped crying long enough to form words. Perhaps I should have felt guilty for leaning on him when Dustin had made it abundantly clear that he wanted more from me, but I didn't.

"I know you like him, Kyle, but it was a vacation romance, remember? You knew It couldn't last forever."

I took a deep breath and slowly blew it out. "It's not about that."

"Well then, what is it about?" There was no agitation in his eyes, only concern.

"He's an escort," I spat out the words like they were acid on my tongue.

Dustin's nose scrunched. "Really? He didn't peg me as a hooker."

My voice came out thick and strangled. "Sapphire hired him."

The combination of shock and pity on Dustin's face was unmistakable. "That's…" I watched him actively search for the right word to describe what I'd told him. Finally, he settled on "shitty."

"You think?" I replied flippantly, finally curtailing the flow of tears and regaining composure.

Dustin looked wounded. "Hey now, I'm not the culprit here." He was right, and I felt a pang of guilt for speaking to him in that tone when he was genuinely trying to console me.

"I'm sorry," I offered, scrubbing my face dry of tears. "Please tell me you didn't know."

"I had no idea, I swear. Honestly, I have a hard time believing that Sapphire would do that."

"So did I," I agreed. "Until Sapphire admitted it to me herself."

"Wow. I'm so sorry to hear that. Did Sapphire say why?"

"She said she didn't want to babysit me. Like I was someone she was burdened with. So, she hired Jax to keep me out of her hair."

I waited for Dustin's reaction, but he gave none. Instead, he asked, "How did you learn all this?"

"I found the check. Sapphire paid Jax fifteen-hundred-dollars and a free cruise, all to keep me out of her hair." That number had been floating around in my head since I'd discovered the check.

"Wow. That's…wow." Dustin stumbled, speechless.

"Am I seriously so pathetic that I need to start paying for

dates?" I realized I was fishing for a compliment, but I didn't care. At that moment, I needed one.

"No," He shook his head. "You are a lot of things, but pathetic will never be one of them. You're stubborn and pigheaded and—"

I glared at him, pulling away. "Are you trying to make me cry *more*?"

"Of course not. If you let me finish, I was going to say that even with those flaws, you're still kind of amazing."

A warm flush brushed my cheeks. "If I'm so amazing, then why do men keep breaking my heart?"

Dustin examined me, his brow quirking, as a sad but knowing grin spread across his face. "Speaking as one of the men who did so, all I can say is that it's not about you. We all have issues that sometimes make it difficult to love people the way they deserve. No matter how amazing they are."

"I thought he was different," I said mostly to myself.

"I didn't," Dustin declared, his expression straightening and a hint of protectiveness creeping into his voice. "There was always something about him. Something I didn't quite trust. I couldn't put my finger on what, but I suspected he was a douche from the moment I met him."

I smiled, even though it was hollow and disingenuous. "I suppose it takes one to know one," I teased.

"Indeed, it does. Besides, his name is Jax. That's a red flag if ever I've seen one. So ostentatious."

I couldn't help but laugh. "You know, there are some who might say Dustin is also an especially pretentious name."

With a hand to his chest, he feigned insult. "You wound me, sir." I laughed again. This time the sound was genuine. "Seriously though, a man who needs a paycheck to want to spend time with you isn't worthy of your tears."

I stared at him, shocked that he was so generous with his words, especially after I had been so dismissive and cruel to him the night of the prom.

"As much as I love Sapphire," he went on, "if she's the one who hired him, then she doesn't deserve your tears either."

I shrugged one shoulder, feeling like a total idiot. "She's my best friend."

"That may be true, but she still doesn't deserve your tears.

Spending time with you is not a burden." Dustin's left hand came up to stroke along my jaw. "You are smart and funny. Getting to spend time with you is a privilege." Dustin's right hand touched my left hand gently, two fingertips against my palm. "It took losing you for me to realize that." He laced his fingers through mine, and I let him.

Reaching for him in return, I pressed one thumb into the hollow of his collarbone, slipping right under the knot of his Adam's apple.

"You deserve so much more than anyone has ever given you, including me." Dustin paused, taking a breath. My stomach twisted. "You deserve love and honesty. I promise I can give both to you this time."

The muscle in Dustin's jaw ticked, and there was the tiniest tilt of his head. He gave me a meaningful stare, and the desire to kiss him bubbled up in my chest. My thoughts drifted to all the things I knew his mouth, lips, and tongue were capable of doing to my body. The visions slid into my heart and mind, uninvited. I shifted my eyes away from his impenetrable gaze, but the desire in my belly lingered. I counted to ten in my head then waited for the feeling to pass. It didn't.

Sexual tension rose like smoke in the room, thick and suffocating. I reached out, resting my right hand on Dustin's stomach. He spasmed slightly beneath my touch. My fingers scratched lightly there, down to the hem of his shirt, and I slipped my thumb under, stroking. The point of contact where my thumb touched his bare skin was suddenly the hottest part of my body. My left hand joined my right, and I ran both of them up under his shirt, over his chest. I'd forgotten how firm his body was. He hummed beneath my touch, and I relished in his reaction.

Then he kissed me.

Dustin's lips were as soft as I knew they would be, and mine received his willingly, pliant against his moving mouth. I pushed my fingers deep into his hair, sucking the air out of him while Dustin wound his hand tightly around my waist, bringing me closer. I couldn't hold back the moan that slipped out. The primal sound seemed to spur him on, and he hugged me even tighter, banding his arm around my back.

We fell onto the mattress. Dustin was careful not to land

directly on top of me, but I longed to feel the sensation of his weight, the heat, solidity and sheer size of him. He hovered over me, on straight arms propped near my shoulders, his gaze roaming across every inch of my face. The way his eyes searched me looked like he wanted to say something. I silently begged him not to ruin the moment with words, especially not any further declarations that would cause my head to swirl with thought. I didn't want to think. I only wanted to feel. Thankfully, he said nothing, and I wondered if he could read my mind.

Dustin carefully lowered over me, groaning quietly when my legs came up along his sides. He knew what I liked from all of our years together. I skirted my hands down his back as he started to move against me. It felt good and familiar, but also wrong. Our history still hung over me like a cloud. I wished I could go back in time and remember what it was like to feel him for the first time, before the disappointment and pain.

We kissed again, with more intensity. Wrapping my hand around Dustin's neck, I opened my mouth to invite his tongue in. We tangled, and with each brush of his tongue against mine, each time his teeth grazed my lips, I felt the heat in my stomach grow and expand to other areas of my body, which were screaming yes while my mind screamed no. I silenced all the warning bells going off in my head, then reciprocated his grinding. After so much time ignoring it, I could no longer deny that I wanted him, especially at that moment.

Then suddenly, we were in the eye of a storm. We kissed madly, pumping, grinding, pulling at each other until Dustin pinned my hands to the mattress, limiting my movement. His palms were soft slides of heat, up over my stomach, to my chest. His fingertips mapping every inch of me. His sounds vibrated against my lips, into my mouth.

Dustin lifted my shirt up over my head then turned his attention to my belt, button, and zipper. Before I knew it, my shorts were pulled open wide, his hands digging into my boxer-briefs, feeling the length of me. He smiled breathlessly, looking extremely pleased with himself.

His hand on my shaft felt glorious, and the pleasure swallowed up my common-sense like a shark would a school of minnows. Maybe it could work, after all. I litigated with myself, running through all the pros and cons I had contemplated a few days earlier. I considered all the possible outcomes. What would Dustin and I back together look like? How would it affect those people around us? We already broke up once, could I put our friends through that again? What about Shawn? Shawn was young but promising. He didn't deserve that kind of betrayal. I pondered more about Dustin and our potential relationship than I ever cared to.

Laying my head back on the pillow, I closed my eyes as Dustin explored the length of me with his tongue. His woodsy cologne wafted over me—all bourbon and musk. Immediately, I noted that I preferred Jax's tropical scent over Dustin's, and I knew that wasn't the time to make that comparison.

There I was, my cock in Dustin's mouth, but I was thinking of Jax and his fragrant body-wash. The way it made him smell like citrus and coconut. I smelled like Jax too, I knew, having spent the night in his bed.

Somewhere through the smoke of sexual desire, I heard a single word escape my lips. "Jax..." If Dustin registered the moan, he didn't react to it, but the sirens had returned to my brain with a vengeance, extinguishing all flame.

My eyes sprung open.

"Stop," It came out as a whisper, but Dustin continued servicing me. "Stop," I repeated louder and with more conviction. I felt him pause mid-suck. His eyes lifted, meeting mine. "I can't do this."

Dustin released me. "Of course we can," he said, his lips swollen and wet. "We love each other."

It would have been so much simpler if that were true, but I knew better, now more than ever before. What was happening between us at that moment had nothing to do with love. I couldn't deny that there was an attraction, chemistry even. Still, what was happening at that moment was about me feeling hurt, sad and wanting to feel anything but the pain. Love no longer fit into the equation. Even Dustin deserved the truth.

"No, I don't love you," my voice came out strong and forceful as I pushed him off of me. "And I won't do this." Pulling my underwear and shorts up over my erection, I swung my legs over the edge of the bed, resting them on the floor. "You have to go."

Dustin looked shocked, as though I had uttered the most ridiculous phrase he'd ever heard. He stared at me with flat skepticism for one, two, three seconds before shaking his head. "What are you talking about?" I could hear a laugh hovering at the gate of his mouth. "I'm not going anywhere."

"You have to go," I said again as I hurried off of the bed before my raging hard-on changed my mind. "Please, go. You have to go." If I said it enough times, I hoped it would sink in.

From the myriad of expressions that crossed Dustin's face, I could tell that it was, slowly. I watched him move from shock to bewilderment to mildly entertained, then finally to wounded. I knew Dustin well enough to recognize that anger was about to follow.

"Are you fucking serious?" His voice was a growl, the train of anger arriving right on schedule. He stabbed each word with condescension. "Is this a joke to you?" He demanded, getting up from the bed.

"Of course not," I replied, picking up my t-shirt, holding it between us like a shield. "I know I made the first move. I'm sorry. I thought it was what I wanted, but it's not. I would be using you to feel better."

"I don't care," he shrugged.

"I do," I protested. "It wouldn't be right. You have a boyfriend. I won't help you hurt Shawn like this. That's not who I am."

He laughed coldly. "Right, because you're so morally superior."

"It's not about being superior. It's about having a conscience. Shawn cares about you. This would devastate him."

"I don't love Shawn."

"You don't love anyone!" I shouted. "You don't know how to love anyone but yourself. You are a very charming person, Dusty, but you're also selfish, arrogant, destructive and cruel. I allowed myself to forget that for a moment, but it's how you are in relationships. You won't ever change. I deserve better, and so does Shawn."

"At least I'm not some pathetic fool who needs his best friend to buy him hookers," he spat the last three words with painful, patronizing clarity. They hit me with the aim of a sharpshooter's bullet. He had intended them to sting, and they

367

did.

"Get out," I ordered, no longer feeling the need to be polite. "Get the hell out of my room." I extended my arm in the direction of the door for dramatic effect.

"Fine," Dustin fumed. On his way to the door, he stopped mid-step, turning to me. "One of these days, you're going to change your mind. When that day comes, it will be too late. I'll have moved on again, and you'll be alone, forever." The blaze in his eyes and in his words frightened me, but I stood firm.

"I guess that's a chance I'll have to take," I replied, pushing him to the door.

"I can't believe you're doing this to me again," he muttered.

I paused. "What the hell are you talking about?"

"You know exactly what I'm talking about. You can pretend you don't remember all you want, but you and I both know what happened the other night."

"What are you talking about?" I asked again. "Do you mean when you kissed me?"

He shook his head. "No. I'm talking about when we almost slept together on the night of embarkation."

I felt like he was talking to me in gibberish. Nothing he was saying made any sense. Embarkation night was the evening of Sapphire's wedding. The man had spent the entire time making me miserable, then threw me into a table of champagne and cake. I most definitely had no interest in sleeping with him that night.

"Have you lost your mind?"

He eyed me suspiciously. "Wow. I thought you were pretending, but you really don't remember shit about that night, do you?" Thanks to Ruby spiking my drink with G, I really didn't. "I ran into you in the hall. Shawn had gone to bed early, and I was on my way back to the room. You were locked out of your suite, something about your stupid keycard giving you a hard time."

That part certainly sounded like the truth.

"Okay, I'm with you so far. Then what happened?" I wasn't sure if I could trust him to be honest, but I figured I knew him well enough that I would be able to tell if he chose to lie.

"You were a little tipsy, so I came in to make sure you were okay. That's when you threw yourself at me."

"I threw myself at you?" I probed with a raised eyebrow. That part was bullshit, and I knew right away, by the way his eyes shifted when he said it.

"All right, I made the first move, but you were totally into it," he assured me. "You took off all your clothes, and we were half-way into it before you started freaking out, demanding I leave. You shoved me out of your room and into the hall."

It suddenly all made sense. That was how I'd ended up locked out of my room naked. I'd shoved Dustin into the hall, and the door must have closed behind me. At some point, I had found my way into the laundry room and fallen asleep. Even given everything his story revealed about the laundry room mystery, something about it really unsettled me.

"So let me get this straight," I started, anger rising in my voice again. "You saw me all sloppy and falling down drunk, then decided that would be a great opportunity for you to try to get me into bed? What the fuck is wrong with you?"

"It wasn't like that," he glared. "You wanted it. I know you did."

"That is the defense used by date rapists everywhere, you pig!" I screamed at him. "Get the hell out of my room!" I flung open the door with so much force, the hinges groaned in protest, then I shoved him out into the hall, a deja vu moment for him, I was sure.

By bad luck or fate, or a combination of both, I almost pushed him directly into Shawn. He happened to be walking past my door at that exact moment, on his way back from his morning workout. Shawn stopped dead in his tracks, taking immediate stock of Dustin and me. My shirt was still off, my shorts still wide open, and although Dustin was fully clothed, he looked equally disheveled.

Heat immediately rushed to my face, so I dipped my chin and eyes toward the floor. I wasn't only humiliated at that moment. I was guilty. It built up within me until I ached from the grit of my teeth to the curl of my toes. As the feeling washed over me, I whispered a silent appreciation to a higher power that, at the very least, my erection had deflated.

Dustin's expression was a lot less smug than it was only a few seconds earlier. He looked downright ashen. For a moment, I thought he was going to make a run for it.

369

"Baby, it's not what it looks like," he said with a note of nervousness. Obviously, that was his go-to response whenever he was caught doing something he ought not to be doing with someone he ought not to be doing it with. My knee-jerk instinct was to glare at him, but he wasn't even looking at me, so the gesture would have been wasted.

"Really?" Shawn asked. "Kyle is half-naked, and your lips are red from friction." I could tell from Shawn's expression that he knew exactly what had happened and what had been happening the majority of the trip. It occurred to me for the first time that Shawn had only been pretending to be oblivious to Dustin's wandering eye.

"Baby," Dustin said, moving closer to him. "Kyle was upset. I came to check on him, and he threw himself at me."

I wanted to laugh at Dustin's version of events but wisely opted for silence. When I examined the evidence, I had technically made the first move, so instead of disputing his claim, I simply glared at him.

Shawn's eyes went ice cold, sharp. A window slammed shut. "You really do think I'm stupid. Don't you?"

"Of course not," Dustin assured him. "Baby, I love you."

Shawn closed his eyes, exhaling through his nose. He was shaking, and I was quite sure that it wasn't from the air conditioning. "I want to believe you. I do, but it's so obvious what's going on."

"I promise, nothing happened." Dustin lied so quickly it should have disgusted me, but it no longer surprised me. He was such a complete dirtbag.

Shawn gnawed his lower lip, looking more disgusted than upset. Then his gaze shifted to touch on me, hitting me like a ninja star between the eyes. "Is this true?"

"I don't want to get involved," I said, waving my hands in front of my chest.

"You're already involved."

Shawn was right; I was. The thought sent rolling discomfort through me. I owed it to him to answer his questions truthfully, so I took a deep breath, steadying myself. "He's lying," I told him, feeling guilt all the way to my breastbone. "He's been trying to get with me the entire trip." Dustin murdered me with eyeball daggers.

Shawn sighed, a hoarse, tired sound in the back of his throat, then scrubbed his face with one hand. He opened his mouth to say something but reconsidered. He closed his lips tightly, swallowing whatever words had been resting on his tongue.

"I'm sorry," is what came out of Dustin's mouth, miserable and earnest. "We never slept together," he tried to justify. "We almost did just now, but I stopped it."

Shawn examined Dustin for a second, then looked to me again. "Half-true," I nodded. "We haven't slept together, but we would have if *I* hadn't stopped it. I'm sorry." I hoped Shawn saw that I was sincere. He seemed to.

Dustin scoffed, throwing his hands, visibly upset that Shawn chose to believe me over him. He reached out an arm to touch Shawn's shoulder, but Shawn quickly dodged his touch.

"It's not my fault," Dustin proclaimed lamely. He looked wretched, forlorn and on the brink of tears. That rare display of vulnerability tilted me sideways. For a moment, I felt sad for him.

"Seriously, Dustin? What does that even mean?" Shawn wasn't buying what Dustin was hawking, and I felt new-found respect for him.

Shawn's voice had started to rise, and I took that as a sign to take my leave. Part of me wanted to stay in the hall to see how the rest of the conversation unfolded, but I was reasonably sure I knew how it would end. Dustin would lie, Shawn would cry, then there would be screaming, followed by cursing. Ultimately, they would both storm off. I'd given a performance in that identical scene with Dustin before. I didn't need a front-row seat to the matinee. Turning, I walked back into my room and didn't even look back at Dustin or Shawn as I closed the door behind me.

TWENTY-SEVEN
JAX

Dropping my head onto the bar, I groaned. I blew it. I bloody-well blew it. The moment Kyle had discovered that check, I knew the jig was up. I had felt something shift between us. Had smelt it in the air like burned sugar, potent and sour. I watched as Kyle deflated right in front of me. His shoulders slumped, his smile faded, and the twinkle in his eyes went dark. Burnt out, like a cactus star.

Seeing Kyle standing there in his grundies that morning, his hair dishevelled and a look of morning laziness on his face, I'd been struck with a massive wave of possessiveness. It had been staggering. I stood there, awestruck, staring at the mouth that had kissed me the night before, at the hands that had clawed at me, at the thick, red hair I had run my fingers through. Then, when Kyle looked at me, the smile lighting his face, that possessive feeling had been reinforced by something I wasn't sure I had ever felt. Something I wasn't quite ready to label, but I knew what it was instantly.

I was falling in love with him. That was never the plan.

The plan had been Sapphire's, and it was supposed to be simple. Arrange a meeting with Kyle, keep him entertained, keep him company, make him feel good about himself and most importantly, keep him happy. Make sure he had a vacation to remember. It wasn't done with any malicious intent.

Sapphire had commissioned me for events in the past. Most often as a plus-one for on-air talent who couldn't secure a date for an awards dinner or an important event. My job was always to fill the vacant seat, charm the other people at the table, and ultimately make the television personality look as good as I possibly could. This time it had felt different, even before I knew the details.

When Sapphire had contacted me for the job, all she had said to me was that she wanted to hire me for a private event. She needed me to entertain an important guest, keep him happy and out of trouble. It sounded almost exactly like all the other times she'd required my services, but when she told me the VIP guest had to never know that she hired me, obviously, alarm bells went off.

That wasn't a standard request. Usually, my dates knew and understood the parameters of our time together. It was business, not romance. For that reason, I had almost declined the job outright. Yet, when Sapphire showed me Kyle's picture on social media, I was glad I hadn't brushed her off. Kyle was exactly my type. Handsome, although a little dorky looking, with red hair, freckles and glasses. Dag-chic, as I liked to call it.

Sapphire told me about Kyle, his ex-boyfriend and how Kyle had shut entirely down, romantically. He needed a reawakening of sorts, and she made it clear that she was desperate for me to help make it happen. She even offered me an additional spending allowance, under the table, as an incentive. I almost wished I had rich friends who cared that much about me having a good time on vacation as she seemed to care about Kyle.

It wasn't like me to stalk people on social media. Still, Sapphire had sparked my interest, and I couldn't help investigating the adorable ginger-haired bloke. She had warned me that Kyle wouldn't be easy to get close to. He had almost zero interest in having a good time on the cruise and even less interest in men or romance. Apparently, he had batted zero out of nine innings and had practically quit the game altogether. That only worked as an aphrodisiac to me. I loved a challenge.

As I scrolled through photo after photo, seeing the books he raved about and the social causes he lent his time and attention to, I knew I liked him before I had even met him. When we finally did meet, it felt like oxygen: natural, fulfilling, and life-giving.

He was different than I had expected. More brutally honest than I'd anticipated, with a sharp mind and wilder heart. A little darker, more neurotic, and definitely a little self-absorbed. He talked about himself heaps, but it wasn't in an egomaniac type of way. It was more like the ramblings of someone who was rarely allowed to talk about himself, so when he did, he couldn't stop. It was frustrating but endearing. I was equally attracted to Kyle's bright wit, his cloudy temper and the millions of shades in between. Spending time with Kyle hadn't felt like work, and I quickly lost myself.

I hadn't gone in with any intention of sleeping with him. Sleeping with clients was frowned upon by the agency. We were escorts, not sex-workers. It was a small but important distinction. The plan was to romance him. Kiss him? Sure. Make out with him? Maybe, if inclined. Enjoy each other's company? Absolutely, but no sex.

I'd known from the moment I first kissed Kyle that we were compatible. In that first kiss, I had felt eons of possibility. Yet, I hadn't anticipated my attraction to him being too strong to resist. Sleeping with him had been an impulsive, spectacular development. I was thrilled it happened and kept happening, but I hadn't even considered that I could develop real feelings for him. I bloody-well hadn't expected to feel so strongly about him so quickly. Getting so wrapped up in how good it felt to be with him, I completely forgot it was a job. I had dived headfirst into Kyle. Now I was going under, struggling for oxygen.

I should have told him sooner. I should have given him all the information the moment it started to feel real to me. At the very least, I should have told him before I slept with him. When I hadn't done that, I should have been wise enough to walk away.

At first, I'd been so convinced I could keep things professional that I didn't see the need to say anything. Then, I had been so smitten with Kyle that I didn't want to tell him and risk ruining the time we had together. I always knew I would have to be honest with him eventually. I kept telling myself I would reveal the truth when the time was right. Like, once we were back in Chicago, and he was too smitten to care about why or how we met. By the end, I was too afraid to come clean because I knew how he'd react, and I didn't want to hurt him or lose him. I already missed him.

Kyle, with his easy smile and dry humour. With his intelligent mind and his guarded heart. He'd built a wall around it to keep everything and everyone out. That had been obvious since the moment I'd met him. Yet somehow, I had managed to crack a fissure in that wall. He'd slowly and hesitantly let me in, but then the truth had revealed itself, and he immediately threw me out. Now I feared he would rebuild those walls, higher and thicker than before. All because of me. That was the last thing I wanted.

Technically, I hadn't lied about my job. I *was* a freelance photographer by trade, but photography was a competitive industry. Everyone with a camera thought they had what it took for their photos to make the cover of *Vogue*. I didn't always know when the next job would come. Working for the agency helped ensure I never had to worry about how to pay my bills. All payment went directly through the agency, but Sapphire had promised me additional funds privately. So, two days into the trip, she slid a personal check under my cabin door, and I had placed it in my passport for safekeeping.

That brought us to where we were now.

Kyle's reaction, when he discovered the truth, had been less than gracious. I had anticipated an adverse reaction, but nothing I couldn't fix. Yet Kyle's response had been such that the potential for any future felt entirely beyond repair. He had panicked. Worse than panicked. He spun entirely out of control, bolting from the room so fast I was sure he'd left skid marks on the carpet. In the blink of an eye, all that possibility had slipped out of my grasp like a bloody eel.

I tried to imagine how I would have felt if someone had lied to me in the same way. I didn't even have to think about it: I would have been pissed too. I had been paid to spend time with him. I had tricked him, virtually stalked him, orchestrated our entire relationship behind his back with one of his closest friends. Individually, those may have been forgivable transgressions. Yet, compounded in that way, it was likely too much. Kyle needed time to digest the truth, and I owed it to him to leave him be. I would have to wait and hope he came around eventually.

The deeper question was, what if he didn't come around? Was I willing to simply lose what I'd found without a fight? The answer which I knew in my bones was no. I couldn't accept that it was over. Not that suddenly. I wouldn't be a dick about it, but I wouldn't walk away either.

I liked him too much to give up. I more than liked him if that was possible. Our romance was brief in terms of days. Yet, when it came to time spent together, almost twenty-four hours a day for ten days, it added up to more time than most new couples spent together in the first few months of dating. Even though he dismissed me like I meant nothing to him, I knew it was a lie. He cared as much for me as I did him. I felt it in my bloody soul.

After he basically told me to fuck off, I spent most of the day by the pool. To the untrained eye, it may have looked like I was tanning. In reality, I was racking my brain, trying to come up with a course of action. Kyle seemed closed off to my apology, but there had to be something I could do. A grand gesture, perhaps? Nothing immediately came to mind. Nothing that wouldn't have involved more scheming with Sapphire or another one of Kyle's friends.

I had fallen in love with him, yet I had destroyed any hope for us through my dishonesty. This was a rather poetic irony since if it not for my deception, I would have never been around him enough to fall in love in the first place.

I wanted to yell. I wanted to cry. I wanted to set something on fire. What I wanted more than anything was Kyle. To see him naked, on a bed or on the floor or bent over a chair, while I pumped hard into his tight cavity. A memory of Kyle with his ankles around my neck while I pumped my cock deep into him, flashed into my mind. I pushed it away, frustratingly. That was no longer an option. That made me want to lay out in the sun and hope that I was engulfed in a blaze of painful death, but the sun was already starting to set, so the only thing left to do was to drink and pout.

I ordered a dry martini, then another.

"Fancy finding you sitting all alone."

I looked over to my left. Dustin. That bloke really did have a way of popping up unexpectedly. I wasn't annoyed by his arrival. I had no beef with the bloke, although I didn't entirely trust him. There was something about his sideways glances and tempered stares that made me uneasy. Like a temperamental dog, he struck me as relatively harmless as long as you maintained eye contact and moved slowly. Still, like that same dog, I worried about what he might do if he felt threatened.

I wasn't really in the mood for company, but I waved, nonetheless. "G'day mate," I nodded, flashing him a smile that passed for genuine.

He positioned himself on the barstool next to me, ordered an IPA, then turned to me, grinning. "You must have got some serious sun today. You look much darker than you did yesterday."

"I didn't see you yesterday." He smelled like a brewery. I'd wager he was too pissed to even remember what day it was.

"Maybe, but I saw you. You're a guy who stands out." He thrust his beer bottle towards me. I didn't want to leave the poor bloke hanging, so I tapped my glass against his bottle, shaking my head. He wasn't even doing anything douchey, but I felt gross sitting next to him.

"Where's your boyfriend this evening?" I made sure to emphasize the word boyfriend.

"To be honest, Shawn and I have parted ways," he said quietly, and I smiled grimly at him. "By that, I mean, we broke up this afternoon."

"That's pretty shitty timing. It couldn't have waited until you got home?"

Dustin took a swig of his beer. "Shawn didn't really give me much choice in the matter."

"I see," I mett his eyes. "Well, I'm sorry to hear that."

"It's actually ok. I'm actually glad it happened. I thought we were happy, but the truth is, our relationship lived on the surface. I don't think it would have worked much longer, anyway."

"I'm still sorry to hear it," I offered again.

"Don't worry about it," he waved a hand flippantly. "It gives me a chance to focus on bigger and better things." He winked at me, then added breezily, "I hear that you and Kyle parted ways too?"

Wow. Lousy news travelled fast within that group of friends. "Where did you hear that?"

"Does it matter?" I didn't respond. "So, what happened?"

I tensed but tried to wipe any trace of it from my face. None of it was Dustin's business, least of all how I felt about Kyle or our situation. So, I decided to make light of it. "It was only some vacation fun," I shrugged. "It would have likely ended when the ship docked, anyway."

Dustin nodded. Whether or not he believed me, I cared not. "Well, cheers to some vacation fun," He said, clinking my glass again. "You're better off anyway. Kyle is difficult."

This tilted inside me, ringing untrue. Kyle had proven to be many things: energetic, passionate, witty, intelligent, kind, maybe even a little egocentric, but never difficult. For the life of me, I couldn't understand what Kyle and Shawn both had seen in Dustin. Maybe he had a giant cock? I had no desire to find out, but it would have at least explained why Dustin could act like a total wanker and get away with it.

Dustin flagged down the bartender for another beer. He thanked her when she delivered it, then he took a foamy sip, still studying me. "You never did show me your package."

His comment caught me mid-swallow, and I nearly spat a mouthful of gin across the bar. "I'm sorry. My what?"

A laugh burst out of Dustin's mouth before he could contain it. "Your portfolio," he grinned slyly. "Unless there's another package you're interested in showing me."

I lifted the toothpick, swirling the olive in my martini glass. "I can e-mail it as soon as I get home," I told him, purposely ignoring the innuendo.

"Why wait? I'm sure you've taken a ton of photos while on this trip. I'd love to see the unprocessed work."

"Are you trying to get an invitation back to my room?" I joked. As irritating as he was being, Dustin hadn't said or done anything I couldn't navigate.

"Maybe a little bit," Dustin winked. "Can you blame me?"

Things were getting awkward. I picked up a paper napkin, folding it several times until it was a small, tight square. Having met Justin, I couldn't believe that he and Dustin were brothers. Aside from looking virtually identical, the two men couldn't have been more different. I had thoroughly enjoyed the brief time I'd spent with Justin. He was quiet but genuine, and I had immediately felt at ease around him. Dustin was more rotten. Like he thrived on making people uncomfortable. He relished in it.

I was starting to feel bloody agitated sitting alone with Dustin. The discomfort was made worse by the fact that he was still looking at me. Not simply looking. His eyes were feasting on me. Dustin looked like he wanted to rip me in half then lick out my creamy centre. If it were any other handsome bloke smiling at me like that, I would have been flattered. Yet with Dustin, it made me feel slimy, like I was betraying Kyle further.

Even though I wasn't meeting his eyes, I could feel his focus on the side of my face. "So, you up for it?"

My mind was immediately buzzing. Was Dustin asking what I thought he was?

"Showing you my work?" I deflected.

He blinked at me. "Among other things."

The husky quiet of his voice made me uneasy. I had a sense of dread, like I was on the back of a motorcycle, staring over the side of a canyon. I suspected Dustin was going to try to push me over the edge. I looked at him over the lip of my martini glass. "Such as?" I was pretty confident I knew exactly what he wanted to see.

"We're both single," Dustin said evenly. "I would really enjoy seeing your hot Australian cock before this trip is over."

Damn it. That left no bloody room for misunderstanding. I pulled my jaw closed once I registered that it had popped open. "You're a charmer," I stated indignantly.

"So I've been told."

I kept my movement small and my voice calm. "Are you always so direct?"

"When I know what I want," he said, breezily, like he hadn't just offered to sleep with me in the most vulgar way possible.

I tapped my chin with a finger, focusing on keeping my cool, and put my martini glass down carefully. It took every ounce of control I had to not use it for violent means. "Thank you so much for the offer." It was a struggle to keep my voice even. "I think I'll pass."

I expected him to look visibly disappointed, but Dustin shrugged like it made absolutely no difference to him. "Some other time then."

I gapped at him. He had brass balls, that was sure. I needed to get away from Dustin and get some air. I took a final watery sip of my martini, then exhaled the fumes of cheap gin directly into his face. "I want to make myself bloody clear, Dustin," I said in a calm tone, standing abruptly, robotically. "I will never sleep with you. Ever. You're not my type."

Dustin squinted at me. "You don't like blondes?" He teased.

"No, mate. I don't like pricks."

Dustin's laugh was a deep and bitter sound that sent vibrations of rage through me. "I can afford it."

I took a breath. "Excuse me?"

"I can afford it," Dustin repeated. "Whatever your rate is."

Mother fucker. Something squeezed inside my chest, but I laughed, even though it wasn't a happy sound. Kyle must have told him. I resisted the urge to shoot him a baleful glance and shook my head. I couldn't even be upset by his comment. To the naked eye, I had accepted payment for sleeping with Kyle. I couldn't even be cranky that Kyle had told Dustin. He was hurt and probably venting. I was tempted to continue the ridiculous exchange, just to see how low Dustin would stoop, but someone had to be the adult.

"I think you're drunk, mate. Let's pretend this never happened." I began to walk away.

Dustin's face went utterly blank for a second, then suddenly, vividly furious. "Funny," he mused. "That's the same thing Kyle said this afternoon when I left his bed."

That stopped me short. I went bloody still. "What is that supposed to mean?"

"Should I draw you a diagram? I should thank you. You've obviously taught Kyle a thing or two since the last time we fucked."

I inhaled. It got caught in my throat, shuddering violently on the way back out. "You're a dammed liar."

"I wouldn't be so sure," Dustin said with a small, cocky laugh. "Kyle and I have a complicated past."

I had no idea what to say. My stomach felt like a concrete block, sinking inside me. "Kyle would never do that. He can't even stand you."

"Yeah, you're right. That's why we did it laying down."

I felt my heart rate spike, blood pulsed in my ears. I didn't even know how to process what I was hearing or the undeniable ache it shoved through me when I considered Dustin might be telling the truth. I felt my breath grow tight as jealousy bubbled to the surface.

My jaw clenched. "I don't believe you."

"You know what they say, the best way to get over someone is to get under someone else."

Something rose in my throat. Unforgivably, I felt like if I didn't hit something, I might have started to cry. I imagined my fist in Dustin's face then removed myself by two steps, out of range. "Good night, Dustin." It took every ounce of strength to turn and walk away.

"He moaned your name by accident."

It took only a split second for me to rush towards him, slamming my hand down on the counter. "What the fuck did you say?"

Dustin crossed his arms, facing me fully. The steel shining in his eyes was nothing short of impressive. "I'm pretty sure you heard me."

"Repeat it! I dare you," I growled. I didn't want to believe it, but I suddenly felt like I didn't know anything. I was thunderstruck. There was a storm brewing inside me, and like lightning, I needed to strike. I wanted to grab Dustin and shake him, wanted to scream in his face, wanted to smash his beer bottle over his fucking head.

Dustin let out a long, low whistle. "Your reaction sure seems extreme for someone who was only having vacation fun." He used my earlier words against me. "Why do you even care? We both know Sapphire paid you to fuck him."

The next thing I knew, Dustin was laid out on the floor, blood leaking from a split in his lip. I didn't even remember hitting him, but I didn't feel guilty. From behind the bar, the server picked up the phone to dial security.

"There's no need," I told her, looking towards Dustin. "We're done here." I huffed out an almighty breath, turned on my heel, then stalked away.

I could feel Dustin's eyes on my ass while I left. As I turned right, I could have sworn, out the corner of my eye, I saw the prick smile.

TWENTY-EIGHT
KYLE

"**W**hy do suitcases always feel a hundred pounds heavier when we leave than they did when we arrived?" I asked rhetorically, heaving my suitcase face down on the conveyer belt.

"Did you buy a lot of souvenirs?" Ruby asked.

"A few, but they certainly weren't made of solid marble, I assure you."

Immediately after escorting Dustin from my room, I had gone in the shower to wash the stench of shame, defeat and prostitute off my body. I felt terrible reducing Jax to that single word. There was so much more to him than that. Also, there was no shame in sex-work. I truly believed that. Yet, my anger and shock needed a way to manifest, so I allowed myself to be intolerant.

Afterward, I went directly to Ruby's room. It was an interesting role reversal for me to be the one banging loudly on her door for once. When she opened it and saw me sobbing uncontrollably, she hadn't even asked what was wrong. She had merely wrapped me in her arms and asked me what she could do.

Thankfully, the timing of the bombshell couldn't have been better. The ship was scheduled to dock back in Miami early the next morning, and it was Ruby who called the airport to arrange my flight. She was even kind enough to sweet talk the service agent and get on an earlier flight than the one she was initially scheduled on with Sapphire and the others.

Although, I rather wished she hadn't. I didn't feel like talking. I didn't even feel like thinking anymore. I only wanted to stare out the window and forget the world. Forget Jax. Forget Sapphire. Forget the pain of my heart tearing in two. As much as I appreciated Ruby's desire to help, I remembered Sapphire, Jax and the entire situation every time I looked at her.

It was exactly what I had known was going to happen. Ok, maybe not exactly. Yet, there had been hesitation in my mind, something that told me it was a bad idea to let Jax in. I had almost run from it. I had almost pushed him away. Still, I had told myself I was being ridiculous and forced myself to accept the potential in front of me. I should have listened to my instincts, but I hadn't. Now my heart wasn't only broken; it was thoroughly humiliated.

I sighed.

Ruby, who was reclined back in her seat with her eyes closed, spoke suddenly. "Are you going to tell me what happened?"

I hadn't breathed a word about anything in the last twelve hours, and thankfully Ruby hadn't asked. She intuitively knew I needed time to process whatever it was. Now, away from our typical cluster of friends and family, isolated on an aircraft where I couldn't escape, Ruby felt it was time to probe.

I continued to stare out the window. "No. Not yet."

"You're going to have to tell me eventually. I know it must be something big. Otherwise, Sapphire wouldn't have texted me this morning demanding I check on you."

"You didn't tell her you were already with me, did you?"

"Of course I did. I had to tell Sapphire something. I needed to explain why I was suddenly taking an earlier flight."

I humphed, and a small silence settled. I had hoped that meant Ruby would drop the line of questioning, but then, "Whatever happened, I assume it has something to do with the Dustin and Jax love triangle."

"Why would you assume that?"

"I could hear Shawn sobbing like a colicky infant from outside their room last night. So I think it's safe to say that they're no longer together."

"That's a safe bet."

She eyed me suspiciously. "What did you do?"

"Technically, nothing."

Ruby was unsatisfied with that response. "Ok then. Technically, what did you *almost* do?" I gave her a guilty side-eye, and she nearly cackled victoriously. "I knew it! You slept with Dustin! I knew you would, you dirty home wrecker."

"Would you please stop? I did not sleep with him."

"You *almost* did, though! I knew you would too. Damn, I'm good."

"Yeah," I drawled facetiously, feeling a glimmer of humor.

"I wouldn't go changing your name to Miss Cleo, just yet."

"You dare doubt my powers, man?" Ruby teased in the worst fake Jamaican accent I had ever heard. Still, it made me smile. "Does Sapphire know you nearly slept with Dustin? Is that why she texted me, frantic?"

"I don't want to talk about your sister."

"Ok," Ruby grimaced. "What about the hot Aussie? What happened there?"

My arms fell. "I don't want to talk about Jax either."

Ruby nodded. "Ok. I'll assume that means something went very bad with him."

"I don't want to talk about it," I repeated, more firmly this time.

"Ok..." Ruby said cautiously. "That doesn't leave much room for discussion."

"That's kind of the whole point."

"You can't give me bread but no butter. Obviously, something is going on. You have to tell me what it is."

"Actually, I don't."

"You're no fun," Ruby pouted, then she softened, throwing me a brief, earnest look. "You know, you can tell me anything. I would never judge. Whatever it is, I can pretty much guarantee I've done worse."

"I know, I know, but I would really prefer not to get into it."

"Ok. Just tell me, do we hate Jax now? I'm prepared to hate him if you need me to."

I thought about it for a moment. Did I hate Jax? No. Many feelings were dancing spastically through my body and mind. Anger, devastation, mortification, even fear, but not hate. I shook my head. "No, we don't hate him. Thank you for your blind loyalty, though."

"It's not blind. I'm perfectly aware that, whatever happened, you're likely at fault, but I like you more and have known you longer, so..." Ruby shrugged.

My eyes narrowed. "Thank you for your brutal honesty, but I assure you I am not at fault for this."

"I wouldn't know," she shrugged again. "You won't tell me what's going on."

"I don't want to talk about it," I said a third time. "It's too humiliating. You wouldn't..." I trailed off.

"I wouldn't what? Understand?"

I turned from the window to look at her quickly. "No one humiliates you without your permission and a safe word."

She laughed. "Oh, honey. How little you know. I'm humiliated all the time. I just don't throw a parade in its honor when it happens."

"Really?" It was hard to imagine anyone as confident as Ruby being humiliated or embarrassed by anything. Ever.

She nodded. "Do you know what happened with Cody last night?" I shook my head. "He finally told me that he and I were never going to happen."

I looked surprised. "What? Why? You're beautiful. He'd be lucky to have you."

She nodded. "Yes, I am beautiful," she humbly agreed. "I'm also Black." My eyes bulged as I slowly realized the weight of her words. "Cody doesn't find Black women attractive."

"That racist pig."

"He doesn't see it that way. To him, it's a preference. Like Coke vs. Pepsi or top vs. bottom."

"That's awful."

"I haven't even gotten to the humiliating part yet. Cody waited until I was standing naked in his bedroom to tell me this."

"Wait," I held up a hand. Something about that didn't make sense. If Cody didn't find her attractive, then... "Why were you naked?"

She shrugged like it was an innocent mistake. "Champagne makes me presumptuous," she said. "He had invited me back to his room to hang out. So while he was in the bathroom changing out of his prom attire, I changed into my birthday suit."

"So he came out of the bathroom, and you were standing there naked?"

"Wearing nothing but a smile." She gave an embarrassed grin. It was the first time since I'd known her that I'd seen her make such an expression. "Then, he told me he didn't find Black women sexually attractive. Just blurted it out like he was commenting on the weather. I was so stunned that I could hardly think. I scurried around the room, gathering my things so I could get out of there as quickly as possible. I put my dress on backward and ran into a wall." I laughed. It felt inappropriate, so I immediately apologized. Ruby laughed too. "It's ok. It is funny. Mortifying, but funny."

"Thank you," I said suddenly. Genuinely.

"For what?"

"For being here. For arranging everything. For—"

"For letting you drag me out of my perfectly good bed at the ass-crack of dawn so you can avoid my sister?" She finished my train of thought.

I nodded. "Especially that last one."

"You're welcome," she said, placing her hand over my forearm. "When you're ready to tell me what happened, and there is no rush, but when you're ready, I'll be here to listen."

It was such a rare display of tenderness and compassion from Ruby that I wasn't sure how to react to it. To my horror, I could feel tears pricking my eyes again. I turned back towards the window, looking out at the sun, hoping its rays would dry them up before they fell.

When the plane landed, Ruby hailed a cab the way only Ruby could do, with a shrill two-fingered whistle. As I sunk back into the leather seats, I felt a wave of fatigue fall over me. I fell almost immediately into a dreamless nap, lulled to sleep by the steady rhythm of the car's engine as it traveled down the busy Chicago morning streets. Faster than I would have liked, Ruby was nudging me awake.

Opening my eyes at the shake of my shoulder, I looked out the window at my apartment building. The thirty-two story building suddenly seemed so cold and lonely compared to the floating city I had spent the last ten days.

"Do you need help getting your bags upstairs?" Ruby asked.

"No, I'll be alright." My voice sounded hoarse, like I was coming down with something. "Thank you, though."

"Text me later?" Concern flashed brightly in her eyes.

Ruby and I had never been close. We'd been friends, sure, but mostly through Sapphire. We had never been the type to hang out together or call or text each other randomly. Yet, after this vacation, I could tell that had definitely changed. I nodded, my throat suddenly too sore to speak. She gave me a quick hug goodbye before leaning back in her seat.

With that, I got out of the cab. The driver carried my suitcases to the lobby door, then I tipped him generously before offering a polite farewell. Standing in the frigid Chicago winter air, I waved to Ruby one final time while the car drove off. Silence permeated the air, slicing into my skin as sharply as the cold Chicago wind.

When finally I got upstairs to my apartment, it felt foreign, and I felt changed. Being alone for the first time after spending almost every second with Jax drew hard, dark attention to my loneliness. Had it really only been ten days? How Could so much have happened in that short time?

Even though it was only mid-afternoon, I went to bed almost immediately, but sleep was elusive. I was haunted by echoing visions of all that had happened from the first moment Jax said hello to the moment I walked away from him. Any one of those dozen memories drew tears from the well of my heart, and I woke up sobbing.

I went back to the office the very next morning, which had been poor planning. It proved to be one of the longest days of my life. My body and mind ached, and I completely lacked energy and focus. I'd returned from vacation more exhausted and in need of relaxation than when I'd left.

The hours turned into days. Soon almost two whole weeks had passed since the cruise, but it felt like a decade. I had spent the bulk of that time trying to get caught up. Simply because I had been away on vacation didn't mean the work stopped. It continued to grow and pile, and no one took over my projects in my absence. It was the second Monday since my return, and I was only starting to get things under control.

I had spent most of the morning sorting through the congestion of emails from needy authors. Several wanted to know if I liked the new pages they'd sent me, which I hadn't yet read. A few others had micro-panic attacks in response to the notes I had sent about the pages I *had* read.

Writers were like any other artist, a peculiar marriage of narcissism and self-doubt. Few things mattered more to an artist than their art. So, when they presented their art for evaluation, they subconsciously assumed that every other aspect of your life would cease to exist. They demanded you give their submission the time and attention they felt it deserved.

Most writers were also deathly afraid that their latest piece of work was self-indulgent garbage. So, if they didn't immediately receive positive feedback or praise, they automatically assumed it was the worse thing to ever see a computer screen's soft glow. They didn't quite seem to grasp the concept of time-off or vacation. Probably because writers wrote all the time. Everywhere. Whenever inspiration struck them. It wasn't a nine-to-five job, so they didn't always respect nine-to-five boundaries.

After a quick lunch, I prepared for a pitch meeting, which was the part of the job I enjoyed the least. It wasn't enough to find a talented author with a gripping story. Part of the job was convincing the publisher's that you had found the right author, with the right voice, and that it was the right time for their story to be told. Of course, you also had to convince them that the project would be lucrative. Publishing was as much about money as it was about art.

The project I was pitching happened to be an adventure romance novel by a first-time author, complete with a treasure hunt, secret societies and government conspiracies. It was *The DaVinci Code* meets *Romancing the Stone,* and it was a fresh, fun read. I felt it was precisely what the current hostile climate needed. The bulk of it was set on the Australian continent, so right away, it reminded me of Jax.

As much as it irritated me, he hadn't left my thoughts. I alternated between being mad at myself for falling so ridiculously far so fast, being furious at Dustin for intentionally clouding my head and then taking advantage of my confusion, sad and disappointed over Sapphire breaking my trust, and absolutely heartbroken over Jax. Our brief romance had left me wanting more, but the sting of his deception tainted any desire I had to reach out to him. He couldn't be trusted. I knew what it was like to date a man I didn't trust, and I had no interest in repeating the cycle.

The worst thing about heartache was it couldn't be ignored. Sure, you could crawl into bed, hide under the covers and sleep for the next month if you wanted. Still, the pain would follow you and be waiting for you whenever and if ever you decided to leave your sanctuary. So, if I couldn't ignore heartache and I couldn't hide from it, I decided I could at least distract myself from it. So I buried myself in work. Since returning from the cruise, I had done almost nothing but reading and editing, but I also started writing a piece of my own.

For years I had toiled with the notion of writing my own book. Ideas had fluttered and floated around in my head but never ever found their way to paper. Jax had been right. Fear had been a significant obstacle. Now, that fear of not being good enough was no longer as crippling as the fear that I would never try at all.

Hearing the way Jax had spoken about photography had inspired me. I enjoyed being a book editor. I really did. Still, I wanted to do something in life that lit me on fire the way photography did for him. I didn't know if my writing was any good. I wasn't sure if it would ever see the ugly fluorescent lighting inside a publishing house. I wasn't even confident that I could persuade my own boss at Pegasus Press to look at it, but I didn't care. The simple act of writing gave me so much joy, it wouldn't have bothered me if no one ever read it. Jax took photos for himself, and I would write for me.

I took everything I was feeling out on the page. All the anguish, sorrow, anger, lingering affection, I poured it all into the plot, the characters, and dialogue, until I was merely a vessel for the words to the story. It flowed through me with a life of its own. As though the story existed entirely outside my imagination, and I was merely the conduit through which it traveled. Writing certainly helped curb the throbbing impulse to collapse on the ground, kicking and screaming. Admittedly, underneath that impulse, deep down underneath, there was a tiny glimmer. Not relief or hope, but acceptance.

I'd accepted that the romance with Jax hadn't been real. It had been an illusion performed by someone who was paid to give a good performance. No one could fault Jax for not being believable. Accepting that helped to put things into perspective. Yes, I was hurt, but I knew it too would pass. I'd survived my breakup with Dustin, and that had been years worth of love and happiness. Theoretically, getting over someone I had known less than two weeks would be easier.

Except that someone was Jax, and it didn't feel any easier. It felt impossible. Yes, I had loved Dustin for many years, but even when our love was at its peak, I never really liked him. Not in the way I should have. Not as a whole person. I hadn't liked the way his coworkers talked about him behind his back at his company Christmas parties. I had hated that he insisted on ordering a bottle of red wine for us at every meal, especially since he knew I preferred white. He often laughed when I cried, or he would act all confused when I made perfect sense. He always made me angry more than he made me happy. Lastly, I had always found his arrogance libido crushing. Looking back with new clarity, I wasn't sure I ever truly loved him in the way one was supposed to.

Even though I had only known Jax for a fraction of the time, I had liked him several times as much after those ten days together than I ever did Dustin. That led me to believe that I would have eventually loved him as much or more.

Would have, eventually.

The more I tried not to think about him, the more he worked his way into my mind. It made me groan. For the hundredth time, I reminded myself that it hadn't been genuine. At least, not on his part.

Our falling out had happened before we had made time to swap contact information. So imagine my surprise when an email appeared in my inbox from one Jaxson Abernathy.

Glowering at my computer, I was determined to listen to the tiny voice in my head that told me to ignore him and his email and focus on my work. Sighing, I turned back to the file on my desk. The rest of my day passed much as the previous part had, with meetings, emails, phone calls and memos. Yet, Jax's email weighed on my mind.

When I got back to my desk in my office and had a sip of my cold coffee, I logged back into my computer. I was tempted to delete Jax's message without opening it. My finger hovered precariously over the backspace key for several seconds. Why should I care? I hadn't even answered Sapphire's calls or texts since returning to real life, and we had a long, meaningful history together. What did it matter what some guy I had known only a week had to say? The damage had been done. He couldn't undo it with a few tender words of remorse.

I pressed delete. An automatic feeling of regret washed over me. The question of why I should care was irrelevant. I did care. I hated that I did, but I cared deeply. As quickly as I deleted it, I fished it out of the recycle bin then opened it. I expected a long-winded apology. Instead, it contained only one sentence with an embedded image.

Jax and I, shirtless, lying in bed, my head resting in the crook of his shoulder. Part of my face was obscured by my fingers, which were drumming against the peeks of his pectoral muscles. Jax had managed to capture the moment right when I must have cracked a joke because the photo had caught him mid-giggle, his attention entirely on me. His outstretched arm knew the buttons of his camera without any assistance from his eyes.

I remembered it well, the encounter captured in the photograph. We had just made love, and we were enjoying the euphoria that came after. We were talking, completely caught up in each other. Lost in intimate, playful conversation about our individual hopes and dreams for the future, things we wanted to try and places we wanted to go—pillow talk. He had taken the selfie without me even knowing. The picture looked so affectionate, so openly tender that seeing it for the first time, with so much wariness in my heart, made me want to look away. It felt like I was intruding on an intimate moment between two people I didn't know. Below the photo, he had typed a single caption:

Sometimes poor choices lead to rich moments.

It wasn't the apology I expected. I wasn't even sure if it classified as an apology at all. It was a statement. That much was clear.

It certainly had been a rich moment. We had shared countless moments equally as beautiful in those ten days of sailing and sightseeing. If it hadn't been for Sapphire's scheming and Jax's lying, those moments would have never happened. That was what he was trying to tell me. He was reminding me of all the joy that had come out of one poor decision on their part. He was asking me to forgive so that more rich moments could be made.

I wasn't sure if I could. The lie had shaken me to my very core. It had been earth-shattering and mind-blowing, and I wasn't sure I could ever look past it.

Trust was a tangible object, delicate and fragile, and it had been broken. I was not the type to pick up shattered fragments of an item and glue them back together. Some people could do so then tell themselves that the object was as good as new. I wasn't wired that way. Trust could not be repaired flawlessly. I would only ever see the soft cracks and the glue. I would only ever see it as broken and in need of replacing.

I sighed, then deleted the image. Then, I deleted it from the deleted folder. It was gone.

For the last few hours of the day, I immersed myself in my work, trying not to think about Jax, his email or the photo of us together, but it was damn near impossible. I went to a staff meeting, which distracted me for a while, but I had the attention span of a teaspoon. I couldn't think or concentrate for more than ten consecutive minutes. The memory of Jax and all the gloriously dirty things he had done to my body kept creeping in at the most inopportune moments.

A few days later, an embarrassingly large, beautiful bouquet of flowers was delivered to my office. It was a stunning arrangement of hyacinths and snapdragons in hues of blues and purples. It was quite possibly the most gorgeous floral arrangement I had ever seen. I knew immediately who they were from. There was no need to read the card, but I did.

You're still sailing through my mind - J

I couldn't help but smile despite my anger. Jax's message was clever, cheesy and perfect. It was almost enough to make me take out my cell and text Sapphire for his number, but I didn't. I couldn't. There were still too many red flags that I would have been foolish to ignore.

Any relationship built on a lie was itself a lie. I had been uncharacteristically forthcoming with Jax about everything. Almost to a fault. I had told him things I would have never even considered telling other men. Initially, I did so because there was security, knowing that we would likely never cross paths again. Then, I did so because I felt a level of trust. That trust had been a complete fallacy.

Our meeting hadn't been by fate or by chance. It had been strategically planned. Orchestrated by Sapphire. Jax had known who I was; my name, where I worked, what I looked like, even my history with Dustin before I had even sat down at that bar.

I was his target. His entire purpose had been to seek me out and romance me. If it hadn't been that afternoon while I sat covered in wedding cake, it would have been that evening or the day after or the next. It made me question the sincerity of our entire time together. It made me doubt the sincerity of his gestures now.

A few days later, another less poetic email came. It simply said;

I want you to know that it was never a job for me. My feelings for you were real. Are still real. I miss you.

I read it over several times before deleting it.

When again I didn't respond, Jax seemed to take the hint, but I wasn't sure if that was good or bad. At least the flowers and emails meant he was thinking about me as much as I was thinking of him. When they stopped coming, the idea that he had given up and was moving on was almost more painful than the original betrayal. That left me feeling very conflicted.

I wanted Jax to chase me since I wasn't the one who messed up. I wanted him to be persistent while I attempted to sort out how I felt and what I wanted to do. It was selfish. I knew that. Yet, I felt justified.

It would have been easier to forget him if he hadn't been so perfect. Well, aside from the lying and the whole being an escort thing. Jax was witty, playful, infatuating, and excellent in bed. I couldn't deny that we were a great fit, which was both surprising and terrifying. Terrifying because I wasn't sure I could trust him, and surprising because a part of me didn't care. I just wasn't sure if that part was my heart or my penis.

I told myself it was for the best. Even if Jax hadn't been part of Sapphire's scheme, Jax was way too gorgeous to have any long-term interest in me. We'd never be on equal footing. I'd always be the nerdier, pudgier one who had to be smart and funny to make up for my lack of physical beauty. Jax was an A-list gay, while I existed almost exclusively on the D-list. I'd already experienced that sort of unbalanced coupling. So, as much as I would have liked it to work, I knew it would be a mistake.

When had I become so self-deprecating? I hadn't always

been that way. If anything, my flaw had always been overconfidence. Even as a child, I had felt so thoroughly above everything and everyone that it never occurred to me to be tactful or reserved with my thoughts and opinions. I was never afraid of how people would react. I rarely worried. I never had any doubts about my worth because I knew, even at an early age, that my value was not dependant on those around me. So what had changed?

I thought about Dustin and his boy-toy. Not Shawn, but the guy with the perfect ass from all those years ago. Had that been the catalyst? Was it possible that being betrayed and humiliated in such a profoundly personal way had resulted in a psychological metamorphosis? Had it caused something sad and self-conscious to awaken within me? Something that manifested itself as bitterness and anger to disguise the feelings of worthlessness that I'd yet to deal with? Was Sapphire right? Was I becoming a bitter, old troll? Was I becoming that way as a means to defend myself from being hurt that deeply again?

The answer was obvious, although I rather wished it weren't. Self-reflection was a total bitch, especially when it revealed truths you weren't ready to accept about yourself.

I couldn't call Sapphire and ramble about any of it either because I hadn't spoken to her in weeks and wasn't sure I wanted to. She had tried texting and calling. She had even shown up unannounced at my apartment building, but I pretended not to be home. The possibility that the rift between us could become permanent made me light-headed. I'd forgive her eventually. Our friendship was too important for me to write it off completely. I knew that much. I also knew that I wasn't ready.

After work, I left the office and walked out into the cold evening. A fresh blanket of snow had fallen that day, making the streets and walkways dangerously slippery as I made my way to the subway station. Around me were the street sounds. Pedestrians walking, talking and horns blaring in the heavy traffic, which always seemed to be clogged up. In the distance, a siren wailed. I made a pit stop at the Asian market for some take-out ginger beef and rice, then stopped at the liquor store for a bottle of Sauvignon Blanc.

I wondered if it would make me an alcoholic if I drank the

whole bottle alone. If it did, then I would have to embrace it since I would likely be spending most of my time alone, for at least the foreseeable future.

So alone.

I had started my second glass of wine when someone buzzed my apartment. I sauntered over to the intercom panel. Fortunately, the intercom was equipped with a front door surveillance camera. This way, when someone buzzed, you could see who it was before you decided to respond. It was Ruby.

"Hello," I greeted.

"Let me up, whore!" Her voice demanded through the speakers.

It was rare that anyone other than Sapphire came over unannounced. "Is your sister with you?"

Ruby released a long breath. "Does it look like she's with me?"

According to the footage, Ruby was entirely alone. "She better not be," I warned.

"Just let me up."

I buzzed her in. A few minutes later, Ruby rapped on the door

"Happy Friday!" She proclaimed, holding up two bottles of wine. It reminded me of our first night on the cruise. Hopefully, those bottles weren't also spiked with narcotics.

I stepped back from the door frame, letting her in. The moment she stepped over the threshold, the entire space felt more alive and like home than it had since I'd returned from the cruise. Since returning, I hadn't been in the best of moods, and Ruby's infectious energy was precisely what the space needed. Maybe she was exactly what I needed, too.

"Thank you," I took the bottles from her hands. "I already have some chilled. I'll get you a glass."

She followed me into the kitchen.

"Have you eaten? I have tons of food left. It's Chinese, so I can't guarantee you won't be hungry again in twenty minutes, but it's there if you want some."

She followed me into the kitchen, pulling out a plate and silverware while I poured her a glass of chilled wine. She filled her plate with rice, ginger beef, and sautéed vegetables. Then we gathered around the coffee table, cross-legged on my Persian area rug.

Ruby poked at her rice. "How are you doing?" Her expression was sympathetic.

"Fine." My tone indicated that I was anything but fine.

"I wasn't sure if you would let me in."

"Why? My issue is with your treacherous sister, not with you."

"I saw her yesterday," Ruby admitted, then waited to see what reaction I would give.

"How is she?" I couldn't help the tightness in my voice. I missed Sapphire so much. Every day I got closer to the moment I knew would come, calling her up and forgiving her, but that moment was not now.

Ruby took a bite, chewing and swallowing while studying me. "She's the same as you." It was a small but loaded comparison. "How long do you think you two will be on the outs?"

"I don't know, Ruby. Let me consult my crystal ball and get back to you."

She looked like she couldn't decide if she wanted to laugh or throw her fork at me. "Snarky much?"

"Sorry," I offered sincerely, brotherly bumping my shoulder against hers. "I don't mean to take it out on you. I honestly don't know how long this will last. It's not like Sapphire and me to go this long without talking."

"The ball is in your court, isn't it? Sapphire made it sound like she tried everything short of the black arts to get a hold of you."

I nodded. "Yeah, she's called, texted, sent emails."

"And?" Ruby asked, poking at her food.

"I'm not ready yet."

The slightest of expressions crossed over Ruby's face. "That's fair. What she did was kind of shitty."

"Glad you agree."

"You should still hear her out, though. Things may not be exactly how you think they are."

"She bought me a man."

"I wish she would buy me one. Hell, if they look as good as Jax, I'd let her buy me two."

I glared at her. There was a question hanging in the air, and we could both see it. I didn't want to ask, but I had to.

"Did you know?"

Ruby didn't look surprised by my inquiry. "No."

"Honestly? Because Sapphire pretended not to know Jax very convincingly. She stood right in front of me, actually introduced herself to him, then proceeded to grill him like she didn't already know everything about him. So, I'm not all that trusting right now."

Ruby looked a little annoyed. "I swear, I had no idea. Still, just think, if it weren't for Sapphire, you would never have gotten to experience all of that yumminess."

I sighed, touching the edge of my glasses. "Is that supposed to make me feel better?"

"It would make *me* feel better! I would have done him just for the experience."

I laughed.

"Seriously," she went on. "I would take the memory of his gorgeous cock and wrap it around myself like a security blanket, every night."

"You are the most vulgar woman I have ever known."

"Thank you," she beamed as though I had just crowned her Miss America. "Anyway, Sapphire's version of the story is a little different."

Acid filled my stomach. A different version? I wasn't surprised Sapphire decided to put her own little spin on the situation.

"What is her version?" I really was curious what Sapphire could have said to make herself seem less guilty.

Ruby must have thought my question was rhetorical because she didn't answer. She turned back to her ginger beef, completely happy to blink her ridiculously long lashes at me and remain nonverbal.

"Ruby!" I raised my voice, demanding a response.

She finished chewing before answering. "You should take her calls if you want to know the whole story."

"Why are you here if not to tell me these things?"

Ruby dropped her fork, leaning back on both hands. "Only to offer you the pleasure of my company."

At that, I was incredulous. "Oh? Is that all?"

"Also to drink," she leaned forward to pick up her glass of wine. "Cheers."

I picked up my glass, clinking it against hers before taking a sip. "I'm surprised you stopped by on a Friday night. Don't you have a line-up of men waiting for you all weekend, every weekend?"

Sighing, she reached up, wiping one strand of hair off her face. "I do," she admitted. "I thought this was more important, though."

"Drinking with me is more important than getting laid? Since when?"

"Since never!" She laughed. "That's not the main reason I'm here." I raised my brow. "Don't get me wrong, drinking is on the agenda, but the real reason I'm here is to help get to the bottom of this issue with you and my sister."

"I figured," I set down my wine glass. "I've already told you, I'm not ready."

"Well, you better get ready," she said with gusto. "Babies are coming in four months. They're going to need their Uncle Kyle. One of them is definitely going to need a godfather."

"I'm not going to be...wait, did she say something?" I felt the heat crawl up my neck and across my face.

Ruby gave me a look that indicated she'd said too much. "That's for you and Sapphire to discuss. If you would only get over yourself long enough to talk to her."

"You're a double agent," I accused, blinking down into my wine glass. Ruby was right though, it would have been better to make peace with Sapphire, sooner rather than later, but I wasn't sure I could.

We'd had so many disagreements over the years, and they all seemed so hilariously minor in hindsight. Yet, some of the things Sapphire had said to me on the ship were downright vicious. I wasn't a vile, narcissistic old troll. I knew that wasn't true about me. I was sarcastic because I was guarded. I was guarded because my parents had loved my brother more than me and had made no secret of it. I was also guarded because Dustin had betrayed me in the most intimate and hurtful of ways. Finally, I was guarded because Sapphire, too, had betrayed my trust. Tricked me into falling for a man who was paid to be there.

So I had to ask myself, could I trust her? Could I put aside the feeling of betrayal and outrage long enough to have a little faith in her? I knew without a shadow of a doubt that Sapphire would never purposely hurt me. Her intentions had been right, rooted in romance even, but her methods had been manipulative and deceitful. Intentional or not, she had hurt me. Deeply.

All of that being said, I missed my friend. As much or more than I missed Jax, I missed Sapphire. She was my soulmate. My sister from another mister. My friend till the bitter end. Even when I hated her, she was still the biggest and best part of my world.

"Look," Ruby got up suddenly, slapping a piece of paper on the glass coffee table. "I'd love to sit here, wallowing with you, but I do have one of those dates you mentioned earlier."

I rose too. "Well then, please don't let me keep you." I picked up the piece of paper she had left on the table. "What's this?"

"An invitation to Sapphire's baby shower," Ruby said simply. "Two weeks from today. I expect you to be there."

"I don't know."

"I *do* know, and you *will* be there," she declared, her voice ominous. "Although I would suggest getting there a little earlier so the two of you can hash all this out. If you ruin the party that I am spending good money to plan by arguing, I will be very upset."

"You know, you and your sister are a lot more alike than either of you care to admit."

Ruby's mouth dropped open. "That is an ugly, vicious lie. I demand you take it back right now."

I laughed. "I can't do that. I only tell the truth."

"So do I," she said, flicking the invitation I held in my hand. "Be there. Talk to her. Trust me, this whole situation isn't exactly what you think."

My jaw actually dropped. "Which part? Sapphire paying a man to date me, or a man actually pretending to like me for cash?"

Her gaze turned apologetic but unwavering. "Both. I know you don't believe me, but you need to talk to her. There is so much that you don't know." I wasn't sure why, since Ruby had also never been notoriously trustworthy, but I believed her. I followed her to the door. "If it makes you feel any better, Sapphire misses you as much if not more than you miss her."

It did make me feel better, but I had to ask, "How do you know?"

"Because the woman won't leave me alone," she whined. "She's constantly calling and inviting me to lunches and dinners."

"That sounds awful," I said dryly.

"It *is* awful. I love my sister, but she is exhausting."

I laughed. "Sapphire tends to say the same thing about you."

"Yes, but I'm exhausting in an exciting, fun way. She's exhausting in the way that involves picking apart my every life decision. That is not my idea of a good time."

"I know she's a lot sometimes, but she only meddles because she cares."

Ruby tilted her head as though she had caught me in a trap. "Oh really? You don't say?"

I heard her loud and clear. Sapphire was a meddler, always had been and likely always would be. She did it because she cared. She loved us so deeply that sometimes she made the wrong choices, chipping away at our patience. I owed it to Sapphire and that love to hear her out. A courtesy I hadn't yet granted her.

"Stop that," I demanded.

"Stop what?"

"Being so emotionally balanced. It's jarring."

Ruby smiled shrugging. "What can I say? I'm trying on a new shade of adult."

"Maturity looks good on you."

"Everything looks good on me," she winked. "You really should talk to her."

"If it's possible, you might be even bossier than your sister."

"It's not possible," she dismissed the suggestion immediately. "Besides, I'm only making a suggestion. I'm not going to force you to do anything you don't want to do. I won't judge you if you decide never to speak to Sapphire again, but I know you well enough to know that you'll be happier if you do."

"Thanks." Before Ruby opened the door to leave, I caught her by the wrist and repeated it. "Seriously, Ruby. Thank you."

She grabbed my face in both hands, squishing it. I groaned but didn't push her off. "You're lucky that I like you enough to get involved. Normally, I wouldn't care."

She was right. I was lucky.

TWENTY-NINE
KYLE

A week later, I had mustered up enough courage to meet with Sapphire. Her neighborhood was composed of row after row of little brown condos, each a carbon copy of the one next to it. Community bike racks sat on each corner. The same shrubs were planted in each yard. I was sure it was intended to be aesthetically pleasing. Architecturally, however, it was rather boring. Although, not any duller than the plain grey exterior of my high-rise apartment building.

With a knot in my stomach the size of Texas, I ventured up the long stairs of her brownstone. There were things I wanted to ask, things I needed to know, but there was a lingering fear that I wouldn't like the answers. I felt unsteady, vulnerable and determined like a Christian coming face to face with a lion. I didn't know how the encounter would go, but whatever the result, I knew something would be forever changed. If it wasn't already.

Things certainly felt different since the cruise. I felt different, like something inside me had cracked open, which was both painful and freeing. My breath still ached from the depths of which I missed Jax. Even a month later, I missed him so much it hurt. With him, I had felt more myself than I had in a very long time. I'd forgotten how light-hearted and easy-going I could be when I let go of the anger and acidity I'd collected throughout my life.

I had been holding tightly to the bitterness like a security blanket. It had kept me safe from additional pains and heartache. Like a wall of thorns, it had helped me keep people at a distance. Potential suitors, potential friends, even work colleagues couldn't penetrate the protective barrier. Some would try, most would fail, and they all ended up pricked and bloody in the process.

Not Jax, though. He had been persistent. He had found a chink in my armor and managed to break through. I knew now that he had merely been doing what he had been commissioned to do, but I liked how it felt, having him there on the other side of the wall. It had been a long time since I'd felt that open and comfortable with someone. I wasn't sure I'd felt that way with even Dustin, despite all our years together.

Being in Jax's company had felt natural and effortless. We had clicked in that rare way that people sometimes did. Being with him had been like spending time with my best friend. He had made me feel seen, respected, valued and loved, just like Sapphire, only with orgasms. Even though it was over, the memory of how right it had felt made me want to experience it again.

When Dustin and I had imploded, it had closed me off. Jax had not only reopened that part of me, but he had also somehow reconstructed it so that even heartache couldn't slam it shut again. Even beyond the hurt, I felt hope. I wanted love. I wanted a partnership. Jax had reminded me that I was capable and deserving of both if I laid my guard down long enough to let it in.

That's what had me climbing the stairs to Sapphire's home. I didn't want bitterness to worm it's way back into my heart. I had to forgive her, my oldest, dearest friend. Or at least, I had to try.

I stood outside, closing my eyes for a moment, gathering my nerve to ring the bell. I had called ahead to let Sapphire know I was coming, so it shouldn't have been so jarring when the door suddenly opened, but it was. She must have been waiting for me.

We'd never gone a month without seeing each other before. Since college, we had rarely even gone two days without speaking. Even with our busy work schedules and obligations, we still checked in with each other once a day and shared a meal twice a week. Our lives were so intertwined. Being without her for the last month had felt like losing a limb.

As soon as our eyes met, all that residual hate melted away. I was still angry, hurt and confused by the plan Sapphire had hatched with Jax, but I no longer saw her as an enemy. She was my friend, my sister. She had hurt me, but we could get past it. Without words, we wrapped our arms around each other, as tight as they'd go. It felt like life. Like the first puff of oxygen after holding your breath for several minutes.

"I am so sorry," she whispered into my shoulder.

"I know. I am too."

"I hate when we fight," she said, her arms still wrapped tight around me.

"So do I." I pulled back, taking a good look at her. Her baby bump had popped in the last thirty days, and she was looking full and motherly. "How are you feeling?"

"Fat," she said simply, turning around, leading me inside. I had always loved her home. It was so open and bright. Luckily Sapphire had impeccable taste and decorating sense. If it had been left up to Justin, I knew it would have looked like a frat house. Her expensive art pieces would have been replaced with dart boards and movie posters. Instead of the furniture of teak and chintz, there would be billiard and foosball tables. Justin was great, but Nate Berkus he was not.

Following her into the den, she gestured for me to take a seat. "Please, sit down."

I felt dread coil deep in my stomach but did as instructed. Sapphire then disappeared into the kitchen, returning with two steaming mugs of tea in her hands. I made a conscious effort to look normal as she handed one to me, then nestled herself on the sofa across from me. It was an obvious indicator of how not normal things were between us.

I looked everywhere but at her face. I knew if I looked at her and got any sense that things really were forever changed between us, I wouldn't be able to hold myself together.

She drew a slow, controlled breath, then let it out, relaxing her face on the exhale. "I wasn't sure you would ever speak to me again."

"Neither was I," I admitted, picking up my mug, blowing across the surface. Sapphire straightened as though she had expected me to say something else. I took a deep breath, adding, "but, if you can forgive me for the cake fiasco, I suppose I can forgive you too."

She nodded, her lips forming a small, sad, sincere line. I hated our new somber dynamic more than I hated the fact that she meddled and lied. I could tell that we both still felt like we had to tiptoe around the topic. So I ripped the Band-Aid off. "I'd like to talk about what happened on the cruise." Then I clarified. "About Jax." I broke a little, simply by saying his name. Every time I thought about him, it pushed a spike of pain through me.

Sapphire took a long drink, then looked at me over the rim of her glass. "I suppose we do need to talk about it."

An ache built and expanded in my throat until I wasn't sure I'd be able to speak further. In an attempt to quell the feeling, I took a sip of my tea. It tasted like sadness and hot water. "I think we have to if we want to truly get past it."

"I'm not sure what more there is to say."

I paused, trying to figure out where to begin. I had rehearsed the conversation a thousand times, but I still didn't have the right words. "You could start by explaining to me how paying someone to date me seemed like a good idea."

"I didn't—" she started, and I quickly shut her down.

"Don't." She looked at me, puzzled. "Don't try to spin it. Just admit it. Please."

"Alright, I admit it," she said stoically. "I hired Jax to keep you company. I shouldn't have, I know that. I thought, at the time, that it was for your own good."

"What makes you the authority on what is good for me or not?" I demanded, managing to keep my voice calm. "I'm nearly forty-years-old. I don't need you meddling like that."

Sapphire pursed her lips together. "I know you don't."

"Then, why do it?" I countered. "Why go through that whole charade?"

"I already told you why," she said, keeping her voice equally calm. "I didn't want to spend my honeymoon making sure you were having a good time."

"If I'm such a horrible friend, then why have me there at all?"

Sapphire laughed like I'd made a silly joke. "You're not a horrible friend. Not in the least. However, you tend to make things about you, and I have a bad habit of mothering people. It's not always a healthy combination."

"I don't mean to make things about me."

"I know that. I've always known that. I know how hard it was for you to compete with your brother growing up: your brother, the doctor, the surgeon, the legacy. The only time your family ever talks about you is when *you* talk about you. I get it. I've also never held it against you, but it's not always easy,

Kyle."

"That's why you hired a prostitute?"

Sapphire's face moved through a series of expressions before settling on a terse frown as if she found something unsightly on the bottom of her shoe. "Would you stop?" She begged. "Jax is not a prostitute. Yes, I technically hired him, but it had nothing to do with sex. I wanted you to have someone to hang out with, and you totally shot down my other suggestions."

"What other suggestions?"

"At Armando's, when I asked you to be my man of honor."

"That's still not a thing," I quipped.

"Maybe not, but I did offer to set you up with a guy from my office. I said, if you hit it off, you could even bring him as your date, but you absolutely refused. You then went on a tangent about how horrible my taste in men was."

That part, I vaguely remembered.

"I'm sorry I went behind your back, but I'm not sorry I hired him. I wanted you to have a good time. Maybe even be reminded of how nice romance could be. After the trip, you were never supposed to see him again. I figured, at most, you'd have a great story to tell people about the Caribbean fling you had. You were never supposed to know that Jax lived in Chicago. You certainly weren't supposed to find out that we knew each other or that I set the entire thing up."

My stomach dropped in a weird burst of confused outrage. "That was poor planning on your part," I snarked. "Does the fact that I wasn't supposed to know make it ok?"

"Of course not," She said, raising her hands in defeat. "Why does it matter how you met or why, anyhow? You like Jax, don't you?" When I didn't answer immediately, she added crossly. "Or were you too busy trying to decide whether or not to run back to Dustin, to really give Jax a chance?" I choked on my tea. "That was really frustrating to hear since it took me four months to pick you up off the floor the last time."

That effectively snapped my mouth shut. Guilty crimson flashed across my face. "Ruby told you about that?"

"Of course she did. I would have preferred if you had told me yourself."

"You were busy."

"Jesus, Kyle. How could you even contemplate it? The guy is an ass."

I was surprised to hear her say that. "You love Dustin."

"Yeah, because I *have* to. I'm his sister-in-law. It doesn't mean I want my best friend to jump back into a relationship with him. You two were awful together."

This snapped my head up so fast, I nearly hurt my neck. "What? Everyone thought we were the perfect couple."

"No," Sapphire shook her head. "The two of you thought you were the perfect couple. To the rest of us with eyes and ears, you were the most irritating couple to be around." I gazed at her like she had told me she hailed from another planet. "All you did was argue. All you *still* do is argue. When you broke up, we all did a little dance of joy."

"When we first broke up, you told me to get back together with him."

"I most certainly did not," she said defensively.

"Yes, you did. You told me to call Dustin."

"When I said that, you were sobbing uncontrollably on the bathroom floor, wearing sweatpants that smelled like moldy cheese. You were going on and on about how much you missed him. I was trying to be supportive."

"So it wouldn't be easier for you if Dustin and I were a couple again?"

"Why on earth would you think that?"

"No reason." Sapphire eyed me suspiciously. "Fine," I exhaled, defeated. "Dustin said—"

"Dustin said?" Her voice rose slightly. "What did he say, exactly?"

I debated whether or not to tell her. Dustin was her brother-in-law. The last thing I wanted was to say something that might cause a rift between them and subsequently her and Justin's marriage, but I knew Sapphire. She wouldn't stop asking until I told her, so there was nothing left to do except tell her everything.

"He said you were going to cut me out." To my horror, I heard something shake in my voice, which I quickly swallowed down.

She tilted her head, confused. "Out of what?"

"Your life."

"That son of a bitch." Anger flashed across her features. "I don't know what's worse, the fact that he said it or the fact that you believed him."

"At the time, he made sense. Dustin and I could barely last two minutes in a room together before waging world war three. It's not really the type of influence you want around a child, is it?" I paused. "He made it very clear that out of the two of us, his position in your lives was permanent, being blood and everything. Whereas mine was entirely dependent on how well I could behave in his presence." I swallowed. "Then the cake thing happened, and I just—"

"Wait," she interjected. "You mean you went the whole cruise thinking I was looking for a way to cut you out of my life?"

"Maybe not looking, but definitely contemplating the idea."

"No wonder you freaked when you found out I had brought Jax along to keep you out of my hair."

I shrugged.

She reached over, covering one of my hands with her own. Then she pursed her lips, choosing her words carefully. "You listen to me," she said, her jaw set, ironclad. It was the game face I'd seen her use a hundred times. Her grip on my hand was steady and robust. "You are more than my best friend. You are my family, my brother. Absolutely nothing Dustin said is true. There will always be room for you in our lives."

Her gaze was serious while she waited for a response. I sat silent for a moment, contemplating her words and how much of them I already knew to be true, on some level. Even still, doubt lingered. I struggled to absorb the sincerity in her voice. "Dustin is blood. Justin will always choose—"

"His brother," she nodded in agreement. "I will always choose mine. Justin and I know that about each other. We've talked about it at length. We're a package deal. Justin married you, as much as I married Dustin."

I raised a brow at her choice of words. As if hearing what she said for the first time, she broke her stoic, motherly demeanor. She grinned a small, crooked, unflattering smile. "You know what I mean."

"Do I?" I challenged. "It sort of sounds like you want us to start a polygamist commune."

She put her hand over her mouth. "I think I'm going to throw up."

"A simple no would suffice."

"No. Seriously. I'm going to throw up." Without a second thought, I rushed for the wastebasket beside the writing desk and placed it in her hands. Sapphire immediately put her face inside. Taking a perch on the sofa beside her, I held her hair back as she started to retch.

Just like that, we were right again. Our friendship had an unshakeable foundation. It didn't matter how much we fought or how severe the yelling; we were unbreakable. When one needed the other, all disagreements were put aside. All the pettiness, disappointment, rage and sorrow, made way for endless support.

When she was finished, I took the bucket from her, dumped it down the toilet, then placed it in the shower stall for me to wash out later. When I returned, I handed her a wad of bathroom tissue then sat gingerly next to her. "Morning sickness?"

She shook her head, smiling, embarrassed. "Morning, noon and night sickness." She dabbed the corners of her mouth. "I haven't puked this much since freshman year."

I resisted the urge to laugh. Instead, I smiled sadly, rubbing her back. "If it helps, you're glowing."

"Fuck off."

Sapphire laughed, and I laughed too. It was a relief, like the air coming back in the room. I smiled at her like everything would be ok between us, but I could sense skepticism lingering in her posture. When she looked at me again, she had a sharpness in her eyes. "Promise me you won't get back together with Dustin," Sapphire pleaded. "You don't love him, and he doesn't deserve you."

"You're right. On both counts." I cringed internally when I thought about it. I had actually considered giving Dustin a second chance. Luckily, I had come to my senses. "I told him there was zero chance of us getting back together while we were still on the cruise."

"Thank Christ," She proclaimed. "Also, promise me that you won't hold that silly plan of mine against Jax."

"What about the fact that he's a gigolo? Can I hold *that*

against him?"

Sapphire's answering silence left my words to echo back to me. I realized how they sounded. So unforgiving and bitter. I recognized the tone and didn't like how easily I settled into it.

Eventually, Sapphire said, "You could hold it against him, but I wish you wouldn't. You liked him. A lot. That shouldn't change because you learned you didn't meet by chance."

As usual, she was right.

"He's an escort."

"You've said that multiple times already. Each time, I still don't understand why that's an issue. You met, and you like each other. Why should anything else matter?"

"Because it wasn't real! You paid him to spend time with me."

"He didn't take the money," She said suddenly, and I eyed her suspiciously. "The check I wrote to him has never been cashed. According to my contact at the agency, he quit shortly after we returned from the trip."

I needed to sit with that information for a while. Sapphire must have instinctively known that because she didn't say anything further. After a long moment, I asked, "He quit his job?"

"Apparently. Does that change anything?"

I didn't know where my head was on that particular question. "Why should it?"

"I don't know," she shrugged. "You tend to pass quick judgment on anyone or anything that doesn't mesh one-hundred percent with your ideals. So I'm thinking Jax's job played a larger factor in your decision to end things with him than his lying to you."

I considered her argument. She was right. When I really thought about it, how Jax earned his money bothered me more than the fact that Sapphire and he had conspired behind my back. Did knowing that he was no longer in that line of work make a difference to me? Absolutely it did. Did that make me an unreasonable prude? Probably.

Sapphire was right about something else too. I did like him. More than like, but I had dismissed all his attempts at reconciliation. Eventually, he stopped trying. That was understandable since only a fool would have persisted after a month with zero progress. Even if he had kept trying, there was still the matter of trust; in that, I wasn't sure if I had any in him.

"Besides," Sapphire went on. "If the choice was really between Dustin or Jax, you have to choose Jax. He's definitely more mature than Dustin, of all people."

I bit back a smile at her determination. She was working extra hard to convince me.

"Dustin was an option I knew better than to really entertain."

"That's good to know," Sapphire nodded approval. "What about Jax? Did you ever really entertain the idea of him as an option?" Had I? I wasn't sure. "I know you feel the way you met was sneaky and underhanded."

"That's because it was."

"Even so," she continued. "Jax is smart, handsome, driven, and mature. He likes kids, he loves animals, he's cultured in music, art and literature, and you already know your best friend likes him. He checks all the boxes."

I shrugged. "I don't know if a relationship can be based on a list of requirements."

"You two were good together. You could make it work if you wanted to."

I made a face. "Make it work? I always thought that falling in love was a natural process. You meet someone when you least expect it, and you fall."

"Didn't you?" Sapphire asked. "Stop trying to be so rational about this. Love isn't rational. You're listening to the wrong organ."

I thought for a moment, trying to channel the hopeless romantic that laid dormant within me. My brain told me that I hadn't known Jax long enough to love him. Yet, my heart said that the loss I was feeling only made sense if I did.

Sapphire was right. I had to let my heart lead my head for a change. I tried to imagine not wanting to kiss Jax, to hold him, to laugh with him, to listen to his stories of constellations and Greek mythology.

I couldn't. Even in my imagination, it was impossible.

My track record with relationships may have been small and unsuccessful. I might have had no idea what the perfect relationship looked like, but with Jax, I recognized that it had felt close. Closer than it ever had with Dustin, even in the earliest stages of our courtship.

I dropped my arms, leaning forward, resting my elbows on my thighs, as old memories suddenly seemed brand new. I tried not to remember that afternoon in the rain, the way we had laid together, soaked to the bone and getting even wetter by the second. I tried to ignore how natural, comfortable, easy and beautiful it was, walking hand-in-hand down that foreign street. I tried to imagine not wanting to do the same thing down Michigan Avenue or the Magnificent Mile. I tried to forget how good it felt and how great he had smelled; fresh and citrusy, like bottled summer.

I realized then that my clear-as-day memory of how Jax's hair had smelled, all wet from the tropical storm, answered any questions I had about the way I felt.

Sapphire snapped her fingers, and I startled to find her leaning in, looking like she wished she had a stick to poke me with. I must have zoned out, lost in my contemplation.

"I'm guessing it's all clicking into place now," She said, smiling meaningfully. She knew me too well. She placed her well-manicured hand on the small of my back. "You have so much in you. You have so many amazing qualities and so much love to give that you're almost impossible to match. Jax is your perfect match. He really is. I saw it that night at the glow party and again at the prom."

My brain was struggling to compute. Reeling from the deep enormity of Sapphire's insight and how exposed I suddenly felt, I saw a need to add levity to the serious conversation. I sat upright. "I feel like your projecting your starry-eyed romantic fallacies onto me," I said to her, sticking my tongue out.

Sapphire knew what I was doing immediately. She withdrew her hand from my back, giving me a crooked smile. "Do you miss him?"

"Yes." There was no purpose in lying. "A lot, but he lied to me. Broke my trust."

"You're forgiving me." Then it occurred to her that I hadn't actually told her that I was, so she added, "Aren't you?"

"Yes," I nodded assurance. "I forgive you, but that's different. We have twenty years of history. You breaking my trust was one tiny infraction in a lifetime of friendship. Jax's very first act, in our very first moments together, was to lie. He continued to lie every moment afterward. I'm not sure I can move past that."

"I think you can."

"I'm not so sure."

"Oh, Kyle," she said it without pity, only compassion. "I think you're scared. I think you've been scared for a very long time. You've been actively searching for reasons not to trust people and not to be happy. I think it's easier for you than taking a risk. You've always been this way."

"Have not," I said insulted.

"Have too," she stared at me, clearly exasperated. "You only started dating Dustin because I pushed you. The same can be said for almost every other date you've ever been on. I push you. I set you up. I introduce you, and when things don't go well, I shoulder the blame. You never actually try." She took a breath. "I love you, Kyle. So many people do, many more people would if you would only let them."

Her words struck me like an invisible fist punching me in the chest. She wasn't wrong. I had always been closed off. Afraid to let people see all sides of me. Afraid to let them genuinely love me. Even with Dustin, I had always kept one cookie in the cookie jar. Hidden from him in case it was a flavor he didn't like. Then it hit me. Jax had gotten through. Somehow, I had felt comfortable enough to show him all my sides, even that final cookie, and he had not only liked it, but he had also wanted more.

Sapphire sat back, her eyes on me, her expression grimly amused. "I can get you his number," she offered.

I laughed then, because I had been contemplating asking for his number, and as usual, she had read my mind. It was her superpower, as we liked to joke. Instead of taking her up on her offer, I shook my head. Part of me was too proud to accept it, and the other part was still unsure if I even wanted it. Even if I did take his number, I had been unforgivably dismissive of him for the last month. I couldn't call him up out of the blue now. I would have looked bipolar.

That was my typical way of thinking, always assuming the worst in people, situations, and possible outcomes. Still, in this scenario, it also seemed the most probable.

"No," I shook my head at Sapphire. "I don't want his

413

number."

She didn't ask why. She just sighed grimly.

No. I wouldn't call Jax. Our time together had been fantastic but brief. That's how it would stay. It was time to forget about Jax Abernathy.

THIRTY
KYLE

B lue and pink balloons, filled with helium and tied with white ribbon, floated at both ends of the buffet table. I had been in charge of the menu, as the only thing Ruby knew how to make were cocktails. I had gone with a prominent theme, making everything baby-sized. The menu consisted of mini crab cakes with lime chive mayo, spinach and cheddar mini quiches, BBQ bacon sliders, and of course a selection of baby vegetables; carrots, zucchini, artichokes and tomatoes. I was a culinary genius. I even folded twenty-five yellow cloth napkins into roses and set them in empty water glasses.

What had Ruby done to help? Well, she had hired a stripper, which I promptly canceled. Who thought a half-naked man gyrating and thrusting at a baby shower was a good idea? What would his costume have been anyway? An image of a muscular man in an oversized diaper and baby bonnet popped into my brain.

On second thought, it might have been entertaining.

I really didn't mind doing the bulk of the work of planning and executing the shower. Ruby may have been Sapphire's sister, but she was notoriously unreliable. So much so that when Sapphire had learned that Ruby was attempting to plan the surprise shower, she had called me up in tears, begging me to take over. Ruby was all too eager to wash her hands of the entire endeavor, so it worked out for the best.

The guest list was a diverse mix of Sapphire's female family members, sorority sisters and work colleagues. I was the only man in attendance. Dustin would have been invited too if Sapphire hadn't forbidden it. She was still pissed at him for what he had said to me on the cruise. I tried to tell her that the vacation had been over a month ago. There was no reason to cling to that anger any longer. Still, she had stood her ground, and I couldn't say I was heartbroken over Dustin's absence.

We hadn't spoken since I'd kicked him out of my cabin. Since then, we'd both gone back to pretending that the other didn't exist. I was reasonably confident that when we had to share space again, Dustin would act like a petulant child, even more so than before, embarrassed by my rejection. So, I had no burning desire to rush that reunion.

The shower was going very well. Sapphire had pretended to be adequately surprised. The guests seemed to thoroughly enjoy personalizing newborn sleepers with colorful fabric paint and even more colorful words and phrases. My personal favorite was *I broke my mom's Vadge*, which someone had written in serial killer letters. I was pretty sure that one was Ruby's contribution to the project.

Most of the ladies had gathered in the den to watch Sapphire open her collection of gifts. They waited on bated breath as she opened every bag and every box. Ruby and I stood on the outskirts of the action. We hovered near the arched passageway leading to the dining room, watching from a distance. Ruby held a glass of chardonnay in her hand while I sipped on a can of coke.

"Have they decided on any potential baby names yet?" I asked Ruby quietly.

"For girls, Savanah and Clarice, after our grandmothers."

"What if they're boys?"

"Onyx and…" Ruby got a gleam in her eye, as though she was about to reveal a treasured secret. "Boomer."

My face squished up involuntarily. My voice rising slightly, my tone disbelieving. "*Boomer?*"

Ruby shushed me before I drew too much attention to our corner.

"That's something you name a dog, not a child," I went on.

Ruby agreed. "I know! It was Justin's choice. Apparently, it's a family name."

"Boomer," I repeated the name quietly to myself, trying to get my brain to accept the genuine possibility of having to call a child that in the future. It didn't sit well on my tongue. "Boomer?"

I noticed the time on the clock behind Ruby. It was almost three in the afternoon, and the party would be wrapping up shortly. "I should get the cake ready," I announced.

"Did you order the gender reveal cake that I mentioned?"

I glared at Ruby lovingly. "No, because Sapphire has made

it very clear that she wants to be surprised. Also, I've explained to you that you can't tell the babies' genders from a sonogram. Gender is a spectrum. An ultrasound can only tell us whether the babies have penises or vaginas. Neither of which is worth celebrating."

"Shows how little you know," She quipped. "My vagina is always worth celebrating."

I rolled my eyes. "You've certainly invited enough guests to the venue."

I excused myself to the kitchen. Once there, I went to the refrigerator, pulling out the costly two-layer red velvet cake with raspberry compote. It was large and cumbersome and had to be refrigerated, or the cream cheese frosting would turn into a sour inedible mess. I had purposely avoided buttercream. I'd had been forced to empty most of the contents of the refrigerator to make room for it.

Hoisting it out of the fridge, I turned to bring it into the dining room. That's when I saw him. I hadn't even realized it was him at first. I had seen a male figure leaning by the pantry, and my heart had a rapid flutter of panic. Seeing me struggle, Jax rushed forward to steady me before I dropped the cake to the floor.

"Careful." He took the dessert from me. My heart jumped instantly at the sight of him, and I struggled to ignore the immediate instinct to wrap my arms around his neck. "If you destroy another expensive cake, Sapphire will likely run you down with her car." He smiled, and how much I enjoyed looking at it sent a sharp pang through my chest.

Only a month ago, I would have made a cutting, sarcastic remark in response, but my brain was full of nothing but heart-eyes and the urge to kiss him, which took all my strength to resist. We stood there staring at each other, forty-some-odd days removed from the Caribbean sun and sand. It almost felt like meeting a new person, like I was seeing him for the first time. I was suddenly far more appreciative of his broad shoulders, square chin, kind eyes and genuine smile. I knew I was missing him, but it took seeing him again to realize how much.

I didn't move or say anything. "Where should I put this?" He asked, adjusting his grip on the serving tray the cake rested on.

Shaking my head, I realized I had been frozen, gaping at him. "On the smaller table in the dining room." I gestured to the arched passageway that led to the other space.

I followed him, in awe. While behind him, I tried to send Sapphire a what-the-hell-is-he-doing-here look, but she wouldn't meet my eyes. She pretended to be engrossed in opening one of her many duplicated gifts. Seriously, did no one even look at her registry? I turned to Ruby, who shrugged both shoulders, equally bewildered by Jax's presence.

He set the cake down on the small circular table, then turned back to me. He looked good. Gorgeous actually, in a collard shirt and a tie that, upon closer inspection, was patterned with little yellow duckies on it. Perfect for the occasion.

My breath turned to hot smoke in my lungs, and I couldn't look away. "What are you doing here?" It didn't come out rude, only straight to the point.

Jax paused, mouth open like he wanted to respond but wasn't sure what to say. Finally, he put the words together. "I miss you."

Hope lit in my ribs, but I didn't stoke it, knowing better than to let myself get too excited. "You miss me?" I whispered. I placed a pile of napkins on the table next to the cake, attempting to act like his confession didn't thrill me beyond measure.

"I do," he said. "I can't even begin to tell you how sorry I am for misleading you."

"Misleading me?" I quoted back to him while placing tiny dessert forks, stem up, into a silver, glittered canister.

"I know I hurt you. For that, I'm deeply sorry."

"Deeply sorry?"

"Are you going to repeat everything I say?" He placed his hand over mine. I dropped the last fork in its holder then pulled my hand away, slowly.

I was trying to play it cool, but I was almost sure he could tell how much our exchange affected me in both an uplifting and confusing way. Jax Abernathy was there, in Sapphire's dining room, professing how much he missed me. It was taking my brain a little time to catch up to my heart, which was jackhammering away beneath my black cashmere sweater. It was beating so hard that my voice shook a little. "This isn't really the time or place. Today is about Sapphire."

He turned to follow my eyes to where Sapphire sat, still pretending she didn't notice our exchange happening in the corner. "I'm aware. She invited me."

"Why would she do that?"

"Probably because she knows you weren't responding to my emails," he replied. "Or perhaps, she wanted another gift."

"You brought a gift?"

He nodded. "I bought Sapphire a breastfeeding kit." His eyes went comically wide. "Did you know you have to buy shields for the nipples? Like you're sending them off to war."

I couldn't help but laugh at that. Jax laughed too, and the sensation was like clearing away cobwebs from a dark corner of a room. As the laughter died, I tried to figure out how to funnel everything I was thinking and feeling into words. Before, I hadn't even been sure what I wanted to say. Now, with him standing directly in front of me, the veil had lifted, and I found new clarity. I knew what I wanted to say. I just wasn't sure I had the nerve to say it.

"I—" we said simultaneously, then we both smirked awkwardly.

"You go first," I told him.

"No, you can go first."

"No, I insist."

"I was twenty-five," he started, "when someone first offered me money for my time. He was an older guy. Sixty, maybe. I had just left Australia. I thought I could make it in New York City, but I didn't have a job or a place to live, and he offered me easy money."

I tried not to judge, but my face had a mind of its own. "Don't look so disgusted," Jax said. "I didn't sleep with him. He was just lonely. We'd sit together, watching old reruns of *Threes Company* or *Golden Girls*. Sometimes he'd order in food, and we'd watch a movie."

"He paid you for that?"

"Well, I was in my underwear."

"Fair enough," I nodded.

"That's the type of service I provided. My talent was making people feel special and seen. Especially those people that typical queer society deemed less worthy: older, overweight guys or the differently-abled. I even had a drag queen as a regular for a while. She got a little handsy sometimes, but she was harmless as long as we kept the gin out of reach." He almost looked nostalgic, telling me about his past clients. "When I moved to Chicago, I got a position with an elite agency. I'm not a prostitute. I don't walk the streets or have sex in parked cars. In fact, I never have sex with clients."

I eyed him suspiciously.

"Ok," he corrected himself. "Maybe not never, but you were different. I was attracted to you immediately. Even on that first night, when you were drunk as a skunk, dancing badly. So, so badly. I regretted taking the job because I wanted it to be real. I wanted to be a regular man, meeting a cute bloke on vacation and having an incredible, fun time. I liked you before I even met you. I knew right away that I wasn't going to be able to keep it professional. Not with you. You were more than a job. You *are* more than a job."

"Sapphire told me you didn't take the money," I breathed. "She also told me you quit the agency."

He nodded. "I knew three days in that I was never going to cash that check. I didn't want it. I didn't want you to be another client. You also helped me realize that I don't want that life anymore. I want something real."

There was another pause before he continued.

"That day, in the gazebo, was one of the best days of my life. Not just the sex, but everything leading up to it and everything that came after. A few nights later, when I fell asleep, cradled in your arms, while we were watching that old black and white movie, that was the moment I fell in love with you. I got a glimpse of the future that I want, and I want it with you." My heart did a tight and twisty maneuver at the way Jax so easily revealed how he felt and what he wanted.

The words hit me hard and inspired two responses in me. One was joyful, the other was terrified. The first felt breezy and light. The second felt familiar and safe, but that was only a tiny fraction of the welling emotions inside me. There was also lingering anger, violation, humiliation, uncertainty and panic. Sapphire's words from the other day echoed in my mind.

You've been actively searching for reasons not to trust

people and not to be happy. Many more people would love you if you would only let them.

I pushed the fear down, willing it away, embracing a fundamental truth instead; he loved me. Jax Abernathy had said he loved me. I had my flaws, I knew them well, and he loved me anyway. Jax had already apologized, at length, and like an obstructive slag, I had refused to give him the time of day. Yet, there he was, a month later, standing before me, vulnerable, still trying to apologize. Still trying to win me back because he loved me.

He loved me.

For a fraction of a second, a whole crystallized life flashed into view. I pictured us living together in Chicago. I could imagine us cuddling on the sofa, making dinner together in our tiny kitchen, and playing with Sapphire's newborn babies. Maybe we'd adopt a baby of our own someday, and by baby, I meant puppy. The image felt comfortable, natural and right. It was beautiful, and it dropped right into the well of my chest and began to spread, like a sunrise over a dark landscape.

I wanted that life too. I wanted it with him. I didn't know if it was normal to fall in love in ten days. In fact, I was almost sure it wasn't, but I had. I didn't know if I could trust Jax not to hurt me again, but I realized with new clarity that I didn't care. It was a chance I wanted to take. The risk would be worth it if it brought that image to life, for even a brief time.

I registered that I was staring at Jax with overt fondness when he reached forward, touching a careful fingertip to my chin.

"You're looking at me like you might love me too," he said. "Do you?"

I did. I really did, and I wanted to shout it from the rooftops. Yet, in true Kyle fashion, I chose sarcasm over real human emotion.

"Did you practice that speech?" I asked suddenly, coolly, crossing my arms.

He nodded. "With hand gestures, but I decided against those." Then he registered my tone. "Wait, did you not hear what I said?"

I cracked a smile. "I can't believe you crashed Sapphire's

baby shower. You do realize that I'm going to have to deal with the repercussions of this."

Jax took my hand, one corner of his mouth also tugging gently upward. "You haven't answered my question," he reminded me quietly.

"Well, you just sprung this on me. It's not really fair."

"You're kind of hot when you get all indignant, you know that?" Jax smirked.

"I do."

"Now answer the damn question."

"What question was that again?"

"Kyle!" he cried, his voice filled with a combination of frustration and humor.

"Alright, I fucking love you too, ok?" I half yelled, finally, irreversibly. "No need to make a big deal about it."

Jax's smile was suddenly so wide and bright that I thought my heart was going to break simply by looking at it. He examined me, gaze swimming, then he reached out to cup the back of my neck. His fingers played with the tiny hairs at my neckline for a beat before pulling me in with a careful hand. I didn't resist. It was almost as if, in hindsight, I'd known this moment was coming forever. I tried to hold the size of the entire moment, the perfection of it, inside my rib cage, but my heart was swelling beyond containment.

We kissed, long and purposeful. It was not only a connection of our lips but of our hearts and minds as well. A uniting of two lives. A launching off point from which our love would sail uncharted waters.

Somewhere outside of the kiss, I heard an eruption of applause. I'd completely forgotten about the baby shower and all the people around us. At some point, they had stopped with the gifts and had sat silently, eavesdropping on our conversation. Sapphire, Ruby and the entire gaggle of women were clapping, smiling and handing each other tissues.

Jax and I briefly looked at them, embarrassed, before turning back to each other, pushing our foreheads together. The simple gesture felt perfectly intimate, and for the first time, I saw that Jax's eyes had glazed over. He loved me, really, truly loved me. We loved each other. It was too perfect to be real, yet it was.

The cruise had been ten long days. Longer still, the forty-plus days that followed our return. In that time, I had discovered a lot about myself and the people around me.

I learned that Sapphire wasn't perfect. She was a woman who loved me but was frustrated by me equally. Like all of us, she was morally ambivalent on occasion, making the wrong decisions for the right reasons.

I learned that Ruby was so much more than she pretended to be. Yes, she was wild and tempestuous, but she was also intuitive, sensitive and smart with unshakeable confidence that I envied. Even though I had known her for years, I had never taken the time to honestly *know* her. Now that I did, hers was a friendship I wanted to nurture and cherish. We all needed those friends who fearlessly told you everything you needed to hear, but no one would say. Those people were precious.

I learned that Dustin was terrified of being alone. That's why he had cheated on me. Dustin could sense that our relationship was expiring, and he had been desperate to find a replacement before we curdled completely. It was the same reason he had been so eager to try to rekindle a romance with me on the ship. Shawn and his relationship had been showing some red flags, and Dustin had clung to the closest lifeline. It had nothing to do with me. It never did. Understanding that had helped me to finally let go of the anger I had for him.

What I had learned about Jax wasn't about him specifically. It was about me: who I was and how I saw life and love. For the first time, I saw myself clearly. I had been afraid. It had been more comfortable to be closed off and mean than admit it. I had been petrified of letting men close, to show weakness, vulnerability or even interest. I had been terrified of getting hurt. I'd find a flaw, any flaw, and use it as an excuse to push suitors away. Not any longer.

I learned that I wasn't afraid of Jax. I wasn't scared of the way he made me feel. I wasn't frightened of loving him or being loved by him. I wasn't even afraid that he may hurt me someday. Love was not a battlefield like Pat Benatar once had me convinced. Love was an ocean, deep, endless, rough sometimes, but ultimately a source of power and life. It had been a harsh lesson to learn, but so necessary.

I'd read once that the past was a place of reference, not a place of residence. I understood that lesson now more than ever before. I felt it in my soul. Obsessing over what was or should have been was a waste of valuable energy. As was focusing on who hurt who and how. It made one stagnant and bitter. The past was a place to learn, not to live. Until one accepted and forgave the past, one could not move forward. I couldn't. I hadn't. I wanted to, now more than ever. For me. For Jax. For us.

With the way Jax held me, it left no doubt that he had never meant to hurt me and would do everything possible to avoid doing so again in the future. I could see that unspoken promise shining in his eyes. I could feel it in his embrace. I could hear it in the gentle way he spoke my name. I might not have known him long, but I knew one thing to be sure; Jax Abernathy was the one for me, and I would never let him go.

Happiness was a choice, love a gift, and I suddenly had plenty of both. Neither of us knew where our relationship would go, and that was ok. What we did know was that we wanted to find out together. We also recognized that we owed everything we had found to my meddling best friend and the adventure she forced me to have, on a good ship, called Lollipop.

EPILOGUE

JAX

"**G**ross. He's drooling."

"He is not."

"Look at him. He's like a St. Bernard."

"Maybe, but he's my St. Bernard."

I tried to open my eyes, but the fog of sleep was still too heavy.

"If he drooled any more, we could row our way to Australia."

"Technically, it's an island. We could do that anyway."

"He better wake up before the plane lands." That was Sapphire's voice, easily recognizable by the air of authority. "We can't carry him off the plane. Justin has a bad back."

"Would you stop?" I heard Kyle beg. "The plane has only started its descent."

Another voice cut through the haze of sleep, this one unrecognizable. "I'm sorry, sir, but he needs to put his chair in the upright position for landing."

"It's ok. I'll wake him. Thank you." That was Kyle again.

Seconds later, I was jostled. "Jax, babe, we're landing. Apparently, that one inch of recline is all that stands between us and certain death, so I need you to wake up before the flight attendant comes back with a blow horn."

I dragged myself out of slumber with intense effort, wildly blinking the remaining sleepy dust away.

"Good morning, sunshine." My vision came into focus slowly. The first thing I saw was Kyle's adorable smiling face. "If it's possible, you look even more handsome when you've just woken up."

I lifted a heavy hand, rubbing my face, trying to clear the fog. "Well then, it must be possible." I smiled lazily, and Kyle smiled back.

"We're almost on the ground," he said.

"I feel like I just fell asleep."

"You did. Five hours ago." On a twenty-four-hour flight,

five consecutive hours of sleep was quite the achievement. I knew my back would be paying for it later. Even in economy plus, sleeping in a chair was still sleeping in a chair.

Kyle was sitting in the window seat, so I looked over to Ruby sitting next to me in the aisle. "At least tell me I wasn't snoring."

"You weren't," she assured me. Then her mouth curled into a sly grin. "Still, the next time I see you release that much viscous fluid, there better be an orgasm involved."

Crikey. I almost blushed. Two years hanging around her, and I still hadn't adjusted to her brazen, say-anything-I-want-whenever-I-want attitude. I suspected she said those things for no other reason except that she enjoyed the shock they caused.

Sapphire and Justin were sitting in the row in front of us. She turned in her chair to chastise her sister. "Why must you turn everything into sexual innuendo?"

Ruby lifted her chin. "Because I'm good at it, and I know it annoys you." She then stuck out her tongue, and unexpectedly but hilariously, Sapphire did the same before returning to her forward-facing position in a huff.

"Now-now, you two. Behave, or I will turn this plane around," Kyle threatened like a frustrated father. "I refuse to listen to you two bicker for the next three weeks."

"It's cute that you think you have any power to stop two feuding sisters," I whispered. "I'm pretty sure they could take you if necessary."

"You're supposed to be on my team," Kyle growled. "Team Kyle-is-always-right-because-it's-his-wedding-trip-and-it's-all-about-him."

"I am on that team," I assured him with a smile. "That team name has got to go, though. It's quite the mouthful." I bopped him on the nose playfully with my pointer finger.

Kyle looked like he was about to say something further on the matter, but the view out the aeroplane window distracted him suddenly. "Oh my," he gasped. "The water looks so blue."

I leaned over him to look out the window to discover that he was right. It did. Below us, the Pacific Ocean was a turquoise gem. The colour of the water hadn't changed in all my time away, and it struck me how much I'd missed the intensity of it.

"Are there always that many boats in the harbour?"

"That's Port Jackson," I said, nodding. I then pointed to a long bridge to the right. "That's Sydney harbour bridge. It connects north and south Sydney. Over there," I pointed to the left. "See those white triangles that kind of look like cones? That's the opera house."

Kyle looked at the landmarks, then back to me, leaning in, kissing my cheek. "Are you excited to be home?"

"This isn't home. It's just a place." I reached up, flicking his ear. "Home is wherever you are, but yes, I am excited to be back. There's so much I want to show you." I kissed him.

Beside me, Ruby strained to look over us and out the window to also enjoy the view. "If you two are going to make out, could you at least lean back so I can see out the damned window?"

She was always such a charmer.

"Tell me again why we didn't go on this vacation alone?"

Kyle laughed but couldn't stop from rolling his eyes. "Because we owed them a trip."

"Sapphire and Justin, yes, but why her?" I gestured to the beautiful vulgar woman beside me.

Truth be told, Ruby was by far my favourite of the three. Don't get me wrong, Sapphire and Justin were fantastic, but Ruby was indeed a wonder to behold. She was a free spirit if ever I had met one. Simply sharing space with her was like a breath of oxygen. There was never any judgment or pretence. With Ruby, you always knew exactly what you were getting. One hundred per cent pure, unfiltered diva. She was authentic to a fault and encouraged us to be the same in return. I thoroughly enjoyed bantering with her. She was the little sister I never asked for and never knew I wanted.

"Because I told you, I can't get married without my best women," Kyle grinned, answering my question. Gosh, I loved that smile, all wide and toothy. He had tried for weeks to decide who he wanted to stand next to him on our big day.

Sapphire had automatically been the top contender, based solely on how long she and Kyle had known each other. Of course, the mutual knowledge that we wouldn't have even met if it were not for her was also a tick in her favour.

Yet, Kyle hadn't been able to count out Ruby completely. Since Sapphire and Justin's twin boys were born, Sapphire's social circle consisted almost exclusively of stuffed lions, tigers and bears—oh my. She worked from home most days, running herself wicked, chasing after winged monkeys disguised as toddlers, between conference calls and video meetings. As a result, she was far too tired to do anything most evenings. For a woman like Sapphire, who preferred to keep a stranglehold on all possible variables at all given moments, she handled the cyclone of motherhood surprisingly well. However, since Sapphire was frequently unavailable, Kyle and Ruby had become practically inseparable. Sapphire was still, without a doubt, Kyle's best mate. Yet, neither could deny their relationship had evolved with the birth of Onyx and Boomer.

Boomer. I chuckled to myself because Kyle still had difficulty bringing himself to say the name. In the two years since the munchkins were born, I was sure I'd only heard him utter it once or twice. He often referred to the youngster only as Boo, which didn't seem much better to me, but I accepted that some things Kyle did, didn't always make sense. Some things did, like choosing both women to stand next to him during our ceremony.

I wish I could say that my proposal had been exciting or original. The truth was, my plan had been spoiled by my lack of foresight. It was our first Christmas living together, and like a tired cliché, I wanted to propose on Christmas Day, surrounded by all of our friends and Kyle's family.

Sapphire had been so helpful. As I bounced from jewellery store to jewellery store, she had stood by my side trying to find the perfect ring for Kyle.

"No, that one is too bold," she said, quickly dismissing the sixteen-diamond signet ring.

"What about something like this?" I pondered, gesturing to a sleek, modern black titanium band.

She made a face. "You have met Kyle, right?" I took that as a no. "It can't be anything too gaudy or flashy, but nothing too masculine either. Kyle isn't really a man, so much as a forty-year-old boy." She didn't say it in an insulting way. She was merely stating a fact. Kyle wasn't a manly bloke. He was boyish and whimsical, and it was one of the many things I loved about him.

Once I finally settled on the perfect ring, I placed it in a tiny bag then brought it home. Our Christmas tree had over fifty different gifts under it, and I hid the bag underneath the pile of parcels so that it would be one of the last gifts we came across Christmas day. I hadn't anticipated Kyle feeling compelled to reorganize the presents on Christmas Eve.

"What are you doing?" I asked, trying to maintain my calm when I saw Kyle kneeling under the tree, shuffling boxes around.

"The gifts aren't spread out evenly. I don't want people judging our gift placement."

"Who would do that?"

He stopped, looking up at me. "Sapphire would accuse us of being heathens if she saw this mess."

"We're not religious, so we technically *are* heathens."

He scrunched his freckled nose. "That's no excuse."

"Do you honestly think anyone is going to be looking that closely?"

"Of course. We're gay. We're expected to be good at this stuff." I wanted to argue further, if for no other reason but to distract him from the task, but Kyle had already returned to his strategic shuffling. Suddenly his brows shot up. "What is this?" He asked, picking up the tiny black bag.

I shrugged. "I think Ruby brought it over. It's probably to both of us. Let's leave it and open it tomorrow when they're all here."

Kyle examined the bag more closely. "Are you sure?" He lifted the package up to look at the bottom. "There's no tag or label."

"Just leave it," I instructed, leaning down, pressing a kiss to the top of his forehead.

"Aren't you curious who it's to, or who it's from?"

"I told you," I sighed. "I'm pretty sure it's from Ruby. Please leave it."

Still holding the bag, Kyle rose from the floor, sauntering over to the kitchen counter where his phone sat plugged into its charger. His finger danced a text message across the keyboard. Moments later, it dinged in response. "Ruby has no idea what it is. She says it's not from her."

He had no idea how profusely I was sweating at that moment. I was struggling, running out of ways to prevent him from opening that blasted bag. "Let's have sex," I practically yelled across the room, panicked.

Kyle eyed me suspiciously, almost comically.

"Excuse me?"

"Right now," I demanded, taking the bag from his hand, placing it on the counter. "Let's go." I started to pull him towards the bedroom.

He laughed, struggling against my tug. "As much as I enjoy making love to you, like thoroughly enjoy it, you're acting very strange."

I bit back my nervous smile. "I am not."

"You are too. Now, what is it with you?"

"Promise me, you won't look in that bag."

Kyle raised one eyebrow. "Why not?" He inched towards the counter.

I growled because there was no use fighting it anymore. I knew the jig was up. "Because it's a bloody ring, you nosey little galah!"

Kyle's face fell instantly in shock. I took the bag off the counter, retrieving the ring box from it myself. Kneeling on one knee, I opened it showing him the contents of the box. "Would you please do me the honour of being my husband, you frustrating, adorable bloke?"

He responded in decibels only dingoes could hear. Still, after he finished screaming the shrill cries of excitement, he gave me an audible, "Yes."

I let Kyle plan the entire wedding. He, in turn, allowed Sapphire to plan the bulk of it.

The only request I'd made was that it be a destination wedding in Oz. This way, my oldies and my mates from school could be there. Kyle had hesitantly agreed, still nervous from the horror stories of giant insects and rabid wildlife he'd read about. After months of planning, we were three days away from being married right on the sand of Maroubra beach, at sunset.

Sapphire assured us she had timed it to the second. We would share our first kiss as legally wedded spouses under a starlit sky and a beam of moonlight. At least we would if everything went according to her plan, and it better if the officiant knew what was good for her. I would hate to be on the receiving end of Sapphire's wrath if the officiant was even a millisecond behind or ahead of schedule.

"I am so lucky to be marrying you." I brought Kyle's left hand to my mouth, pressing a delicate kiss to the finger that bore his ring. Two emeralds set side-by-side on a brushed platinum band with a gold inlay accent. No boring traditional diamond for him, no sir. When I popped the question, I made sure to present a ring that was entirely and uniquely us. The platinum represented Chicago, its grey concrete and cold steel, while the gold inlay represented Australian sand. It was supposed to mirror our two worlds, blending together. As for the emeralds, that was solely a reference to one of Kyle's favourite childhood films, *The Wizard of Oz*, which was doubly symbolic considering I was technically a man *from* Oz.

"I'm the lucky one," Kyle whispered back.

It was right then that I held my camera up, snapping a selfie of us together. Even though Kyle looked tired from the flight and I looked groggy and dishevelled, it was quite possibly the best fucking photo. It was a great picture because we were together and we were genuinely happy. Also, we really did look so good together.

The floor rumbled as the landing gear lowered, and we began our final descent into Sydney. Still, it was nothing compared to the rumble in my chest and the growing excitement of what was to come. A future with Kyle. My future husband. Legal and forever.

They say a heart is not judged by how much it loves, but by how much it is loved by others. If that were true, Kyle indeed had the purest heart in all the land because I couldn't imagine ever loving anyone more.

ABOUT THE AUTHOR

This is Patrick Benjamin's second novel. He was excited to try his hand at something lighter and more humorous than his debut novel (The Road Between). Patrick can most often be found spending quiet evenings at home with his Husband, Jarrett and his puppy, Dax. When he's not writing, Patrick can often be seen performing on stage as his glamourous drag persona Tequila Mockingbird. He also volunteers on the Board of Directors of a non-profit organization that has proudly served the LGBTQ2S+ community for 45 years.

Follow him on Facebook

https://www.facebook.com/PWBenji

Made in the USA
Middletown, DE
06 March 2021

34419889R00245